W9-AJT-740

HER ROYAL
DESTINY

HER ROYAL DESTINY

Carol Maxwell Eady

Harmony Books

New York

Cautionary Notice: The herbs, spices and remedies listed throughout the book are for historical interest only and are *not* for contemporary use in the form given.

Published by Harmony Books, a division of Crown Publishers, Inc., One Park Avenue, New York, New York 10016 and simultaneously in Canada by General Publishing Company Limited

HARMONY and colophon are trademarks of Crown Publishers, Inc.

Manufactured in the United States of America

Library of Congress Cataloging in Publication Data

Eady, Carol Maxwell.
  Her royal destiny.

  I. Title.
PR6055.A3H4   1985   823 '.914   85-965
ISBN: 0-517-555654

10 9 8 7 6 5 4 3 2 1

First Edition

For Allan, of course

Contents

History is the deeds of great men,
not gossip from the bedchamber.

Thomas Carlyle, 1852

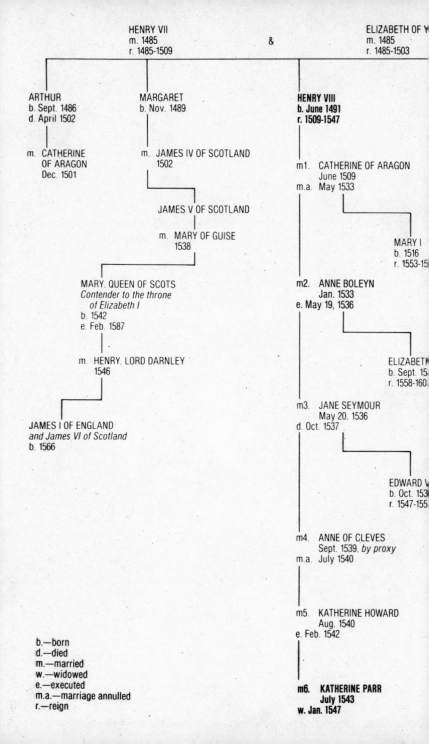

HENRY VII
m. 1485
r. 1485-1509

&

ELIZABETH OF Y
m. 1485
r. 1485-1503

ARTHUR
b. Sept. 1486
d. April 1502

m. CATHERINE
OF ARAGON
Dec. 1501

MARGARET
b. Nov. 1489

m. JAMES IV OF SCOTLAND
1502

JAMES V OF SCOTLAND

m. MARY OF GUISE
1538

MARY. QUEEN OF SCOTS
*Contender to the throne
of Elizabeth I*
b. 1542
e. Feb. 1587

m. HENRY. LORD DARNLEY
1546

JAMES I OF ENGLAND
and James VI of Scotland
b. 1566

HENRY VIII
b. June 1491
r. 1509-1547

m1. CATHERINE OF ARAGON
June 1509
m.a. May 1533

MARY I
b. 1516
r. 1553-15

m2. ANNE BOLEYN
Jan. 1533
e. May 19, 1536

ELIZABET
b. Sept. 15
r. 1558-160

m3. JANE SEYMOUR
May 20, 1536
d. Oct 1537

EDWARD V
b. Oct. 153
r. 1547-155

m4. ANNE OF CLEVES
Sept. 1539, *by proxy*
m.a. July 1540

m5. KATHERINE HOWARD
Aug. 1540
e. Feb. 1542

m6. KATHERINE PARR
July 1543
w. Jan. 1547

b.—born
d.—died
m.—married
w.—widowed
e.—executed
m.a.—marriage annulled
r.—reign

■. LOUIS XII OF FRANCE
   Oct. 1514
Jan. 1515

2. CHARLES BRANDON, DUKE OF SUFFOLK   &   **LADY CATHERINE WILLOUGHBY, DUCHESS OF SUFFOLK**
   April 1515   m. Aug. 1533
1545   w. 1545

                                      m2.   RICHARD BERTIE
                                            1546
                                      Took custody of Lady Mary Seymour in 1549

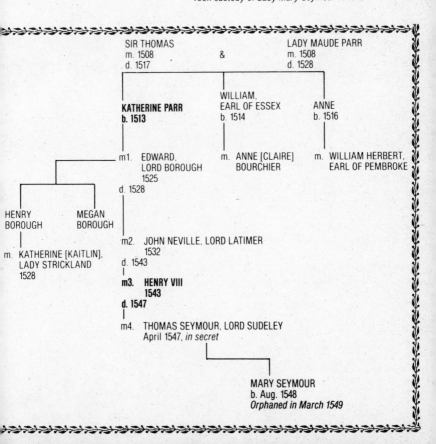

SIR THOMAS   LADY MAUDE PARR
m. 1508   &   m. 1508
d. 1517   d. 1528

                           WILLIAM,
                           EARL OF ESSEX   ANNE
KATHERINE PARR   b. 1514   b. 1516
b. 1513

          m1.   EDWARD,   m. ANNE [CLAIRE]   m. WILLIAM HERBERT,
              LORD BOROUGH   BOURCHIER   EARL OF PEMBROKE
              1525
          d. 1528

HENRY   MEGAN
BOROUGH   BOROUGH

m. KATHERINE [KAITLIN],   m2. JOHN NEVILLE, LORD LATIMER
    LADY STRICKLAND   1532
    1528   d. 1543

                             m3.   **HENRY VIII**
                                   1543
                           d. 1547

                             m4. THOMAS SEYMOUR, LORD SUDELEY
                                     April 1547, *in secret*

                                            MARY SEYMOUR
                                            b. Aug. 1548
                                            Orphaned in March 1549

PART I

A
Country
Wife

Chapter
1

The cart, for you could hardly call it a carriage, was a ramshackle affair with hard leather seats and dusty canvas. Atop a slight hill, it shuddered to a halt. Ned, my driver and an old family friend, turned to shout down, "That's Borough Hall down there, Miss Katherine, in the valley beyond the trees."

I gazed with scant interest, for my heart was back home at Kendal Castle in Westmoreland, whence we had departed some three days before. Depressed by this cold, miserable journey across the breadth of England to Lincolnshire, I was jolted out of my lethargy by the sight of the building—a large manor house of timber and mortar, without a thread of smoke coming from either of its two chimneys.

"Looks cold in the valley," grunted Liza, who, just a few days before, had joined me as my attendant. She had peppered our journey with her gruff country comments, making me laugh despite my deep-seated anger.

My mother, Maude Parr, had arranged this unwelcome marriage, thrusting me from our family home into the arms of a stranger. I was to be married to Edward Braintree MacIntyre, Lord Borough of Gainsborough, a man of some fifty-three years. I was not yet thirteen. Yet I was to be stepmother to his daughters of ten and fourteen, and to a son I believed to be nearer twenty.

Although I knew that my life would not really begin until I was a wife, I was quite happy where I was and not eager to leave the joys of childhood. I had succeeded a few months earlier in thwarting another plan of marriage with a Lord Dacre, in Yorkshire. But when Lord Borough approached, Mother brought my brother William in on her side. William might have been younger by one year, but, lacking a father, he was the man of the household.

Red-haired and slight for his nearly twelve years, the new voice he practiced as a man held sway over the great hall of Kendal Castle. William had commanded:

"You shall be wed, Kate. You and Anne both. No more nonsense. This castle is too costly for our continued upkeep, as well you know. Mother is working on a prenuptial agreement for myself with Claire Bourchier, through whom the title of Earl of Essex will pass. It will be advantageous for our family and guarantee me a good position at Court. Once there I shall call you to London. As the wife of Lord Borough, you too will have a pleasant life. I am sure we could find you a position at Court, if you so wish."

On my last evening at Kendal, I had begged my mother to swear she would come and rescue me from Lincolnshire if I so needed. But she had only laughed and brushed my fair hair with her lips.

"Katherine, you are my firstborn and my favorite. I would never do anything to hurt you. Lord Borough is a fine country man with good sound morals, and plenty of money. Elderly, yes, but you may inherit much property and jewelry. He is accepting you, Kate, with no dowry. We must be grateful for small mercies."

As I gazed into my mother's beautiful face, I realized how she had struggled to keep up the ancestral home in the wild Westmoreland district.

Mother's fine fair hair framed a gentle intelligent face. For a second I had wondered whether she regretted never marrying again. I was sure she had led a happy life without a husband, since her own heart had veered more to the glamour of Court life. If only I could be widowed without having to marry first! Then I too would enjoy the freedom Maude had known as Lady Parr.

But that was not to be. Instead, the cart carrying me to my

betrothed clattered over the cobblestone driveway, through the gateway, and up to the door of the bare and graceless house. Through the last rays of the sun my eyes made out windows on two floors and an attic turret at each corner of the house. The brown-and-white wood-and-mortar frame was common enough in low-lying areas such as Lincolnshire, though Westmoreland was too wild and windy for such flimsy structures.

The month was February, the year 1525, in the reign of the mighty King Henry VIII and our beloved Queen Catherine of Aragon. We had made the crossing from Westmoreland, through the greener pastures of Lancashire, across the wild Pennine range, into Yorkshire and southward to Lincolnshire, battling snow and icy conditions. But here the snow lay thinly on the ground, and the air seemed dry and freezing.

The heavy oak door opened, and I rose to greet my future husband as befits a gracious lady. But the figure that appeared was an old woman wrapped in a woolen shawl.

She squinted in the twilight at the cart and grunted, "Which one of you is Lady Katherine Parr?"

"Why, I am," I answered haughtily, for I was annoyed at such a rude greeting. "We are cold and tired from our long journey and are looking forward to a warm fire and some refreshment."

"Huh, didn't say nothing about two of you to me. Who's this?" the old crone asked as she pointed a finger at Liza.

"My attendant, of course. I am Lady Katherine Parr."

"To be sure, come in then. Man, get their bags and boxes. The northeasterly winds rob a house of any of its warmth. I'll have you brought some supper. The master is out at this moment." Abruptly, she turned her back on us, leading the way indoors.

The hall of the house was dimly lit by a couple of candles and a small fire that was dying in the hearth. We followed the elderly lady, whom we later learned was Abigail, the housekeeper, up the wooden stairs to the first floor. At the end of one long corridor, she opened the door to a small chamber.

"Here. You and your attendant will have to share this until the marriage. I was given orders to prepare only one bed."

Turning once or twice about the room, my heart sank as I thought of my own pretty chamber in Kendal with its decorated coverlets and embroidered pillows, its books and papers piled everywhere. I observed the plain wooden poster bed with white covers and linen counterpane, the hard bench stools, basic earthenware jug and bowl for washing, and the small leaded windows.

"We will need more candles, more pillows, and a trundle bed for Liza to sleep on. We will also need a table and chairs for me to write letters or continue with my studies, and more cupboards to store my clothing and goods," I commanded.

Abigail huffed and disappeared through the door. But I brightened somewhat as Ned lumbered up the stairs bringing box after box of my wardrobe and favorite possessions. By far the biggest bundles contained my books and papers. Following the custom of Court people, my mother had hired tutors to school us in Latin, Greek, French, German, and philosophy, leading our minds beyond the narrowest confines of social convention. I lovingly unpacked my most recent poems.

Liza, however, had no such comforts and distractions. Seeing the abject misery on the girl's face, I summoned up a courage I did not feel and said, "We will try to be happy here, Liza. We have only just come, and perhaps they were not completely prepared for us. And if things do not work out, we will return home."

Cheered by my words, she managed a weak smile.

"I miss my home and family right now."

"So do I. But things will get better. They have to! Now . . . shall we dress for dinner?"

We hurried to get out of our dirty travel-worn clothes into something prettier and altogether more comforting. Soon we were giggling together as though we didn't have a care in the world.

But the optimistic mood changed when I went to open the door and found that Abigail had turned the key on the outside, locking us in.

I tugged at the door angrily, shouting out to Abigail that our door was wrongly fastened. But all I heard in return was the hollow echoing of her footsteps.

The door was unlocked on our second day. But psychologically the damage had been done. We were scared and submissive. Meals were delivered to our room by Borough's younger daughter, Edwina. She seemed sweet and demure— pretty in a kittenish way—but she barely said a word in response to my questions. We saw nothing of the elder daughter, Megan, nor of my intended spouse, Edward Borough.

But by the third day, my courage had returned. "I have had enough of this prisonlike existence. I no longer care what is expected of me as the future Lady Borough. Next time Edwina brings a meal, we shall go out and explore the house."

Later that afternoon, holding on to Liza's hand, dressed in my finest blue woolen dress, belted with a gold chain and decorated with a white lace shawl at the neck, I stormed out of the chamber. I might be small, slight, with no bosom to speak of as yet, and my fair hair might be long and naturally curly, not in the fashion of titled folk, but I felt buoyed up with my sense of righteousness. I, Katherine Parr, would not take such treatment in this strange household. I must find Lord Borough and express my outrage.

We moved cautiously along the upstairs corridor and descended the plain wooden staircase into the hall without meeting a soul, not even a servant sweeping or arranging the rushes. I opened door after door, found Borough's library— bare of books, unlike Father's old library at Kendal—a small withdrawing room, what appeared to be a chapel, and a dining room. Stumbling down another corridor we came unexpectedly into the kitchen, where a group of women, including Abigail, were sitting around the square pine table munching away at a pile of freshly baked cakes and sipping what I guessed were jugs of ale.

"Abigail!" I fairly shouted. "I must meet with Lord Borough this minute. I will not be kept a prisoner in his home another day. I am about to write to Lady Parr at Court and report his disgraceful behavior."

The words were spoken more in despair than authority, for I knew they were falling on deaf ears. Abigail put down her jug of ale, and as she turned, I saw her face was beet-red, her swollen eyes almost the color of her cheeks.

"Sorry, my lady," she slurred. "The master's still not home. You'd better speak to Megan." And then she slumped forward onto the table, her head falling on folded arms.

Backing out of the kitchen quickly, I clutched Liza's arm as I pulled her to my side. "She's drunk. The old biddy is blind, ripping, snorting drunk!"

"Lady Katherine!" Liza said sharply, shocked at my language.

"I'm sorry, but to think I was scared of the old crow, and the fact is she's sozzled, flat out! That's why she's been leaving us alone so much. Come on, let's go find Megan Borough if we can. Someone around here *must* be in charge."

"You need look no farther," a voice called from the end of the corridor. "I am in here."

The voice was throaty, youthful, and my heart lifted at the prospect of meeting my other future stepdaughter.

Liza and I swept down the hall. We were greeted by a young woman, taller than I, with wild red hair and hazel eyes. Her face was white as ivory, with eyes that seemed to glow in the dim light of the passage. Her red hair flowed around her in a river of tiny waves. Truly, the hair had a life of its own—uncontrolled and uncontrollable. Like me, she had foresworn hiding her hair timorously under a cap as young ladies were supposed to do. *How different she was from her shy young sister!* Strength and determination seemed to emanate from the straight line of her nose. She concealed her developing womanhood under a dress of brown wool that hung over her body. She was slim, graceful, elegant—like an arrow.

"Megan Borough." She stuck out a hand.

"Katherine Parr." I smiled in return.

Megan was standing by a table piled with yellowing pages of neat quill writing. She was holding a battered and crumpled book in her hands. She said quickly, "This room is my private study. Or at least I have made it that way. Edwina and I are not supposed to need a private place, other than to practice our embroidery or play the spinet. But I like to study, to read. Do you, Katherine Parr?"

Flushing, I answered haughtily. "I was fortunate to receive an education fit for a man. I would say modestly that I am the most educated young lady you could meet."

Megan's eyes snapped, and her lips pursed. "Then maybe we can teach each other, my lady."

"You may address me as Katherine, or Kate, as do my friends and family. I am not your stepmother yet." Then, feeling a coolness between us, I went on, "Where is your father? I have been here for three days now and still have not been greeted and welcomed formally into his home. You must appreciate my disappointment."

Turning swiftly to glance at the closed door, then moving away to a seat by the window, she beckoned Liza and me to join her, as she settled comfortably on the velvet-covered cushions. She spoke so low I could scarcely hear her.

"I must be careful what I say. Are you content to become Father's wife? I mean, is your heart set on this union?"

"Why, Megan!" I was caught off-guard.

"Father's last wife was a fool, but that made little difference. He is not a good man, Katherine. He is cruel to women, and especially to those he marries. I don't know why your mother has arranged this marriage. You seem too good for it to me." And she took my hand in her own cool firm grip.

Full of misgivings, I tried to stutter something about my mother's impatience and the family's financial plight.

"I must warn you, then. Father thinks I am an evil influence. He has forbidden me to speak with you, until you are his wife. I have refused to be married, and he has threatened to keep me locked up. But I will fight him!" Her eyes sparkled with fire.

"Why, you make me feel like a child!" I exclaimed. "I too tried to object but you can see the result."

"In some ways a father is probably easier to overrule than a mother." She grinned unexpectedly. "I'll help you all I can, but we must be friends in secret. Look." She thrust the book she had been holding into my hands. "Have you heard of this?"

Taking the tattered worn pages and turning them gently for fear of ripping them even more, I was immediately enthralled. The neatly shaped letters fairly jumped off the surface. This must be one of those new printed books from Germany I had heard about. I saw the author's name on the title page—"Martin Luther."

"It's called *The Babylonian Captivity of the Church*," she told me proudly. "By the German priest, some say heretic, from Wittenberg. My brother, Henry, lent it to me. This is the new learning, Kate. Don't you know anything about his ideas? So much for your fancy Court education."

Eager to know more, I confessed I did not.

Now Megan stood up and paced the room, nervous, taut with the intensity of her thoughts.

"Luther is turning the Church upside down. He believes the Pope and the monks, and much of the priesthood, are decadent and profligate. They have forgotten the true meaning of the Bible. They are merely interested in worldly matters and are besotted by greed. They disobey the laws of celibacy, openly living with women and their illegitimate children! Luther believes we don't need the Pope, and all the priests, to help us with our faith. They have filled a life of faith with icons and rituals and rules to keep ordinary men and women powerless. Luther believes that the Bible should be available to each and every man or woman in the vernacular, and that we should pray to our Lord ourselves, without intermission of the priestly hierarchy."

Then she sat down, exhausted by her speech.

I heard Liza cough. Being a devout churchgoer and hardly a rebellious soul, she was offended by Megan's words. But I was fascinated. My mind already flashed to the scene at Jervaulx Abbey, where we had stayed on our journey. There the monks had made of the abbey a profitable industry, with guest houses, an infirmary, cellars, and workshops. We were charged a goodly sum of money for our stay, and when we ate dinner, even I had been shocked to see the monks indulge in fatted calf, pheasant, quail, larks' tongues, rich pork in Madeira sauce, and quantities of ale and red wine.

"That book sounds very interesting," was all I said for the moment. I wanted time to let the new thoughts sink into my mind.

"It's dangerous even to say so much," Megan warned me firmly. "The King has denounced Luther as a heretic, and anyone found reading his words, or speaking them, could be brought to trial for treason."

I shrugged my shoulders. "We're a long way from the King in Lincolnshire. May I borrow this book someday?"

"Are you sure?" She sounded triumphant and, without further ado, took another book from a shelf and tucked Luther's little one between its pages. "Here, and don't forget to hide it from Father. He would have me flogged if he knew what I was up to!"

Clutching her books in my hand, reminded with a chill of the reason for my presence in this strange house with this even stranger young lady, I asked, "So, then, when am I going to meet the great man?"

"He'll be back soon enough, and then you'll wish he'd never turned up. Life is not so easy when he is around. He must be in Lincoln with his friends. They often spend days at a time there, deciding which of their peasants will be thrown out of their cottages for failure to pay tithes."

"Megan," I scolded. "Don't you have one good word to say for your father?"

"No." And she stared me in the eye.

✤

After dinner that evening, I gladly returned to Megan's chamber. I felt comforted by the familiar sight of books and papers, so like my own room at Kendal.

Megan was in love with Robert Prince, a young man in Lincoln, but her father had forbidden their marriage. Her lover was a poet and musician, but the union would bring Borough no financial gain. He had insisted she marry a local squire, which was the cause of her rebellion. Robert Prince was in Lincoln waiting loyally for a favorable resolution, which of course was not to come.

Now I was both impressed and envious. To have one true love who would go against your father's wishes and wait for you sounded wonderful. At that point in my life, the notion of love, true love, was only just beginning to take seed in my simple heart.

"And what if nothing will prevail with Lord Borough?"

Megan shook her wild mane and shrugged with nonchalance, before saying cheerfully, "Who knows? Maybe I'll run away to a nunnery. I have a friend in these parts, Anne Kyme, who is so clever, a real devotee of Martin Luther . . . and she has a notion to run away from her husband. I should introduce you."

I was about to ask how a woman could run away from her husband when Megan jumped off the bed. The house trembled with the sound of doors slamming and boots thundering up the stairs.

"Where is everyone? Abigail! Edwina! Megan! Come here this minute."

"That's done it." Megan stamped her feet on the floorboards, swiftly slipping shoes back onto stockinged feet. "Let's hope he goes straight to his chamber, and you can get to your room unseen."

I was standing stiff and straight, ready to meet my fate. Hearing another door slam, we both heaved a sigh of relief. Megan ushered me away.

"Now you'll get to meet your Lord Borough." She held my hand to say goodbye.

"Wish me luck," I pleaded.

"Go, quick, before you get us both into trouble," was her only reply.

Chapter 2

Liza had already prepared my best cambric dress. It was pale bone color, not as pretty as the blue one I had been wearing that day, but it was my most formal gown. She brushed my fair locks, bringing a shine to the mass of soft blond curls. I feared my appearance was less than stunning, for I had not been careful to wash my face during these bone-chilling days in Lincolnshire. What would Lord Borough expect of me? What would he make of me?

Abigail stood at our door, noticeably less red in the face. She led me by candlelight down the oak staircase to the great hall. A fire was burning in the hearth, as though by miracle now that the master was returned. The face of the man I was about to marry slowly became clear as I descended step by step.

Edward, Lord Borough, was tall, maybe six feet to my slender five feet. The man I was supposed to love, cherish, and honor stood before me, warming his haunches against the fire, a glass of brandy cupped in his hand. He was white-haired, red-skinned either from the cold night air or from too much wine, thick-set, firm-shouldered, and not, at a quick glance, kindly-looking. But, I sighed with relief, not the picture of the ogre Megan had painted either.

Glancing me briefly up and down, he spoke to Abigail, not to me. "Is this the girl? Good Lord, couldn't Maude have delivered me one with some flesh on her? Take her away, Abigail. Feed her up and deliver her back to me when she's a bit plumper. Can't stand scrawny girls. You should know that. Get the girl into the air. Anything to improve this meager dish."

I was set to drop in a curtsy before him, though his insults had added flame to the fire already ignited by Megan. Abigail took me back up the stairs, grumbling to herself.

"Feed her up, he says. And never mentions where the money is coming from to feed two more mouths."

But back in our chamber, after gazing at Liza's mournful tear-stained face, for she had overheard everything, I slammed out of the door again, straight to the staircase overlooking the great hall. From the third step down I called his name. When he did not answer, I took more steps in long strides and walked toward him. His back was turned now, the glass of brandy still in his hands.

"Lord Borough." I spoke firmly to hide the hint of fear in my voice. "I must speak with you."

Turning, he yawned, and placed the glass on a small table.

"Yes, Lady Katherine, what can I do for you? Your mother told me you had a wayward spirit with a mind too fanciful for itself. What do you have to say to me?"

"That I am distressed by my welcome here. My attendant and I have been in this house nearly a week and we have not yet been formally greeted, nor treated with the courtesy we deserve."

"And you'll not be till you've proved yourself worthy to be my wife. You must first learn humility before your husband."

Anger steaming in my soul, I said, "Then I shall write to Mother to break off the marriage negotiations right now. I cannot live in this house."

"Lady Katherine." His voice registered a slight change. "Come here. Let me take a better look." Taking my hand, he pulled me toward him near the fireplace.

I stiffened, letting my hand lie limp and ungracious.

"You will write no such letter, do you hear me?"

"Sire, you cannot prevent me." I held my head high.

Then, suddenly, he relaxed his grip, and sighed deeply as though all the cares of the world were upon his shoulders.

"What would you have me grant you? What does the lady desire to improve her life here?" His voice was mocking, but I had already decided I quite loathed the man.

"If I could take some rides with my attendant and with your daughters, I would become better acquainted with the city of Lincoln. To visit the fine cathedral, and pay formal visits on some ladies of rank and note would benefit us all, sire."

"So Megan has got to you already, has she?"

"Father!" a voice yelled out, echoing across the hall, resounding from oak beam to beam.

Lord Borough raised his head toward the gallery.

"Well, Megan, what do you have to say for yourself?"

"Father, you must not treat Lady Katherine so. We have shared a few words, but she is a fine, righteous, devoted person, who has only encouraged me toward the true and virtuous path. Her example will be good for me. Who knows, I might even condescend to marry one day under her good influence."

He dropped my hand. "Not likely! Go on, Katherine, back to your chamber. You may take rides with Megan and Edwina *only* to visit their aunt in Gainsborough. Your mother told me you were a good religious girl—that's one reason I wanted you here . . . put some sense in my daughter's head. Get to bed, all of you. Now!"

❖

I saw little of Lord Borough in those first couple of weeks. But my days did take on a different routine. Early mornings Liza and I had to attend chapel, where my husband-to-be would prostrate himself in a showy affectation of devotion.

I spent most days secretly reading the book by Martin Luther. I became convinced that what I was reading mirrored my own secret but never expressed beliefs. The priesthood was largely corrupt and often downright obscene.

Sometimes, in chapel, on my knees, my head bent in prayer, I would glance sideways at Borough, in the pew reserved for him across the aisle. I began to associate my religious misgivings with my antipathy for him.

I soon became bored with our ladylike existence—doing embroidery, playing the spinet, and walking in the gardens when the weather permitted. I was delighted when Megan told me she had arranged a trip to Gainsborough. Borough believed we were off to see his sister, but we were really going to pay our respects to Megan's friend Anne Kyme of the nearby village of Stallingborough.

Anne was waiting for us by the glowing fire of her palatial

drawing room, furnished in much more splendor than was ours at Borough Hall, overlooking the vast stretches of fields that belonged to her husband. She tinkled a little brass bell to greet us and ordered warm ale and biscuits from her servants. I was immediately struck by Anne's radiant beauty. Her glowing dark hair fell down her back. Her skin was pale and pure, and her eyes seemed to melt me with their luminescence. She was taller than I, with a firm strong back, a fine long nose, and a bright rewarding smile. Who would have guessed she was anything other than a good and contented country wife?

"Katherine." She held out her hand graciously, in the manner of Court. "How pleasant to meet you. I believe we might have crossed paths as children at Court?"

"I was there from time to time with my parents Sir Thomas and Lady Parr," I returned politely. "But I gather from Megan," I added, "that neither of us is as pleased to be in Lincolnshire as we might have been at Court."

Anne turned a delicate shade of pink and leaned to kiss me on the cheek. Glancing at Megan, then at me, she laughed lightly. "We are a terrible band of women, aren't we? What will become of the world if all women are as disobedient?"

Megan guffawed, and I tittered nervously, unsure of my place here.

But Megan showed me their intent by saying boldly, "Kate, Anne Kyme has so distressed her husband that he is threatening to throw her out of the house!"

Anne Kyme showed her pretty teeth as she flashed one of her nice smiles. "I believe you have read *The Babylonian Captivity* too, Kate?"

I nodded eagerly.

"In Court circles you'll find many people reading Martin Luther, some even openly, despite the King's attitude, which must surely change one day. But my husband does not agree with my readings. He was horrified to learn that I had been in Lincoln Cathedral, arguing with the bishops there. Yes, he has threatened to throw me out of his home, but what he doesn't know, Kate, is that I am planning to leave *him*. There are ways a woman can survive alone. I intend to prove it can be done."

"Katherine. Will you join us when *we* run away?" Megan put in.

"Please," I answered lightly, for I thought they were teasing. "I am not even married yet!"

We all laughed, but not exactly for the same reason. Anne Kyme intrigued me, as did Megan, but I felt ill at ease with both of them and a bit frightened by their strange ideas.

Then I felt my friend's strong hand on my shoulder. "It's all right, Kate, we'll stick together. Everything will be for the best."

"I hope so, Megan, I hope so," I said rather shakily.

✛

Borough sent for me later that evening. I entered the library and was met by an angry face.

"I know you did not visit Megan's aunt," he stormed. "You have disobeyed me—as I knew you would!"

"Sire, please," I begged him. But then a quiet voice inside me bade me say no more. Let him rant and rave. He did not want to hear my excuses. He needed to vent his anger. I sought the easiest solution for Lord Borough was impossible to deal with under the circumstances.

So I hung my head and whispered, "Yes, sire," to everything he bellowed.

"Go to your room. Abigail has a fresh dress ironed for you. We will be wed this night. I have called for a priest to come by after dinner."

Not fully aware that my last strand of freedom was now about to be cut, I again murmured, "Yes, sire," and retired to find Abigail laying out the gown and a pile of rich accessories upon my bed.

Made of gossamer silk, the gown was white, trimmed with lace, and decorated with tiny pearl buttons. There was gold thread embroidered at the throat, waist, and around the wrists of the long elegant sleeves. Impressed, I fingered the delicate material and decided I would enhance it with several cotton petticoats to make the skirts stand out nicely and my figure look more womanly.

Abigail helped me on with the dress, easing it over my hair. She grumbled when I sent Liza searching for petticoats and silk hose. The dress fitted well over the bust but was tight at the throat with its embroidered lace ruff. It fell to the floor in great folds; I was obviously much shorter than its previous owner.

Liza pulled up the skirt from the waist and encircled me with a belt of gold chain strung with pearls. The billowing effect was lovely. We found satin slippers in one of my chests, and I pirouetted around the room, elated. Liza insisted on combing out my hair while Abigail stood by impatiently. As a final touch she strung another gold chain through my hair, whispering in my ear, "There, ma'am, now you look really beautiful. Your husband can't help but be enamored."

We giggled foolishly until Abigail put her dry old claw over my hand and took me from the room.

Sitting in the great hall alone, I shifted my cap so that the gold chain Liza had put in my hair would show. For the first time I felt passingly pretty. My blond hair was shining as it fell around my shoulders. The waves that had made my mother despair now seemed a virtue. My brow was smooth, my skin clear and healthy with a pinkish glow. For perhaps the first time in my young life, I felt a sensual warmth of physical satisfaction spread over me. I was a woman able to attract a man. With a shudder, my girlish self came to its senses. I pictured Lord Borough, my husband-to-be. I should be thinking of him, yet he was certainly not a man who inspired fantasies of love.

The marriage ceremony took but five minutes. The priest read the vows, to which Lord Borough and I responded. Immediately afterward, Borough led me, in my fine gown and gold chain, up the staircase. This time we headed away from the little chamber I had shared with Liza, down a different corridor, toward his own room.

It was a dark room, severe, without the soft touch that a woman usually adds. A large oak bed with four columns, draped in coverings of dark red damask, took up the center of the room. The only other furnishings were an armoire and a wardrobe, also made of oak. The chamber was bare and unforgiving, as was the man I had just married.

Borough bade me be still while he prepared himself for bed. He disappeared through a small door and called to me from his dressing room.

"Did your mother prepare you for this day, Katherine?"

"No, sire."

"Good Lord. Will these women never learn?" he said angrily and reappeared wearing only a long cambric nightgown.

The skin on his legs and neck was white and red, which is the only way I can describe the motley effect I noticed. My husband was not a handsome man, though he was tall and strong. He had a shock of snowy white hair crowning his head. He was a heavy man with a spreading middle. But what disturbed me most were his eyes. They were deep-set, almost hooded. It was as if he never really looked at me. I sighed to myself, for I had just been dreaming of perfect love and now I was to bed this man for whom I had no feeling.

"Do you know why I determined to marry you today?" he snapped.

"No, sire."

"Because you were becoming unruly. I decided I had better take you in hand now. Though in truth I was waiting for you to come of age before we wed. How old are you—not yet thirteen?"

"Very nearly, sire."

"Cannot you speak more than two words, girl?"

"Yes, sire." Then I added deliberately, "When I so choose."

"You're an insolent girl, Katherine. You have to be controlled. I am going to teach you to be more obedient. Your trouble is not having a father. You've grown up with too much uncontrolled spirit—under just a mother's hand."

"I had a father, sire."

"Died when you were a mere tot."

"I was nearly five, sire."

"Exactly."

He was convinced by his own argument. Then he slid into bed, while I remained sitting in the chair. To my amazement he said no more to me. I was left in that chair all night long. I woke at dawn to find myself lying on the floor, mocked by the finery of my wedding gown.

Abigail came into the room at daybreak, bringing Borough his medicine. She did not seem at all surprised to find me on the floor at the foot of the bed.

Tearily picking myself up, I said to Abigail, "Might Liza be allowed to join me so that I can repair my dishevelment?"

"Ask the master," was all Abigail would say. She slammed the door shut.

The man in the bed moved. Borough raised his head from the pillow.

"You have learned an important lesson in obedience this night, Kate. Just never forget I am your master. Do as I say and you won't find me unkind. Now come into my bed."

He reached out and pulled me to the edge of the bed. He undressed me carelessly. The silk gown and many petticoats were soon on the floor, leaving me in only a cotton underslip. Tired and defeated as I was, I felt nothing when he finally took me as his wife—no fear, no apprehension, no interest. Total indifference. I had lost all sense of myself. What he did to me scarcely lives in my mind. I remember it was long and painful. My mind has mercifully blotted out the memory of the few times Edward, Lord Borough, took me between the sheets.

I was Lady Borough now, I said to myself, with grim determination. I would find a way to be happy.

Chapter 3

I sat in the ladies' parlor the following day, working on a piece of embroidery. Although I was scathing of women who thus spent their time, I was trying to accustom myself to my new position. The day had brightened, and we were experiencing fresh and sunny weather, rare for early March.

Megan pushed the door open and peered her head around. "March comes in like a lamb." She smiled at me and I at her. We were slightly awkward with each other, now that I had become her father's wife.

"Am I ever to call you Kate again? Would you prefer me to address you as ma'am, or Lady Borough?"

"Names mean little." I spoke lightly. "Only labels from the outside world. I am no different from the girl you met a few weeks ago. Only now, as they say, I am a woman."

I stared out the window at the first buds on the willow trees, buds that would soon turn to blossom and blessedly transform this eerie, barren landscape.

"Megan!" I cried, jumping out of my seat and letting the embroidery fall to the floor.

"Why, Kate, whatever is the matter?"

"It has just dawned on me, looking at the leaves about to bud, now spring is almost here, that what has passed between me and your father could mean I will be with child."

"A thing to rejoice in, I am sure," said Megan, still unsure of me as her stepmother. "Father will be delighted to welcome a young son into the household."

"Megan!" I was in panic. "I cannot have a child."

"Father will wait. You are probably too young."

"No, you don't understand me. I am scared of it . . . I don't want it . . . I don't want to be a mother to another human being. I'm so young. I cannot, I will not. . . . Oh, no, I could not let that man—I am sorry he is your father—but I could not give nourishment to growing his seed in my body. I would die at the horror of it."

Megan was stony-faced, and I was sure she despised me now. But at last, she spoke kindly.

"Kate, arrange to take a walk this afternoon. The weather is balmy, so no one should be questioning. Walk through the gardens that way," she whispered, pointing in a southerly direction. "Pass through the lych-gate at the far end of the kitchen garden and then follow the path for at least two miles. The area is wooded. You are going to pay a call on Old Nell in her cottage. She is our local healer. They call Nell a witch . . . at least I have heard my father say so. He threatens to burn her cottage down at least once a year! In truth, she is a wonderful woman who heals the poor. She reads the stars, too. She will know how *not* to have a child—if that is what you desire."

I put out my hand to grasp Megan's. In silence we pressed palms, sealing our silent vow to help and support each other. My stepdaughter had turned out to be a true friend.

✤

Old Nell's cottage was easily found. Liza followed lazily behind me as I raced ahead. Walking through the woods before they burst into greenness was like exploring the rooms of a large house that has not yet been furnished. The thin silvery birches were very tall and silent, their white trunks glowed like ghosts in the clear March air. I was happy that no one had seen us and elated to be out of that wretched house.

I saw a thatched roof with a thread of smoke rising out of its chimney. I beckoned to Liza to make haste. The cottage was just a hut made of mud and wood staves, covered with creeper vines. It looked as though it had been there forever. I rattled the door, and it opened. A voice told us to enter.

"Shut the door, girls," Nell said. "It's still winter even if the sun has graced us today."

As she spoke I followed the line of a sunbeam entering the window. It lit Nell's hands, which were gnarled like tree bark from years of usefulness. She worked quietly and with self-assurance.

Nell was not the image of a witch I had in my childish head. She looked very normal to me as she mixed herbs and divided them into several pots. Her only distinguishing feature was her thick red hair, which was as wild and untamed as my stepdaughter's. It hung over her eyes and fell across her face, causing her to scowl and push it back. She picked up a green-and-red handkerchief, rolled it up tight, and tied it around her forehead to keep that hair still. I had never seen a woman wear such a head covering before.

Nell was short and plump—or at least she looked so. The fullness of her brown woolen dress hardly concealed a body not bound up by belts or girdles. She worked slowly, methodically, at one with her actions. I was almost envious of the freedom her life seemed to hold. Why, she had her own little house and work to do.

"Megan Borough suggested I come," I offered hesitantly.

"You sound foreign. Not from these parts."

"I come from Westmoreland, many miles away. My home was Kendal."

"Ah, 'tis a beautiful dialect ye have, my dear." Nell raised her head. "You in trouble?"

"My name is Katherine Parr—I mean, Lady Borough. I am newly wed to Megan's father. We live just two miles away. I, I . . . came to you for advice."

"How long married?" Nell was pouring a fine green powder down a wooden funnel into a small clay jar.

"Two days."

"You with child, dear?" Nell sounded sympathetic even in her indifference.

"No, no, at least I hope not. I mean, surely . . ." I was stumbling for words when at last I found some courage. "I want to know if you could help me *not* be with child."

Nell now raised her head and fixed her piercing black eyes upon me. "You're just married and don't want to be with child."

I flushed again, but Nell had not said it as a criticism, only as a statement. I nodded dumbly.

"How old are you, child?"

"Not quite thirteen."

"Do you have your bleed yet?"

"I don't think so," I stuttered, and I heard Liza snigger. Nell let out a hearty laugh.

"You'd know if you had it, girl." She rocked on her heels. "I doubt you have. You won't get with child yet—not till the moon has taken your body for hers and the red foam gushes out. They say it is a sign of our shame for not being with child. But we, my master and I, we call it the Red Princess— it's our sign of freedom. Tell me where you were born and when," Nell demanded, taking my hand in hers.

As I spoke she turned my hand over and over. She looked into my eyes, even at my eyelids, and passed me a tankard of some herbal mixture and bade me drink. Then she put her hands to her forehead and said in a strange low voice, "Katherine Parr, I am sensing an aura from you. I am going to read your future. Pass me the tankard back when all the liquid is drunk and I will tell you your destiny."

Nell sat down in a rocker by the fire and took the cup I handed her. After a few minutes of silence she began to speak again in a strange voice.

"You have the sign of leadership, my dear. You will have a fascinating life. You are born for great things. I see a house, a fine house, the house of Kings. I see a crown and a large man at your side wearing a crown. I believe you have been born to wear a crown on your head, dear girl. You should live long and happy; you will know love and sadness. There is one word of warning—beware a girl child who may not be your own, or may be."

Confused, I asked if the leaves told of my having any children of my own.

"I can only tell you what you have heard. The words come from my master. If you want to avoid children, take dittany, and aristologia. Here, I'll give you a sachet of the herbs. Mix the dittany with pork grease and anoint yourself with it after your husband has been with you. Rub the infected area. Drink the infusion of aristologia each night mixed with water of rue. You can rinse yourself with vinegar, or you can apply vinegar, honey, and butter into your passage. Do you know yourself in that region yet, girl?"

Blushing, I said, "No."

"Then learn fast. Or your husband will own your body too."

Nell looked cross and turned back to her work. "Go now, I am tired."

"Can I pay you?" I asked nervously.

"Why, do you have any silver?" she asked sharply.

My head lowered and I said, "No."

"You married girls are all the same. Husbands give you nothing but babies. Run away, girl, run away."

✢

"Do you think she was telling me to run off and leave Borough?" I asked Liza on our walk home, clutching my sachets of dittany, aristologia, and rue.

"Surely not," said Liza. "How could you?"

"I don't know. But Mistress Kyme might leave her husband. There must be some way a woman can be on her own and have her own money."

"It doesn't sound as if you'll be staying long anyway, mistress. If you are to wear a crown!" And Liza giggled.

"Liza, wasn't that strange? Imagine her telling me I'd be a Queen. Foolish woman. I hope all her advice wasn't as false. How would I look in a crown, Liza?"

I ran ahead, carrying my head straight, putting a twine of leaves on my hair and walking back to her as if I were indeed a Queen.

"Do you think she was talking about our dear King Henry?" I asked.

"Why?"

"Well, she said a large man."

"The King is tall, but he's not large," said Liza. "Not according to your mother. Lady Parr always describes him as youthful and athletic."

"And handsome, Liza, the most clever and handsome man in the world. I adore him. I'd love to be his wife."

"You wouldn't!" said Liza, surprised.

"Why not? To be Queen and have all those beautiful dresses and jewels, all the riches and power to do whatever you want to. Oh, surely it's a better life than this," and I waved my arm around me.

"Well, Queen Catherine is not so happy, as your mother tells it," pointed out Liza.

I shrugged. "Catherine of Aragon let him down so, with

those babies. You know the King wants a son—he has to have one."

I ran ahead. "I want to be as free as a boy—and as a Queen!" I ran laughing between the trees. "Come on, Liza, catch me if you can!"

✣

Borough had been away for a whole month, and my life had become quite happy in that house with the two girls, my friend Liza, and even Abigail. She had become used to my presence and I to hers.

Then a letter bearing the proud insignia of King Henry's Court arrived. My mother, as lady-in-waiting to Queen Catherine and Princess Mary, used this seal.

"How wonderful!" Megan said with what sounded like envy.

Mother's letters were always full of Court gossip and tales. I never had written to complain to her, biding my time to see if life improved. Instead I had addressed copious letters to her full of the small details of my new life.

Maude Parr's letter, dated June 1525, raged at first about the dreadful sweating sickness that had attacked London sending up a foul stench that infected the air of the city.

There seems to be no escape from it, other than luck. In a recent very hot week, more than fifty people died in one day! The malady has just reached King Henry's Court, and he is so fearful for the life of his new young mistress, Anne Boleyn, that he is sending her back home to Hever Castle in Dover. Mistress Boleyn will never die of the sweat! She is too tough for that!

That Boleyn woman. She puts on all these airs and graces, but she is no beauty. The King has only recently pushed her family into the peerage. A commoner, my darling Kate. Why, you would have more chance with the King than this little upstart! But all the men seem to favor Anne Boleyn. Thomas Wyatt, the great poet, is also besotted.

Dearest Kate, you know Queen Catherine has been my friend for years.

I've gone through all these problems with her before—first it was Bessie Blount, and then Mary Cary (née Boleyn!). Catherine never really recovered from the sadness of the death of her little son, Henry . . . or all those dreadful miscarriages. My child, I have been blessed to have loved none but your father, borne my three wonderful children in good health, and, cross my heart, I still feel hale and hearty. But Catherine does bring problems upon herself. She is not a happy woman. It is hardly surprising the King looks elsewhere. She has her religion, I know—but, oh, I remember the days when she and the King were so happy—dancing, laughing, playing like young children. And there's Princess Mary. Such a sweet, shy little girl. The King does love her as he would a daughter. But he so longs for a son—he talks about it all the time!

There is talk the King wants a divorce granted by the Pope. How can that be possible? Where will this mess end? Anyone I talk to thinks that divorce is impossible. Yet maybe King Henry is powerful enough to institute laws to make it so. Oh dear, Kate my darling, the poor Queen has done nothing but cry all week. Henry is threatening to send Princess Mary off to Ludlow Castle to begin her duties as the Princess of Wales. I know Catherine feels she will be left alone and deserted—the child Mary is all Catherine has in the world these days.

Ah well, I thank God to have been blessed with you, Kate. I pray this letter finds you happy and healthy. My love to you always.

"Never believe in love, Kate. Never!" Megan's hands were clenched so tightly that the blood seemed to have completely left them.

"Robert Prince is to marry. I learned yesterday. I have not seen him in months, for I am not allowed to meet him. He has found another love . . . he has broken our vow."

"I am truly sorry," I gasped. I was indeed heartbroken, for I had been dreaming of finding a true love, as Megan had described hers. I did not want to hear this distressing news.

She grimaced. "Sorrow won't help. He was unworthy of our love. That is all there is to say. He vowed to remain true to me. I have kept my vow. He has not."

"Don't be so hard on him," I cried. "He has a life to live too."

"If we are speaking of perfect love, then it must be perfect." And she flounced off to the gardens.

⚜

Edward Borough and I had somehow become used to each other. Although I had been plunged into womanhood well before my time, I was still very naive. Many nights I quite enjoyed the caresses from the old body that lent me its physical warmth. If, in our daily lives, Borough was often cold and sometimes downright cruel, in bed he was strangely tender. He fondled me as if I were his own child. My body still had none of the properties of a woman, and I often wondered what pleasure I brought him. I guessed he knew other women, for his absences from the house seemed to cheer him up.

One night the linen sheet had a red stain upon it, as dark as a stain from the butcher. I felt weepy and scared. Borough woke to hear my sniffling. Angry that I had disturbed his sleep, he told me to be quiet immediately or I would be sent back to my room. But, glancing at the red stain, he grinned and said, "Now you can give me a son, Kate."

But I could not halt the tears of misery. I felt that I had lost something very important and precious.

As I lay there, I dared to ask him, "Sire, good husband, why did you choose to marry me?"

Borough growled on his pillow, "That was the arrangement made between me and your mother."

"But was I not *very* young to be wed? Why would you want a wife *so* much younger than yourself?"

"Ask your mother that, not me, girl," he said brusquely.

"Are you content to share your bed with a wife younger than your daughter?" I carried on, indifferent to the outcome of my persistent questioning.

"You are no longer younger in wisdom than Megan, mistress wife. She has disobeyed me. You have now become a good woman, by virtue of being wed. Women need a strong ruler. They have to be yoked. They are wild and bad on their own. Megan is already a lost soul."

I was silent, for he had called me wife for the first time.

"Get with child, Kate. Then I will honor you with everything I have. I need a son, young wife, someone to replace that wastrel young man Henry, who purports to carry our family name."

Quietly, more as though I were speaking to myself, I whispered, "Can I not have a happy life without a child, sire?"

"No," he snapped, turning over with his back to me.

But I reached my arms out to hold him. I knew this was the way to soften that surly exterior. I had learned, in the few months of being Lady Borough, one of the first lessons of survival.

⁜

Summer became fall, and the Lincolnshire countryside turned golden, then purple, then dark brown, readying itself for winter again. The skies clouded over and were soon heavy with snow. The walks and playful times with Liza were forgotten, as we retired more often to our chamber during the somber afternoons. I had learned to pass my time, secretly, in study of the books Megan lent me. After the first Martin Luther epistle smuggled into my chamber, there followed one or two more—as soon as she could borrow them from Anne Kyme. I also continued studies of my own, in Latin and Greek, translations from French and Italian, and poems that I penned with my own hand, which always brought me great pleasure.

And always there were letters to be written—long letters to my mother Maude, to my sister Anne, who had joined her at Court. Their life seemed filled with everything mine lacked. The marriage plans for my brother William, with the Bourchier clan, were going well. Surely now Lord Borough would bring me to town, to be introduced at Court. I was envious of the arrangement Mother had drawn up for marrying Anne. She was nearly eleven and betrothed to Willie Herbert, the bastard son of the Earl of Pembroke. Maude expected Willie to inherit his father's title, for Pembroke had only sired daughters to his legal wives.

I clung to the faint hope that my life as Lady Borough would improve, that I would soon be at Court with a place of privilege as a wealthy and respected wife of the nobility. In the meantime, however, my friendship with Megan was flourishing and I found our secret discussions about Martin Luther stimulating, even exciting.

Chapter 4

Shortly before Christmas, nearly a full year since my arrival in Lincolnshire, I was standing in the great hall marveling at the bright sun that was pouring into the room and listening to Edwina's spinet playing, when Megan came running in the front door. Her long velvet cloak fell to the ground as she tripped in her haste.

Her words came tumbling out in frosty breaths as she blew furiously on her hands. "He's coming! He'll be here in under an hour!"

Edwina jumped down immediately from her stool and ran to embrace her sister.

"What is happening?" I cried.

"Henry, our brother, is on his way from Fountains Abbey. He'll be spending Christmas with us."

My brow furrowed slightly, but my heart seemed to be

thudding loudly at the prospect of some excitement in our mundane lives. We all rushed to our rooms to prepare for the guest. Minutes later we heard the galloping horse and the boys closing the gates behind the breathless steed. Through a windowpane I could see the stallion being led to the stableyard by a tall figure in a long black cloak. We all burst from our chambers, hands taming stray locks of hair, and descended to the great hall.

Megan and Edwina were already out the front door running to greet the man who almost ran into their eager arms. Then all three came running up to the door, one of Henry's arms around each pair of shoulders.

Henry Borough was tall and handsome in an almost god-like way. His hair was thickly blond, hanging straight about his ears. His was a face from tales of ancient Greece, of gods and wood nymphs. The high cheekbones lent him a princely grace, the narrow eyes twinkled and sparkled as though permanently afire with humor and intelligence.

Megan shared much of that native aristocracy with her brother, and Edwina had his natural charm. How did their father so lack in all these qualities? Their mother must have been a beautiful woman indeed to have borne such children. I tingled in anticipation of meeting such a good-looking, appealing, altogether fascinating personage as Henry Borough. Maybe life would not be so bad here after all.

When Edwina and Megan had stopped chattering, and hugging, and tugging at his sleeve, Henry laughed, caught sight of me, and pulled away.

"Pray introduce me, Megan. This must be Katherine, Lady Borough. My new stepmother, I believe?"

He held out a long, thin, elegant hand to me, and I bowed low as I accepted his greeting.

"Henry, I hardly feel content to be called your stepmother," I said, quite in awe of this attractive, obviously urbane, older man.

He was in good spirits, and continued teasingly, "Well, stepmother you are, so I shall address you thus. Come on, sisters, let's go and explore the garden. I haven't been in the old house and grounds for so long."

I found myself gazing longingly after their three diminishing figures. I wished I could run out and play too. I had never before set eyes on someone as altogether beautiful as Henry Borough. Blushing, I tore myself away from the window and went to the kitchen to discuss the special dinner planned for that evening.

The next few days passed in a whirlwind of energy and entertainment. At Henry's command, we forsook morning chapel. He too was an avowed Lutheran and loudly proclaimed—in his father's absence—we should have none of that "devilish Popery." I laughed and clapped my hands with glee to hear him speak so boldly.

"We have another reformist in our stepmother?" he asked.

"Yes, Henry." I was able to hold my head proudly over our breakfast of oatcakes and light ale. "Megan introduced me to *The Babylonian Captivity* in my first few days in this house. I was enraptured by its message. Though I will confess to you that sometimes the fact we have to be so secret in our new faith frightens me—does it not you?"

Henry Borough's face seemed to alter at my words. "Why, Katherine," he exclaimed, as though his use of "stepmother" was no longer right, "I am moved by your words. I had no idea you had taken the reformist faith so seriously."

Megan chimed in, "Henry, you should not take women so lightly. You, of all people, should know that much of the reformist work in Lincolnshire is being led by Anne Kyme—and me."

"Yes, yes, Megan, sweetheart," Henry mollified her. "I know you young women these days are all *full* of ideas and good works. But you still need the men to put the ideas into action, don't you?"

Megan was insulted by his words, and she flounced out the door, slamming it behind her. "Men!" we heard her shout as she marched off down the hallway.

Henry leaned back in his chair, laughing again, at ease with his sisters.

"I presume you have come to know my impassioned sister well, Katherine? Megan is *never* to be taken lightly."

Edwina too got up to leave the room, and I felt a rush of pleasure to be left alone with Henry. His presence had brought a new lightness to my days, a new spring to my step.

"I count Megan as one of my dearest friends, Henry," I said carefully. "But she is certainly one of the most *definite* people I have ever met. There is no gray in Megan's world, only black or white. But she tells me you write poetry? I try my own hand at verse sometimes. I would be honored, sir, to show you my verses someday soon, and to hear your learned comments."

Henry beamed at me with that noble aquiline face. "Why, of course, Katherine. Bring them to the library this morning. We'll compare notes. It would be a great pleasure to me."

My heart skipped several beats, for I had not dared to imagine he would take such an interest. "Are you sure I won't be in your way?" I asked.

His eyes were speaking to me in words I would not dare interpret, yet his speech was gentle.

"You won't be in my way, Katherine. I will be the one who is honored by your presence."

✢

The next few days passed as in a dream. Most mornings, I brought my poetry to Henry Borough in the library. He perused it carefully, occasionally correcting a spelling error, or improving my script. He had been educated at the University of Cambridge, for which opportunity I was most jealous. His recent passage of time at Fountains Abbey had been purportedly to improve his religious education, but, he informed me, during those quiet mornings in the library he had really been in collusion with others of the reformist faith, helping to translate Martin Luther's writings into English.

"That must be wonderful work." My eyes were wide open with interest.

"It certainly is, Katherine. If ever I can think up an excuse to take you to visit Fountains, would you care to come? How far will you go in rebelling against Father's ban on Lutheranism?"

Frowning, sitting next to him on a bench at the wooden table in the library, I said truthfully, "Right now, I feel very brave. But your father is absent. When he is here, my courage sometimes escapes me."

Henry placed his hand over mine, and I felt tinglings rush through my whole body.

"I don't blame you for lacking courage, Kate," he said, suddenly using the name only my closest friends and family used for me. "Father is not the easiest man to manage. I have a hard time with him myself, as you may already have heard. I admire your strength, as it is."

His hand was still over mine, and I did not think to take it away. I turned to face him, and his eyes stared boldly down at me. "Henry . . ." I stammered, shifting my hand now, as his own seemed to press down harder. "We must not be seen like this." And without knowing what I was doing, I dragged myself away and ran from the library.

I did not see Henry for the next few days. Perhaps I was scared of him, or scared of myself and my own feelings. His mere presence made my heart lighter. To see him lifted my spirits in a way I had never experienced before. Everything about me felt fresher, younger, more alive and more interesting. Yet he frightened me, not only because of the strength of my feeling for this man who was my stepson but because he seemed to threaten a certain safety in my existence. I avoided our shared family breakfasts, avoided going to the library, and only met with him at the dinner table before I quickly disappeared to my room.

Henry seemed unperturbed, bantering with his sisters, teasing Abigail, whose whole personality changed with Henry in the house.

The morning we heard that Borough was expected back the following day, a pall fell over the household. The laughter vanished and I noticed even Henry paled at the news. The weather was cold, but I was determined to walk in the gardens, bracing myself for the return of my husband.

I chose the topiary. I was walking between the strangely shaped hedges, tightly wrapped in my blue velvet cloak, when I saw Henry up ahead. His head was buried deep in a book. Perhaps I stepped on a twig, or perhaps it was the gasp of surprise that escaped my lips, but something made him raise his eyes at that moment, and our gazes locked.

His face was soft and warm, the skin supple and tender, the eyes like pools of light on a dark afternoon. Something in his eyes glinted, speaking to me from the depth of his soul. He rose to meet me, his eyes never leaving mine. He smiled at me, and I smiled in return. All the while my heart was beating, thumping against my chest, which I feared he might hear. What would happen if I fainted at his feet? With great effort I lowered my gaze.

"Well, Katherine," he said in a deep voice. He took my hand in his. I said nothing, not knowing what I could, or should, say.

I loved the look of his hooded eyes, the crease by the edge of his mouth where a smile formed, the furrows of that noble brow that had been so buried in learning. I wanted to stroke the forehead, kiss those eyes. Oh, how I yearned for passion!

"Kate," he said sharply, disturbing my reverie, and I blushed lest he might have read my mind.

"Father is coming home," he said urgently.

"I know. Does it worry you?" I asked softly.

"Only that I . . . I never meant to hold your hand the other day. . . . But I wanted to touch you," he said, and his fingers tightened against mine.

A shiver ran up and down my spine. What I had dreamed about was coming true. Was I brave enough to meet the consequences? To fall in love with one's stepson was dangerous and foolhardy.

"I was hoping you would never let my hand go," I said shyly.

Henry held my arm, for I had turned as though to walk away.

He whispered into my hair, "Shall we continue to meet even with Father in the house? Dare you, Kate?"

"What about you? Wouldn't such actions be just as dangerous for you?"

I was ready to flee now, unable to accept all this.

"Wait." He pulled back my straining body. "Meet me here tonight," he said hotly into my velvet hood. "Father will not be back until the morrow. After dinner, here at the back of the garden, we can walk in the woods and continue our talk."

My hand flew to my chest to quiet the unsteady breathing. Foolish, impetuous, wild, stupid girl, I said to myself as I nodded my agreement and ran back to the house.

❖

When Megan and Edwina had retired to bed, I slipped out the garden door and found Henry waiting for me, nervously pacing up and down. Flinging his large cloak around both our shoulders, I was hidden from spying eyes. He led me the length of the gardens, until we came to a copse of trees quite a distance from the house.

He leaned toward me and whispered, his breath hot behind my ear, "I want to kiss you."

The very sound of his voice unleashed a fire within me. *Oh, Henry.* I was ready to die in his arms. *Take me, take me anywhere, away from here, I will follow you to the ends of the earth*, I wanted to say.

"You must not," was all I *did* say.

"I shall." He sounded deep, dark, and insistent.

"But you must not." My voice was weak and feeble. And what was that feeling between my thighs? Why was I feeling so hot in my blue velvet cloak? I tossed back my hood, shaking my hair free in the cool night air.

His hand held my head and began to stroke. "Such pretty fair hair," he said thickly, and again my heart skidded.

"Do you think so?"

Henry kept that hand upon my head and slowly turned me around to face him.

Gazing into my eyes with his own blue ones, he said, so surely that I knew I loved him, "Now I shall kiss you."

Closing my eyes, I pursed my lips and held myself ready for him. But he took me off-guard, by dragging my face to his, devouring me with kisses, nibbling at my throat and mouth, eyes and forehead, as though he were a starving man.

"Henry," I groaned, caught by the soft sensation that was now descending from my breasts downward. I yearned for his caresses, yearned for those kisses all over. "Oh, Henry." I struggled with my conscience, my sense of right and wrong— and my desires. "I cannot, I should not."

But his hands were exploring my body and tracing the curves of my dress, beneath my cloak. He stroked my small breasts, making them tingle with desire. I could hardly stand; my legs were weak and shaking.

"Sweet girl, sweet, sweet girl," he groaned as his lips brushed my head, and he ran his hands through my hair, then down my back again, all the while breathing in hot furious breaths. I was shocked by his ardor, awed by his strength of feeling, terrified at the prospect of what might become of me should his breathing intensify any further.

As he wrapped the cloak around us both, I let myself be

held close and buried my nose in his warm chest. The smell of wool and leather, the tangy aroma of a body not my own, was overpowering and is a scent I can recall even now. I whispered a thousand times into his chest that I loved him. I scarcely had time to be unhappy about the future. I was so happy in the present.

"Look after me, young Kate." Henry shivered, holding me even more tightly. I could feel his lips kissing my hair as he promised himself to me. "You are so pretty, so good, so honest. I don't care if you are my stepmother—I am going to wait till he dies, then you shall me *mine*." Now I looked up at his long face, tears wetting my cheeks.

"Do you mean that?"

"Of course, sweet Kate. He cannot live forever."

"Oh, I hope not." And we looked startled in our shame.

We stayed in perfect harmony for so long my neck became stiff and out of joint, until eventually we agreed to part. People would surely notice my absence—if not his.

I walked back alone through the woods and the garden into the house, lost in a trance. Now I was whole. Now the house in Gainsborough and my strange life here had some meaning. Fate had led me to Henry Borough. My dreams forged far ahead of me. All thoughts of going to London had vanished. As soon as my husband was dead, I would marry Henry. We would devote our lives to the cause of Luther, and our selves to each other. Maybe we would travel the country spreading the reformist word. Such a good life we would have together. I was almost dancing with pleasure as I entered the darkened house.

Chapter
5

bigail came by early the next morning to tell me, "Your husband is home. He waits for you by the fire in the great hall."

Trembling still from the excitement of the night before, I felt as though I could conquer the world. Borough's back was turned to me as he stood beside the fire, whipping the air with his crop as was ever his custom.

"Greetings, wife," he said curtly.

"It is good to have you home again, sire."

Edward Borough then turned sharply, and I saw his face was red with anger. "When did you meet with Old Nell back there in the woods?"

I wished to faint. "Old Nell?" I repeated her name weakly.

"Yes, Old Nell—the witch who practices medicine. When did you meet with her, and for what?"

"I . . . I scarcely remember, sir. It was at the beginning of my stay, when I was new here and looking for something to do one day."

"Speak up, girl, I can't hear you," Edward shouted. "Who told you to go see her?"

"Why, no one." Struggling to find a good story, I changed track, to divert his attention. "Why, sir? Why do you ask?"

Edward drummed his feet on the floor. "The woman is a witch. She has been exposed. Yesterday she was arraigned at Lincoln and she bought a slight pardon by giving out names— yours was among them."

"My lord . . ." I was rigid with fear. "I remember now how Liza and I came across her hut by accident as we were walking together one day. Such a dirty run-down old place."

"Are you sure Megan had no hand in it?"

41

"Why no, sir. I hardly knew Megan then. It was just Liza and myself."

"I and some others of this town will do our best to see that witch burned. The old devil is a nuisance and a threat to our lives."

"Burned, sir? Old Nell is a healer, not a witch. Who said she is a witch?" Her kindly face and manner were still vivid in my mind.

"Are you sure your acquaintance with the woman is not deeper than you like to say, young wife?"

"I saw her but once," I asserted in truth.

"Phaw," he snorted. "You women are all the same. Love to keep your secrets. Well, this old woman must die. She has affected the minds of too many good women in these parts. You shall stay in your room, Kate—until her trial and sentence are over."

"What?" I cried in anguish, my concern for Nell forgotten. How would I ever meet Henry again if I was banished to my room?

"I cannot, sir. I cannot and will not stay in my room."

"You will do as I say." He stared at me angrily.

"No, sir, I will not do as you say this once. I have to be out in the fresh air. I need the cool clear air each day. I am ill, sir." I searched my mind desperately for some excuse to maintain my freedom.

"What kind of illness needs cold air, woman? If you are ill, all the more reason to stay home."

Frantically, I clutched at the very thing the memory of Nell evoked.

"Sir, I am with child." Knowing it was untrue, I prayed it would appeal to his mercy.

"What? With my child?"

"Why yes, sir. How else?"

"My dear wife. If you are with child and the doctor says you need the outside air, so let it be. I told you once that if you got with child I would be your very servant. I am a man of honor. I stand by my word."

"Of course, my lord. I never mistrusted the sincerity of your word. I am indeed honored to be bearing your child." Seeing the effect my words had upon him, I could not resist a parting barb. "I count myself a lucky woman to have conceived so young. May I now be excused?"

He gave me permission to leave, reluctantly, as if he wished to say more but did not know how.

My head was bursting. All I wanted to think about was Henry and our love for each other. But once alone my worries about Nell increased. I had heard before of witch hunts and the terrible fate that is met by women so chastised. But of course it was not until I had met a woman denounced as a witch that it carried any meaning in my life. I had to speak to Megan, as I doubted if even my dear Henry would appreciate the urgency of Nell's situation.

Hearing Borough retire to his chamber, I guessed for an afternoon nap—his face showed evidence of drinking that forenoon—I crept down the stairs and hunted for Megan. The young woman lay with her red hair fallen over her face, flat out on the ottoman in the little ladies' parlor.

I sat beside her and gently stroked her hair, whispering, "Is it about Nell you grieve?"

"They'll murder her. I know it. They are calling her a witch."

"But how can they kill her? Do they have proof she is a witch?"

Megan raised her lovely head. She was becoming more beautiful as the days passed.

"What proof do they need? Think, Kate, how can you *prove* someone is a witch? All they have to do is say she communes with the devil. That they have seen her in a trance, chanting curses, that because of her so-and-so died, or a child disappeared. They'll say anything. Father will testify. So will all the other men. They're scared of women like Nell—because she has power to heal and to influence girls like you and me, Kate. They'll burn her to teach us a lesson."

"What does Anne Kyme say?"

Megan shook her head. "I met with Anne last week. Now I dare not leave the house. Father has his spies out. He believes we are all against him, Kate. You must be careful. Anne Kyme would tell us all to leave—that we should run away together. I wish we could."

Megan was so hopeless she cast me into a deep melancholy. I desperately wanted to see Henry again.

"Have you seen your brother recently?"

"Why?" she asked suspiciously.

"I have something to tell him. Something he asked me to bring him this morning."

"He's in his room. Across the hall from mine." Sullenly, she lay back across the ottoman.

Secretly I wrote a note and slipped it under Henry's door, asking him to meet me before lunch in the woods where we had been last night. Then I disappeared into the garden, walked sedately past the topiary hedges, and hid myself among the trees. Within a few minutes I spied Henry's lithe form hurrying down the garden path. As his eyes lit on mine, they shone in greeting—but he indicated we should go even farther back into the woods. Falling at last into his arms, I responded to his eager mouth as he kissed my face all over.

"Have you heard?"

"About Father and the woman they call a witch?"

"That he greeted me this noon accusing me of seeing Old Nell, which was, sadly, true. My name has been exposed and he has threatened to banish me to my room. I was so scared, dearest Henry, of not being able to see you again that I lied, in the only way I knew, to assure he would let me do as I pleased."

"What was that, sweet Kate?" Henry whispered playfully in my ear.

"I told him I was with child."

I watched the smile fade from Henry's face as he groaned, "Oh, no! Is it then true?"

"No, of course not. I told you I lied. I do not want a child . . . not with him. You know I cannot love him, Henry. You must understand that."

But now he was lifting me up to his face so our lips met. "Oh, my darling girl. I didn't believe it, I really didn't. But you scared me so. If you have his child I can never marry you—you would be mother to a brother of mine."

"Henry," I said solemnly as he let me down again, "I doubt we'll ever be allowed to marry. Stepmother to stepson. It's against the law of the Church. Just think what problems the King is having because he married his brother's widow— though Queen Catherine claims she was a virgin bride." Then suddenly I brightened. "I could vouchsafe the same. I could swear I had not broken the sacred bonds of wedlock. If Queen Catherine triumphs in her case against the divorce, then maybe we shall be able to marry also."

But even as I spoke I felt the despair of our situation, though my heart lifted as he tugged my hand and drew me down to the cold ground. I had been so looking forward to our next meeting. Indeed my thoughts had encountered no other dreams. My heart was already his, and as he pulled me onto his cloak laid out in readiness, all thoughts of the impropriety of our strange relationship vanished with the late-morning mists.

"Henry," I whispered, my heart throbbing most uncomfortably. "I have been desperate to be with you."

"I, too, my love." He was covering my mouth with kisses. "I do not want to live without you."

Again he awakened dormant feelings in me, tracing my slim form, feeling for my budding breasts, tenderly brushing the line of my back, past my waist, until he was stroking my nether region. I quivered and shook in his arms.

My body drew imperceptibly nearer to his, brought there, I believe, by an attraction between us, for I swear I did not move an inch, yet there I was resting myself against his warm frame.

His hands stroked and caressed, until I became a seething mass of desire, undisturbed by the damp cold ground. My thighs jerked and kicked like those of a young horse. My bosom raised itself as if leaving my body to find his. Now all I wanted was to be with him, forever, every minute of every day, to be his in all ways.

"Take me, take me," I groaned, but he silenced me with his soft sensual mouth, diddling the inside of my mouth with his long delicate tongue. We melted into each other.

He drew my hand down the front of his jerkin, past the leather belt that crossed his waist, down to the top of his leather breeches. My hand pressed tightly against his thighs, became aware of a solidness beneath those breeches, and a blush rushed the length of my body at such frank intimacy.

Henry loosened the top of his breeches and slipped my hand down inside. I felt the softness that lay within, and, though somewhat scared of where this would lead us, and whether we should be so indulging, my hand groped and stroked his muscled stomach. My fingers left a burning trail as I explored the dark recesses of his body.

He groaned, for I had lighted upon his member, behind the soft silk of underbreeches. He begged me in hot whispers to caress him, begged me not to stop. So I stroked and played with my delicate hands, pressing and gently tugging at the hard mound beneath his breeches.

Henry turned his face to me with such a look of adoration that tears flooded my eyes. Quietly taking my hand from its warm dark home, he kissed the fingers gently, and, in a hoarse voice, bade me hurry inside before it was too late. I skipped across the gardens, happy in my soul, more alive than I had ever felt.

‡

I was called down from my room early one morning in the same week by a distraught Megan. "Do you want to come to Lincoln? Old Nell is to be burned at the stake come eight o'clock." The matter-of-fact way Megan spoke terrified me.

"Where is your father?"

"He's already there," she said. "He was up all night organizing the verdict. Her trial was nonexistent. A few of the gentlemen of Lincoln came to an agreement and signed a paper ordering her death at the stake. They are determined to rid the country of the devil's influence. Father is no doubt piling up the stakes."

I hurriedly dressed and raced to catch up with Megan, who had already ordered the horses out. I mounted my steed and felt a thrill of excitement, never having had the freedom to go by horseback such a distance since my arrival. Megan flicked her whip across her horse's rump, and we both trotted down the avenue, breaking into a gallop as we hit the bridle path, which was totally deserted at this predawn time of day.

The frost bit my cheeks as we raced over snowbound wastes through the icy stillness of the early morning. The countryside was bathed in half-light as dawn slowly rose over the distant horizon. A few peasants were out digging at the hard, empty soil, making ready for spring and new planting. But I had little time to take in the beauty of the morning, as this journey was for such a horrible cause. Burning at the stake? I had no idea what that entailed—but it was not hard to imagine.

The ride was long, and soon I was breathless and numb with the cold. I leaned down over the horse's neck as Megan did, our two young bodies hurtling through the gray morning.

The crowd looked strangely out of place in the main square in Lincoln. There were no more than a hundred people, conspicuous perhaps for the number of women among them. The only men were the row of dignitaries who circled the huge pile of wood built into a tall conical shape. The men wore gold chains on their chests as if to prove their authority in this matter. The women stood, in their drab peasant clothes, holding a child's hand or a lover's arm, shivering in the cold but transfixed by the occasion.

Megan and I led our horses to the holding posts outside a hostelry, dismounted, and tied them in place. I admired her confidence. I had spotted the white hair of my husband and feared our confrontation. Megan beckoned me to join her at the back of the crowd. I noticed Anne Kyme's slight form and nodded silently to our acquaintance.

Within moments, one man, the mayor, read the proclamation against Nell. Two men offered their signatures as witnesses. Someone called for an official to lead Nell to her punishment. I stood frozen with fear as two burly men held her by each slender wrist in case she should try to escape. She was led to a small platform.

"Do you admit to being party to the devil, Nell?" shouted the mayor.

I could just make out Nell's defiant eyes glaring at him as she spat on the floor.

"I mixed herbs that healed the sick," she snarled. "I have told you ten times and more. I picked the herbs as grew in the ground, and following the wisdom of my grandmother I gave physic to the poor, who cannot pay for doctors. I befriended the common folk and was a comfort to the dying. If that is being party to the devil—then yes I am."

"Then, Nell, we have no alternative but to carry out this warrant for your death at the stake. Do you have any last words to your Maker—begging his forgiveness?"

"None for you to hear," she growled again, proud to the end.

"The only hope for you then is to purge your sins by fire.

Ye shall burn till you scream for forgiveness—only then may the good Lord listen and offer you sympathy. Your soul must suffer the agony or you will be condemned to perpetual misery in the fires of hell. Begone, evil woman!" he intoned, his voice reaching a high-pitched squeak.

Nell was pushed onto the piles of wood. I watched two men reach for torches from attendants, and I also watched as my own husband took the torches and lit the fire that so quickly shot to the heavens. Nell did not so much as scream—not one word came from her lips. I was struck dumb myself at her courage, tortured at the image of this woman.

Seeing Anne Kyme run from the scene of the burning, her dark hair in disarray, her eyes streaming with tears, I chased after her, catching her by the arm.

"Anne, Anne, is there nothing we can do?" I begged, my heart breaking with the senseless murder I had witnessed.

"Have faith," she replied, her own eyes burning with belief. "Have faith in all you do."

I desperately wanted Anne to stop and tell me more. I wished I could prevail upon her to teach me more—some way to deal with the injustice I had just witnessed, some way to cope with a world that held women so powerless. But she was gone in a trice, presumably to avoid the wrath of Thomas Kyme. And, looking around, I became scared of Edward Borough. I ran back to where our horses were tied and, with Megan, mounted in haste. We rode back, our souls deep in the mire, our spirits completely deflated. Such an experience was enough to fill any woman with fear. The path between dire misfortune and easy contentment seemed to be hazardously crisscrossed.

✠

Waking from a troubled sleep late in the afternoon of that dreadful day, I was surprised by a tapping on the door. Liza had gone out, so I tiptoed to the door and cracked it open. There was Henry, one hand to his forehead, leaning against the wooden lintel. He pushed open the door and pulled me roughly to him by the shoulders.

"Oh, Kate." He kissed me fiercely on the mouth. "I know what you have been through. Don't lock me out in this fashion. Megan is beside herself, hysterical, and you shut yourself away in your chamber. I want to help you. What can I do?"

Brushing the hair off his forehead, I could see his eyes were glistening with tears. He hugged me again, and I felt some comfort in his arms.

"Borough will not be back here today. He is bound to stay in Lincoln after such a monumental event. Come with me to my room, dear Kate. At least there we can talk in privacy."

I followed him, like a lamb. Somehow, all fears or misgivings about my actions had been banished by the sight of those flames eating up Nell's flesh. He led me to the bed and ripped off his outer clothing before he jumped in between the linen sheets, beckoning me to follow. It seemed so simple, so pure, so honest that the two of us should find solace together, wrapped in each other's arms. I had no difficulty joining him.

We lay together for the long hours of the afternoon, watching the daylight disappear. Henry got up to light some candles and rekindle the fire in the hearth. We said very little to each other, but maybe our silence spoke more than words ever could. Comforted at last, I crept back to my bedroom late that evening. My husband returned the next morning.

❖

Many times in the early mornings when Borough was absent, I would creep out of my bed before the sun came up, tiptoe down the hallway in the dark, and enter the door Henry had left open for me.

Though he never tried to take advantage of me, sometimes my hands would caress his member beneath his nightshirt. I enjoyed being able to make him happy while fearing no threat to myself. Our love was simple and pure, like that between boy and girl.

We had to keep our voices low in case we were overheard, especially as Megan's room was directly opposite. Instinctively I did not want her to know of my trysts with her brother. Yet I suspected that she already knew, for she had turned quiet and circumspect. Megan had begun to make visits again to Anne Kyme, now in open defiance of her father.

Her attitude toward everyone was changing as the days passed. Even her adoration for her brother seemed to diminish. And one day, the inevitable confrontation occurred, when Henry teasingly accused her of witchery rather than trickery. Megan's face turned stony white, her lips the color of chalk.

"You call me a witch without thinking about the meaning of the word. Not two weeks ago we attended the burning of our dear friend accused of being a witch. And our father set the stakes alight. Think again about the power you have. Call me a witch but a few more times, Henry, even if only in jest, and I swear there will be ten more men eager to testify against me. Ask your lady friend how Nell looked when she was burning. . . ."

Megan fell silent, and we all stood rigid around the lunch table.

"Megan," said Henry sharply, "whom are you calling my lady friend?"

Megan turned her head away from his eyes. But she threw an arm out pointing at me.

"I hear you every morning. Not only do you have the indecency to dally with her, but you both have the insensitivity to disturb me in my sleep. Don't worry, Henry, I won't tell Father. Though you should have thought of that before you began this foolish jape. She's but a child, Henry, and you know better."

"I think I had better leave the room." I moved toward the door, not liking the tenor of their angry voices.

Megan threw her words violently after me. "Fool, Katherine. Fool. You would throw away everything just to have a place in his bed. Have you no shame? Have you thought what will become of you should Father find out?"

Tearfully I left the room. I could not stay in the house now. I felt like a stranger. Everyone hated me. I had known it would happen. Henry would desert me too.

I ran out of the house, and into the garden, little heeding my direction or that I was without my robe and the rain persistently fell, turning the dank winter vegetation sodden and malodorous. I hated this part of the country, so flat, ever rain-soaked. The people were trapped in their claustrophobic emotions, just as Lincolnshire was trapped at the end of the land before the ocean. I yearned for the mountains of Westmoreland, for the peace and shelter the lush green hills had afforded me as a child. Here there never seemed to be a place to hide.

I watched a rabbit playing in the woods for most of the afternoon, as I crouched under the trees, sinking into the soft wet mulch of the rain-damp leaves. At long last I heard the sound of feet squelching over the leaves and Henry's shape came into sight. Keeping my head down for fear of his response, I felt his long arms around my shoulders. He kissed me tenderly, then gathered me in his arms.

"Come back to the house, poor Kate. You will catch your death of cold out here. Megan promises to apologize. She is not very happy these days. We had a long talk. It was good for both of us—we used to be very close. She is jealous of your position in my life. I told her we love each other. She understands now."

I clung to Henry's neck and sobbed into the prickly wool of his robe. He picked me up in his arms and carried me back through the rain to the house, where, without stopping to speak to sister or servant, he led me straight upstairs to his chamber.

It was evening, the candles were dim, my husband was nowhere to be seen, and Henry was taking me to his bed-chamber. This time I knew there was no turning back. He would take my body as man does a wife, or I could no longer continue these visits. My body yearned for his, yearned for fulfillment of those emotions kindled by being with him.

This time it was I who whispered in his ear, "I must stay with you tonight."

He laid me on his bed, ripped off his jerkin, then his cotton shirt, revealing his chest, hairless and broad. "I shall have *you* tonight, Kate."

Cold and damp from my stay out in the woods all after-noon, I found it warm enough just to watch him strip off his clothes. He pulled down his breeches, pulled at the ties holding his hose to his underbreeches, kicked off his leather boots, and with a final tug to his underclothing, stood before me in all his slim, graceful, erect beauty.

"Why, Henry," I said. "You are more beautiful than I ever imagined."

His eyes glistened. "Then let me see you, sweet Kate. Let me see you."

Now I giggled. We were so at home together. Carefully he peeled off my damp clothing and laid it over a chair by the fireplace. Then he brought rags bathed in warm water from a basin by the fire and thick cotton towels. With his gentle hands, he not only rid me of my petticoat, hose, and the camisole that protected my breasts, but he washed my body caressingly, lovingly, and tenderly, drying it with towels, sprinkling me with rose-scented water as he progressed from chin to toe.

All this time I was lying on the rich damask cover on his bed, luxuriating in the feather mattress, writhing in exquisite agony on the soft down of the material.

"Please, Henry, do not tease me anymore," I begged, knowing no more shame.

Henry turned from replacing the washcloth, towel, and bowl by the fire. He walked over to me with a pewter tankard of wine in his hands and bade me sip. Before my eyes I watched his member rise, and I could not stop myself from smiling.

"There," he said. "You know he is all yours."

"Do you mean that?" I said shyly.

"My dear girl, why do you think I have risked life and limb to be with you? Just imagine Father's face if he should find us like this."

I could not stop myself from laughing. The idea of our complete awfulness, naked together in this room, was so wild, so funny, I threw myself back in fits of laughter. Henry climbed upon me pretending to stifle that laughter.

He had straddled me as he would a horse, so his knees were by my waist, and his hands were side by side with my shoulders. He begged me to make him feel happy. And I did. I cared no more. Let whatever would happen in life be. I had no more control.

Henry devoured me with his tongue from top to toe. Then his mouth found its way between my thighs.

Breathing hotly, he cried, "Don't let me hurt you."

As he spoke he worked those graceful fingers between the thatches of hair in my groin. "Kate, you are so lovely." He massaged and caressed and lightly pressed my throbbing lips until I was moist and welcoming. Then, arching himself over me, he drove his member into its pulsing home. I bucked and reared like a young filly, begging him for more, yearning for complete ecstasy, terrified but loving it all, hating him and his father for putting me in such a position, sobbing, crying, and tearing at his hair, until he too began to groan, and sob, weep, and growl.

Then we were riding through the frosty dawn, the cold wasteland turning to burning meadow as we came down the mountainside together on the same horse, peaceful and harmonious.

Chapter 6

Winter now was almost gone, passing on the rod to spring. I felt optimistic about our life here in Gainsborough. My husband was more and more away from home. But one morning he unexpectedly arrived and called us all into the great hall.

"Greetings, wife and children. I have some tidings you will be pleased to hear. Megan, I have arranged a fine marriage for you—it will take you to an excellent house in Yorkshire. No refusals this time, eh? You will be much happier for it. Kate, your kinswoman Kaitlin Neville, Lady Strickland, on your mother's suggestion, is coming here for a visit in April. I think you will enjoy that. Edwina, no more spinet playing and more time on your studies, please. Henry—well, you will find your place in life soon enough. I have no orders for you. Come with me, Kate."

I followed my husband as I would follow a complete stranger, since I was now so accustomed to being Henry's partner and lover. Once in his chamber, Borough proceeded to take off his clothes, first his riding boots, then his stockings, until with horror I realized his breeches were shortly to follow.

"Sir," I coughed.

"Get a move on, girl. Help me with these breeches. Get your dress off. I haven't had your sweet body for these weeks—I've missed its tender little soul."

"Sir, if you recall, I told you I was pregnant. Well, the baby is still there, and I fear for its life if I were to . . ."

"Fooey." My husband stamped. "Old wives' tales. Of course you can. Come here, girl, and help an old man out."

He tore my hand almost from my body and forced it down into his breeches. "Come on, sweet Kate, fondle me, stroke me as you used to."

I had to do as he bade me, though in my heart I tried to pretend he was Henry.

Afterward he beat me on the rump. "There, see if you lose the child any faster that way. The baby won't budge—they never do—not if he's a boy, at least. If you lost a girl, all the better."

"Yes, sir," I said wearily, wondering whether I should now kill off this fictional baby. After all, he had given me a perfect excuse.

"You've changed, Kate. Something about you is different. You seem more grown-up. Being with child must be good for you."

Then he sat down, half naked, on a chair and propped me upon his knees, rubbing my flat belly and jumping me up and down while he sang nursery rhymes.

"I'm a sick old man, sweet Kate. Take care of me," he said in his singsong voice.

He was definitely turning senile. He retired to bed, and I escaped to the sanctity of my room.

When there came a rapping at my door some short time later, I was terrified Borough wanted me back. But when Liza opened the door, Megan came flying in, her face streaming with tears, her red hair wild about her.

Megan closed the door and said in a low voice, "I won't let him do it to me. I won't marry. Anne Kyme has told me how to escape. I shall be leaving tonight. Will you come with me, Kate?"

"I cannot, Megan, I cannot," I replied, avoiding her eyes.

"So much for your beliefs, Kate. You won't leave because of my brother, isn't that it?" I nodded, gazing at her squarely at last. She seemed so wild, so distraught, I worried for her.

"Megan, you're surely not going now? You haven't taken even a bag of clothes. If you wait a day or two, maybe we can arrange something, gather jewelry together. You will need money. Oh, Megan . . ." I began to feel anger and envy, and fear, rising in my chest. "I won't let you go like this."

"Then come with me," she shouted over her shoulder as she marched resolutely down the corridor, taking the stairs three at a time, racing through the kitchens, and straight to the stableyard.

I grabbed my cloak and ran after her. I had to stop her.

Once out in the stableyard, the night was chill. Where was Henry? I thought frantically. Why couldn't he be here to stop his headstrong sister? Megan had a horse already by the reins.

"Megan Borough, get down from that horse," I commanded in my best authoritative manner. I was her stepmother and she was bound to obey my word.

"Goodbye, Kate. I'll write to you!" she whispered, for fear Borough would hear us. "And if you dare mention a word to him of where I have gone, I'll see he knows everything about you."

Turning to the boy, I shouted for another horse and within minutes was mounted. Galloping off down the lane, I cursed to myself that Megan had made me do this. She could leave, yes. She could refuse the marriage, yes. But there must be better ways of doing it. Megan was about half a mile ahead of me, and try as I would, I could not catch up with her. My cloak was flying wildly behind me, and I struggled to wrap it around my freezing chest. I had to keep her in sight, because alone I doubted I would know my way to Stallingborough. The roads were dangerous at night for young ladies. We all heard tales of highwaymen and robbers out on the prowl.

Just before Anne Kyme's house, I finally caught up with the wild young lady. I was tired and sore from the ride. Cantering by her side, I was able to ask, "Does Anne know you are coming? What will Thomas Kyme say?"

"Anne told me last week she was ready whenever I was. I just had to send a messenger with the word 'Midnight' and she would have the necessary clothing and jewels for our departure," Megan shouted breathlessly across to me. "We shall dress as young men for the first part of our journey, going to her brother's house. Francis Askew has always been sympathetic, and Anne knows he will take us in until we have decided what to do."

"And what will you do?" I said angrily again. "What about the rest of this year, the next five years, your life?"

"We'll enter a nunnery. Anne and I are agreed on that. At least a convent will give women such as ourselves, fleeing an evil father or husband, sanctuary. There we can decide in the due course of time our next actions."

Her words relieved me. At least behind a convent's walls I knew she would be safe. We were dismounting now, outside the walls of the Kymes' mansion. In their yard, we could alert the dogs with our horses. Crouching by her horse, Megan let out a strange bloodcurdling sort of cry. It whistled through the dark night as though some monster were outside the gates. There was a long silence, while Megan chewed her fingernails and I was scared. Then we heard a hooting, rather like an owl cries.

"That's it!" cried Megan triumphantly. "That's Anne. She's ready. Well, Kate, will you come?" Her voice sounded less urgent now.

I shook my head. "You know I cannot. Not only because of your brother, whom I do love, Megan. But your father. I could not do it to him. But listen to me, I have as much faith in reform as do you. *Never* forget that. I just can't make this wild, crazed move right now. Don't forget me, Megan. I am your sister in spirit and have always loved and admired you. I hope we can continue to be friends, and stay in touch— though God knows how!"

We hugged each other, with more honesty than ever before. I felt a dampness on my face, where her cheek had rested against mine. "Why, are you crying, Megan?"

"Just a few tears," she confessed.

"Are you scared?"

"Of course I am."

"Oh, this is too awful. If only your father could be made to understand you better," I cried. "Shall I send Henry after you to see that you are all right?"

"No, Kate. Tell no one. Keep my secret, please. Or all will be lost. Henry is in no better position. I hate to warn you like this, dear Kate, but I have a feeling Father is arranging to marry him off too."

"What?" My heart began to thud loudly with a new fear.

But then we saw Anne Kyme's slight form creeping around the gate. She had come without a horse, for fear of disturbing old man Kyme. But over her back was a large sack, and she grinned, totally unafraid. We kissed each other again, and I helped Anne mount behind Megan. We all rode together part of the way back toward Borough Hall, until a crossroads where I stood waving to their disappearing backs as they cantered off into the unknown. Shivering with cold and fear, for now I was truly alone in the night, I whispered, "Goodbye, and God bless. May the Lord look after you, Megan and Anne."

I galloped home to Borough Hall as fast as the horse and

the wind would let me. I led the horse to the stables, and crept wearily up the kitchen stairs to bed. No one seemed alarmed at the slight noise outside, nor at our absence.

The next day I was quite ill, which mercifully allowed me to rest in bed and recover. I heard the news, from Liza, from Abigail, from Henry; even Lord Borough came in to see me—Megan had disappeared, with one of the horses. Had I any idea where she might be? Shaking my head, unable to speak, my head hot from a raging fever, I cowered with my secret, grateful that nature had come to my rescue.

For days, Henry led the search, believing perhaps Megan was dead or surely would be found. Neighboring families and relatives were contacted. But as the days turned into a week, they grew to believe Megan had vanished without trace.

Borough had the stableboy flogged for letting Megan take a horse in the night. Then he retired to his room. For the first time ever, I actually went uninvited to his door and offered him any help or comfort I could muster. Borough, the ogre, the bad-tempered old man, was prostrate on the bed weeping and beating the pillow with his fist. Never would I have expected such emotions from him. Megan was gone and he could not forgive her.

❖

"Lady Borough," she murmured, and dropped a tiny bow, as she stepped down from her carriage.

"Lady Strickland," I echoed and likewise bowed.

Recently widowed Kaitlin Neville had kept her title and possession of Sizergh Castle through some loophole in the inheritance laws. She was now very rich, very young, and quite attractive. An eligible widow. Megan's words of warning about Henry, and a marriage, echoed in my mind as I emerged from our front door to greet her.

Kaitlin was dressed in a rich tone of burgundy wine. Her long black hair shone like the night sky. She had a neat figure, good bones, but her nose was too long and pointed and her mouth too thin and too narrow to be considered a real beauty.

"Kaitlin, my dear, how lovely to see you." I hugged her close to me. "Have you seen Mother recently?"

"No, oh, no. She sticks to London now. Your home is all closed up. But, my little Katie, look at you all trim and wifely. I can't believe my little girl is already a man's wife. Are you *very* happy, darling?"

"I'm all right, thank you. Though life in Westmoreland seems a long way distant. How are the mountains, and how is the smell of heather?"

"Same as ever, sweet girl. My little Willie, he's a little man now, you know, four years old—he loves the mountains too. He calls them 'big ones.' Ah, my life has been good to me, Kate. I hope it treats you as well. No babies yet? No, too soon, I'm sure. You really are only a child still." Kaitlin's voice, for all its sharpness and false tones, rang with the sweet melody of Westmoreland.

Ironically, Kaitlin's visit liberated Henry and me. With my cousin as chaperon, the three of us were able to take long walks in the lovely fresh spring air. Yellow primroses pressed our feet, and white daisies shot through the new blades of grass. The peasants were out sowing seed in their narrow strips of land. The horses had produced foals, the fields were full of frisky lambs. It was a festive season, if still quite cold. Henry enjoyed our walks and would place himself between us, one arm around each of our waists. Edwina, now our constant companion, ran a few steps in front explaining the wonders of nature as we walked. Kaitlin giggled and complained about her aching feet. I gloried in the sense of harmony with Henry.

One afternoon about a week after Kaitlin's arrival, I suggested we walk through the woods. Strangely, my feet led us on the path to the cottage where Old Nell had lived. I was not surprised to see the house had been burned down.

"Henry, that was Old Nell's house," I said excitedly.

"They burned Old Nell as a witch not long ago," Henry explained to Kaitlin. "Kate took it hard—Megan did too," he said quietly.

"They burned Old Nell for disobeying the law—and acting as a healer," I said, "but Nell was a clever woman."

"Nonsense," said Kaitlin, irritable and bored. "She was no doubt a stupid old woman with a lot of superstitious nonsense in her head. I'm not surprised they had her burned. Her type is dangerous."

"That's a terrible thing to say." I was tiring of Kaitlin's company every day. "Henry, what do you say?"

"Ha!" laughed Kaitlin victoriously. "Henry won't speak up for you anymore, Katie. Not now he is to be *mine*."

"What do you mean?" My head turned from face to face. You could have cut the silence with a scythe. Henry and Kaitlin stood together like conspirators in a crime.

"Go on, tell her, Henry," said Kaitlin. Henry turned his face away, avoiding my eyes, his mouth tightly closed.

"Very well, I will. Henry and I are to be married, Kate dear," Kaitlin announced proudly.

My hand went immediately to my breast to try and quiet my thumping heart. "Why? When? I don't understand."

"Why, that is what I came for, my dear girl. Henry Borough, beautiful young man that he is, needs a good wife. Your mother and Lord Borough fixed up the marriage contract on my behalf."

Barely able to keep my legs from buckling under me, I uttered the first words that came to mind. "Are you coming to live here?"

Kaitlin's shrill laugh struck through my body like a sword. "Heavens, no. In this godforsaken place? Remember that I am Lady Strickland of Sizergh Castle. Henry is returning with me. He will receive a title and share of property. He is very pleased at the prospect of our marriage. We expect to be very happy, don't we, Henry?"

Henry's voice was scarcely audible. "Yes, my dear."

My Henry the toady of this woman? There must be some explanation. Ever proud, I was not going to show my emotions in front of my cousin.

"I wish you both every happiness. I shall return to the house now."

I ran to be alone elsewhere in the woods. Once more heedless of weather and time, I stayed out till nightfall. But this time no one came to comfort me. I was left alone.

Unable to think, barely able to feel, I picked my way back to the house through the fields and gardens. I should have gone with Megan, I lamented. At least I would have been spared this fate. As I approached the house, I saw candles going out. It was late and they were retiring to bed. A chink of light, however, shone as a door opened. Out of the house a tall figure came toward me. Before I knew what was happening, his arms had picked me up and we were running back over the fields to the sheltering blackness of the woods. Henry covered my face with kisses and sobbed into my hair as he lay me down upon his cloak and knelt beside me.

"Kate, what can we do?"

I swallowed my own tears, but my resentment reared. "How can you ask? You decided to marry her."

"No, no, it's not true," He raised his arms to the heavens. "My decision was made for me, as was yours. I have to make a good marriage. Father intends to cut me out of his will. He has nothing but contempt for me. Dear Kate, you will inherit most of his property, and any son you carry will bear the title. I will get nothing. This way, at least, I shall be Lord Strickland of Sizergh. Ugh, I don't even *like* that woman."

"But we talked so much of our life together, of spreading the new religion."

"Sweet Kate. All I hope is to continue my work translating Luther's Bible . . . waiting for you, dreaming of you. I shall write to you, Kate, every day. And you will come visit us."

"As your stepmother? Don't be foolish. We won't be allowed to meet again."

"Oh, sweet Kate. I love you so much. Come lie with me."

But I would not. I struggled against him. "No, it is cold and damp. Kaitlin will suspect your absence."

His face was long and miserable. "You never objected to the cold before."

"I never felt so hurt before."

He pushed me against a tree and held me there, forcing his mouth upon mine. Angry though I was, as he worked his lips on my face and pressed his body against me, the passion that we had shared could not be denied. I groaned in misery, and anguish, and elation.

He whispered into my neck, "Don't leave me, don't let me down. I must have you."

Holding me against that tree, the damp evening mist playing on our backs, Henry lifted my skirt and petticoat, unfastened his own breeches, and, in a gesture of defiance I once would have admired, he kneaded my frozen thighs. He felt with his hand between my legs, knowing I would be waiting for him.

Grunting and groaning as though with rage, he pushed himself at me, and forced an entry, and, oh, even if I had wanted to stop him, my own body would not let me. I screamed at him that I wanted, needed him. Though he hurt my back, pushing me relentlessly against the tree trunk, he made me admit that I still loved him and always would.

Henry fell limp, with his head on my shoulder. My arms were wrapped tightly around his back. I held on to him as he sobbed in broken, pained, heart-wrenching heaves against my neck. I stroked his hair and promised to remain faithful to our love even if we could no longer be together.

Then, smiling sadly, he wiped his eyes and bade me go alone into the house. He would continue his walk into the night, for he had no desire to return to that place of misery and torment.

A low mist hung over the fields, between the woods and the house, a mist like a thick white blanket dividing our lives. A roll of thunder boomed in the distance, and lightning lit up the skies.

Chapter 7

enry left the house in Gainsborough early on the morning of May Day. Kaitlin had overseen the packing and chosen which pieces of furniture Henry might take from the house. Their marriage was to be solemnized at Sizergh, but the main arrangements concerning the inheritance and division of property were documented, witnessed, and sealed.

I could not even nurse my heart in solitude, for I was to preside over the traditional May Day ceremonies in the village.

The maypole was already erect in one of our gardens. The long colored streamers made of woven linen hung down from the top of the white pole in stripes of red, orange, blue, green, and rich purple. Servants were putting up old wooden tables on trestles around the edge of the lawn. Out of the kitchen streamed platters of bread, cheese, freshly churned butter, pastries, fruits, tarts, and cakes. The frivolity seemed strange in Borough's household. He had refused to leave his bed, declaring the peasant children a noisy abomination.

But Edwina was excited, and her enthusiasm lightened my spirits.

As the whole village gathered before us, I announced the proceedings open, took a cup of ale, and stood on a bench by one of the trestle tables, calling on the musicians to play. The flutes piped up, the fiddles squeaked into action. They broke into a popular ballad, and the children formed lines to take part in the maypole dance. Edwina and I were in the first group. Holding our long streamers, with the other dozen boys and girls, we threaded our way in and out, around and around. We wove the streamers into a neatly latticed covering to the pole.

Breathless after the dancing, the children took cups of apple cider and the adults drank ale or mulled wine, spiced with cinnamon and dates. They crowned Edwina Queen of the May, perching on her silken hair a crown of catkins and primroses.

The afternoon turned to dusk, and the candles on the trestle tables lent the evening an exotic glow. The musicians turned to slow romantic ballads. One tune impressed itself upon my heart:

> "Grene grouth the holy, so doth the ivie
> Thow winter's blastys blow never so huge.
> As the holy grouth grene and never changeth hew
> So I am—ever hath bene—unto my lady trew.
>
> Now unto my lady, promys to her I make
> From all other only to her I me betake.
> Adew myne owne lady, adew my specyall
> Who hath my heart trewly, be sure, and ever shall."

I turned to a peasant woman standing close by and asked her what the song was.

"Why, Lady Borough," she said with a laugh. "Surely you know. It's the King's. He wrote it for his lady love, Mistress Boleyn. A song of Constancy."

❖

Henry was gone—though he lived on in my dreams as a pleasant memory. For several months I fantasized I was with his child, and I cradled my belly and sang songs to the spirit of our love. I knew I could pretend to my husband it was his child.

But by the autumn, as the leaves were falling, turning the ground into a rich golden carpet, I once again became sad. I was not with child. Even Lord Borough had accepted that my "pregnancy" was no more. By the look in his eyes, I knew that he felt it a mark of his own failure. I was lonely and bored, and all set to be utterly gloomy, when a most welcome letter came by messenger. Ripping open the seal, I devoured its contents.

We have arrived safely at the home of Francis Askew! After three days and nights on the road, dressed as young men of fortune, we stayed in hostelries, drank lots of ale, played cards, and disappeared to our beds if any local men became too friendly. We have moved to the convent at Nunmonkton in Yorkshire. It is owned by a relative of Kaitlin Neville's (whose name I learn you may not wish to hear), a Lord Latimer. He was kind about my request, and both Anne and I have been given pleasant rooms. No one is forcing us to take vows. We shall do some work here to help the nuns and, in time, will decide to leave or stay.

I have heard of Father's illness, but I do not feel I can come home to visit him. I shall be in touch with Henry. In the event of Father's passing I will learn the details of my inheritance (if any). But for the present, I choose to remain behind these walls. I trust we will not lose touch with each other.

You might be interested to know that "Anne Askew," as she now calls herself, is becoming quite notorious. She recently engaged the Dean and some priests at Lincoln Cathedral in a debate on religion. She was bold enough to state that the bread and wine of the sacrament do not turn into the flesh and blood of Christ! Whatever will become of her?

I wonder how you are feeling, dearest Kate. Maybe one day we will meet again. I think of you often, with my dearest thoughts. Your loving Megan.

Edwina read the letter and wept, for she missed her feisty sister.

Abigail had turned quite sick, and so the duties of attending my increasingly debilitated husband fell to me. I cared for him as best I could, despite my previous feelings of animosity. Now he was in my care, things improved between us. The more ill he became, the more pleasant was our marriage. To his horror I made sure he was bathed at least once a week. This was a severe shock to a man who stuck by the old tradition of bathing once a year. But I had grown up with more sophisticated habits. Even through the cold winters in Gainsborough I made sure I bathed myself in warm water at least once every week. Liza too.

To ease my husband's discomforts, I would mix mint and other fresh herbs into hot water and afterward rinse his crumpled flesh with warm rosewater. I rubbed him down with pork fat to keep the winter chills off his bones. Lord Borough found it difficult to eat, as no foods sat easily in his stomach, so I would make him drink marigold tea first thing in the morning to keep down his fever. I made tea of anise, fennel, and coriander to purge his system, or of clary to cheer him, or of hyssop to clean his blood. A paste of mandragora leaves was used to rub his chest and legs, to cool his body when it was feverish. I even mixed up an infusion of sage and made him gargle it to relieve the inflamed throat.

When Borough asked me how I was so skilled as a doctor, I told him I used to read Dioscorides' *De Materia Medica* and Pliny's *Historia Naturalis* in my Latin studies back home. The books were part of my father's library. I did not tell him I had read the great English physic Bartholomew's work *Liber de Proprietatibus Rerum* for fear he might talk against his own wife as a witch. It was against the law of the land for women to practice healing.

My husband almost grew to love me. I cared for him so well.

He would lie in bed and insist I stay there with him. We would hold hands for hours on end. I read to him from the great Latin writers. One winter's afternoon, he admitted he enjoyed the fruits of my learning, which he had always dismissed before.

Liza and I often talked about what we would do after he had gone. Liza expected me to stay there in Gainsborough, while she preferred to go back to Westmoreland.

I laughed at both ideas, gripping her hand tight. "No, we'll go to London. Mother is there, and my brother and sister. William promised he would find me a place at Court. Wouldn't you fancy some of the grand life, the exciting life, after all this? You'll come with me there?"

Liza looked surprised. "What about your young man? Henry Borough?"

I blushed, for I had already forgotten him. "He's another woman's husband. I don't want to go anywhere near him. I don't want the pain stirred up again."

"You should be thinking of doing things for the poor—charity work such as other married ladies do," Liza admonished.

"I'll do that in London. I have ambition, Liza. And the only way to get on is to marry well. But I shan't marry well in this nowhere land. I need to be in the center of powerful men. Oh, Liza, I can't wait."

Edward Borough clung on to life for nine long months, coughing heavily, unable to swallow or hold food down, through one of the worst winters I could remember—when even the oceans froze. Lincolnshire, so open to those chill east winds, stayed frigid in the face of the frost and snow.

Abigail died first, and then finally my husband found peace just as the winter was coming to an end. Edwina, tearful and somehow matured by the experience, went to live with her aunt in Gainsborough, while I set to the task, with Liza's help, of clearing out the ghosts from the house.

I wrote to my mother as soon as I could of Borough's death, expecting her to come up the Roman Road to take us back to London with her. I was surprised then when a letter came from my sister Anne, and not from Maude.

> *Dearest Kate, I have delayed writing so long hoping Mother would take a turn for the better. But I now have the sad task of informing you she passed away last night after another attack of the "sweating" sickness. The only relief I can offer you is that she died peacefully. Both William and I were there with her at the end. She spoke of you and said she wished to see you. Dear Kate, be brave. Your loving sister, Anne, Lady Herbert.*

I threw the letter down as the tears shot to my eyes. How could she have let Mother die without sending for me? William and Anne! How could they keep her for themselves like that? I was Mother's favorite. I was the firstborn. Oh, no, not Mother . . . not Maude. For all that we fought sometimes, I loved her more than anyone.

I wept for three days. Only Liza was with me in the house. She cared for me and comforted me. Slowly I emerged from my sorrow to realize I was now totally alone in the world. I began to doubt we would ever get to London after all.

The next morning a messenger arrived at the house. He came with a litter and spare horses, and Liza brought me his note. It was from Kaitlin Neville, Lady Strickland, and her husband, Henry, Lord Strickland.

> *Hurry, dear Kate. We heard the terrible news about Borough, and now about Maude. You must come to Sizergh and live with us. Bring Liza. We're waiting.*

I looked at Liza's sorrowful face. She nodded. I sighed and nodded back.

"Tell the messenger we shall need the rest of the day to arrange the house and our belongings. Then we shall go with him back to Sizergh. You will be happy to return to Westmoreland. Edwina already told me she will stay with her aunt, as a marriage has been arranged for her. There is no other choice—nothing else I can do. Goodbye, London." Nervously I said to myself, *Hello, Henry Borough.* I was excited at the thought of seeing him—and partly terrified.

PART II

The
Wild
Moors

Chapter
8

As we approached Sizergh Castle, it stirred my heart to see the firm solid girth of the castle walls. Constructed around a keep, a tower built so strong and sturdy that it would forever hold at bay those evil raiding Scots who bothered our borders, Sizergh appeared like a refuge to those in trouble. The manor home attached to the tower was in fine proportion, gracious, elegant, a reminder of our noble lineage up here in the wild northwestern counties of England. The former Lord Strickland had had a great hall built in the manor, with fine wood carving and high strutting beams. The grounds around Sizergh were vast, filled with ponds and streams that abounded with fish. Fruits and vegetables flourished in the long meadows in summer.

Kaitlin's servants came running out to greet me. Many of them remembered me as a child. Now I was the fifteen-year-old widowed Lady Borough. I had a string of properties in Lincolnshire and adjacent counties, some jewels and fine plate that Borough had bequeathed me, and, if not wealth in my pocket, at least a good enough dowry to attract another man.

Before Liza and I had left Borough Hall, I had gone through my late husband's will and testament with the chaplain. Henry, as he had guessed, was all but disinherited save a portrait in charcoal of his mother and one of her gold rings. Megan was taken care of, should she ever return. Certain property was to be kept in trust for her until her death was ascertained, and then it would pass to Edwina. But the bulk of his holdings had gone to me. Though I was a widow of much property, my wealth was hidden unless the many houses and stretches of land could be sold.

Liza and I were shown our quarters. They were so handsome, so ample after our bare accommodation at Gainsborough. I had my own room, and Liza a smaller adjacent one. There was a sitting room for our personal use. It was an apartment of size and luxury, the like of which I had never had for myself.

As I twirled around the spacious chamber, I sang to Liza, "This is going to be different. We shall enjoy ourselves here."

"I hope so," she said grumpily.

"What's wrong with you, lass?" I laughed. "I thought you were thrilled to be home."

"That I am," Liza said gruffly. "I feel mighty strange to be staying in something so grand."

"Oh, it's nothing. You'll get used to it. Anyway, now you can visit your little nieces and nephews. And you can have Sundays off to yourself to go to church and play with the little ones. Oh! Things are going to be *different*."

I fell onto the bed and sank into its deep feathery thickness, feeling the soft cambric touch my face.

"Kaitlin, for all her faults, knows how to live well," I told Liza, just as my cousin appeared at the door.

"I'm pleased you think so," she chirped.

Jumping to my feet, I dropped a curtsy. "Kaitlin! You surprised me!" I ran to kiss her. She held me slightly at bay, allowing me to peck her cheek.

"Come now, Katey. No childish pranks. You are a lady and a widow. Remember your decorum. You shall stay dressed in black all the rest of the year, lest you forget. And there's to be no skipping and jumping in public."

All year? But it was only March. The news made my heart sink. But then Kaitlin was ever the lady of propriety. She lived her life as it *should* be, by a book of rules. We stood staring admiringly at each other, as young ladies of title do.

"You look beautiful, Kaitlin." In truth she did look rather stunning in a dress of emerald-green velvet with red trim.

Slightly overdressed to my mind for midday on a Wednesday, but nonetheless stunning.

"Marriage to Henry must be suiting you." I let the comment slip without thinking.

Kaitlin's face clouded over. She dropped my hands. Kaitlin was suspicious of my feelings for Henry—and Henry's for me. She was nervous, no doubt, that her husband's fancy might stray my way again. I tried to say something that would make her feel better.

"Is he settling in, and just *loving* Westmoreland, Kaitlin?" But again that was the wrong thing to say. I knew Henry would hate it, being essentially a serious-minded young man.

"He's as well as can be expected, Katey my dear. Henry took a while to adjust to our way of life here. It is more busy and social than he was used to in Gainsborough. But then we live among the titled and important people in the North of England. He is fitting into his position as Lord Strickland very nicely. Of course, we are *blissfully* happy."

"Of course," I murmured, my head down. "I shall be concentrating on my studies while I am here, Kaitlin. I intend to perfect my Latin, Greek, and German."

Kaitlin turned to leave the room. "As long as that's all, Katey. No more of this religious nonsense. I don't want to find you dangerously involved in some underground group. The Pope and the Church are sacrosanct. I don't want to hear you have been blasphemous. Blasphemy is a dangerous charge, you know. So study by all means. I intend to find you another wonderful husband before long. You cannot sit around here as the widowed Lady Borough. We can't have you wasting your life."

The door shut sharply behind her. Kaitlin was gone. I turned to look for Liza, but she was in her own room, sorting embroidered cloths and putting things away in her closets. I returned to the feathery bed and sank again into the warm security of its pillows. Was life not to be so deliciously easy here after all? Was Kaitlin going to be my enemy? I was banned already from my two passions, the new reformism of the Church and Henry Borough.

I missed Megan very much, sorely sometimes. The prospect of life in close quarters with Kaitlin Neville seemed dull and stultifying. She would expect me to play the part of the lady. I would be dragged around the social circle, forced to attend house parties and dances. I winced at the thought of being introduced to every eligible man in the neighborhood. I was slowly coming to the conclusion that marriage *was* the only thing for me. I stamped my foot angrily on the wooden floor and wanted to beat my fist against the finely carved oak door.

✛

Sizergh's gardens were more sophisticated than the wilderness we had enjoyed at Kendal. Many years before, the family had employed the services of a proper gardener, and now there were formally laid-out flower gardens, pathways, trellises, duck and fish ponds, and a beautiful lily pond not many yards from the main doorway, down a little slope. I wandered down the hill, wrapped in a thick robe. The air was chill, as it was a wintery day, but at least there was no snow, and the ground was hard and dry. Spring was coming, for I could feel the trees about to burst into bud. Sitting by the water's edge staring idly at the pool, gazing at my own reflection, I wondered what life would do to me in the next few years.

As I trailed my hand in the icy crystal, I saw another face staring into the water. It was a man's. It had straight blond hair and a long face. It wore no smile but gazed seriously, as did mine. My heart leaped like a butterfly. It was Henry Borough.

What was he doing out here? He must not try to speak with me alone. Oh, why had I come here? I groaned, unsure of how to deal with all this. I fully intended to be Lord Strickland's demure and correct relative. I had no wish to resume our love affair in Kaitlin's house.

Then there was a splash, and I saw a pebble hit the surface of the pond. Another, and then another. While still at Gainsborough, Henry had said to me, "If I throw three pebbles against your bedchamber window, it means I want you to run away with me right there and then. Would you do that?"

"What, without warning, or time to prepare myself?"

"Yes, just on the spur of the moment."

Then I had flung my arms around his neck and vowed, "Oh, yes, Henry. Oh yes, of course, anywhere." But I had been madly in love then and full of fancies.

I heard a low whistle. I glanced over my shoulder to a clump of bushes nearby. Under the bushes I made out one slim ankle, neatly shod in black leather. The whistle continued, high and piercing.

I got up nimbly from the pond. Glancing carefully around me, I made for the bushes. A hand dragged me among the winter foliage, and suddenly I was pressed against a warm cloak, hot air breathing in my face. He was devouring my face with kisses, like a man drunk or thirst-starved from the heat.

"Stop, Henry," I cried, fear in my voice tinged with excitement. "We must not do this. It's terrible. Worse than before. We're in front of the house. Kaitlin is within. She'll have me hanged, or burned." I pushed him away, and he looked shamefaced.

"I'm sorry, Kate, I couldn't help it. I was so thrilled by seeing you. I thought I never would again! I've been in a state of pent-up excitement this whole week. Forgive me, darling girl. But I've missed you so much. I was just . . . well, hungry for you."

He stopped talking, and we smiled at each other, crouched

there like a couple of thieves in the bushes, on the front lawn of Sizergh Castle.

"Good heavens," I said. "When I used to play here as a child, I never imagined this would happen to me!" That made us both laugh, and we were able to talk a little.

Henry told me he was desperately miserable. He hated Kaitlin, hated Westmoreland, hated the sort of life he was being made to lead as Lord Strickland of Sizergh.

"I was not made for the social round, Katey. You know that. She drags me to hunts, and I cannot stand to see a fox or deer killed. She makes me go to these dreadful sessions of wine drinking with the local men, most of whom I abhor. They talk only about murdering animals. Then we attend numerous formal dinner engagements, balls, and banquets. The people have no culture, little education, and absolutely no refinement. They frown when I say I attended the University at Cambridge. I doubt any of them know what a university is—nor do they care. They only want to know how many of our sheep died in the winter storms, and whether we have had any raids from the Scots.

"I have been in despair, Katey. Then, when I heard you were to live with us, my heart leaped several steps up the church tower. I have not read a new book, or heard the name Martin Luther pass anyone's lips, since arriving here. Kaitlin has ordered me to drop that line of study and argument. You know I'll never drop it!" he said with a new fierceness. Carefully, after his frank admission, I told him how I was only prepared to be his friend here at Sizergh. I reasoned with him. "We must learn decorum, Henry. If nothing else, at least we can benefit from each other's company. Kaitlin is a true and trusted relative," I said, pushing his hand from my arm. "I cannot, will not, do anything to hurt her. You are married. There is nothing we can do to change that."

It was so still you could hear the leaves crackle on the frosty ground. Henry stared at the hand I had just pushed away. As I looked upon that face, I became torn with misgivings. I was flattered that he still felt so deeply for me. He raised his intense blue eyes and gave me the look of a pitiful little boy, lost. I knew with a sinking heart that my resolve was melting away.

"Can you do this to me, Kate? Can you break my heart with yours of stone?"

His voice was so tender, his face so beautiful and pained, that I had to fight not to reach out my hand to caress him.

"I have to, Henry," I said desperately. "It would ruin both our lives. You must know that as well as I do."

"But I love you." He said it so simply, as though in those words lay the answer to the universe. "I need you at my side."

Frowning and unhappy, I rose to my feet determined to run inside. He grabbed me with one of those long-fingered hands. "Be kind, sweet Kate, be kind to a wretched man."

"Let me go, Henry. Let me go in and think about things. I have only just arrived."

Trembling, I tore myself away from him. My shameful passion was rekindled. The touch of his hand on my arm had brought back everything—I would have given my soul to resume that joy.

I flew across the beautiful lawns, up the carved stone steps to the front entrance of the magnificent Sizergh Castle. Kaitlin was standing in the imposing hall. She looked oddly out of place and small against the enormous carved fireplace. Her hair was carefully piled up on her head. The thick dark tresses were hidden from view under a cap of starched linen. Her dress of rich emerald velvet with red trim had been replaced by one of ruby damask, shot with gold silk. My black damask looked dingy by comparison.

Kaitlin had something on her mind, that I could see without asking. Her face was red, though the color could have come from her closeness to the blazing fire. I shivered with fear lest we had been seen.

"Where have you been?" she asked through those thin, tight lips I remember so clearly chastising me as a girl.

Frowning, I looked innocently at her. "For a walk in the garden. To remind myself of the smells and beauty of Westmoreland. Oh, Kaitlin," I carried on, hoping to infect her with my enthusiasm, "I haven't been here at Sizergh since I was eight. It is just lovely to walk through the gardens and run my hand in the lily pond again."

"Do you forget your manners completely, young lady?" Her voice still sounded threatening. "You are expected to dine with us at this hour. At Sizergh we conduct ourselves with decorum. We breakfast in the forenoon, lunch at two, and dine at seven o'clock."

"I had forgotten, Kaitlin," I said honestly. "At Borough's household, we dined nearer five, and that was often the only meal we all partook together. Things were not so formal there."

"They certainly weren't. Though I do feel it was your position as lady of the house to arrange things on a more proper level. There has to be order, Kate. I will not allow slovenliness in my home. Do you hear?"

Nodding my head in agreement, swallowing my anger at being treated like a child, I suddenly realized I too had rights and status.

As she turned to march off, her ruby dress billowing behind her, I could contain my feelings no longer. "Shall we talk someday soon about my position here and what you expect of me? I'm not little Kate Parr, Maude's daughter, being looked after while Mother is away in London. I'm Lady Borough, a woman in my own right, staying here at your gracious request. You are the nearest I have to a close relative and friend in the world. I am not sure of my role in life, or my duty to be performed in this house."

But Kaitlin paid scant attention to the dignity I claimed for myself. "Child, I don't know what you are talking about. You will do here what any young lady of means and title would do. You will sew, embroider, practice the piano. Maybe paint. You will exercise your mind with French and Latin. Attend church. Sometimes we will grace local village functions and give the peasants something to talk about. You will find your time full enough. Once we introduce you to some fine upstanding men, they will decide between themselves which one will take you as his wife."

"You make it sound as if I shall be up for auction, Kaitlin." I tried not to sound sarcastic.

"Well, you will be, won't you, my dear?"

Chapter 9

Glumly, I returned to my room, and Liza helped me comb my hair and tidy my dress before I descended. As I passed through the hall and entered the dining room, my heart sank as I recalled the cozy kitchen at the back of the house where we used to eat as children, with Bess the cook and all the other domestics. Even the little ladies' parlor at Gainsborough, where Megan, Edwina, and I would eat, seemed infinitely preferable to this austere room and its dim lighting.

The oak dining table was as long as the tallest tree in the forest. Obviously it was the finest table in the district. Around it were two long benches and several upright chairs, for important guests. Candles were lit the length of the table. Before each place was a wooden platter. Kaitlin even had pewter knives and spoons, which were the latest court fashion. Pewter goblets, ringed with ivory, sat by each place. Three musicians stood in a corner waiting to play. There was a stillness of expectancy in the room. As I opened the double doors to find my place, Kaitlin called out to me from the anteroom.

"Come here, Kate. We have guests to celebrate your arrival. We shall enter together. Tonight is a special dinner in your honor. Come and be introduced to our friends, who I trust will soon become yours."

Putting on a brave face, I drew my shoulders up, trying to appear taller and more self-confident. I did not have to be cowed by Kaitlin. I was Lady Borough, a widow of independent means. I had a sudden realization that Kaitlin was determined to treat me like a poor relation, and a childish one at that.

As I straightened my back to confront these strangers, I was aware that my once flat bosom was now more healthily endowed. The black damask dress was by far the most fashionably cut of all my gowns despite the chaste mourning cloth. I knew it showed off the rich yellow of my hair in stark contrast.

My hair fell in lustrous waves down my shoulders and back. Something in me had wanted to emulate Megan's carefree, self-confident beauty, and my abundant hair seemed symbolic of a free spirit. So, with twinkling eyes and a heart set firm, I walked slowly yet jauntily into the crowd of guests.

Making sure I had a polite smile on my face, I looked into three or four faces, and saw only polite smiles like my own. Henry Borough was nowhere to be seen. Slowly my grin faded. Surely Kaitlin would say something to explain his absence?

"Kate, Lady Borough, is newly widowed and has moved here from Gainsborough to live with us," Kaitlin said to the assembled few. "She was Kate Parr, of Kendal, if you recall.

But then she was just a little girl, not the blossoming young lady you see before you. I'm sure you'll grow to love her as we all do. Kate has a bright mind. But watch her tongue. It can be sharp!" Kaitlin let out one of her insincere tinkly-bell laughs.

I shook hands with the high and the mighty of Westmoreland. With Thomas Denton, Lord Dacre's son, and his wife, Rosamund. I felt a blush rise to my cheeks, as this was the man I had first been betrothed to and should have married rather than Edward Borough. He looked passingly attractive. I pondered for a moment whether my life might have been more smooth had I married him. Rosamund seemed dumb and tame. Then I was introduced to Lord and Lady Levens, of Levens Hall, who lived only a couple of miles away, and to the Beethams, Sir George and his good lady, Margaret, a solid, God-fearing country couple. The Levens were considered the highest-ranking in the district. Bored, I searched the corners of the room for Henry.

A man stood by the fireplace whom I had never seen before. Kaitlin turned, as if she had quite forgotten him, and exclaimed in a childlike voice, "Oh, good heavens, John, I am sorry. Kate, Lady Borough, do meet a cousin of mine, John Neville, Lord Latimer. He is from Snape Hall in Yorkshire and has been traveling around the country for a while. Kate, Lord Latimer," and she lowered her voice, "is also recently widowed."

I dropped in a little curtsy and said politely, "I am most sorry to hear that."

"As am I, dear Lady Borough, to know of your bereavement. To have your mother die at the same time as your husband must have been quite a shock."

He was fairly attractive, and his voice was appealing. I instantly wondered if this was Kaitlin's scheme, to marry me to a cousin, a widower, another man old enough to be my father, though Latimer had only hints of gray at his temples and a fine figure for a man of mature age. In my heart I was determined against any such arranged marriage, and I forced a smile at this John Neville. I turned, letting the black dress swing, hoping it was obvious I was ignoring him.

Kaitlin looked pleased with her social engineering. She ushered us into the dining room, to the coos and cries of admiration from our guests.

"For a winter table, Kaitlin," admired Lady Levens, "you have done wonders. With so few fresh flowers about, and so little in the way of fruits, I see you have decorated the table beautifully."

"Why, thank you." Being a gracious hostess was her favorite occupation.

Kaitlin clung to my arm as we walked into the dining room. "Don't say a word," she hissed in my ear as we entered the double doors and set foot on the slate flagstones, covered with tapestries of finely woven cloth. "Don't ask me where Henry is, because I don't know. I can't stand it, Katey. I can't stand it. He does these things to embarrass me. He knows I need him here. I want him by my side. Already everyone in the area is talking about him. Help me get through tonight, Katey. I *need* you."

So there I was, trapped between the devil and the deep blue sea. Both Kaitlin and Henry needed me. Both were hoping I'd help rescue them from the situation they had chosen for themselves. And I, caught between buffeting waves, had naively hoped they would help me.

I squeezed Kaitlin's arm, to show my strength and support. Whatever my feelings for Henry were, I respected hers, and felt for her pain and suffering at this moment.

Kaitlin sat me at her side as the honored guest. I found it hard to swallow the mouthfuls of veal and larks' tongues with any enthusiasm, choked by my own pottage of emotions. The guests studiously ignored Henry's absence, making light conversation, though Lady Levens became heated when the conversation turned to heretics of the Church. She vehemently believed any blasphemer should be executed without further ado. Kaitlin threw me a pointed glance, and I blushed slightly into my pease pudding. The Beethams questioned me on my former marriage and my adjustment to widowhood. Lady Beetham smiled at me, through her three teeth.

"But you are so young, dear. Almost a child. You will have no problem finding another husband."

"I trust not, Lady Beetham," I said demurely. "And thank you for your confidence in my ability to attract a new proprietor. I mean patron, I beg your pardon. Slip of the tongue."

"You need a husband, my dear girl," the good solid lady continued. "For all these functions. It's a lonely life for a woman as a widow. You never get invited out as much."

"Oh really?" I still sounded polite. "My mother, Lady Parr, existed for ten years or more after my father's death, quite happily. She did not want to remarry because of the strong feelings she still had for my father."

"But your mother, the revered Lady Parr, such a good lady, so clever," went on Lady Beetham, taking the sting out of my tail, "had a position at Court. I think any woman with such a position could survive on her own."

"You mean she had some paid employ and her time was filled. Do you agree then that some women need not be married?" I asked sweetly.

"Kate," snapped Kaitlin, obviously angry with me.

"Katherine." A soft, rather droll voice attracted my attention. "You seem to have argument with the married state. Is that a tenable position for a young lady of your status? Or have you been influenced by your erstwhile stepdaughter Megan Borough?"

Frowning, I turned to John Neville, Lord Latimer, who sat at my left. Of course, now his name rang a bell. Megan's letter had described entering the convent at Nunmonkton, owned by a cousin of Kaitlin's, John Neville.

I smiled in my most charming manner for the company and replied, "I admire Megan a great deal, but she has never been married, whereas I have. Her views on matrimony, therefore, may suffer from a lack of experience."

Then, dropping my voice to a confiding whisper, I asked Lord Latimer, "Did you meet Megan? Is she all right? I do miss her so," I found myself confessing.

He laughed and sat back, holding his wine goblet tenderly as he spoke to me. "No, we only corresponded. I gather she is a fiery young woman who has totally disobeyed her father. Surely you do not agree with such behavior?"

"Of course I do," I said hotly. "Lord Borough was about to marry her off to an elderly gentleman in Yorkshire . . . and she told him she would refuse."

"Not all elderly gentlemen in Yorkshire are so bad!" he said lightly.

"It wasn't *you*, was it?"

"No, no, no." He beamed at me, as though enjoying our conversation. "Did you refuse your mother's arranged marriage, Lady Borough?"

Annoyed with him, impatient even, I did not want to have to explain myself. So I said rather smartly back, "No, I'm a well-brought-up young lady. Not half as strong-minded as Megan Borough."

Before he could reply, Kaitlin called out to Latimer, "Tell me, John darling, tell me about the King. You were so recently in London. Is he really trying for a divorce from the Queen?"

And I took great pleasure in watching Latimer's face turn quite red, as his own anger rose to the surface. "I sincerely doubt he will be allowed to, Kaitlin. This business is a shame for the whole nation and could be ruinous to our peace and well-being. King Henry is notorious enough for his treatment of the poor, for the heavy taxes he levies on even the commonest peasant. Now he threatens to cut our Church off from the Pope's jurisdiction in Rome by divorcing our dear Queen Catherine and bastardizing Princess Mary. All for the young . . . the young lady Anne Boleyn . . . well, it makes my blood boil."

Kaitlin supervised the servants who were bringing in the next course, and I whispered across to Lord Latimer, "You don't approve of men who break the rules either, eh?"

Still angry, he did not beam at me this time.

"Don't be frivolous with what might be a very serious matter, Katherine."

"But if the King can break the rules, so can young ladies, can't they? Things have to change sometimes. Why must we carry on living the same lives, by the same laws, generation after generation? One day, I'll wager, young ladies will all refuse to marry whom their parents choose. They'll marry for love . . . or excitement . . . or wealth . . . or for whatever reason of their *own*. Or they won't marry at *all*."

"Katherine, Katherine . . ." Lord Latimer was about to protest further when there was a loud crash outside the doors, a scuffling of horses' feet, and men's cries. Kaitlin leaped to her feet in fear, her hand to her chest.

"What's that?" Her butler and several domestics came scurrying in to alert her.

"Ma'am, I don't think it's serious, but Lord Strickland has just this minute come home at a gallop and his horse has skidded to a halt and slid in the mud, throwing Lord Strickland onto the grass. Benjamin has gone to look after him. As I said, I don't think he's hurt, ma'am."

"Oh, my poor Henry," cried Kaitlin, and excusing herself from her guests she hurried out of the room.

I was left to take over the dinner party, as anxious as his wife that Lord Strickland should have come to no harm. I smiled fixedly and continued to eat. The Levens and the Beethams talked among themselves. I tried to engage the young Dacres in some friendly chitchat, avoiding further conversation with Latimer.

But there was a loud voice outside, a male voice, which we could not help but overhear as it screamed in rage.

"Get off me, woman. How dare you handle me so! Get thee hence! Fie on thee, and a pox on your guests, the mealy-mouthed idiots. You've got Kate in there, toadying for you. You can't expect to have me as well. Not two toadies in one night. That's *two* much to expect, ha, ha!"

I raised the lids of my eyes to the ceiling and prayed for help for Kaitlin, and for me. I had guessed Henry might turn to drink in his despair. His father, I knew, had spent much of his time in Lincoln drinking with his friends. Henry had shown the same weakness and frustration that seeks comfort in the wine cask.

Coughing, I turned to our mealy-mouthed guests. "I must go to the aid of Lady Strickland. Perhaps Lord Strickland is hurt about the head and is out of control. I remember seeing such an accident in Lincolnshire. Excuse me, gracious guests."

I ran for the door and was pushing it open when I saw Kaitlin strike Henry a whopping blow across his cheek with the back of her hand.

"I hate you for bringing me such disgrace. How could you do this to me? It is a celebratory dinner for Katey's arrival. How could you, Henry Borough?"

I came forward to hold her hand, whispering, "It'll be all right. We'll make up some story. The Dacres and Levens are too highborn to mention the truth, if we furnish them with a convincing enough tale. They would not gossip in public. We'll keep a proud face on it, never you mind."

"Thank you, my dear. What a help you are. Like having a little sister."

She wiped tears from her eyes as Henry's bent-over figure staggered up the stairs, crashing against the banisters, tripping and sliding in his drunken stew.

I whispered again to Kaitlin, "His father used to be like that. I nursed him through the most evil drunken bouts. I could nurse Henry too."

Even as I opened my mouth, I knew with a sinking heart that I was finding a loophole, a way I might be alone with him. Whether it was the fact I myself had drunk two pewter tankards of wine, or whether it was deep within me, I knew not. But right at that moment I craved his warm body, his eyes, his beautiful mouth to be kissing my own. Embarrassed, I took Kaitlin's hand so that she would think me her friend, and we returned to the dining parlor together.

Chapter 10

Later that night, when the guests had departed to their homes, I tiptoed into Henry Borough's chamber. Only one candle was still burning. The room was very dark. Like most of the aristocracy, Henry and Kaitlin had separate chambers, for those times when they needed or desired privacy.

Kaitlin had already retired for the night, depressed beyond measure at the humiliation she had suffered. She begged me see to Henry's comfort. Of course, I was nervous about entering Henry's room in this way, nervous, too, at what I might behold there. Still, forgiveness was foremost in my mind, and a terrible sympathy for the condition he was in. I really wanted to help him.

I entered the dim chamber. There was such a terrible noise of snoring that I almost giggled. Henry had not taken off any of his clothes. He lay sprawled, spread-eagled across his bed, his cloak tangled uncomfortably around his legs and waist. He was on his back, his mouth wide open, in such a deep sleep I doubt infernal thunderbolts would have wakened him.

I knew he was going to feel very sick the next day. I gingerly removed what clothing I could, piling the stained and splattered garments on a stool in his dressing room. He really was a sight of degradation and defeat. I took off the leather upper shoes, and the stockings, the thick hose, the doublet, the undershirt. Searching among his closets, I discovered a cambric nightshirt, which I deftly put over his head, cradling the neck and shoulders in my arm as I pulled the long garment over his face.

"My poor Henry," I whispered into his ear, feeling great waves of pity for him. "My poor darling boy."

Despite the ugliness of the scene, I loved him all the more for being so helpless and so vulnerable. He had been placed in an unbearable situation. He did need my help and strength, I could see that.

Then, placing a jug of water and a mug by his bedside, I slipped under the sheets beside him, an arm around his shoulders and my head upon his heaving breast.

Oh, Henry. Nothing could keep us apart. I loved him so terribly, with an ache that seemed to fill my soul. He groaned occasionally but did not wake. I drifted off, dreaming of our happy times together.

I woke in the chill before dawn, realized where I was, and began to kiss his face and throat. I stroked his chest beneath the nightshirt, hoping he would awaken.

"What? Who's that? Oh no, you smell like Katey. My Katey. My Katey," he began to cry in his sleep. "Oh, good Lord, why did I marry the wrong Kate?"

"It is me, it is your Katey." I cradled his head in my arms. I lifted him to a sitting position, then turned his head to face mine. "See, it is me. It is your sweet Kate, the one who loves you passionately."

Gradually his eyes began to focus, and he stared at me as though at a stranger. Scarcely moving his lips, he managed to say, "You are real?"

"Who do you think took off your clothes and dressed you so nicely in your nightshirt? I looked after you in your sickness. I wiped you down. I gave you water to drink. I have infusions that will ease the sore head and refresh the spirit. You will feel better in no time."

Henry lay back against the feather pillows and sighed. "You are an angel. It was no dream."

I kneeled against his body and kissed his fevered brow as I wiped away the perspiration that had gathered there.

"Oh, Henry. We will make life good for each other. We will be happy. We have our love. But I *am* scared of Kaitlin's finding out our secret. If ever I appear cool it is because of that."

At that moment, we heard the clatter of the maids with their buckets and cleaning mops. I scuttled off Henry's bed and made a dive for his dressing room, where I hastily concocted my herbal remedies. One of the maids entered without so much as a knock at the door. Emerging, my face full of proud annoyance at her rude entrance, I chastised the girl while walking over to Henry.

"There, sir. This should help clear your head. That was a terrible fall you took from the horse last night. You are lucky you did not do more permanent damage." I adjusted my dress surreptitiously and hastily left the chamber.

Kaitlin came to me later that day. She was humble and grateful. Henry had recovered remarkably and was even being nice to her. Secretly I smiled to myself, knowing it was because I had brought joy back to his heart.

As she left my room, instructing me on lunch and my manners, she added, "Henry won't be around very much for

the next few days. He is going to take up his studies at
Cartmel Priory. I am so pleased he has returned to the Church.
He is very clever, and I am proud of his ability to write
beautiful devotional material. I feel it will be best for him to
have a place of retreat and study, away from the social pell-
mell here. The pace of life can be too much here in Westmoreland. Don't you think, Katey?"

"Oh yes, Kaitlin," I said shyly. "I have been enjoying my
own studies. By the way, may I take a horse out on my own
or with Liza for rides over the fells? It is such a long time
since I had the freedom to ride alone. Borough would not let
me. That way I find my head is clear to think."

Kaitlin did not seem unduly worried. She looked at peace
with herself; she nodded and said as long as I graced her
table at mealtimes, I was free to do as I pleased.

The hills surrounding Sizergh—fells, as we call them in
Westmoreland—were beautiful and familiar. I soon found
many opportunities to escape the tension and bad feeling in
the castle. Cantering my own horse, a solid but speedy brown
mare, whom I named Daisy after the carefree white flowers
that spotted the early spring meadows, I found peace and
contentment way up in the hills, beneath the trees.

※

Walking Daisy carefully down a hillside on one such day,
I was startled to see a lone rider galloping our way, along the
dirt road that led from Middleton Hall. Why was a rider
coming to Sizergh? The horse was thundering along, paying
no heed to my own mount. Certainly there was no chance to
make my voice heard, so I prepared to follow the mystery
figure back to the castle. However, Daisy slipped at the last
foothold, over the roots of a gnarled tree, and we ended up
colliding with the hasty messenger.

Throwing back the woolen hood that had covered my face
against the breeze, I smiled at the stranger.

"What brings you in such a hurry to Sizergh Castle? We have not had a visitor in days."

The man was young and exceedingly handsome. He jumped down from his horse and crossed to my side. He gazed up quizzically to where I sat astride and said heatedly, "I did not expect to be accosted by a solitary woman in these wild lands. Surely it is unsafe for a lady to be so unescorted?"

Unaffected, I shrugged off the danger. "I live here. Who is likely to harm me?"

"Considering that I have been dragged from civilized London to protect you folk from the rebellious warmongering Scots, I should have said the danger was high."

"You're right. I probably should not have strayed so far on my own. But I love to be alone with nature."

The young man laughed, a deep throaty sound. He was of medium build, with a dark complexion, as though he spent most of his days outdoors on horseback. His brown skin was offset by shining jet black hair. His teeth were gleaming and his smile was broad, accommodating, and genuine.

"Is Henry Borough, Lord Strickland, at Sizergh?"

I cocked my head. "Why, I believe so. He is just returned from Cartmel Priory. Do you have business with him?"

The young man restrained his eager horse.

"We're old friends, Henry and I, from Cambridge. Thomas Seymour is the name, ma'am."

"Seymour?" I questioned, not recognizing it. "That's a strange accent you have."

"Not so strange as yours," he shot back archly.

I bristled. "Mine is quite normal in these parts."

Seymour smiled disarmingly. "So is mine back home in Wiltshire. My father is Sir John Seymour of Wolf Hall. Brother Edward is one of the King's henchmen. My elder sister, Jane, is a maid of honor to the Queen, though"—he frowned—"I believe she has recently moved allegiance to Anne Boleyn."

News from Court! Now I was genuinely elated at the prospect of his visit.

"Lady Strickland, my cousin Kaitlin, will be delighted to receive you."

He stepped forward to take my hand in greeting.

"You have not given me the honor of your name, dear lady."

"Oh, I am Katherine Parr—I mean, Lady Borough. I was born and bred over there, at Kendal Castle."

"Married?"

"Widowed."

"Are you not rather young to be in widow's weeds?"

"My husband was older."

He grinned at me.

"Well, Katherine Parr, since you are plucky enough to be out here on horseback, I'll race you to Sizergh. I have little time to call on Henry, but I was riding north and felt I should take this opportunity."

"Are you really a soldier?" I wondered what sort of friends he and Henry were, for Henry was not at all a man to brandish a sword.

As he leaped agilely back on his mount, Thomas Seymour's eyes seemed to smile with deviltry.

"Aye, it's a great world for a young man of adventure."

Tugging at Daisy's reins, I retaliated to that bragging manner with my own bravado. "Let's see what you are made of then, Seymour. I'll beat you to the gates."

Daisy careened off over the path, into the moorland heather, for of course I knew the shortest route to the castle. Daisy and I tore through clumps of bracken and fern and over rocks. I felt the bubbles of adventure and excitement frothing in my veins, as I galloped, elated, determined to win this race.

Imagine my mortification when I rounded a large rock, came face to face with the gates of Sizergh, and saw Thomas

Seymour dismounted, requesting permission to enter from the gatekeeper.

"Good try, Katherine," he said mockingly. "My! Watching you and that horse go filled me with fear. I should hate to be against you in a tournament."

But I was angry and disappointed. The young man was a foolish braggart. Tossing my head in annoyance, I said nothing but led my horse back to the stableyard.

Thomas Seymour stayed for dinner, and Kaitlin was charmed and delighted. He had such a handsome face and charming manner. I could tell that despite his youthfulness, he was well experienced with women. He was full of flattery and compliments to Kaitlin, who blushed and primped to be thus treated. I sighed and retired to my chamber early that evening. I was quite sore from the daredevil horse ride and could scarcely sit straight through dinner.

The next morning we lined up to bid our hasty visitor farewell. He strapped a sword to his side, the perfect picture of a brigand. His eyes seemed afire with passion, presumably for the fighting ahead. Approaching his horse, I reached up my hand and could not help myself from saying, "Be careful, Thomas Seymour. Fighting the Scots won't be as easy as beating me at the race. Don't let yourself get hurt. You are not invincible."

He leaned over and kissed my hand. I was embarrassed, knowing both Kaitlin and Henry watched.

Chapter
11

enry Borough and I met once or twice in secret, at Cartmel Priory. We sat together in his study, talking, reading, holding each other tight. Our meetings were intense, but not indiscreet. I made poor Liza ill at ease with the monks and fearful for her health in the cold. I knew she had run out of sympathy with my actions. There was quite a distance these days between Liza and myself. I had put her attitude down primarily to her return to Westmoreland and rediscovery of family and friends.

By the time Liza and I were riding back that night, I could see she was upset. As we walked our horses through the damp evening mist, over Cartmel Fell, which was too steep to ride, I asked her if anything was wrong. "Not that I can tell thee, ma'am," she grunted. For Liza was never one with words.

"We used to be such friends. In Gainsborough we told each other everything. Please."

"You won't like it," she said, her eyes down at her feet.

"Try me," I said, wanting to draw it out of her. "I'm tough. I've been through a lot."

She paused, fearful to go on. "First off, I don't like what you are doing with Henry Borough. I think it's dangerous and foolish. And not worthy of your place in life. He's not worth it, ma'am. He's not worthy of you. I don't see how you can ruin your life for him. If Kaitlin Neville finds out, which she surely will one day, I'd hate to be in your shoes."

I held my breath, angry at her presumption. But I told her to go on.

"Second of all," she said, gritting her teeth, "I don't approve of your dallying with this new Church thing. It's blasphemous, and you ain't got no right to truck with the holy word."

"Liza!" I exclaimed. "You never said such a thing to me in Gainsborough. And all that time you knew I was discussing it with Megan, Anne Kyme, and Henry. So why the change of heart now?"

"Because I'm home, ma'am. And my people is God-fearing folk. And I'd hate for them to hear you was a blasphemer and a traitor. And . . . and because I've a new young man, Stephen, ma'am. We're walking out. And he is very God-fearing. And he says folks that listen to this Martin Luther are crazy and foolish, and should be put to death, ma'am."

"Oh, Liza!" I was so shocked I didn't know what to say. I wanted to laugh, in part, at her ignorance. But I could see she was serious. Our disagreement strained further conversation. And so, I tired of the awkward silence and rode on ahead.

When I neared Sizergh, its masterful shape stood out from the dark night sky as if it owned the valley and the hills. The sky was thick with low-hanging clouds. I knew I should be in trouble if Kaitlin found me riding this late alone.

My bad temper had abated, and I regretted leaving Liza behind. I hoped nothing would happen to her. There were many poor and starving folk these days, as there seemed to be too many people striving to make a livelihood off too little land. Only a few parts of Westmoreland were rich and fertile. Tilling the soil was difficult here; the country was unlike the rich flat lands of Lincolnshire. As for keeping sheep, or mountain cattle, well, that was a life fit for a dog, chasing the beasts up the snow-covered wastes, or rescuing them when they strayed into the cold winter night.

But I reached home without mishap. I slid the horse in through the stables at Sizergh without being seen. I had already bribed the stableboy to keep silent when I took the horse out. He staggered out of bleary sleep, and I saw him leer at me with a most unpleasant look. I ran inside the kitchen entrance of the castle, bidding him a swift goodnight.

I realized, however, that I was gambling dangerously. Perhaps I should not go to Cartmel again, at least not in this fashion. Anyway it was clear Liza would never accompany me again. I threw off my overboots in the kitchen. As the roads had been muddy and wet, my dress was splashed around the hem, so I slipped it off to leave in the laundry room, knowing one of my dear old friends in the back kitchen would wash it for me in secret.

Standing in the kitchen in my underslip, the black dress that I had become so accustomed to wearing no longer covering my form, I heard a scuffling noise by the door. I called out to Liza, hoping she was back safely. But there was no reply. More than likely rats, I said to myself, and lit a couple of candles from the fireplace to see my way upstairs.

The castle felt eerie this late at night. I wished Liza were with me. Any minute now I would go and wake old Jessie, one of the maids, and ask her to light my way upstairs.

I hardly had time to think as a hand grabbed my throat and an arm pinioned me stone-still where I stood in the middle of the kitchen floor. Another hand came down over my mouth, preventing me from calling out to Jessie, who slept only a few yards away.

From the smell of the intruder, I guessed it to be the stableboy. Fear flashed through my body. My mind went blank. I thought not of my safety, or of my impending danger. Since Henry had departed Borough Hall, we had not made love. My worst sin, on living at Sizergh, had been to kiss and hold his hand warmly in mine. Now it was as though our previous acts were mocking me. Was this my punishment?

The room was pitch black, as the candles had blown out when his arms took me with such force. I could feel him breathing down my neck. The smell of him was awful. He stank of hay, horse excrement, and perspiration. He slept, I knew, out in the stables among the horses. How I loathed the vile creature!

Without saying a word, he forced my body into a corner and tried with his one free arm to pull my underslip from my body. The only sense I could muster told me to do everything to prevent his free arm working. But as I started to show signs of struggle, he asserted his strength and that merciless grip on my throat tightened.

His hand was over my mouth, his thick stubby coarse fingers grating at the skin around my lips. I tried to bite him once, but he just shoved his fist farther down my throat. Again his free arm pulled on my underslip. It fell to the ground. His grip slackened slightly on my mouth. Now I had only a camisole top and my loose cotton shorts, plus hose held up by garters, between me and nakedness.

Prying his hand from my mouth, I managed to speak. "Please unhand me. Or I'll die for want of air." He let his hand slip a minute, and I turned quickly to face him.

In a few seconds my eyes became adjusted to the darkness. I stared at his stumpy form, his broad shoulders and short-cropped blond hair. I watched him kick off his breeches. This young stableboy had no shame whatsoever, and my anger riled up within me. Why, his thing stood out before him like a sledgehammer determined to beat me. I shivered in the night air.

"You don't want to do this," I said firmly. "You know I am a widow, and if I get with child Lady Strickland will have to assume it was one of you men, because my husband has been dead for over a year."

Still standing before me, and swaying slightly so that he made his thing move in the breeze, he laughed, showing me his yellow broken teeth. "You! You who sneak off with the master whenever you can, behind Lady Strickland's back! You tell me she'll point the finger at us? Lady Pomp and

Glory, that's what they call you in the stables, when we fancy we've got you in the haystack, your dress up over your thighs—you should hear what we say about you, Lady Muck. *We'll* point the finger at the master. I'll just tell the lady how you's sneaked off on a horse and came back at night, and tipped me with silver not to tell."

"I'll give you more silver. Pewter. Gold. Anything."

"No way, girl. I'm gonna have you this night. For mine. I knew it this morning when I saw you go off on that horse. I says, when she comes back, I'll take her. I'll show her. Come here, lass, sit on this. You ain't never had one like this. You ain't never known how *good* it can be."

I stared at the boy with surprise, he had such confidence. He was not scared at all.

"What if Liza should come back in now? What if I should scream and wake old Jessie up?"

He reached into his shirt pocket and drew out six inches of cold steel. "I'll show 'em this," he snarled. "That should keep them all quiet."

Then he made a move toward me, flashing the cold steel. I backed away. "I'll use it too, make no bones about it, lass. One peep out of you, and I'll be across that throat like a razor over a chin."

He grabbed my hand and pulled me to him, and though I expected him to throw me on the floor, I was pushed against a wall so the jagged pieces of stone pierced my back. Brutally he tore at my shorts and pushed his thing against my thighs.

"I told you to sit on this, lass." He laughed. "Just give in and you'll enjoy it like they all do."

"How many ladies have you taken like this?"

"You'd be surprised, young lass. They love it," and he licked his lips.

"Please don't hurt me," was all I could say as his dirty coarse hands rammed his thick banger inside of me. The boy was quick, obviously pent-up by our long delay. It was over and done with in a short time. He had bruised my thighs, and my back was sore from the stone wall. As for my insides, they felt as though they had been ripped apart with his knife. The sight of the boy revolted me as, wilting and spent, he picked up his breeches and began to make for the door.

"Mention a word of this and I'll tell Lady Strickland about your horse ride," he warned before he left the door. "You'll thank me later. After one of those namby-pamby men marry you. One day you'll come begging at my door for more."

I heard him run as the sound of horses' hooves clattered over the stableyard. Sobbing heavily, I was sitting on the cold stone floor, my shorts around my knees, my hair in tangles, when the kitchen door opened and someone stumbled in. She must have heard my sounds, because even before she could light a candle, I heard Liza's voice call out, "Who's there?"

"It's me," I said mournfully.

"My lady, where? What on earth . . . ?" She lit a candle from one outside the kitchen door and turned to see me on the floor.

"What happened to you?"

Within seconds, she was on her knees helping me stand up. "Are you hurt? What has happened?" she gasped. "We must get help."

"No, stop. That boy. He must have taken your horse in, too. He . . . he violated me here, in this kitchen. I was taking my dress and boots off because they were muddy and I did not want Kaitlin to see them, when he came in and caught me by the neck."

"He forced himself upon you?" cried Liza.

"I suppose," I said wearily, "I have been raped. But I let it happen. I was so scared he would hurt me with his knife if I put up a struggle. I let it happen, Liza, and that shames me."

"That boy has an evil reputation. I've heard them talk

about him in the village. We must tell Kaitlin immediately and have him punished."

"No. I can't. He knows about me and Henry. He has threatened to tell Kaitlin if I breathe a word of this."

"Oh, ma'am. I told you so. I told you it would lead to trouble. Are you all right? Are you in pain? Oh, I shall get my brothers to go after him." Liza wept, wringing her hands.

"Don't do that. He must be stronger than any of our folk. He hates me. They all do. He says the other stableboys all talk about me behind my back, and call me rude names." The shame of it all filled my heart, and I began to sob again.

Liza helped me to my room, and my spirits were so depressed that the next day I stayed in bed. Liza cooked up a story about my falling off a horse the day before to explain the bruises on my legs and face.

All that day I was so morose, everything about my body and soul felt violated. I no longer knew what to think, or believe. Was it not all a sign that my life was wrong? That I should not carry on the alliance with Henry. I was thankful Henry was not around to witness my degradation, and that Kaitlin refrained from visiting the sick chamber.

There seemed to be no way out of the depression. When Henry returned from his visit to Cartmel at the end of the week and asked permission to visit me, I could not refuse. But equally I could say nothing to him.

He sat by me on the bed and leaned over to kiss me. "What's wrong, little Katey? Did your fall dull your spirits?"

"A lot happened on my way home, Henry." I sobbed. "Liza disapproves of my meeting with you, and of my interest in the new religion. She said we could no longer be friends and she certainly would not accompany me to Cartmel anymore. So I rode home alone, and . . ." But I had determined not to tell him, ever, of my degradation.

Henry brushed the hair off my brow, where I had combed it forward to hide the worst bruises. He was staring at one of the ugly purple marks on my head when he seemed suddenly concerned. He began to search down my body, looking beneath the nightshirt, for more bruises. He lifted my nightshirt above the waist, inspecting the bruises to my inner thighs. No one had seen those except Liza.

"These are not the bruises from a horse fall, sweet Katey. No fall could bruise you here, in this manner. These came from the hands of some beast. What has happened, Kate? Whatever has happened?"

To hear his gentle, pitying voice let loose my tears as I melted against his warm chest. Now I wanted to tell him, I dearly wanted to tell him.

Henry covered his ears as I spoke, the words were so offensive to him. He cried with rage as my story ran its course. "We must have the boy punished! Such a disgrace to a member of Kaitlin's family. She will at least banish him from her grounds, if not have him flogged. Katey, my dearest . . ." He stared at me with a new fascination borne of his dawning horror.

"You cannot tell Kaitlin. The boy knew I had been to see you. He gave me the horse in the morning. He is not stupid. He had seen us together at other times in the grounds. The stableboys and gardeners watch our every movement. He threatened if I mentioned a word of it to Kaitlin, he would tell her about you and me." I fell silent.

"We have to stop meeting, Henry. We are breaking too many rules, upsetting too many people. If we are causing so much pain by our futile attempt at happiness, ought we not to stop?"

I was resolved.

"But, Katey, sweet dove. How can we stop meeting?" Henry was stricken with fear. "You know what my life is like without you. I would be dead here. Dead. Dead of a dying soul. Stultified. I cannot go on without you. You're my lifeline. I have my studies, but you are the only living thing that means anything to me. I should kill myself, I know it."

"How can you say that, when this love of ours brings pain, and evil everywhere?"

My decision was tearing me apart. I cried in desperation, wanting him to let me go, wanting him to release me from our bond together. I needed him to make the break.

If he begged and refused to break off our liaison, I knew I should have to continue with it, regardless of my fate. Never before had I felt so swept up by fate and circumstance, so out of control of my own life. Why had I not run away to London when my mother died? I had known it would be dangerous coming to Sizergh, with Henry married to Kaitlin. Yet I had been spurred on by that danger, egged on by that sense of adventure and excitement at not knowing what the outcome would be.

Then Henry was crying on my lap, and I was stroking his hair, as if he were the wounded one.

Chapter 12

Henry grabbed hold of my arm in the corridor near my chamber, as though it were pure accident we had met in such forbidden quarters.

Before I could ask an explanation, he was furtively whispering, "Kate, I need you!"

My mind was fuddled, it being so early in the morning, but I was caught by the strength of his feelings.

"Let us go away together," he was saying wildly.

He almost made me laugh, for, in truth, the idea was exciting and appealing to me too. Worse, a messenger had just the previous evening delivered a letter to me from my brother William, saying he would soon be coming to Kendal Castle to sort out our family affairs, and that I should try to meet him there for a few days. When I confessed this perfect cover to Henry, his eyes were wild with anticipation and happiness.

"We could take our horses and ride into the hills and lake district, look at Westmoreland together. I have only seen it under Kaitlin's dull tutelage. You would bring my eyes alive, my darling."

I forgot myself and hugged him about the neck. Just at that moment we heard a scurrying of feet, and I ran from him, down the corridor, hurrying to the dining hall for my breakfast.

Later that afternoon, fixing my hair to look very neat and proper, I went to find Kaitlin, who was sitting in her parlor, to tell her of the letter and my desire to visit Kendal the following week.

Kaitlin was mildly interested. She was suffering from her headaches again. The heat of the summer often brought them on. Poor Kaitlin was unable to enjoy life.

"It's been such a long time since I have seen William, or Kendal. I am longing to hear all about Mother's death and William's life at Court, and . . . about the King. Don't you think it would be wonderful to be at Court with King Henry, Kaitlin?"

"In a position such as your mother had?" she asked, looking down at her long fingers and perfectly groomed nails. "I suppose so. But all that gossip about Henry and Anne Boleyn must be tiresome."

"What do you think will happen, Kaitlin? Will he marry Anne? Will he divorce Queen Catherine? What will become of Princess Mary?"

Kaitlin came to her feet sternly. "Really, Kate. How could you talk such nonsense? The King *cannot* divorce Queen Catherine. It goes against the rules of the Church. How can such a thing even be talked about? That Boleyn woman is just a schemer."

"But the King *is* talking about divorce very seriously. Deputations have been sent to Rome to discuss it with the Pope. King Henry spends hours every night studying his case for a divorce. Rumors in London are strong that he will leave Queen Catherine."

"Rumors from whom, girl? The guttersnipes?" Kaitlin was angry now. But then, of course, if the King managed to obtain a divorce, and with the Church's blessing, it would put women like her in a vulnerable position. It would destroy the sanctity of marriage, tear down the century-old laws by which they saw themselves protected.

"My sister Anne tells me. She is now Lady Herbert, with a place in Queen Catherine's Court. I wonder what will happen to Anne and William Herbert if Queen Catherine is removed and Anne Boleyn becomes Queen."

"Anne Boleyn will *never* be Queen. Mark my words. The day a common slut becomes Queen—a girl who would lie down with the King, a married man and a father, and expect to be made Queen for her sins—that day will mark the end of this great kingdom!"

And with those thunderous words, majestically, Kaitlin Neville left the room.

❖

Liza and I clacked and clattered our way into Cartmel's courtyard, after having visited and left my brother. I was still so angry and incensed by our meeting that I was scarcely in a fit state for a romantic rendezvous with Henry.

William had, of course, inherited Kendal Castle from my mother, for although I was the eldest child, he was the son. In letters from Anne, I had learned there was little money left for us after William had taken his share after Mother's death. I had determined to question him closely about his handling of our affairs.

William was much taller and broader now. He had just turned fifteen, and the hint of a red fuzz was growing along his manly jaw.

"Well, brother, it is good to meet with you again," I greeted him warmly. "And how have you been since your marriage to Claire Bourchier? I trust the good lady serves you as well as the title she will bring you?"

"Katherine, remember your place," he said sharply. "I hope to become the Earl of Essex quite soon, though Claire and I still await the birth of a son to cement our union. I know you're here to find out about Mother's will. Let me warn you now, you won't like it. So let's sit down first and enjoy some wine together."

Taken aback by his cool reception, I followed him with trepidation into my childhood home.

It was so strange to be sitting together before the fireplace of our beloved Kendal Castle—both adults, married people. Strange to be back in those familiar halls that now echoed hollowly. A couple of our servants remained, looking after the empty rooms for us, but William had never opened the castle up and, indeed, told me he intended to keep it closed, for Kendal was too costly to run.

"Frankly, Kate, can you see yourself coming back to live here? It's cold and damp. You are better served at Sizergh. Your sister and I both love city life. What about you? I thought you were hankering to join us at Court?"

His attitude still annoyed me, so I would not give him the pleasure of thinking I was miserable.

"I changed my mind after Mother's death. Maybe when I am next married, I will come down to visit with both of you. For now, strangely, I am content to be in Westmoreland.

But why, William, why is there no money left in the Parr name? What on earth did Mother do?"

He hugged the old cask of wine on his lap, as though seeking support from its wooden frame. His belly had spread, despite his youth, and I guessed he drank like all those at Court. The cask was dusty and smelled of mildew, like everything else in the castle.

Sighing impatiently, he spoke as though I were a naughty child.

"Really, Kate, you know all about it. To make this marriage of mine with the Bourchier family, Mother had to promise a large sum of money. Although Claire herself brought a normal dowry to our union, they knew the title was what we were after. Old man Bourchier was forever broke, so they made Mother put money down. To guarantee my steadfastness, Bourchier was supposed to pay it back each year, in agreed sums. If we had a son within the first year, he was supposed to give it all back at once. That was Mother's arrangement. But you know the rest—Bourchier drank and gambled most of it away. He paid Mother very little, and now that she is dead and we have not yet had a child, there seems little I can do to extract a debt from my own father-in-law."

Shaking my head with disbelief, I said angrily, "So Bourchier drank and gambled away whatever family fortune we had. Did no one think of my sister and me? You were, after all, the man of the house, duty-bound to provide *something* for your sisters. While your father-in-law gambled and you tumbled in bed with his daughter, *my* father's daughters were left stranded. Now our only hope is in the men we marry."

Unable to bear the sight of William any longer, I gathered my skirts behind me and swept from the room. I spent the rest of the day walking the grounds of Kendal, and then departed hastily with Liza first thing the next morning for Cartmel.

✠

We arrived around midday. Liza stayed only briefly to greet Henry, placing a forced peck on his cheek and announcing she would continue on to her family in the village of Oxenholme before nightfall.

"Shall we be on our way?" Henry asked as we watched Liza leave. We rode all afternoon, until we came to Lake Windermere. Henry was so struck by its wild beauty that we stayed in a hostelry by the lakeside.

Relieved of the restrictions of life at Sizergh, all the love we had felt for each other promptly returned. I happily resumed my position in his bed, glorying in unbridled lovemaking. We spent every minute of every day together, walking through the fields, perched on large rocks overlooking the lake, reading in the crisp fresh air.

One sunny afternoon, I began to run down the hillside, but tripped over a rock and fell on my nose into the masses of tiny white daisies. Henry came racing after me, most concerned, then fell at my side, and we rolled around laughing. He picked me up and carried me back up the hill to a copse of trees, under which was an entrance to a cave. Henry walked calmly into the cool dankness of the underground room, where in the dim light from its entrance he laid me on the soft clay floor and took down my skirts so they rested on my ankles, and there we made love, while I complained that surely this was dangerous and we would be buried alive for our sins! Henry just laughed as he let himself down over my body, muttering he could never be so happy as to be buried here alive, for we should then make love until Eternity.

Back in our room at the Red Lion, the serving wench came with hunks of fresh bread, country cheeses, and a big pot of pickled cucumbers. Hungry from our activities of the day, I hurriedly ate the cheese and pickles, stuffing the food into my mouth by the handful.

Then suddenly, without any warning, I leaned over the

edge of the bed and, to my horror, threw up all over the floor.

"Oh, I'm so sorry," I murmured to Henry, who was cradling me in his arms. "I don't know what's happened to me. Every time I eat something rich or spicy these days, I become quite sick. That's the third time I've vomited like this." I shivered, and he held me tight.

"Oh, Katey," he whispered in my ear. "I'll look after you." We fell asleep in each other's arms, oblivious to the fate about to unfold for us.

The morning we were to leave for the ride back to Cartmel, and so to Sizergh, an awful thought flashed into my mind. Words of Liza's, spoken in jest, about an unmarried sister and how the foolish girl had vomited her dinner and tried to hide the mess from their mother. Could I indeed have become pregnant that night with the stableboy? For Henry and I had indulged as man and wife only these last few days.

Oblivious to my agitated state of mind, Henry stood strong and peaceful in the casement window, overlooking the lake, and said, "I wish we could be married, Kate. I can't face going back to her. You know what some men do? They poison their wives. There is a poison you can buy that makes it look like a natural death. How else can I escape this imprisonment?"

"Don't speak like that, Henry."

Then he turned to face me, hope lighting up his face. "Come away with me, Kate. I'm sure we could find enough money. We could live in one of those cottages by the lake. I can write poetry. Oh, darling, will you come?" He held my hands so tight they hurt.

"Oh, don't talk like that." Tears streamed down my cheeks, for I did not want to go back to Sizergh either and resume our stiff and secret life. But running away was no answer. Grimly, we mounted our horses for the trip home. I knew I lacked the courage to live as a social outcast. Henry was a dreamer, but, in my despair, I did not see how we could live on his dreams.

fter eating almost a pound of apples, I was discovered by Liza vomiting in my room. She said sternly, "That's the second time in two days."

"How do you know?" I asked petulantly. I had been keeping it such a secret.

" 'Cause I smelled it the last time, and cleaned up after you."

"I caught a disease in Windermere. I think it must have been the water. I seem to get sick every other day or so."

Liza came up behind me and put her arms around my shoulders. She brushed my hair back from my face.

"Ma'am," she said, her voice very soothing, "have you considered as you might be with child?"

Of course, by now I had distinct suspicions myself. There had been no bleed since the incident. The moon had come and gone, changed and requartered itself, and no sign of any blood. I had kept very quiet, not wanting to admit to myself what might be happening.

"Nothing's happened, this moontide. . . . Maybe it was the excitement of the incident. Oh, Liza!" I grabbed her arm. "What will I do?"

"Stay calm, ma'am. How long is it since that lad hurt you? I'll ask the midwife in my village. Lord, I'm pleased he's left this castle to work elsewhere."

"Go there tonight, Liza. Find someone to help me. I wish Old Nell were still alive. I'm going to try all my herbal remedies. Something must work."

"Herbs won't be any good for you now, ma'am. Not if a babe has took hold. Even a fall from a horse won't shift a babe well lodged. You've heard about these desperate girls that throws themselves from church towers, from the shame of being laid up with child? Sometimes they die from the fall and the babe lives."

"Don't tell me stories like that!"

"I'll speak to my mother," said Liza abruptly, as though that was the final answer.

∻

We left Sizergh under the cloak of night. Disguising ourselves, we headed for Liza's family home in the village of Oxenholme. The rendezvous, and my leaving, took place without problem. Liza took the reins like a seasoned driver. Crouched under a blanket in the back of the cart, I felt relieved to be in her careful hands.

Liza whispered to me when we were a couple of miles down the lane. "You can sit up now. No one saw us. They must just think I'm sneaking off for the night to see my boyfriend!" And she giggled. This time she was leading me. I knew she was enjoying herself.

We had driven for only fifteen minutes or so when I saw the lights of a house behind the trees and heard voices laughing and singing.

Liza brought the horse to a halt and helped me down from the cart.

"They're all in the kitchen. After eating, most evenings are spent drinking ale and singing. My brothers are a fine old lot." She laughed. "You're like them. Pity you couldn't marry Rob. He's a right 'un. Good for you."

I blushed in the dark. How could she talk of marriage now? "What would they say if they knew, Liza?"

"They'd be out with their sticks to get that lad, that's what," she said sternly. "I wish you would give me the word, ma'am. We'd have that boy before he could open his mouth to squeal. My brothers are strong. They are."

I was clutching her hand as I stumbled up the crazy-paved path to their door.

"This brings us to the hall. Mother may be there sewing or she may have gone to bed. Father, like as not, is down at the alehouse. He seldom comes home before they throw him out."

Liza's father was a man of some means. He traded in horses. The family lived in a fair-sized manor recently built, with her four sisters, three brothers, some of their children, all the father's apprentices, and the family servants. Liza often described her home life as a maelstrom. "It's so noisy there," she would say. "Your life is like a convent one compared to that."

Liza opened the door, and I stepped onto rush matting in the small hall. A fire was burning, though it was a summer's night. We never had fires once summer came at Sizergh— part of Kaitlin's economies. There was a youngish-looking woman sewing in a rocking chair before the fire. She looked up and smiled, and Liza ran to hug her. I dropped a bow, but to my horror, she rose to her feet and curtsied before me.

"Lady Borough," Freda Harris said. "It is a pleasure to meet you. I loved your mother so."

"Please, good lady, do not drop before me," I stammered. "I am here as Liza's friend and your humble guest. I cannot express my gratitude deeply enough that you may be able to help me in my hour of need."

Freda Harris looked embarrassed, and shifted from one foot to the other. She whispered, "Ma'am, I was very sorry to hear of the dreadful thing that happened to you. I hope it works itself out fine. Our house is yours whenever you need it."

Tears came to my eyes at the woman's words. I leaned forward to hug Freda Harris, wishing I too had a mother at this moment.

Liza took me into the kitchen and introduced me to her brothers and sisters. I was surprised by the lively animated atmosphere in there. Six or seven young men sat around the table, two with young women on their knees; a third young woman stood by the fire. The men drank from huge leather mugs, which they swung on the back of their arms, holding their mouths wide open, pouring the ale down their throats without stopping to swallow.

I smiled nervously when Liza introduced me as her friend Kate. She could not tell them my identity or assuredly some word would get back to Sizergh. I was offered soup, and with Liza's urging, I accepted a mug of ale. I took a hunk of bread and cheese and soon I found myself laughing with the others well past midnight.

Liza led me up the stairs to the bedroom. The floors were of new and shiny wood, and as the brick-and-clay house was only recently constructed, it had a wonderfully sweet-smelling roof of thatched hay. Bunches of fresh daisies were in vases all over the place, and there were fresh rushes in every room. Liza had told me before that all the women slept in one room and all the men in another. I could hardly believe it, though I knew it to be the custom of country folk.

Freda was already in her bed. She had a wooden frame bed in one corner of the room, near a window. There was one other bed in the room, which belonged to the eldest sister. Other sisters and the female servants slept on mattresses.

I slept at the top of the room between Freda and Liza.

The next morning, a lovely summer's day with the sun pouring in the casement windows and the breeze bringing the fresh smell of daisies to my nostrils, Liza and I hurried off our mattresses to help the other girls clean up the kitchen. Liza had told me we would have a proper talk with her mother as soon as everyone went about their duties in the farmyard.

Freda came in, looking somehow older this morning. She hugged me warmly, as if I were one of her own daughters in trouble. My face certainly looked pale and wan.

"My reckoning is you should go into hiding, with Lady

Strickland's blessing, and then we'll find a village girl who's lost a baby and pass it on to her, as her own," said Freda.

That sounded a reasonable idea. I had no intentions of claiming the child as my own, not in my position—a widow for over a year and a woman of status at that.

"How am I going to tell Kaitlin?" I asked weakly.

"Don't know, my lady. That you'll have to work out for yourself," said Freda calmly.

"But I can't," I murmured, knowing it would force the truth out into the open.

Freda voiced my fears. "Maybe it's time Kaitlin knew about you and Lord Strickland. Maybe it would be best if you admitted what you have done and asked her forgiveness. It'll spare her more pain."

Liza had become very quiet. She offered nothing to the discussion, which puzzled me, as she had arranged the meeting, until suddenly she cut Freda off in mid-sentence.

"I'll take the babe when it's born. I'll care for it. I can't bear to see a child of Kate's being given away. Let me have the babe. I want it, Ma."

Freda was furious. "Don't talk rubbish, girl. And have my daughter shame me in the village? Never."

"You won't be shamed, Ma. I'll get Stephen to marry me. He's said he would. He's a God-fearing man. He'd go along with it to save the child's soul. We could marry now and disappear for a few months—he has to go preaching over the moors somewhere. When we come back, we would be with babe in arms."

Freda was silent. "And what's Katherine to do for the next few months, till she has the child?"

"You can hide her out here, sure enough, with all the girls you got here. Take her on as an extra hand. Then I'll come back all quiet and we'll do the switch-over."

My heart had sunk somewhere between my ankles to hear these two good women speak.

"Liza, stop," I ordered. "How can you ruin your life to be so good to me?"

"It won't ruin it. My life's not worth half as much as yours. I'd marry Stephen anyway, and you know I love babies. It'll be all right. I'll care for your child, ma'am."

"Then you won't work for me anymore, Liza?" I said, foolishly worrying about such a little matter in such a grave crisis.

"Not when I'm married and have the babe to care for, no, ma'am. But you can come visit us. That way you may know your child."

"Oh," I groaned. "I don't know if I'm ready for any of this. I feel more like jumping off the church tower."

"You'll do no such thing, my lady," snapped Freda. "If Liza can work it out, if Stephen will go along with it, then I'll give it my blessing. Heaven's sakes," and she laughed in that way women who have had to care for many worldly woes learn to laugh. "I've plenty of mouths to feed around here, without worrying about one more."

Then I swallowed hard to mention something still so hateful to me. "Don't you mind about the stableboy's being father to the child, Liza? That hateful boy?"

Liza shrugged. "Can't say as I would choose him to father a child of mine. But with love the baby will be better than the father."

These people were so good, so strong. I was a helpless waif in their hands.

We returned to Sizergh and carried on life as normal. The growing child did not show beneath my full black dresses. The bouts of sickness began to wane as the days turned to weeks. I started sewing, not for the baby as other women do, but for the castle. Somehow my fingers felt like sewing on those long days. I began work on an enormous counterpane for my room and a toilette cover which I was making as a gift for Kaitlin. I worked on white satin, embroidering flowers from the fields. In the center I designed a spread eagle in full heraldic glory. I made the pattern rich with large blossoms in gorgeous colors, highly embossed, and glistening with gold thread. Kaitlin supplied me with the materials. She was so pleased to see me turning to industry worthy of female hands. Henry knew nothing of my plan.

PART III

A Pennine Crossing

Chapter
14

O ne afternoon before dinner, Kaitlin warned me that her cousin, John Neville, would be joining us. "I feel sorry for him. He is quite lonely, dear soul. He requested the pleasure of dining again. I think he was quite taken by you."

By then my mind was lost in far different concerns. I had little energy to waste on her cousin from Snape Hall.

Both Kaitlin and I were surprised by the noise of cantering hooves in the yard outside. Surely Neville was not here yet? Kaitlin sprang to look, and I groaned at the thought of another social responsibility. But it was Henry's cheerful voice we heard.

"Thomas! My man! I did not expect you back this way so soon. How was the campaign? You look fit and well."

There was the noise of men slapping each other's backs, of shared laughter.

"Oh, no," groaned Kaitlin under her breath. "It's that Thomas Seymour. I'll lose Henry to him again, no doubt."

Then, turning brightly to me, her social smile already firmly implanted, she said, "Why, Kate, I do believe it is that charming young man from Wiltshire who passed by here on his way to Scotland some months ago. Do you remember his name?"

Despite myself I was flushing red.

We had gathered our skirts and our senses about us before Henry Borough led Thomas Seymour in. Kaitlin ordered a room made ready for our visitor.

Thomas Seymour looked wilder and more dangerous on this day. His black hair had grown long, down to his shoulders, ungroomed in the weeks of fighting. A beard of long, sleek dark hair graced his chin. His skin was more ruddy, his gait more firm, his manner more confident. With a smile of ease and instant recognition, he kissed Kaitlin's hand and spoke over it at me.

"Still with your cousin, Mistress Katherine? I would have thought you remarried by now."

"It is but some months, sir." I put him in his cheeky place.

For a moment I panicked, thinking that Kaitlin had invited him here as a potential suitor for my own hand. But then as quickly I reassured myself that Thomas Seymour was only the second son of a Wiltshire family. His elder brother had a place at Court, but this wild young man was but a soldier with little fame or fortune. No, Kaitlin would never dream of marrying me off to him.

Later, Thomas Seymour joined me on my early evening stroll in the gardens, while we awaited John Neville's arrival. He chatted easily about the grotesqueries of war, and I complimented him on his bravery and success. My heart was certainly not in my words. Then he caught me off-guard.

"You've certainly plumped out since we met last. What have you been doing, indulging in too many sweet cakes?"

Blushing furiously, for no one else had ever hinted at my condition, I smarted, "I thought it becoming for ladies of fashion to be full-figured and well endowed."

"I was not suggesting I did not approve, dear lady," he said, indicating with a sideways glance of his head that he had already made visual explorations of my bosom. "Just strange that you should have so changed in such a short while."

I felt tears coming to my eyes. The girl who had met this young man before was indeed gone, gone forever. Then I had been wild and carefree, racing over the moorlands on horseback. I had since learned a very harsh lesson about the price of freedom. How could I joke or tease with this man now?

Suddenly despairing of my position, I made my excuses and ran from him. My mind was too perplexed with problems to have time to deal with light talk. I needed a way out, not idle flattery.

When John Neville arrived, Thomas was well ensconced with Henry in the library. We could hear their laughter vibrating down the hallways.

I presented myself to John Neville at Kaitlin's side and smiled sweetly with surprisingly real pleasure. I still liked his easy attractiveness, the long thick black hair, gray at the temples, the tanned face, and fine-boned features that gave him a strong profile. He had no spreading girth, stooping gait, or slumped shoulders like most of the men I had recently met through Kaitlin. There was something appealing about his dark eyes too.

Over dinner, Neville, who was again newly returned from London, regaled us with further news about the King and Queen Catherine. King Henry had already summoned the Queen to a divorce court set up at Blackfriars by Cardinal Wolsey.

Thomas Seymour upset our guest with caustic comments about the Queen's virtue—Queen Catherine had claimed she and Prince Arthur had never consummated their marriage. Neville obviously had no patience with our soldier braggart and swiftly quieted him.

"Our devout and worthy Queen, you might be interested to know," Neville said, flashing Seymour a fiery glare, "had the courage to refuse to attend that court, for it was not legal. Forced to attend, she refused to stand when twice her name was called. With her ladies behind her, she circled the courtroom twice, finally falling on her knees before the King and pleading with him. She spoke with enough eloquence to move the hardest of hearts—except the King's, of course. The Queen then rose to her feet and made for the door. The crier called her back. The Queen whispered to her supporters, 'I hear him well enough, but carry on.'

"Then the King tried to persuade us that only his conscience was urging him to divorce this woman who has been such a devoted wife, full of gentleness and virtue."

"Why, sir," riposted Seymour, "you take strong arms against the King. Have you considered the danger of those foolhardy words should report of them get back to Court?"

"I trust, Thomas Seymour, that idle gossip would not pass your lips."

The mood between the two men was icy.

"Both you and Henry," Neville went on sternly, "take it lightly that our noble Queen Catherine should be thus treated. But does she not represent everything we believe and love in the Church of Rome?"

Now Neville had done it. He knew he was deliberately treading on dangerous ground, flushing out the Lutherans in our midst.

"Ha, sir," Seymour parried his thrust. "Do I detect an anti-Lutheran soul here?"

"You do. I would hope all of us in this room are still attached to the only true religion and beliefs."

Kaitlin piped in with her pretty voice. "Of course, John, dear. Henry and I are both determined in our faith. And so is Katey."

Henry threw me a glance that I dared not return. Could I speak up? Should I?

Seymour got in first, caring less than any of us what Neville, or Kaitlin for that matter, thought of him.

"Can't say I've signed my name to any papers yet, but the Lutheran ideas certainly interest me, as they do my brother Edward Seymour, one of the King's right-hand men, and, indeed, they interest many leading courtiers in London. The King has not outright admitted he disagrees with Luther. It's the Pope he wishes would vanish from the face of the earth."

Neville seemed to recover his stance. "Seymour, I wonder if *you* should not be more careful in the way you too speak about the King."

"You don't have to worry about me." Seymour laughed heartily. "I've my sword to protect me! The King knows that I have my own views on things . . . he's already forgiven me many sins."

Seymour rose from the table, and Henry quickly jumped to his feet and begged Kaitlin to forgive them if they retired to the library. Kaitlin nodded, anxious to be rid of their disturbing presence.

"Goodnight, Katherine." Thomas Seymour bent over my hand and pressed it to his lips. I snatched it away, caught at this moment between the various political machinations at work in our home.

I no longer wanted to sit with the anti-Lutheran set, Neville and Kaitlin. Nor did I wish to be trapped with Seymour and Henry. Feeling faint again from the rich food and the strain of keeping up polite conversation, I made some comment about feeling too much concern for the Queen, and quickly exited.

Taking a wrap, I walked down the front steps of Sizergh, anxious for some fresh air and the cooling night breeze. As I approached the lily pond, John Neville came up behind me, his feet padding softly in the grass. I was most startled at hearing his voice.

"You seem in deep study."

"I have much to think about," I said rather sharply, not wanting to be drawn into conversation.

He seemed ill at ease. I wondered what was on his mind.

"You are quiet tonight. Not as argumentative as when last we met. I rather enjoyed sparring with you and had hoped for further conversation."

"Oh," was about the brightest and most provocative comment I could muster.

"Can we talk some more? Maybe on another visit soon if you are tired tonight?"

I turned to glance sideways at him. "I shall be going away soon, for a few months."

"Kaitlin did not mention it."

"She doesn't know it yet." I blushed. "I may go to London to visit my sister at Court."

"For the winter?" He frowned.

"Why not? I hate winter up here."

"Well, if you do, please call on me. I have two homes in London, which I use often."

"Maybe I will. I haven't made any plans yet."

"May I call on you again, Lady Borough?" he asked gently.

He perplexed me. What on earth did he want to talk to me about? We had nothing in common, and I found him slightly boring.

"Of course," I said warily. "Anytime. But ask Kaitlin first whether or not I am here."

"I would love for you to see my home, Snape Hall. It is very beautiful. I'm sure you would find it a rewarding visit. Why don't you come with Kaitlin someday?"

"Yes . . . of course. . . ." Now I was trying to be rid of him. "Please, you must excuse me. I feel faint, all these people and the rich dinner."

"Let's take a walk. It would be good for me too," he replied gallantly.

Unable to think of any other excuse, I let myself be walked around the gardens in the night air by John Neville. I was surprised he too liked the chill of the evening. He was not like other men who only wanted to sit by a fire and drink ale. He held my hand lightly in his own and rubbed the fingers.

"There," he said, "we can't have you catching cold."

"You are very kind." I was feeling embarrassed by this attention, particularly in my condition. He seemed so sympathetic I had an urgent desire to tell him my problems. But luckily I stopped before my tongue waxed too loose.

"Thank you," I murmured. "I don't find many men are kind these days."

"Except Lord Strickland?" He said it so gently, I did not believe at first he spoke other than in jest.

"He is a kind man. Of course, he is a relative." I frowned.

"But now he's not so much a stepson?"

"No, now he's more like a stepfather!" I tried to throw it off with a laugh.

John Neville had slid an arm around my back, and I instinctively grew rigid with suspicion at the first touch. What was he trying to do to me? But he let his arm rest there.

"Be careful, young lady," he whispered in my ear. "Be careful. Kaitlin knows." And there he stopped.

Turning in the crook of his arm, I gazed at him in holy terror. "You mean she knows about me . . . ?"

He nodded. But what exactly did Kaitlin know? All or nothing?

"Knows what?" I decided to bluff my way through.

"That you and Henry have a little pact together. She knows there is affection between you. She called me here to try and talk some sense into you."

"She didn't!" I exploded. The cheek of the woman. "Why doesn't she talk to me herself?"

"She's scared of what she might do or say to you. You know how she can be. If she believes you are really having an affair with her husband she could get very angry. She believes it's more a question of romance and love's young dream. But deep down she hates you both for it."

I knew it, of course. It all rang so true.

"So you came to warn me? How kind of you!" I said coldly, without admitting to my guilt. I had imagined Kaitlin was arranging a marriage for me. A scolding was more like it.

"Well, now what do you think? Should I be sent to a nunnery or beaten on the stockade?"

He laughed gently without answering, though I sensed there was something more urgent on his mind than this idle bantering. I had the uncomfortable feeling his stare was more than avuncular, more than interested on Kaitlin's behalf. As we stood there, his arm on my back, I was aware of its pleasing pressure, of some bond between his arm and my inner core. As if he had become part of me. The man wanted to dig too deep. I had to keep him at bay.

Since being with child, my breasts, which had been developing slowly, had burgeoned fully. They fairly burst from my dresses. This evening I had worn my black satin, which was cut square and low over the bosom. In my present condition it was wildly dramatic, leaving little to the imagination. I recalled Thomas Seymour's comment that afternoon, and flushed. What must they all be thinking of me?

My hair was also more glossy, longer, fuller, and more abundantly wavy. Deliberately, I let it hang loose and careless. It had grown so long it reached down my back. I could sense Neville's fingers itching to stroke those locks.

I shifted in the night air. "Lord Latimer," I began, "is there something else you wish to say, some other message from Kaitlin? Perhaps some moral homily on the deportment of a young woman in these times? For I must go in. I am now cold." My pretty speech seemed ineffectual as I unwound myself from his arm and ran back to the house.

Kaitlin knows. Lord Latimer had been brought here expressly to chastise me. I was burdened with child. I had to leave, oh, how I had to get away from Sizergh.

I was fleeing up the main stairs, as Henry came out of the library door. He had been drinking with Seymour, and caught sight of my tear-stained face. He ran to throw his arms about me.

"Henry, you must leave me alone! Everything is terrible. I have to depart Sizergh quickly, immediately."

Now I was sobbing and speaking like a lunatic, while Henry was devouring my face with kisses, himself wild, intoxicated.

"Katey, I have been looking for you all over. Where have you been? We must run away together," he said happily.

"The situation has become impossible for me too. Now is the time. We shall go back to Windermere together and find a house to live in."

"Henry," I said flatly. "I am with child, from that terrible night of violation. How can we live in a cottage by Windermere and raise a baby? It's all a dream, Henry. A dream. Kaitlin would find us. We would be disgraced. The child would never live to smile and sing. No, no . . ." I broke into heavy sobs.

"Be strong, my darling," he urged. "Kaitlin has her suspicions about you and me. The only way out is for you and me—together. Will you come now?"

"You'll go nowhere, Kate Parr."

My body turned rigid, and Henry's hands went limp. Kaitlin Neville, in her gown of rich blue damask, embroidered with pearls, stood regally at the bottom of the stairs.

"Take your hands off her, Henry, and go back to the library. Before I am shamed and humiliated any more before my guests."

Meekly, like a lamb, Henry turned and walked away. He managed to speak sullenly before he left the hall. "Katey *will* come with me. She has promised."

"She will do no such thing. The only promises that matter in this world are the vows between husband and wife. Go inside, Lord Strickland."

It was time for Kaitlin to learn the full story. But I had little time to think, before she slapped me across my cheek, again, and again.

"Slut! Whore! Trollop! How dare you!" she screamed at me. "How dare you come into my house, as my guest, and steal my husband away?"

"Kaitlin, please . . ." I begged to get my words out. The only excuse was the true story of the baby. She had to believe me.

And the story stumbled from my lips, about the stableboy, and the rape, how I was with child, that the baby was the stableboy's, and I was terrified to tell her because she would assume it was Henry's when really it was not. How Henry and I had been such close friends at Gainsborough that we found it impossible not to speak to each other. We had never been intimate, we would never do such a thing, knowing he was married to my dear second mother! I wept, acted humble, and for a moment I thought Kaitlin would soften. But her face clouded over.

"Don't tell me your lies. If you're with child, Kate Parr, it's because you seduced Henry behind my back and made him loathe me. I know your type. Just because you are a widow you imagine you can get away with anything. Well, by the sound of it, your sins have caught up with you. How could you lie about a stableboy? I *know* about you and Henry. Don't think I haven't been watching. Kissing in dark corners. Horse rides together. Secret meetings. It is hardly surprising my marriage is so miserable when my own husband is being seduced under my roof! No, Kate Parr, I had hoped John Neville might marry you. I actually managed to interest my kinsman in a good-for-nothing, sinful beast like you. But no, now even that is too late, he's gone. Ridden off into the night. Horrified to learn how evil you are . . . and angry at me for nearly passing off such damaged goods."

Kaitlin turned on the heels of her dainty little shoes and prepared to reenter her drawing room.

"I'll find you a husband within a day or so, Kate Parr. You are not staying under my roof a minute longer than necessary. I would cast you out tonight but for the scandal of it. How could you, how could you . . . ?"

She stormed through the door, her ranting voice echoing down the long corridor.

I was stunned and miserable, leaning against the stone wall of the stair well. How had my life come to this sorry state? My body heaved and rocked with sobs. Then there was a comforting hand on my shoulder, and one of my old woolen wraps enveloped my body.

"Come, ma'am," Liza whispered. "Come with me. We'll go to Oxenholme tonight. Mother will care for you."

"Oh, Liza," I wept, resting my face in her chest. "Thank God it's you. I couldn't stand to see anyone else. I *want* to go to Oxenholme. I *want* to go there more than anywhere in the world."

Arms around each other's shoulders, heads down, lest we should see anyone, Liza and I made our way beyond the drive to Sizergh, where she helped me into a cart. This time there was no need for pretense. We were leaving Kaitlin's home, forever. Tomorrow we would make some arrangements to have our luggage sent after us. My head fell onto a bale of straw at the back of the cart, and I gave in to the comforting darkness of the night as we rolled slowly down the country roads to Freda's humble home.

Chapter
15

Oxenholme was dark as we entered; not a light burned in any of the houses. The people were all in their beds. Surprisingly, I felt refreshed and not so tragic, just to be away from the doom and gloom of Sizergh. My life had become an adventure seemingly out of control.

Liza hurried me up the stairs into the great bedroom where all the women were sleeping. I fell onto a straw mattress and slipped gratefully into sleep.

Freda Harris said little the next day but managed my affairs with practicality. I was given my own mattress, and certain chores to do in the house. I had to keep the dining table polished with linseed and beeswax, until the surface reflected my face. I brushed out the rushes on the floor to keep the insects and ticks from our clothes and hair. Everyone was told to say I was a cousin from Lincolnshire way.

My one lack was for money. Our escape from Sizergh had been so sudden, I had brought little money with me, or valuable plate. Liza had managed to sneak out some of my clothing, my most recent poems, and my dearest possessions, such as the Lutheran books, especially the one given me by Megan, and jewelry that had been left me by Maude. But if I owned property as Lady Borough, it did not help put food on the Harrises' table.

My belly in full bloom, I had forgotten about hiding my condition and was in the garden sitting on a bench when a rider came galloping into the village. Rob, the brother who always seemed to be on hand, rushed to the road to greet the messenger. He returned with a letter for me. *Please don't let it be from Kaitlin*, I prayed as my nervous fingers trembled to open the seal. Yet I knew the seal was not hers. It was far more grand, and noble.

John Neville, Lord Latimer, heaven knows how many spies he had working for him, had tracked me down here in Oxenholme. His brief note read:

> *Dear Lady, I was grievously concerned about your welfare that night at Sizergh. But I could not come between you and Kaitlin and Lord Strickland at that point. I believe you are staying with the family of your attendant, Liza Harris, in the village of Oxenholme. Should you wish to see me, I can arrange to meet you—halfway—on the Snake Pass, where a hostelry awaits to greet the brave traveler. As you will understand, I may no longer extend a formal invitation to you. But I beg you to forgive me for the unusual meeting place. Yours, as ever, John Neville.*

Rob told me frankly I was mad. No woman several months with child would ride by horse over the Pennines. I retorted that my mother Maude, seven months pregnant, had accompanied my father all the way from London to Westmoreland, on their return from Court to Kendal Castle, and that the baby so carried was myself.

Rob went inside to ask Liza. Together they agreed to accompany me. The messenger was sent back with my note of acceptance.

✦

We left Oxenholme before dawn on that autumnal morning. I had given up wearing the black dresses of widowhood, but I hid behind a long woolen brown cloak lent me by Freda Harris. She was worried but did not stop us on our mission.

Rob, Liza, and I rode all day, rested overnight in a hostelry, and by late afternoon the next day, Liza told me we were rounding the bend where the only hostelry on the lonely Pennine pass stood. With but one lodging and place of refreshment in miles of bleak moorland, the innkeeper was bound to be friendly and welcoming.

Liza dismounted first and said she would enter to see if Neville was waiting. I stood outside shivering, but marveling at the stark beauty of this landscape.

The moorland already appeared wintery, brown and pale green the predominant colors. Rocks were scattered about the moors; occasional sheep, hardy animals, grazed at the stumpy blades of grass. On the other side of the muddy route that had been our road was a stream, and I crossed to stand beside it. The clear trickling water soothed my tortured brain.

I had no idea what to say. What would John Neville want to hear? As far as I knew, he had left Sizergh angry at my "sinfulness," as Kaitlin had put it, determined never to cross my path again.

I heard a door swing and nervously held my breath, to see if it would be him or Liza coming to join me. Hearing no voice but only the sound of footsteps, I assumed that Liza had stayed behind inside the hostelry, sitting close to the roaring fire to allow me to meet Lord Latimer in privacy. My back was still turned, for I dared not look him in the eyes.

John Neville, Lord Latimer of Snape Hall, a man in his late forties, twice married, twice widowed, father of a son and daughter, owner of much property in Yorkshire and London, respected man of his area, one of the leading Catholics in the whole of the North of England, was standing beside me, trying to glimpse the face behind my hooded cloak.

Neville broke the silence. "Well, Katherine, how have you been?"

When at last I turned to look at him, I had to return his smile. Neville looked excited and eager to see me. Without saying anything, I indicated we walk away from the hostelry. He helped me over the steppingstones, across the stream. We walked through the moors and I talked, at first lightly, about life in Oxenholme. I watched his serious face gazing far into the distance as if he was not listening to a word I said. Why had he wanted to meet me? Did he have some message from Kaitlin, some more words of warning? Something in his eyes moved me and relayed a warmth I knew came from his heart.

Suddenly, I felt the need to touch him. My hand went out to rest on his arm. We stood still together for what seemed like hours but was maybe a few seconds. Neville broke the peace.

"I had wondered, Katherine, Lady Borough, whether you would consider becoming my wife."

The words struck me slowly like so many chimes of a church bell. The man must be out of his mind, I thought.

But then he was not aware of my condition, only of my shame concerning Henry Borough.

I stammered and stumbled over my words, before taking a deep breath and saying, "I have first to tell you something, John Neville, that will certainly alter your mind about me. This is by no way an apology or an excuse, or plea for help. You have to know what has happened in my life.

"Kaitlin was right about Henry Borough and me. We fell in love at his father's house. We were both outcasts in the home of Edward, Lord Borough, and we clung together in our loneliness. It had never occurred to either of us that his father, with my mother's help, would arrange marriage between him and my kinswoman Kaitlin Neville.

"As you also probably know, Henry and I share an interest in the new reformist religion and the writings of Martin Luther, which Kaitlin abhorred, as, I know, you do too. When my husband died, I fully intended to go live in London, where my brother and sister are, but my mother's death left me at loose ends. Then Kaitlin invited me to live at Sizergh with them. At the time it seemed sensible and proper.

"I swear to you, Lord Latimer, I had no intentions of carrying on the love affair once at Sizergh, but, of course, I had not taken into account Henry's feelings. When I got there I found a man desperate, lonely, and suicidal in his misery. He insisted we continue our relationship. At first, I would be nothing more than close friends. But shortly, seeing how lonely and vulnerable he was, I agreed. Other people guessed at our intrigue and were able to use that knowledge as a form of bribery."

Here I paused, not daring to tell all, and I grasped for words.

Still without looking in his face, I bade him listen a little longer. "To be brief, I am five months gone with child."

I felt his arm stiffen but motioned him to be still as I continued: "But not, as you imagine, with Henry's child. I had an . . . accident. One of the servants at Sizergh knew about our secret meetings, and he used this knowledge to force me to do certain things with him. I could not bear to think of Kaitlin's finding out, and the consequence is this.

"With the help of my dear friend Liza I have been offered the only solution. I am to stay with her family at Oxenholme, until I give birth. She and her husband will take my child as their own, and I . . . I will be free again to live my life. . . ."

I stopped, stunned by the seriousness of what I was saying.

John Neville breathed deeply and delivered his words as though they were judgment in the local court.

"Why not come live with me and we will give the child a name of its own?"

Not wanting to meet his eyes, I shook my head beneath the brown woolen hood of the cloak. "Would you want to give your name to a child of such a . . . misdemeanor?"

Neville swallowed hard. "I cannot say that I relish the thought. But I would like to help you."

Tears came to my eyes. I could feel myself losing this man who was trying so hard to be kind and to help me. Why could I not say "Yes!" and scream with joy at the crutch he was offering? But it did not seem right, and in truth, I did not want this child.

Still shaking my head, I said low and clear, "No. I'll remain at Liza's. I'll tell folks I've gone to London to visit my sister Anne for a few months."

I felt the pressure of his hand on my arm as he said quickly, "Katherine, am I right in thinking you are turning down the idea of marriage with me?"

Now I had to look at him. His face was so mournful in repose. I could not believe he really desired this union.

"Sir," I replied gently, "I am aware that Kaitlin was trying to arrange such a marriage for me, and I am duly grateful that you would even consider it, in the light of circumstances. But I really do not think I can be such a burden to you."

And then suddenly Neville dropped one knee to the ground.

"I want you to know, dear lady, that I am not making this proposition for Kaitlin's sake. We have not spoken since that dreadful night, and I doubt I will ever speak with her again. She was rude and callous to a kinswoman. Your sins were not so great, for her husband is the foolhardy one. I am proposing this marriage, in all sincerity, because it pleases *me*. I know you must think I am old, or perhaps rigid in my thinking. But I will try my best to accommodate your own ideas. There is much work to be done in Yorkshire, no matter if you are a reformist or Papist. I work among the poor, Katherine. I try to act as their intermediary with the King and his commissioners. Even now trouble is brewing, especially here in the North, for the King is threatening to close down many of the monasteries that offer charity and aid to the starving, to the homeless. It seems to me you have a good mind, and a kind heart. You might find a life devoted to such work appealing, even"—and his eyes glinted for a moment—"even if you do not find this man, himself, so very appealing."

He brought a smile to my lips. Neville had managed to drive my own mournful thoughts from my mind, and the smile spread. I dropped down on my knees, on the damp grass, to join him, unable to bear seeing him so humble before me.

"I'll be your wife if you still want me after . . . after the baby is born. I'll try very hard to make up for this mess. . . ." My voice trailed off in fear and apprehension.

Neville took hold of one of my hands and pressed it to his lips. "I don't want to lose you," he said gently. "Go back to Oxenholme if you want. But I'll not let you go for long. Katherine, you need someone to take you in hand."

He drew me toward him so my nose was hidden in the thick velvet of his jacket. The strength I felt from those arms dried up my tears. I raised my eyes to meet his for the first time that afternoon. He was looking down at me, his heavy-lidded eyes full of concern and compassion. I knew I was very lucky.

"Thank you, Lord Latimer. Thank you. I can't believe you are going to support me through this. I have been so wicked."

"It's not you that is wicked, young lady, it's life. There are many things to try and test us. You have still a lot to go through. I only wish it didn't have to be alone. I'll pray for you, as the months pass."

"Thank you for asking no questions about me and Henry Borough," I whispered. *Goodbye, Henry. We can bring each other nothing but pain.*

"Henry is foolish and headstrong. He's no good for a lass like you. All wind and air."

"And you're all earth?"

"Ay. What's wrong with that, Katherine? You'll find Yorkshire a fine place, with good soil. We're men of the earth with our heads set firm on our shoulders. I'll give you a good life. Hurry to me!"

So saying, he kissed me. A kiss so soft and gentle that I was afraid I had imagined it. He kissed me as a mother might a child. Surprisingly it awakened some sense of excitement in my body.

I made solemn promises to Neville that afternoon. I pledged myself to him with bracken and fern. I marveled at my fate. Hand in hand we crossed the stream and came back to the hostelry where Liza and Rob waited. We entered the creaking door. Liza looked up from her seat by the fire to catch us both smiling.

Latimer departed on horseback, while Liza, Rob, and I decided to stay overnight before our journey back to Westmoreland.

PART IV

Valley
of
Hope

Chapter 16

S pring was already in full glory when I took my few belongings from Oxenholme and made ready for the journey to Yorkshire. Liza reassured me everything would be all right. The child would have a good home and I would go to Latimer and begin to lead a proper life. I birthed without too much trouble on a winter's night in the February cold. Freda took the baby from me that dawn before I could see her. She maintained a mother should not see her child if she was not to keep her. There was a lot of blood after the baby was born, and my body and breasts were sore. But Freda wiped me down, and Bessie, the midwife, brought cold rags for my breasts to send the milk away.

After Liza had been given the baby, I hardly saw my friend again. She was tied up with nursing the infant. I heard the child was sickly, and yet I did not care. I never thought to ask what name they were giving it and was even annoyed when Freda told me it was a girl. Heeding Old Nell's warning, I wanted to know nothing about this child of my body. She was no child of mine. Nell had said to beware, and indeed I was more than wary of this terrible mistake in my life.

Once fit enough to leave my bed and walk around, I made ready to leave Oxenholme. I wanted to be off to Snape Hall. I had received only one letter from Latimer, in his curt style, wishing me well and a "speedy recovery," though I had written letters to him whenever I knew of a messenger going that way.

The air was rich with the scent of sweet spring flowers. Daffodils and daisies blew in the windy dales. The day I was set to leave Oxenholme, before dawn, I walked around the village streets in the gentle mist that comes before sunshine. I felt sad to be leaving this comforting home— this village that had welcomed me without prejudice.

Freda hugged me; we both had tears in our eyes. Liza stood crying in an upstairs window. In her arms I glimpsed the small body, wrapped in a white shawl. I turned my head away. I refused to be held back by sentimental feelings. I asked Freda to say goodbye to Liza for me.

Liza's brother Rob was to accompany me on the long ride, over the Pennines, back over the route traveled by Liza and myself. I could not help but shiver on that soft spring morning, wondering what my life as Lady Latimer of Snape would turn out to be.

❖

Rob made me ride hard. I was surprised at the speed of our journey. It took us barely two days to reach the high moorlands which lay like soft carpets of green crisscrossed by gray stone walls. We urged our horses on to greater speed. John Neville's home lay between Wensley and Bedale. Neville would not be expecting me this evening, but I was thrilled to surprise him.

As we approached the gateway to Snape Hall, my heart rose to my mouth with apprehension. Before my eyes, I was gazing at the most beautiful castle I had ever seen, stately and picturesque, built of a smooth gray stone, washed by years of soft rain. Within the estate was also a large mansion or hall, the roof of which was adorned with delicate chimneys, the walls studded with more windows than I had imagined possible in a house.

In the gathering dusk, the windows of the hall seemed ablaze with candlelight. The building was immense, with the side wings forming a square surrounding neat gardens lovingly laid out. I reached for Rob's hand across the saddle.

He grinned at me. "Not bad, eh?" He whistled between his teeth. "You should be pretty fine here, ma'am."

Rob steered our horses to the main entrance of Snape Hall. We could hear laughter and music within, the sound of many people's voices. The clatter of horses' feet brought out stableboys, and a servant eventually came to the door.

An elderly man, dressed formally in doublet and hose, raised a lantern to our faces. "Yes?"

Rob introduced me, and I watched the man's face turn ashen. My heart skidded with fear. Was Lord Latimer not ready to receive me? Had he changed his mind?

"Stay here," the man said hurriedly and turned indoors. "I'll find the master."

Rob and I looked at each other. My heart seemed to stop beating as I remembered my ungracious welcome at the home of my first husband. The voices, laughter, and music continued within.

At last the door opened, and there was Neville, dressed impeccably in a black velveteen doublet and black hose, a white shirt left loose about his neck, his thick dark hair brushed so it gleamed, standing angrily in the doorway.

"What in heaven's name, Katherine?" he sputtered.

I ran forward, pulling my cloak about me, wanting to drop to my knees before him to apologize for whatever wrong I might have committed.

"Sire, I know we are unexpected. But Rob and I made the journey so fast, we decided to delay no further and come immediately here. Are we intruding?"

Latimer pushed his hand through that dark hair touched with gray at the temples, a look of distress passing over his face.

"Why did you not forewarn me, young lady?"

"I wrote you over a week ago. To say my . . . my mission was complete and that I would be here within days, as soon as Rob could arrange horses to bring us. Was that not right?"

Neville seemed to realize the awkwardness of our situation there at the open doorway, and he ushered us in. But his tone continued cold and formal.

"Katherine, a man in my position does not have his future bride turn up, unannounced, on horseback, with some village boy, in the middle of the night, while he is entertaining the local dignitaries. This is most embarrassing. I'm afraid I shall have to send you to a room for the night, and keep your presence very quiet.

"I was waiting for you to write to me," he continued. "Then I should have sent for *you*. I had intended to send a litter to bring you. A woman in your condition should not have been horse-riding such a long distance. I had planned a welcoming party, and all the necessaries the following day."

"Sire, I am very sorry." My heart was thumping. "I was so excited to come and felt the need to get away from Oxenholme so fast, that I just upped and left on the spur of the moment."

"I hear even your language has been sadly affected by mixing with the good people of Oxenholme, Katherine. If you are to be Lady Latimer, you must learn to act with decorum and desist from this behavior."

I nodded, and with as much dignity as I could muster, followed the butler upstairs. I was near tears at the disappointment of my arrival.

Alone that night, sitting on the edge of a chaste little bed covered with crisp white linen, dangling my gold chain between my fingers, I realized that this was not going to be a quick and easy transformation. Kate Parr, Lady Borough . . . Katherine, now had to merge into a new being—Lady Latimer. John Neville was everything I had feared—stiff, formal, conservative, strongly opinionated, though no doubt a hard worker. Before retiring for the night, he had briefly visited my room.

Instead of love, he spoke of the dinner he had given this

night for the local dignitaries. He was trying to persuade them not to enclose the peasants' common land for their own larger pastures. The King had allowed them the right, but if they exercised it, it would force the ordinary tenant farmer into dire poverty, as he would have nowhere to graze his sheep or cattle.

"This is my work, Katherine. You have to learn to fit in with my sort of life. These are idle, rich noblemen who live off peasants' backs, but who trust me and respect me, for I also represent their needs to King Henry. We are in for hard times in the North in the next few years. I don't know if the King or any of these quite stupid noblemen even appreciate it."

With that he stooped to kiss my forehead. "Goodnight. I am sorry this has been so difficult, Katherine." Then he put a hand under my chin, raising my sad face to look at his own.

"Don't be too downcast. I am really most pleased to see you here. Delighted to have you in my home, if not yet in my bed. I'll have you wakened bright and early in the morning. Sleep well."

And so saying, he left my room. But I was restless all night, confused at what I had done and what I was about to do.

M y thoughts that night were full of escape. I would flee to London. My sister Anne would help me find a home. I would use some of Borough's inheritance, have wealth of my own, meet the King, be a person in my own right. Rob was still here. I would find him and persuade him to saddle up two horses and meet me outside. We would gallop off into the darkness together, just as Megan and Anne had galloped off that night.

Then a hand was rocking my shoulder. A voice said sharply, "Katherine."

Opening my eyes, I saw the sun shining in through a casement window. I was lying in a beautiful bed with white linen sheets, a cambric cover embroidered with the finest needlework thrown over me. My clothes were in a heap on the floor.

"Katherine." The voice sounded even more urgent. The figure of John Neville stood over me.

"Good morning," I said sleepily. "I love the morning sunshine to enter my room. It augurs a good day."

"You must wake now. The minister is downstairs to marry us. He's been waiting half an hour already."

My face broke into a smile. "You don't mean that? I thought I was to be banished for bad conduct, for failing the first test in how to be Lady Latimer!"

Neville grinned. "Don't be fresh, young lady. I apologize for my behavior last night. But I was somewhat put out, as maybe you can imagine."

John Neville stared at me as a man would stare, since I was wearing only my camisole. My body thrilled to the idea of meeting with his. I felt myself squirm in my bed.

"Don't look at me that way. You embarrass me."

"I'll do more than embarrass you before the day is out."

"Not till I'm Lady Latimer," I retorted with a smile, my self-confidence returning with the sun.

"Come here, woman. Get out of bed now. We've no time for bantering. I like your strong will, Katherine. But don't forget, mine is stronger. Don't put up too much of a fight with me, or we'll never get along. I want us to be happy. I was very much struck by you, or I'd never have gone out of my way to wed you."

Silenced by the depth of his confession, I rose from my bed, nervously covering my body. He turned to leave the room, pointing to a dress laid out on the chair. "Put this on. I'll wait for you downstairs. Hurry."

The dress was beautiful, made of heavy white damask, shot with gold thread and silver. It was decorated with pearls and rubies. When I tried it on, I was amazed that it fit, though it scarcely covered my breasts. I was ashamed. I had never worn a dress quite so revealing. I knew from my sister Anne that such dresses were the fashion at Court. A maid came in to dress my hair. She wove lilies and pearls through my fair locks and painted charcoal on my eyelids.

Staring at my face in a mirror, I felt pleasure and happiness at the picture I presented. My normally pale blue eyes were shining and brilliant. Cheeks that had filled out with the pregnancy still carried that rosy hue. My features were neat and my face, framed by a cloud of wavy blond hair, had an almost angelic quality. I felt a mounting excitement at the prospect of this marriage.

Our wedding was merely an exchange of vows, in the presence of a minister. In the following weeks, the banns would be read in the chapel at Snape. For now, however, I was grateful to become Lady Latimer.

After the early-morning ceremony, he took me into the grand dining hall for a celebratory breakfast. We ate well of fresh fish and game birds. He plied me with the best red wines, which he maintained were imported from France.

Latimer was no longer attired in his exotic black velveteen doublet. Indeed, as soon as the wedding ceremony was completed, he changed from the formal clothes to a fustian outfit of brown and green, "more fitting my life as a farmer," he teased.

"Make no mistake, Katherine. We might have lands and income exceeding that of the common poor, but you are nevertheless a farmer's wife."

He assured me he would impose no pressures on me this first week. I was to learn the ways of the household, and my role as its mistress. I would meet his children, John and Margaret Neville, both nearly my age.

John was shortly to be married and leaving Snape, and Margaret was betrothed and soon to go to Court. It was with relief I realized my role as stepmother would be very limited.

All I did manage to say was, "Sire, which is to be my chamber?"

He looked surprised. "Why! The same as mine, of course. You're my wife. We share a chamber."

My heart fluttered with excitement.

"And where is your . . . I mean, *our* chamber?"

"Come, I'll take you there."

I followed Latimer through the maze of corridors in his stately home, convinced I would never know my way around without a guide. He held my hand, and the servants stared and smiled at us.

Latimer pointed out the changes he was making in the house. He was putting in new fireplaces, and more stair cases, as many of the old staircases were outside. The windows were relatively new, following the latest fashion in architectural design. He had more chairs, made of the best oak, than I had ever before seen in a house. Everywher there were rugs of tapestry or weavings on the walls. The place had comfort, style, and charm.

We entered a long corridor that appeared to lead to the last room at the end of a wing. From the windows, I could see the neat gardens and farther downhill into the dense woods beyond.

"Here's where we'll spend our happiest times," Latimer said gently, pushing open the door.

Latimer's chamber was spacious, with windows that stood wide open, allowing the autumn sun to filter inside. He had a wall of books, a desk with pen and paper. There were the usual armoires and chests for clothes, and a table and chairs, as though he ate his meals there. In the center was a large and beautiful bed.

"This is our private space, Katherine. You will find Snape Hall a busy place. Over a hundred people work here. Part of your job is to manage the staff, their payments and welfare, as well as help with my work. We can hide away here unbothered by anyone. Go sit on the bed. . . ."

I bounced and sank into the soft feather mattress. The coverlet was made of finest silk, embroidered with a rainbow of colors. There were pieces of needlework all over the walls, and paintings of people dear to him. I glanced at a portrait in charcoal of a woman that hung over the bed, wondering if that was a former wife, or love, but dared say nothing. I was rendered speechless by this efficient, organized man.

"Lost your tongue, Katherine?" He smiled. "Come here."

I rose from the bed to stand by him where he sat at the table. He raised his hands to hold my head and drew my face to his, kissing my eyes, nose, and mouth. Then he began to unbutton my dress, and it fell to the floor.

"You'll be comfortable with me, Katherine. I want to enjoy you and for you to enjoy me."

"I will, sire."

"And you won't call me *sire* for long either," he quipped as he placed a hand inside my camisole and located my breasts, which were still full from the milk. Suddenly the memory of those bad times flooded over me, and my eyes swelled with tears.

"Never mind, sweet girl," he said gently. "I won't hurt you. I know you've been through a lot. One day, when you are ready, you can tell me about it. Don't speak now—I don't want to drag unpleasant memories back."

"I want to tell you," I blurted out, surprised at myself, not knowing until that moment I had such feelings. "I want to tell you . . . I can't bear it. . . . Maybe I should have stayed living in Oxenholme. I don't deserve all this . . . Snape Hall and you. You're so good. I don't know what to do."

I started to cry, so hard I fell at his feet sobbing. I had not felt like crying since the day after the birth, and here I was on my wedding day, supposedly happy, crying as if it were the end of the world.

Latimer stroked my hair. I feared he was already regretting his mistake in marrying me. He wanted a good time, he wanted a wife to bed with, and look at me . . . in such a state.

"It was a difficult decision you made, Katherine. I would have taken the child. I offered you that choice. If you still want to, I will. If not, well, we'll just have our own babies."

I raised my head, my tears drying miraculously, and said with deep conviction, "No, Lord Latimer. I don't want that baby here. And I don't ever want to have another baby."

"Come, Katherine. We are man and wife, and children are bound to come along, if I'm going to enjoy you as much as I intend to." He spoke lightly and happily.

"No, I never wanted to have a child. I don't know why, but I don't. And I was sick all that time being pregnant. I was scared of the birthing. I don't want to die in childbirth. An old woman once told me to beware a girl child. I've run that risk once. Not again."

Latimer looked at me coldly. "And how do you expect to be a wife and *not* have a child?"

I didn't want to tell him about the herbal remedies given me by Old Nell, or of my own medical skills, as men seemed so suspicious of them.

I just hung my head and said, "I go by the moon. You can work these things out, if you would grant me the privilege of taking some care. Would it disappoint you too terribly if I did not bear you children? I'd rather be fit and well to help you in your work, to be available for efforts of the mind rather than the body."

Latimer lifted me onto his knees and began fondling my breasts.

I teased him. "They aren't usually this big, only since I birthed. They'll go down again."

Lowering his face to place a nipple gently in his mouth, he said, "Then I'd better get you with child quick. They're lovely."

I squirmed on his knees. "That's nice, isn't it?" he said softly. "Has any man done this to you before?"

"No," I lied to him. Now was hardly the time to mention my knowledge of men to my powerful new husband. My body was becoming very agitated. "But I wish you would take the other breast and do the same to that."

He laughed again. "It's all right, Katherine. I shan't mind if you enjoy what I do. I'll make you feel good." So saying, he rubbed my belly and slid his hand between my legs. "See how warm and moist you are already? What a healthy girl you are."

Then he slipped off my camisole and underthings. I lay naked on the bed, while he stood at the bedside fully clothed, staring at me.

He pointed down to the area between his legs, which was tight and bulging. "Do you know what this is?"

"Why, I guess so."

He unfastened his breeches, and they slid to the floor. He wore nothing underneath, and my heart pounded at the sight of the mass of soft dark brown hair that surrounded his erect member. I was scared of the fact I could not say "No!" to him, and of the pain he was going to cause me. He looked big, strong, and robust. Yet my body itched for his advances, and my legs drifted apart.

Clothed in his shirt, stockings, and shoes, naked only from the waist to the knees, he knelt beside me on the bed. Once more my husband played with my breasts, at the same time working his hands down to my own mass of sticky hair. Forgetting all fear or shame, I let Latimer bring me to a frenzy of desire.

Then, breathless and happy, I lay smiling up at him. His member ever strong and threatening, Latimer looked proud and content.

"I won't enter you, Katherine. I know it's not considered safe by you ladies after giving birth. But come here. You can make me happy all the same."

To my utter surprise, he lowered my head down to his lap and instructed me to take his member in my mouth, to hold it gently, to lick and stroke him with my tongue. I had never expected to treat a man in such a way. I was mildly horrified by my own inhibitions. But he too began to writhe and squirm and moved from kneeling to lying down.

"Come, Katherine," he said urgently, "put your hand there and be sweet to me."

It was Latimer's turn to lie back, exhausted and happy. "I love it, Katherine, sweet wife. We are going to be very happy together, I promise."

He fell into a deep sleep. I tiptoed around to find a basin and water. No one had ever warned me that being a man's wife might include such excesses. Though, in Latimer's favor, I had to admit I had enjoyed the strange experience, and quite looked forward to a repeat performance.

My husband took an inordinately long time to emerge from his sleep, while I sat on a bench looking over his prostrate body on the bed. Would I be happy here? Misgivings about this new way of life as Lady Latimer continued to shroud my feelings that long afternoon. The spring sun had turned full circle, and now I watched it play on the apple blossoms in the garden beneath our window. Yorkshire seemed attractive enough. Latimer appeared sympathetic—though confusing and dangerous.

"Katherine! How could you let me sleep so long?" He interrupted my reverie suddenly. "The sun is almost going down. I have much to do."

His face clouded with anger. "I'm a busy man, Katherine. Your role is to protect me from such a waste of time. Never, never, never get in my way, woman . . . or we'll neither of us be content. Go along, Katherine. Make yourself busy."

So abruptly dismissed, I exited and wandered down the same long corridor we had used to approach our chamber. In search of something to occupy my own time, I made my way down the magnificent oak stairway into the great hall, where I spied one of the ladies of the household. She looked up and smiled to see me. I proffered my hand in greeting.

"I'm sorry, my husband has not introduced me to any of you good ladies. I really must get acquainted with the work of running the great hall," I murmured shyly.

"Why, ma'am, that'll please us all." Delia Turpin, as she introduced herself, seemed quite genuine, though I blushed to see her wise face, covered with the wrinkles and lines of experience.

Delia took me by the hand, sensing I was ill at ease. She brought me to the kitchen area, which was enormous, made up of scullery, pantry, laundry, spicery, chaundry, bakehouse, brewhouse, butlery, and the grand cellar where wines and liquors were stored. There was a separate small room which was almost filled by a large table with piles of empty books upon it.

Delia designated the room as mine. This was my head-quarters.

"Who has been caring for such concerns since the death of the last mistress?" I asked politely.

"Why, ma'am, I've been doing it, in the bestest fashion I could. I have no education, nor learning, but I can read and write tolerable well, and so the master made me head of the women of the household. He put me in charge of the books. I'll show you what I've done another day. I hope it's all in keeping, ma'am."

She led me into the main kitchen, where, around an oak trestle table, a group of women sat, some with children playing at their feet, drinking what looked like jugs of ale.

"To your feet, ladies," Delia said sharply, as they eyed me curiously, wondering if I had come to join them scrubbing the floors and cooking the meals.

"This is the new Lady Latimer . . . er-um, Mistress Katherine. What are we to call you, ma'am?"

"Kate is what my friends call me. What's wrong with that?"

"Oh, no, ma'am. That won't do. We'll call you 'my lady.' I'd like you to meet"—and they stood, one by one, as their names were mentioned—"Mary Chamberlain, Jane Whittington, Anne Clark, Dorothy Turke, Mary Hall, and this is her daughter Frances, the one at your feet, and Ann Cannock, and the old 'un over there, sorry luv, is Alice Hatch. Alice has been here longer than any of us. You'll find her a real help and friend."

We talked lightly of the weather and the differences I found in Yorkshire from Westmoreland. Finally I bade them all well and hoped we would enjoy working and living together. I left them, knowing they were staring at my back, thinking, How can a young girl like her lead us around?

In my antechamber, my schoolroom as I called it, Delia showed me the pages ruled and inked in. These ladies I had just met were paid 13s 4d a quarter, and not a penny more was to go to them.

"Not even if a child is sick, or hungry?"

"No," said Delia firmly. "They do well, dear. All the lower menservants, the gentlemen ushers, gentlemen waiters, clerks of the kitchen, clerks of provision, yeomen of the cellar, butler, pantler, and yeomen of the wardrobe, only get ten shillings a quarter. The cooks get twenty-five shillings each, to prevent squabbling. There's over one hundred employed in this household, Lady Latimer, and the master has to pay all of 'em, each quarter. That money has to come from somewhere too."

Together we worked out a menu for the day and ordered in food for the next few weeks. We filled out lists for beef, mutton, lings, salt fish and white herring, for salt herring, veal, capons, cocks, hens, woodcocks, partridges, figs, yeast, butter, and salt. Then Delia rethought and added red deer, geese, eggs, mustard seed, and oatmeal, knowing where deficiencies lay in the household.

I was thankful that the day's meals were covered by Delia's firm hand and that the ordering for the next two weeks was also organized.

"Are you here every day?" I asked hopefully.

She nodded, her thick brown hair framing the wrinkled face. "Aye. Where else might I be going?" She grinned at me. "To London town, or sommat?"

Without thinking, I hugged her. I sorely needed a friend in the world.

Nervously Delia brushed me off, in case we were caught in our embrace, crossing social barriers that were never intended to be breached. She smelled good to me, warm, fustian, and honest.

"Yous'll meet some company around here pretty soon. Master is a sociable type. He has all sorts of guests and friends come visiting. Often he travels around the country. He owns properties far and wide. Yous'll enjoy yourself, lovey."

"I know I'm being silly," I confessed, as tears came to my eyes. "Lots of young girls have been through the same, and I have no need to fear. Maybe it's because my last marriage was so unhappy. I was but thirteen years old. Lord Latimer is a good man, I know that."

"Was there some lad back home, lovey?" Delia asked.

I blushed by way of answer. I thought of Henry only fleetingly now, and yet I almost hated myself for forgetting him so easily.

"That often plagues a young bride's heart more than anything else. Yous'll get used to your new position. Yous'll be happy here," Delia went on.

She took my hands in her own rough, work-hard grip and held them tight. "You'll be all right, as all right as any of us, my lady."

Delia went back to the kitchen, to the friendly group of women, while I went back to the little room that was to be my office, all alone.

Chapter 18

During the next few days, Latimer and I spent a good deal of time together. I met his brown-haired serious-minded son, John, and flaxen-haired daughter, Margaret, and we exchanged formal greetings. They seemed honest, but dull.

On horseback, we toured the area around Snape, from Bedale through the wild Yorkshire moors, to the incredible valley Latimer told me was Coverdale. I had never seen an area so bleak and stark, yet so majestically beautiful. The hills rolled sparse and clear away from the river, with lonely cottages perched on the hillsides.

I learned that my John Neville was part of the great Neville family, once kingmakers and leading aristocrats. King Richard III had married Lady Anne Neville and lived briefly at the ancient castle at Middleham, some decades ago. Middleham Castle was perhaps the most important in the area, and other Nevilles, related to my husband, continued to live there.

We traveled back down the tortuous pass through Coverdale. I had a lovely horse, and felt refreshed and at ease in my new life.

John Neville took me to Topcliffe, where, he explained, the great Percy family lived. The Percys were much talked about, as Henry Percy had been Anne Boleyn's first lover at Court. Henry VIII had become so angered that he forbade their courtship, banished Henry Percy to his home, and forced him to marry his betrothed.

Yorkshire was full of the big and the mighty, very different from my homeland in Westmoreland, where the gentry were still rugged and hearty folk.

Finally, we traveled south. Neville pointed out the main route to London, some two hundred fifty-one miles and six furlongs away. The great road, constructed by the Romans, passed by us, through Northallerton, on its way far north into Scotland.

Taking my hands in his own, for we had dismounted by the side of the London Road, he whispered into my hair.

"Sweet wife, soon I will take you to London, and introduce you as the fair Lady Latimer. All the courtiers will die of jealousy to see me with such a young and beautiful bride."

"Oh, Neville," I giggled, my hands tingling in his grasp.

Out there, in the midst of the moors, gazing at the fresh green of tree and fern, the wild patterns of clouds in the later afternoon sky, my body rushed with a new excitement, a new promise.

"I have an awful feeling, Lord Latimer, that I am falling in love with you. And that scares me. When I agreed to become your wife, as you know, it was for my own selfish reasons. I had no intention of loving you . . . but fate seems to have taken me by surprise."

His arm went around my shoulders, and he drew me to his bosom. "You know I never dared expect so much," he breathed into my hair.

Looking up at his gentle face, I murmured, "Am I worthy of you?"

"Dear wife, I fell in love with you the first moment I saw you. I never asked for passion from you. All I hoped was to keep you warm and contented, and that my kindness would extract a sort of devotion from you. I fear your strength of feeling terrifies me too!"

Then he drew his head down toward my expectant face, glistening with tears, and kissed me softly on the mouth. Breathing deeply and steadily, he said as though he spoke to himself, "You know I love you, Katherine."

I took one of his hands and pressed it to my mouth.

Then we stared silently at each other, in the late-afternoon light, awed by our revelation.

"Let's race back to the house," he said happily. We mounted our horses. He whipped my steed on the rump, and I chased off before him. Laughing crazily, he came up behind me, pulling at my horse's rein and leading me back to the stableyard at Snape.

He lifted me down, and we ran up the back stairs, even passed through the kitchens to the amazement of the ladies there, and panting, reached our chamber at the end of the long corridor.

"Tonight will be our honeymoon," he said, laying me graciously on the bed. "After this we will be man and wife."

Contented, I let him disrobe me, bathe me with warm water, rub me with oils of flowers from the fields and even with a strange scent he claimed was imported from the East and brought specially up from London. Adoring, I watched as he snuffed the main candle, stoked up the fire, brought wine to the bedside, and rang for our supper here in the chamber. Thrilled, I watched as he stripped off his clothes and dressed himself in a thick damask robe.

Then I washed his body and rubbed him with the oils, too. He lay back on the bed, and I worked my hands over his strong, brown body. There were crevasses of dark tufts of hair beneath his arms, between his thighs, and all over his chest, even going down to the belly. I stroked and combed the hairs, rubbing my nose in them, for the natural scent of his body was quite exquisite. I took his member in my mouth and kissed and stroked it. My husband began to groan as though in agony and, after a time, bade me stop. Pushing me down on the bed, he brought his soft sensuous lips over to me, coming to rest in that place between my legs that knew no shame.

I was moist and velvety in expectation of his caresses. He nuzzled his head in that space between my legs, and within seconds I cried for mercy. The man was making me delirious, making me pant with pleasure, writhe in the agony of our special love together.

Then his hand entered me, and I bucked and spread my legs, thanking the heavens for this joy. John Neville rose up on his knees and buried himself deep within my body. I was small and helpless in his arms. He held me, cradled me, moved me, plunged into me, until I cried to the night skies.

Exhausted, he lay at my side, his head on my chest, a smile of release and pleasure on his face.

"Do I make you content, good husband?"

Latimer raised his head on one elbow. "Oh, passing so."

Before I had time to argue, he pulled me over on top of him, placing me so that I straddled his wide girth, and instructed me this time how to bring him pleasure.

"But I should not," I protested, until he fondled my breasts in his large hands and I lost all control. I laughed to myself as he drove me again to that point of our mutual happiness.

✤

The next weeks brought true contentment for us both. Often I accompanied John Neville on his rides about the countryside. Sometimes we held hands as he discussed business. People gave us strange stares, for such scenes of affection were not usual.

Much of Latimer's business was conducted in his farm office. It was there the peasants came to bring their complaints, knowing that Latimer would do his best to intercede with their master. I learned now, at first hand, what he had been talking about. Most peasants owned nothing, not even the hut they lived in. Grazing land was usually on the village common, but the noblemen were enclosing the stretches of common grazing ground to make their own pastures wider.

I saw Latimer hand bags of coin to many of the stooped men who came to see him. Others he advised to turn to the monasteries or abbeys for help.

At the end of a long morning, Latimer sighed and pushed back his chair. "See, Katherine, I told you there was going to be trouble one day soon. How does the King expect these people to survive? Now he wants to extract another tax from them and close down many of the monasteries for his own gain. Our majestic King Henry maintains the monasteries are centers of corruption and worldly greed. He claims that the priests who are leading celibate lives are amassing wealth in gold and statues. But, dear wife, I know that the King sees the gold in those walls, which he desires for his own use. Fighting wars in France is not a cheap business. King Henry is running out of coin. He intends to bleed the people of his nation for that money. Do you now understand why I take offense at some of King Henry's actions, including his attitude toward his wife? Do you really think I speak with no sympathy for an older man who has fallen in love with a younger woman?"

Taking his hands in my own, I kissed them fondly. "Don't describe yourself as an old man, Neville. I think of you as young. I did not criticize your comments about the King that night. I just shared Thomas Seymour's contention that it might be dangerous if you were reported saying such things."

"Oh, so we listened to Seymour's braggart words, did we, wife?" He pretended to be teasing. Why did he have to bring up that man's name? I prickled all over with a sense of annoyance. I immediately changed the subject.

"Shh, my dear," I said. "You have one more man to see. Will Turpin, my friend Delia's husband. You know Delia Turpin on our staff?"

Latimer frowned. "I don't have the time for Will. A lazy drunkard if ever there was one. He comes here begging for money, or alms. He has not lifted a hand since he sent his wife to work at the hall. And by all reports he drinks most of her pay in the hostelry at Tanfield."

"Neville," I said curiously, suddenly aware of a disturbing connection I had never before considered, "did you know I had inherited property in Great Tanfield, from Edward Borough?"

"Yes, of course I did."

I frowned. "Did you marry me to enlarge the property?" I asked with trepidation.

"Katherine," he scolded, putting an arm around my waist as we left his farm office by the back door to avoid Will Turpin. "Any marriage is a union of properties, isn't it? I had to make some gains. Your dowry, as I recall, was one gold chain and a small bag of clothing! Besides, any aggrandizement of my property will become yours when I die. John and Margaret will inherit their share, and so will our children." He patted my belly as though he really hoped a babe lay in there. "I own vast acreage in the North and Midlands, and in London. Would you prefer that I was foolish and squandered my wealth in the tavern at Tanfield?"

"Shh, and don't talk about dying," I said sharply, disturbed that I should have so reacted. I had developed a strong affection for Neville—falling in love was dangerous, I already knew that.

I changed the subject. "Neville, if the King is closing down the monasteries and abbeys, will that include convents? What will become of Megan Borough?"

I had tried to make contact with her now that I was living so close to the convent at Nunmonkton. But no letter had come in response. I wanted to know of her but was wary of discussing her situation with anyone.

Neville slammed the farm door shut and turned the big old iron key in the lock. We walked gingerly through the muddy yard, my skirts hitched up above my knees.

"Don't worry about Megan. She and Anne left the nunnery about six months back. That Anne Kyme woman has become a preacher for the reformist faith, I hear. And Megan is married. I don't know to whom. But Kate . . . take care. I know you once knew Anne Kyme. Don't ever let me hear that you have seen her again! Do you hear me? I warned you when we were married to drop this Lutheran nonsense. I cannot have my position here entangled in that dangerous business. Do you understand me?"

His cheerful eyes looked dark and threatening, I wished I had not opened my mouth after all. There was nothing I could do. I had made my decision about my role as a reformer when I accepted Neville as my husband.

Chapter 19

Although I spent much time in Lord Latimer's company, sometimes he was away for days on end, leaving me lonely on his great estate. Of course, there were always Delia and the other women. We passed the long afternoons and evenings gossiping. We talked about the King and Ann Boleyn. Everyone knew that Queen Catherine had been banished from Court for almost a year and was living, in semi-imprisonment, somewhere near Cambridge. But we womenfolk in the dales of Yorkshire knew little that was up-to-date. We relied on visitors from Court and scraps of news from messengers riding north.

Late in October, Latimer instructed me to buy material for new gowns for myself and robes for him. He was planning our trip to Court over Christmas and New Year's, when festivities in the city were at their peak and life up here on the Yorkshire moors would be cold and forbidding.

Unaware of how much to spend on such items, I read back through the ledger to find entries: 10 oz. of Granada silk for Master's shirts—24s 8d; pair of Valentia gloves for Master—10d; for silks taken by Master—£28; fine Holland for ruffs and borders for Master's shirts—7s.

It delighted me to see one item, sneaked in, no doubt, by Delia: shoes for John Turpin—7d. Farther back still, I found entries for her grace's gowns: for the winter gown—£5 13s; material for a black velvet gown for her grace—£5.

My entry read so huge, I trembled at the outcome: for sundry silks and velvets—£178 6d. But prices had risen considerably, especially up here in the North, and surely Latimer, who worked with the poor in the region, was aware of that.

✤

I was busy sewing when Delia Turpin appeared at my chamber door. Feeling low and slightly dejected, I smiled at her tired face. "What can I do for you, Delia?" Latimer had been gone for three days, away on business he would not discuss with me.

My friend fidgeted, wringing her hands, hesitated, and finally stuttered, "I need leave of absence, my lady. I must go back to the village right now. There's a problem at home."

"Why, Delia!" I jumped to my feet in alarm. "Whatever's the matter? Can I help? You may have as much time as you need . . . take a horse from the stables. I'll instruct the boy."

Tears were brimming in her eyes.

"Come here, dear friend. Sit down and tell me what is wrong," I said.

Delia began apologetically. "I'm real sorry to bring you any trouble, my lady. You's so good to me. Back home, Will my husband, he's a good man at heart, and kind and loving. But he's been thrown off the land he used to farm, told he can't use those fields no more. We had to sell our one pig recently and our cow, and we had but a few shillings left. I just got word he's in the hostelry in Tanfield, drinking our last few pennies away. I'm so upset, ma'am. I don't know what to do. I have to go down to the hostelry and get him away from there. They'll never stop a man supping ale, even when they know he's no coin in his purse."

"Why, Delia," I cried, firmly grabbing her hand. "Come with me. We'll go down to the stables together. I'm sure Will Bryant can saddle you a mare, and I'll come with you to Tanfield."

"My lady!" she blurted as she ran behind my swift gait. "You can't do that. Not a lady in your position."

"Yes I can," I said, proudly aware of my own power. "I am Lady Latimer. I can do as I please."

As we thundered through the kitchens where Alice Hatch was busy making bread near the hot ovens, I knew they all thought me strange. But Will Bryant, a nice enough young man who was head stableboy, accepted my demand without comment. When he heard I was accompanying Mrs. Turpin to Tanfield, he gallantly offered to ride behind us. The three of us quickly trotted out from the great gates of Snape Hall.

The hostelry lay squat and comfortable, facing the pond and green, beside what used to be the peasants' common land for their grazing cattle. Lights glowed through the casement windows and smoke rose from the chimney. We could hear voices within, and I, for one, found my heart jumping in my chest at the prospect of adventure.

I was determined to take action. "Lead me inside, Will. Introduce me to the hostelry keeper."

Bryant reappeared with an elderly woman called Rose, who shook my hand nervously and bade us all come in out of the cold.

Rose had given me a hard seat by the huge fireplace. I felt warm and welcome. Glancing out the window, I saw a group of people moving around the courtyard by the inn. They seemed to be constructing a platform and placing wooden benches before it. A table was set up to one side.

"Whatever is going on outside, Rose?" I called to her as she bustled with platters of bread and cheese for her customers.

Rose looked shiftily about her and then, dropping her voice, said, "If you promise not to tell your husband, ma'am, for I know he's dead against these people. I don't want no trouble here. I don't want him closing down the inn or nothing."

I nodded, and she told me.

"There's a lady come to live around these parts who's keen on this new religion business. She comes a-preaching about how we don't have to listen to Latin in church. How we can pray to God ourselves, and not be minding with the priests. I think she says we don't have to drink the wine and eat the wafer of the Christ. Sure to heaven I'm not all that certain what she's on about."

Rose sighed. "The devout Catholics in these parts have it in for the lady, who stirs up the folks with her talk. If they know she's holding a meeting, they come along to break it up. They say the devil sent her."

"Who is this lady you speak of? She must be brave to be doing such work in the face of such danger."

Rose coughed and with her hand before her mouth muttered, "Calls herself Anne Askew. They say she was a married lady once, Mistress Kyme of Lincoln. She comes from a knight's family over in the shire of Lincoln who are so shamed of her they have banned her from their home and cut her off without a penny."

I had guessed as much. My heart fluttered with excitement. "Does she travel with a friend, another lady?"

Rose looked puzzled. "Why no, ma'am. Just herself and a group of men she has gathered around her. Like the apostles they are, ma'am. They worship the ground that woman walks on."

There was a noise of clapping hands outside, and I saw perhaps thirty men and women turn in to the entrance of the courtyard. Four men surrounded the slight, slim figure of a woman. Her head was held straight and erect. She was dressed all in black, her dark hair cropped short. Her beautiful face shone with a strange light. She clutched a book in her hands. It was certainly the same Anne Kyme I had known five years ago.

Watching through the window, I could scarcely hear her words. But I was struck by the magic of her performance. I was so struck, indeed, that I did not hear the door open or notice Will Bryant standing by my side.

"Speaks well, don't she?"

"Very well," I agreed. "I met Mistress Kyme years ago in Lincolnshire, before she became a speaker. She was a believer in the new religion even then."

Bryant coughed and shuffled his feet.

"Ma'am, I think we should leave. It could get dangerous here. I mean, I've heard word that Lord . . . your husband . . . Latimer is coming with a group of men to break the meeting up. You wouldn't want to be found here, would you?"

In panic, I said hastily, "Bring me paper and a pen."

He returned with a scrap of parchment and a quill. I scrawled a few words, leaving the note with Rose to pass on to Anne Askew.

Will Bryant had the horses outside the inn door. We left by the side entrance. As we mounted, we heard the sound of galloping hooves approaching fast. Forgetting all about Delia and Will Turpin, we fairly jumped on our horses and dashed down the lane.

"They won't hurt her, will they?"

"I doubt it," he replied gruffly. "They just like to break the meeting up. Sometimes the men get into fights. But so far they've treated her with the respect due a woman. Someday, though . . . someday she'll be hurt."

As we rounded a bend, entering the safety of the trees, I dared to look back. The horse that was galloping toward the inn was ridden not by my husband, nor by any man, but by a tall and striking young woman, whose mane of bright red hair escaped from under her black hood.

"Does Anne Askew have a friend, another woman with her?"

"Not that I know of," Bryant said, as he led my horse through a secret track in the woods back to the hall.

I slipped into our chamber, dressed, and even bathed myself to disguise the adventure. Then I returned to my private drawing room.

Hunting in my closets, I found the one prized possession I had brought with me from Borough Hall and Sizergh Castle. Buried inside an ordinary book were the tattered and yellowing pages by Martin Luther that Megan had lent to me. I had never given them up—never forgotten my true belief. Now a spirit of renewed faith came over me as I sat, in total secrecy, reading those pages in German print—knowing that I was taking a step away from my husband, flouting his will. I could never be as submissive or obedient as he would wish.

There was a banging at the door, and I froze. Was I found out so soon? Closing the pages and resting my hand on the book, I gave permission to enter. One of Latimer's servants put his head in the door and said my husband awaited me in our chamber.

Breathing a sigh of relief, I quickly replaced the book in its hiding place and went to meet my husband. The long gallery that led to our marriage chamber was cool this winterly night. I kept my skirts wrapped closely around me.

The door to our chamber was closed, so I knocked gently. There was no reply. Pushing the door open, I came into a room flooded with light from many candles and the warm glow of a blazing fire. The thick tapestries were drawn across the windows, and after the chill of the corridors, it was a haven of warmth and comfort.

My eye fell on the table, which was laden with food, jugs of wine, and set with two pewter platters and two pewter goblets. The benches were pulled neatly up by the sides of the table. There was an eerie stillness about the scene.

Latimer was stretched out on the bed. His head was buried in the thick damask that I had recently embroidered as our counterpane. This was the bed upon which he had so often taken me in love. The scene of our happiest times. Yet I felt a new distance between us.

"Sire, you called for me?"

He did not answer, and for a moment I hoped he had fallen asleep. But his head moved on the counterpane, and I knew he waited for some action from me. I tiptoed over to the bed and leaned over his quiet form.

The long hair fell over his shoulders—its color had turned a silvery gray—and I could not see the face with its noble cheekbones. The firm line of his shoulders and trunk were rigid in a stiff pose reflecting some disturbing state of mind.

Nervously I stroked his hair. "Sire, your man came to tell me you wanted to see me."

"Why should I have to send a man to tell my own wife I await her in our chamber?" he commented tersely.

Sitting on the edge of the bed, rubbing his shoulders, I moved my hands down his backbone, feeling it hard and unrelenting.

"Are you tired, my lord? I have not seen you in these many days. You are so busy."

"Busy!" he cried sarcastically. "You don't know what is going on here, Katherine. All hell is about to let loose!"

"Whatever have you been about, Latimer?"

"Oh, Katherine!"

I bent low over his head, kissed his hair, and rubbed my cheek against his ear.

"Tell me, my good lord, tell me."

"They are to bring battering rams and huge iron blocks to tear down the walls of one of our finest monasteries. They'll throw many of the monks out forcibly. The women with children who live there will be cast out screaming and crying into the snow! Just before Christmastime. And there is nothing any of us can do. The King's commissioners are already on their way."

Latimer turned to face me, his eyes red, his cheeks puffed up, weariness etched into every line in his face.

"We have tried everything to stop them. We have talked to the commissioners. We sent our own messenger with a letter to the King. We even threatened to stop the demolition men with our own bodies. But we were told that the King has issued orders to hang anyone obstructing the work. King Henry is known for sticking to his word where treasonable acts are concerned."

Latimer laughed sardonically. "He thinks *he*, the *King*, can be head of the Church. He is to separate England from Rome. The Pope, I believe, will excommunicate him. Can you imagine it! The man is quite crazed and dangerous."

"My own dear husband. I did not know. I thought you had been nearer to home, at the village of Tanfield. Someone told me they saw you riding there, to break up a meeting of Anne Askew's."

"I had no time for such dalliance. She's becoming a menace to the area, but I have more pressing concerns."

I kissed him on the forehead, ashamed of my own petty fears and preoccupations. We may not agree eye to eye on our beliefs, but I did still love him. In this moment of calm assurance, I told him of the affairs of my day and suggested that I make Delia my personal maid, so that I could protect her more effectively.

Then, relaxed, we snuggled like young lovers. The glass of wine I had taken from the table warmed my head and heated my body. At that moment I wanted my husband to take me as his wife, and as if he could read my mind he bade me remove his boots.

"Come here, Katherine." He stretched out his arms, as I struggled to take off his heavy leather boots. The boot suddenly came free, and I wound down his hose and massaged his feet.

A bowl of water had been in the fireplace, warming in case we should need to wipe our hands, and I placed his feet gently in the soothing water.

"Does that feel better?"

"Wonderful," he sighed. Several minutes passed before he ordered, "Take off your dress," and quickly I stood before him in camisole and petticoat.

He helped me move the table closer to the bed, then pulled me quietly onto the bed by him.

Knowing he was tired, I determined to do much of the

work. Having washed his feet, I tenderly undressed my husband, neatly folding up his clothes as I knew was his custom.

Kneeling to pick up the water bowl, I found myself on my knees between his legs. Then, gazing adoringly into his face, I whispered, "You just sit there, and let young Kate see what she can do, sire."

He leaned back on the palms of his hands, welcoming my touch. First I used my hands to knead his flesh like pastry dough. Then I pressed my lips to that soft mound of lustrous dark hair in his groin. I used my tongue to lick and taste the saltiness of his secret dark flesh. Soon I was writhing in exquisite agony myself, although no hand of his had touched me.

"Katherine," he choked. "Come here by my side."

"No." I wanted to torment him. "Let me stay here, let me make you fully contented."

Before I knew what was happening, he had leaned over, put his hands under my shoulders, and pulled me onto the bed beside him. Ripping at the front of my camisole to reveal my flushed breasts, he buried his head between them, biting and chewing at the skin. I could not cry out, for I was lost in my own desires.

Chapter 20

When I woke in the morning, Latimer had already departed our bed. I lay there feeling quite happy. Suddenly, the door burst open and he strode in, fully dressed, as if he had been up and about since before the dawn.

"Out of bed, Katherine. I have instructed Delia to put away clothes for you. We are going south to Lincolnshire today."

"Whatever for?" I did not want to leave my comfortable home.

"I have to visit some important people. I would like you to come with me. We have done little socializing together. It's time we were seen about more."

Quickly I dressed while my clothes were packed, and Delia came to fix my hair for the journey.

"Will you come with me?" I asked hesitantly, knowing she would hate to journey away from her home, and from Will.

"No, ma'am, I cannot. I really am not fit for a long journey. Young Mary Chamberlain will go with you. She looks forward to meeting new faces and, secretly, to finding a beau!"

I admired Delia. She stuck by her man, despite his foolish ways. I had raised her pay since she became my maid. Latimer had given Will a stockman's position at the hall, though he grumbled against it. We hoped the Turpins would fare better now.

My new clothing had been ordered and sewn over the winter. I was dressed in a green velvet gown. We packed away many others of rich damask embroidered with seed pearls and brilliants, chokers of gold, caps of pleated linen, the new fashion at Court, and my mantle of sable, a special gift from Latimer for our wedding.

Will Bryant helped me into our carriage, an expensive and very modern luxury. He was to be my driver. Latimer rode ahead with some of his menservants. I wished I were up there with him, astride a wild stallion, galloping over the hard turf and through the frost-covered countryside. We came down from the high moorlands of Yorkshire, slowly winding our way into the flat plains of Lincolnshire.

After two days and a very long third one, we came to a rest in the dead of night at a fine mansion which Will informed me was the manor of Grimsthorpe, near Bourne, and the residence of the Willoughy family.

Latimer came to the carriage door to hand me down. Because it was late, he said he would carry me into the house and take me straight to bed.

"Who are these people?" I whispered furiously, held babylike in his arms.

"You'll meet them tomorrow. They are all abed. The young lady is not yet married, but I imagine you will get on well. She is known for a tongue that heeds little politeness, just like yours, sweet wife!"

With that, he pinched my behind, so I let out a squeal in the cold night air.

"Shh." He placed a hand over my mouth, which I duly bit. "Remember, you are Lady Latimer here, and none of your games."

In the morning, a light breakfast was graciously brought to our chamber, with a vase of greenery from the estate's own fields. As we ate, Latimer informed me that this was one of the homes of the Dowager Lady Willoughby, Maria de Salinas, and her daughter Catherine, Baroness Willoughby, who had been wife and daughter of the late nobleman Lord Willoughby d'Eresby. The estate had now passed into wardship of the Crown and had been bought by none other than Charles Brandon, the Duke of Suffolk, the King's closest friend.

Ruthless, brutal, callous, charming, witty, the King's right-hand man—many were the tales told about Brandon on long winter nights. Latimer confided as we dressed that he had come to meet with Brandon to put Yorkshire's case against the dissolution of monasteries before the King's friend and commissioner.

Excited and nervous at meeting such a personage, I took special care with my dress. My outfit began with a silk chemise, and stockings of silk that were gartered at the knee. I wore a leather corset laced so tightly by Mary Chamberlain that I could scarcely breathe. Above the corset was a fitted bodice to which the sleeves of my luxurious gown were tied. Then a petticoat was dropped over my head to hang from the waist. It was of soft cotton, very full and bunched-up at the sides. Over it all was my beautiful gown of deep blue velvet, embroidered richly with pearls and brilliants.

The dress had cost Latimer far more than he intended to spend, but he was determined I should appear very grand among this company. The neckline was cut quite low. I knew this was the style at Court, and that unmarried ladies wore theirs cut even lower. But I was not really comfortable revealing my breasts to this degree. For the first time, I wore a stomacher, which was encrusted with silver, gold, and pearls. I even had a small ruff of pleated cambric around my neck, which was the height of fashion. I had never dyed my hair, as Latimer maintained he loved its natural color, but I curled and teased the locks so that they stood out from my face like a crown.

Latimer made me proud to be at his side. He wore an undershirt and short breeches of soft cotton, and a snugly fitted jacket bodice to which long close-knit tights of deepest black were laced. His shirt, of the finest lawn with silken needlework, fell from a yoke at the chest. His breeches were of deep midnight-blue velvet, to match my own dress. And he wore a very fashionable short cloak of soft ivory perfumed leather, the latest style from Spain.

Latimer wore no ruff, even though our King Henry had set the fashion for men to follow. He would have none of such frippery. That was for soft men from the South, those empty-headed courtiers who caused so much trouble for the rest of us.

Arm in arm, aware that we presented a striking couple, Latimer and I strode through the elegant long gallery in this ancient manor house at Grimsthorpe. Latimer whispered that this was by no means their finest house. Brandon was a collector of land and houses. He owned many more in the county of Suffolk. He was shortly to acquire all of young Catherine Willoughby's Lincolnshire property, having purchased her wardship.

"If Brandon dies before the girl, the property will all go to young Lord Charles, his son and heir. The boy and Catherine are betrothed. The only problem would arise if young Charles turns ill and dies." Latimer fell silent.

He brooded for a few minutes, no doubt pondering his own situation and the fact that he, too, had only one son and heir. "Because then the property would go back into wardship to the Crown."

Latimer stopped to look out the window at the frost-covered fenlands. He laughed cruelly. "After all, Brandon paid King Henry handsomely for this wardship. He won't let it go."

"What do you mean?"

"I hear tell he paid over the odds for it. More than two thousand pounds. He must have wanted Grimsthorpe and Tattershall Castle badly." Latimer chuckled cynically. "Or something more precious."

"Whatever do you mean, dear husband?"

He turned to me, taking my face in his hands, pinching me as he said, "See this pretty face? We old men will pay anything to get our hands on such a face and have it for our own. I'll never let another man touch this face, not now or ever. I'll never die, sweet Kate, because I never want to let you go."

I was so moved by this moment that I quite forgot my position and wrapped my arms around his waist, burrowing my face into the soft folds of the lawn shirt.

"My dear Latimer, I love to hear such sweet words from you."

He gently stroked my hair and whispered almost contentedly, "I have not confessed half my feelings to you, Kate. Just think for a minute how I procured you for my own."

"Is that what Brandon is trying to do with young Catherine Willoughby? I thought she was betrothed to his son?"

"Aye, the betrothal is a truth. But it was made many years ago before the wench grew into her bloom of womanhood. She's a beauty, that's for sure. Brandon has a fierce appetite for women."

He paused and looked down at me, then laughed again. "But I shouldn't be telling you this, Kate. It's men's talk."

We descended the wide wooden staircase that led down from the gallery into the great hall.

As I increased my pressure on Latimer's arm, he whispered confidingly, "You'll be all right. Just smile and look pretty."

Indeed, my heart beat at the sight of all the fine ladies who mingled on the thick rush matting over the stone slabs of the great hall. At the far end of this magnificent long room, with its cavernous vaulted ceiling way up in the sky, was a roaring fireplace, the kind I seldom saw in the North, as wood was an expensive luxury.

"How can they afford to burn down all their trees in one season?" I whispered in Latimer's ear.

He turned his face so that no one could overhear his remarks. "Brandon is here for a few days. So what if he uses up all the local forests? He doesn't care. The peasants may have nothing left for firewood for the rest of the winter, but that's not his problem!"

The noise of the guests, the musicians, buffoons, a group of tumblers and actors, the chatter of cutthroat jibes, the splashing of wine, mead, and ale into pewter tankards and goblets, was enough to deafen ears. I clung to my husband's arm.

Latimer wore a fixed smile. I knew that he felt nothing but disdain for this crowd and would stay no longer than he had to.

His hand was shaken by a tall, elegantly dressed man who

slapped him on the back and would have taken him in a bear hug were it not for my arm securely placed upon Latimer's own.

"Good Lord, old Latimer! How the devil are you?" the man bellowed above the din.

"Married again, Wyatt," Latimer said proudly. "And you? With your good wife?"

The man roared with laughter. "Still married for sure. But not with her. Lord bless us, Latimer. We're not all as fortunate as you," and he dropped me a mock bow, obviously the custom of courtiers, but one that took me aback.

"Katherine, Lady Latimer, meet wily Sir Thomas Wyatt, court poet, wit, and jester!"

Wyatt was a friend, and some said former lover, of Anne Boleyn's. My ears pricked enviously as the two men spoke in low voices.

"Come now, Latimer. Temper your comments about Mistress Boleyn or we won't know what will become of you," Wyatt was teasing.

"I shall say what I like about another person."

"Since when does anyone ever speak the truth before the King?"

"Ah, Wyatt, you tread too deep for me. I would never last long at Court."

"You'd lose your head within a few weeks!" Sir Thomas Wyatt laughed and waltzed off into the crowd.

With a fanfare of trumpets dinner was announced. From all corners people made their way to their preordained places.

Latimer led me to the top table, for the heavy oak benches were laid out in the shape of a T, with one huge table making the cross, placed up above the rest on a dais. The stem of the T was made up of several tables, end to end, each loaded with meats, bread, wine, and fruits, alongside of which men, women, and some children sat, from the high and mighty to the lowest peasant in the village.

At the center of the table sat Charles Brandon, Duke of Suffolk, king of his own domain. At either side of him were two graceful women, one an elderly lady whose head was covered in a black mantilla. I guessed she must be the Dowager Lady Willoughby, Maria de Salinas, former lady-in-waiting to Queen Catherine of Aragon. The other lady, on Brandon's right hand, was petite, with shining dark hair, piercing eyes, and a sad expression. She was attired in the height of fashion, her clothing heavily encrusted with the most expensive jewels. I assumed she was young Catherine, Baroness Willoughby.

Charles Brandon was a large uncouth man, solid of girth, merry of disposition. Yet one could sense the burning anger and fiery temper just beneath the surface.

Young Catherine winced as her guardian told bawdy jokes and moved about the table entertaining or criticizing his guests.

We had eaten our way through several courses of meats and fishes, and were now about to tackle fresh boiled larks and nightingales, a delicacy I was sure I could do without. Brandon wiped his greasy mouth with the back of a velvet sleeve. He waved his arm around his head, holding a bird's wing and dropping gravy all over his white ruff, staining that symbol of elegance with rather nasty brown spots.

He turned to Latimer, with a look of seeming innocence that seethed beneath the surface with spite.

"I hear the poor folk up North don't like our new taxes, my dear Latimer," breezed Brandon.

Latimer choked on his gravy.

"They probably would like the taxes had they money or food to pay with, my good Duke," he replied.

"Ha!" jumped in Brandon. "Would you have us make separate taxes, one for the rich and one for the poor? Ha! Ha!"

Several people around the table laughed with him.

I kicked Latimer gently on the ankle, to remind him I was on his side.

"As I said, Brandon, it would be pleasant to think all the people had sufficient to eat, live on, and pay the King's taxes."

"So you think we're starving the people, do you, Latimer? Are you saying Henry's commands are unjust?"

The silence following this question was thick and heavy. I feared for my dear husband. I was desperate to speak myself—to tell Brandon from my heart how miserable was the plight of many peasants.

"Suffolk, you enact Henry's wishes on these matters, not I. I have no reason to concern myself with the justice or injustice of the King's commands. I take care of whatever local matters arise."

I relaxed slightly. Surely Latimer had enough wit and strength of character to hold his own in this crowd.

"Knowing you to be such a good and honest man, my dear Suffolk," Latimer continued, "and one who knows how the people of this country live, I doubt very much that you would take taxes from people if it were an unjust act. I know you would *hate* to see people suffer unnecessarily."

I heard a small cough, and Catherine Willoughby not only sputtered but choked on a mouthful of food. Her cheeks flushed bright red and she deftly placed a linen napkin to her face.

Latimer had trodden on very thin ice. Charles Brandon indeed knew how the people lived. He had been elevated to the aristocracy by the King just recently.

Luckily Brandon was bored with Latimer. He ignored Latimer's last comment and turned to another nobleman at the end of the table for teasing and more lighthearted repartee. Latimer picked up his napkin and wiped his brow.

Catherine Willoughby seemed to want to catch my eye. She politely offered me some more wine.

"Lady Latimer. It is very pleasant to have you with us,"

she welcomed me. "I have heard much about your husband, and was looking forward to meeting his new wife."

"The pleasure, Baroness Willoughby, I assure you is mine."

"Tell me about Westmoreland—is that where you were born?" she added decorously. "I have never been to the northern mountainous districts, having spent all my years in the calm meadows of Suffolk or Lincolnshire. It must be frightening out in the wilds of the moors and fells."

I looked at her curiously, wondering what I was supposed to say. How boring such conversations are. How I wished to talk properly, to see if she and I thought alike on important matters. I sorely needed a friend in my new life.

"I should rather hear about your life in London," I answered at last. "I understand you have spent much time at Court. You must have fascinating stories to tell."

She looked at me with those piercing blue eyes. I returned the gaze with as much honesty and plainness as I was able.

Looking down at her plate, on which most of her uneaten food still rested, she said, "Perhaps you would like to come for a walk with me, in the gallery and then to my chamber. I have some pieces of embroidery I would be proud to show you."

"I should very much like to look at your embroidery. You know needlework is my *greatest* passion."

Catherine Willoughby nodded in my direction, and I rose quietly to my feet. We dropped a curtsy to the Dowager Maria de Salinas and I excused myself from Latimer.

Following Catherine's slim form, I wove my way through the great hall, back toward the staircase. Catherine's dress was of glowing ivory damask. She wore a high ruff around her neck, and her jet-black hair was crowned with a tiara of jewels. Although young and slight, she walked with grace and held her body with pride and elegance. She was a woman of power at fifteen years of age.

Catherine opened the door into a beautiful chamber, oak-paneled and decorated with rich tapestries on the walls. The bed, chairs, and tables were covered with embroidered fabric. She had large pillows, also embroidered, strewn around the floor, and she indicated that I lean myself against one of them.

Deftly, she closed the solid oak door behind us, then opened the shutters of the casement windows to let in whatever dull light was left on this cold winter's day. The room was lit by a blaze from the fire.

For a long time, we chatted about our lives. She told me about her betrothal to Lord Charles, two years her elder and a close and dear friend. I expressed my happiness for her.

"You were married before Latimer?"

Suddenly, and without caution, I found myself describing the horrors of my marriage to Edward Borough. Catherine broke into peals of laughter and I was close to tears myself.

"I was not even your age then. Why, I was widowed by the age you are now!"

Maybe it was the wine, the rich food, or the cozy warmth of the room, but soon we were holding our sides in mirth. I realized I had not felt so happy in a long time. I felt so relaxed with my new friend. Catherine insisted I call her Willy.

"Tell me about Anne Boleyn," I asked, my curiosity unrestrained. "Do you know her? Have you seen her at Court?"

Willy's face clouded. She rose from her pillow to draw the shutters across the windows now that darkness had fallen. Her voice was low as though she feared someone might be eavesdropping.

"You must be careful what you say about Mistress Boleyn in Brandon's house, for he has to defend her hotly in front of the King. My mother is the Queen's closest and oldest friend, you know. She came from Spain with the young Queen when she was betrothed to Prince Arthur. My mother breaks into tears at the very mention of this trouble."

Willy's face brightened. "But I can tell you much."

We both giggled.

"I've been in London recently, with Brandon escorting me as his prize catch. You know that Brandon's wife, Mary Tudor, is quite ill, and I do believe he has tired of her."

I frowned to hear all these tales. Mary Tudor was King Henry's favorite younger sister. She had been the Queen of France, and, when widowed, had romantically and excitingly eloped to marry the dashing young Charles Brandon. Their marriage had struck my girlish heart with passion and envy. Now Willy described how Brandon had no time for her, preferring to show off his young ward in public.

"Shouldn't you have been escorted by your own Lord Charles?"

Willy smirked and shrugged her shoulders. "Brandon has rules of his own. He's like the King. He doesn't really have to obey anyone's orders."

"Did you mind?" I wanted to talk honestly.

"Did *you* mind going to live with Kaitlin Neville once she was married to Henry Borough, your lover?"

Horrified, I gasped, "How do you know that?"

"Oh, most tales get around in the end. It's a small country, isn't it?"

"But what would Latimer say if he knew people were talking?"

"He saved your reputation. He knows how much people gossip."

"Willy," I groaned, "you don't know half the story. One day I'll tell you the rest, but please forget what I said about you and Brandon. Tell me about Anne Boleyn. Go on, please."

"She's living at Windsor Castle now, in apartments next to those that were the Queen's. She's been made Marchioness of Pembroke, as you must know. King Henry has given her land and property.

"She holds court there, and you'd be amazed at how many of the courtiers go in, bow, scrape, and pay lip service to her demands.

"She's popular among the men—she always was. Most people are surprised she's made such a strong play for the King. She could have any of the other leading men at Court. Sir Thomas Wyatt was supposed to be in love with her, until Henry chased him off. Wyatt backed off pretty quickly, from what I hear!" She laughed. "It's not the safest thing to be battling with the King over the woman he loves." Willy laughed merrily, though I sensed bitterness.

"Why do you think Anne's doing it?"

"I really don't know. Maybe she just wants to be Queen."

"She must love the King," I added romantically.

Willy looked cross for a minute. "Oh, come on, Kate. He may not be old, but he's not exactly handsome. He's getting fat, and his legs hurt him. Since he fell in love with Anne, he has turned rather stupid and cowlike."

"I always imagined the King as a wonderful person, quite the most handsome, the most clever, and the wittiest man in Europe."

"Not the cleverest," Willy commented dryly. "Only the most powerful." Then she knelt down beside me and grabbed my hands in hers.

"Promise not to breathe a word of this to anyone, but I heard from one of her ladies that Anne has started to go to his bed at night. All the latest rumors at Court have it that she is already pregnant."

"How awful!" I gasped.

"If she can give him a son, he'd give her the world," Willy continued. "But I wouldn't fancy being in her shoes right now."

"The King still has to sort out his problem with the Queen?" I asked, not taking her meaning.

Willy whispered really low in my ear, "I wouldn't be surprised if the Queen is killed off. King Henry will have to get his way someday soon. Especially if Anne is with child."

A faint tapping at the door made us jump apart guiltily. Willy opened the door, and there, in the lintel frame, stood my husband with his arm around the frail Dame Maria de Salinas.

"Why, Mother!" Willy was aghast. "What's wrong?"

"Lady Willoughby needed rest, Baroness. She refused my offer to escort her to her own chamber, and begged to be with you."

Willy's attitude changed within seconds in the presence of her mother. Latimer led the ailing woman into the warm chamber and laid her on the bed. Willy indicated that I should depart with my husband.

When we reached the long gallery, Latimer pretended to point out paintings of their noble ancestors. "The dowager had something of a set-to with Brandon, about the Queen, of course. He called Catherine of Aragon a stubborn old ox!"

"Willy just told me about her mother. Why does Brandon act so insensitively?"

I watched Latimer's face cloud over. "Katherine, get your things. We are leaving tonight. We cannot stay any longer."

"But why?" I didn't want to leave my new friend Willy. My thoughts flashed to the fine ball to be held that night. "Please let us stay." But Latimer's eyes glared a stormy gray, and his lips tightened and curled in a scarcely concealed snarl.

"Brandon is impossible. He called me to his library, plied me with his best port, and more or less threatened I would lose my head if I had anything to do with the peasant uprising we all more or less expect."

Frightened, I squeezed his arm and retired to find Mary Chamberlain.

We mounted our fine carriage in haste. Will Bryant had his orders to depart immediately. Latimer talked with men in the dark courtyard, making ready his own horse to ride abreast of us. Quite unhappily I gazed at the lighted windows. I felt the warmth and excitement of that day in the presence of the high and mighty fade from my life.

Chapter 21

I kept this from you at Grimsthorpe, Katherine, but Brandon gave me the news. Nunmonkton has been ordered to close down. The forty or so nuns who live there are to be thrown out into the village. The children, orphans every one, are to be cast adrift. Brandon maintains that commissioners discovered young ladies whose families had forced them to enter the convent walls, that nuns were leading secular lives, some with babies born out of wedlock. It's a pack of lies, and I know it."

Bryant reined in the horses sharply, as our carriage halted on a bend. Latimer's voice sounded hard and stern as he spoke to me through the velvet curtain of the carriage.

"We'll go by horse from here, Katherine. Will is preparing you a mount now. I hope you don't mind the cold. But we must get there fast. The snow is too deep for the carriage. We'll meet Mary and Will at the manor tonight."

In grim spirits on this cold winter morning, dressed in a long fur cloak and a woolen wrap around my neck, with gloves, overboots, and thick stockings under my skirt, I cantered by Latimer's side, our horses snorting, their nostrils flaring in the icy cold. We rode over the hard frozen land to the site of the nunnery.

From a distance I could see crowds of stooped figures wandering beyond the walls of the building. My heart leaped to my mouth. Carpenters had arranged a mantel of wooden props the length of the walls, which, nailed into place, created a scaffold around the building. Groups of laborers dug in the frozen earth under the foundations of the stone church and outhouses. Three men stood aside, presumably the King's commissioners.

Huddled for shelter by a lit fire was a group of women in long brown cloaks. Several wept at the monstrous sight. The small fire was the only point of warmth in an otherwise cold and cruel scene.

Other men climbed barefoot up the walls of the building; local plumbers hunted for salvaged lead, and smiths tried to take whatever scrap iron they could find.

From horseback, I saw people scurrying away with windows, doors, iron, glass, and lead. One young boy carried a pile of books as he clambered out of an empty window frame and ran off in the frosty morning. At least he was stealing books. But Latimer pointed out that he would take them home as fuel for the fire.

"Don't fool yourself they want books for reading. These people need the paper to make a fire, to line their boots, to plaster the walls of their huts, to keep them warm."

A loud cry came from the group of nuns. They stood with their hands in the air. Three men were carrying flaming torches over to the scaffold and, without a word, set it on fire. Alcohol had been poured onto the wood to make it burn, and within seconds, flames leaped heavenward.

"May the Lord have mercy on you!" screamed one of the nuns. "For burning down His temple."

"God forgive them," wept a much younger woman who cradled a baby in her arms beneath the dark brown cloak.

My throat ached with anguish. Tears filled my eyes. I watched with horrified fascination while the scaffold burned. As the tight frame of wood turned to embers, the walls began to crumble and fall down. The air was acrid with the smell of smoke, and cinders flew in dangerous circles over our heads. One man screamed as he fell from the wall of the building, clutching in his arms a bundle of lead taken from the roof. A woman cried out in fear as her child ran too close.

"Latimer, I'm scared," I sobbed. "Take me away from here. I can't stand to watch the misery anymore."

Taking my horse's reins, he pulled me around and slapped the animal on the rump. Together we cantered away from the horror and destruction.

⁘

Latimer's dogs and servants came running out to greet us. It was hard to return the smiles of happiness, but I was cheered to be home again.

A gentleman waited in our own great hall to talk with Latimer. Delia Turpin, who had been first to greet us, looked worried when she announced the news to my husband.

"He says his name is Robert Aske from over the moors," she said hesitantly. Gentlemen did not usually come calling on a noble lord without prior arrangements.

Latimer's brow furrowed. "Aske? Ha! How timely. Tell him I'll be right down, Delia. And thank you."

I tripped through the gallery on the way to our chamber, following Latimer's heavy footsteps.

"May I join you in this meeting?" I asked. "I have a feeling he's coming about the state of affairs in the North. And I vowed this morning, watching the ruins of Nunmonkton, to become more active in whatever is going on. Please let me be a part of it, dear husband."

Latimer sighed as he strode on. "Aye. I know you mean well. It's not usually ladies' work. But you may join us. I'll meet with him in the library. I could do with a drink."

The library at Snape Hall, in the new building, was one of my favorite rooms. Cheerful, warm, comfortable, it had a gentle view of one of the pleasant gardens that surrounded the house. It was a square room, with casement windows that had tiny leaded panes of glass and huge wide windowsills on which you could sit and stare out. I had spent many happy hours with Latimer in the library, while he read or wrote and I perched at the window.

Robert Aske was not a good-looking man. Tall, thin, with a gaunt face, he had hollow dark eyes and a staring expression that comes from the depth of some passion. He coughed and acted nervous in front of Latimer. My husband ushered him to a chair by the fire and offered him a mug of port.

"Lord Latimer, I trust you will forgive the intrusion, but I have been traveling around Yorkshire assessing the feelings of the people, doing my best to alleviate some of the damage the King and his men are creating. Lord D'Arcy informed me you might follow my plan. But I had to visit you personally to judge your level of interest . . . and your mood."

Latimer acted impatient. "Go on, man, go on."

"What I am about to suggest might appear treasonable. I do not know how you stand with the King. . . ."

"I said get on with it, man!" Latimer was now irritated.

"A group of us, representing the northern counties, are planning to meet with the King, or one of his advisers, to do something about the poverty. We mean to have a conference with King Henry himself. The Archbishop of York is with us, Lord D'Arcy, and several others."

Aske paused and shifted his feet. "We also intend to make it known to the King that the people of the country disapprove of his plan to divorce the Queen and all the Lutheran cant that is being spread about these days. We want to go back to the old times. We want the Catholic faith, good and strong. We want the Queen and Princess Mary back in their place. We want grazing land and enough to eat for the peasants."

Latimer laughed loudly. "And you intend to tell King Henry all this yourselves?"

The man nodded.

"You must be off your heads. At least your heads will be off before the King can say 'Get out.' No one can broach such private matters with the King. Aske, I have just returned from Lincolnshire, where I met with Charles Brandon, the Duke of Suffolk, who, as an old friend and colleague, I hoped might put such a case to the King on my behalf. But I received no sympathy from him. He warned me seriously to tread carefully with such ideas before the King."

Robert Aske now looked uncomfortable and angry, as if Latimer were a dilettante who really did not care.

"That's all very well, Lord Latimer. If you do not want to join us I'll go elsewhere. But the people will rise up in arms sooner or later, if something isn't done. You wouldn't want civil war, would you?"

"I warned Brandon of that, good man. He laughed me out of his home. The King has arms and army enough to crush the peasants in days. We have to work at a local level. I'm doing all I can." Latimer looked tired and dejected.

"Good day, Lord Latimer." Robert Aske bowed his way out of the room, as if the nobleman were suddenly abhorrent to him.

As the door closed, Latimer stormed up and down the room. "I won't have some downtrodden gentleman coming here and organizing my life. I can plan things better than any of them. He, in particular, is laughable. They call him the Earl of Poverty around here. He takes himself so seriously. I doubt very much there'll be civil war. The people haven't got strength or weapons to fight. But there will be trouble, I can see that."

I ran to my husband when I heard his words, longing for the feeling of security and comfort I could always find wrapped in his arms. "I love you, dear husband. Don't let anything happen to you."

"Katherine, I am happy if I have made you so. Maybe that's all a man can hope for in life. To love a good and pretty woman, and make her happy."

Taking his face between my hands, I kissed his tired eyes. "You could do worse, Latimer dear, you could do much worse."

"Go to your room, Katherine. This visit from Aske is just the beginning. It seems I have Lord and Lady D'Arcy about to call on me soon. Something has finally set all these people afire. For a long time it has just been me. I don't know what you will make of the D'Arcys. He's something of a sop, a flyblown bookish man. As for his new wife, well, rumors are rife about her. Many think she is half crazed. They are both avid reformists, but we came together on our news of the King. So keep the conversation away from the Lutheran business."

"Oh dear." I sniggered. "You'd better lock me away."

I skipped away from him as he playfully slapped the back of my skirt. The evening sun was filtering through the library windows and I felt quite content.

✠

"What is the matter, Mistress Turpin?" I asked cheerfully, as I dressed carefully for dinner despite my tiredness.

"This note was left here the other day to be given to you."

"What does it say?"

Delia's back straightened visibly. "Ma'am, even though I can read, I would never look at a note to you."

"Does Latimer know of it?"

"Of course not, ma'am. That's why I've been so nervous."

"You may leave, Delia. I'm sure it's nothing, just a letter begging for money. Leave it on my dresser, and I'll see to it in a minute."

No sooner had Delia closed the door than I pounced upon the soiled piece of paper folded carefully in four. My fingers trembled to open it. I had several guesses as to the person behind this mysterious missive. It was with no disappointment that my eyes scanned the words.

> *Lady Latimer, I was truly pleased to receive your message. If we can meet, I should be most happy. You may be of great help to us. I have a friend who can bring us together. Your faithful servant, Anne Askew.*

Before I had time to make plans, I was called to dinner. I stuffed the note in my bosom and ran down to the great hall, where Latimer awaited me.

Latimer and I were chatting with Will Bryant about our trip to Lincolnshire and the hazardous return home through the snowbound wastes when the D'Arcys were announced. I turned from my position facing the fireplace, aware that my face must be quite red from the heated embers.

There was Lord D'Arcy, an aesthete, well groomed, well dressed, tall and spare, with fine hair tied behind his neck. His long elegant hands reached out to touch my own. At his side stood his wife, her elegant dress covered by a cloak and her hair hidden beneath a hood.

My face turned dark red as I instantly recognized Lady D'Arcy. She was none other than my own dear stepdaughter and true long-lost friend, Megan Borough!

Megan held out a cool hand. We touched fingers as strangers would.

"I am charmed to meet the delightful Lady Latimer," she said, and I replied with similar politeness.

The evening was not a particularly pleasant one, because Latimer, the staunch Catholic, and Lord D'Arcy, the confirmed reformist, clashed many times. Latimer told me later that he and D'Arcy worked well together, against the King. They tolerated each other's religion. I glanced occasionally at Megan's face but saw no emotion cross those eyes or lips. I wondered if we should own up to our friendship, but felt, as presumably she did, that it was better not to. When Lord D'Arcy rose to leave, I looked at her carefully.

Megan rose gracefully from the table, her tall thin form delicately outlined in a simple but striking dress of deepest emerald that shone luxuriously, as did her bright red hair. Her face was ivory-white.

"Lord Latimer, I would be charmed if your good wife would join me some afternoon for social conversation at our home."

Latimer was flattered and intrigued by this cool person. It was arranged that I should visit the D'Arcy mansion the following week. I could hardly conceal my excitement.

❖

In the intervening week, Latimer received a brief letter from Sir Thomas Wyatt at Court in London. He advised his good friend that King Henry and Mistress Anne Boleyn had been married in secret on St. Paul's Day, in an attic in the west turret of Whitehall.

There had been five or six persons present for the predawn ceremony. King Henry swore that his divorce had been granted and that he had received a Papal dispensation. As daylight just began to glimmer outside the tiny window, King Henry had kissed Anne Boleyn on the cheek and they departed separate ways. Mistress Boleyn, declared Wyatt, was almost surely with child. Latimer read the letter angrily. He stormed up and down our great hall and threw the letter into the fire, with such force it nearly vanished up the chimney.

"Now the country is set for trouble," he said grimly.

Latimer insisted I never repeat a word of this to anyone ir

Yorkshire until the King made the news of his marriage to
Anne Boleyn, and divorce from Queen Catherine, public.

The Court seemed very far away as I set out to visit Lady
D'Arcy. I hardly noticed the surrounding Yorkshire moorlands on that balmy February day. The winter sun shone on
the bleak hills. A rider came up behind Mary Chamberlain
and me as we rode in our carriage toward the D'Arcys' mansion. I was surprised to see Will Bryant's friendly face.

"Good day, Lady Latimer," he said happily. "I have come
to escort you to Lady D'Arcy's."

I settled back comfortably in our old carriage seats, the
ancient leather creaking and smelling of dusty old stableyards.

A short time later we pulled into D'Arcy's gateway and
drive. Dogs raced out to greet us noisily. Stable lads ran in
circles to bring in our horses. Peering out the carriage windows, I saw my dear Megan standing in the stable courtyard,
her dress hitched up to her knees, in a most unladylike
pose, chatting happily with Will Bryant. I was surprised she
knew him, let alone would speak to a servant in this way.
But then Megan was full of surprises.

She turned to help us down from our carriage. Megan
looked stunning. Her long red hair was tied back and wound
up in a coil on her head. Her dress of thick deep purple
brocade was pinned up so that it hung above the muddy
yard. The top of her dress was covered with what appeared
to be one of her husband's waistcoats and a jacket of rich
Spanish leather. Her feet were shod in heavy boots that
probably belonged to one of the stableboys. I wanted to
laugh—she presented the embodiment of a woman who did
not care what others thought.

Megan approached, stepping gingerly over the muddy pools,
a smile on her face.

"Katey Parr! Katey Parr!" she cried as I stepped out of the
carriage. I fell into her welcoming arms. We kissed each
other on the cheeks, then held each other at arm's length.

"God, let's not stay out in this cold. Come in, do come in. Bring your maid with you. My husband is dying to meet you again. I've some other guests coming over too. We'll have quite a tea party!" And she broke into peals of laughter.

As she marched me into the kitchen entrance of their manor house, I noticed she turned to wave to Will Bryant. He delivered a mock bow in our direction.

I came up the back stairs, Megan holding my hand, to meet Lord D'Arcy in their hall.

He rose, in his beautiful elegant way, to take my hand. They were quite a match, he with his graceful elegance and she as the nonchalant and dramatic free spirit.

"My dear Lady Latimer, it is a great pleasure. I was surprised your good husband let you come alone to this house of iniquity."

"I promised him not to be swayed by any of your religious beliefs."

Megan stood by smiling. "How could you have married one of the North's leading Catholics, Katey? How could you?"

Megan stood aside, her arms folded as if she were scolding me.

"I had to marry again, or I should have stayed forever with Kaitlin Neville and your dear brother, as you well know Megan." I answered archly. I was bursting to ask questions myself.

D'Arcy made it easier. "I think your old friend is wondering how you ever managed to end up here, Megan. You must have been surprised, Lady Latimer, to see none other than your stepdaughter on my arm."

"Lord D'Arcy . . ." I was hesitant at first. "May I speak the truth?"

"Of course, dear lady."

"Then spare me the misery of waiting, Megan. How did you come to be Lady D'Arcy? The last I heard of you, you were locked behind convent walls. Oh, Megan." I felt a rush of feeling for her. "You must feel so sad. Only the other week I witnessed the tearing down of Nunmonkton. I knew from Latimer that you were already gone from there."

"And I had tried to locate *you*, Kate. What a surprise for both of us! Lady Latimer, meet Lady D'Arcy. Oh, I wanted to die laughing there in your husband's library. But we were all so serious. And now, Kate, I have another surprise for you. Anne Askew is coming to visit us this afternoon."

My hand flew to my mouth. "So you are in league with her?"

D'Arcy exploded, "In league?"

"I have asked everyone around here whether the speaker Anne Askew had a woman friend, with red hair. You may not know, Megan, but I saw Anne myself, from the hostelry windows in Tanfield. And from that moment I was certain I would catch up with you."

D'Arcy spoke again. "Anne has been a good friend to us, Katherine . . . she introduced me to my beloved Megan."

"Darling," Megan cajoled him, again astonishing me at her change in manner.

"Anne was brave enough to leave the walls months before I did. I stayed on there, in charge of the vegetable garden. I rather enjoyed it. She began her secret career as a preacher, and met up with all the reformists, from the lowborn to the nobility. D'Arcy became one of her friends. Our beloved Anne connived to bring D'Arcy with her to the convent to help a poor friend in distress."

"I expected to find some starving orphan." He guffawed. "I knew the woman in question was a reformist, thrown from her father's home for her beliefs. I did not expect this strong, dramatic figure I discovered in the vegetable garden yelling her head off at a village boy who had dug up her potatoes instead of weeds."

"And so you fell in love and married?" I sighed, now quite lost in the romance of it all.

We chatted happily far into the evening. I learned that Henry Borough was still, in name, Lord Strickland, Kaitlin's husband. They still had no children. He now spent most of his time at the University of Cambridge. Edwina Borough was a happily married young woman of property in Gainsborough.

When Anne Askew finally arrived, in the secrecy of a covered wagon, we kissed in frank intimacy, having always had a fondness for each other. I had to confess to them my position was awkward. I had vowed to Latimer I would have nothing to do with Anne, but in my heart, I was a reformist.

"I still have your book, Megan. I read it in secrecy."

Knowing they must think my marriage peculiar, I leaped to Latimer's defense.

"My husband is a good kind man. He has made me happier than I deserved. He is a Catholic, true. But he fights for the poor, and in that I can help him."

Megan cut me off abruptly. "Kate, we have a small band of reformist sympathizers around here. We are working together, and we want you to be one of us. There is D'Arcy and me, of course, and Anne. I believe you met Rose at the inn at Tanfield. Will Bryant, who works for your estate, is good and always to be trusted. He will deliver messages between us. Latimer has no idea of his beliefs. Will is so sensible I cannot believe he would give our secret away."

Swallowing hard, I vowed with feeling, "I will do what I can. You know I am a believer, all of you. But I will do nothing to upset Lord Latimer."

PART V

Young
Wives

Chapter 22

S pring returned to Snape Hall. The meadows were full of daffodils and bluebells, cowslips and butter-cups, ragwort, and daisies. I discovered the joys of the gardens and of the expansive parks and charming ponds. In the afternoons I helped the gardeners with their work, cutting and rearranging, and, of course, planting herbs for my medicinal stocks.

It was late April when we received a directive addressed to Lady Latimer from the King. The letter declared that as the wife of a peer I should henceforth address Mistress Boleyn, Marchioness of Pembroke, as our Queen, and pray for her in church.

We had heard that Anne was now beginning proudly to show her belly. As far as we knew, no word had been made public about the divorce from Queen Catherine.

The rumors were confirmed by a message from Willy. It seemed that Queen Catherine had been formally divorced from the King on May 23, by Archbishop Cranmer, at a public tribunal in Dunstable. The marriage of King Henry and Queen Catherine was now null and void.

Then, Latimer received instructions from Court requesting our attendance at Anne's coronation in June. Highborn nobles would be attending Anne's procession from Greenwich Palace to the Tower on May 31. Latimer was against the idea of attending, but I very much wanted to make the trip to London.

"I won't allow you to ride behind the new Queen like many of the other ladies," he replied petulantly to my pleading.

"No, but Willy will be there, and I'd love to watch. It will be so very exciting."

Latimer finally gave in, and we had a hurried time preparing fine clothes and making all the arrangements to move to one of Latimer's town houses, at Charterhouse.

Carriageloads of food, clothes, and furnishings were sent ahead of us, including all our silver and gold plate, pewter tankards, and gifts of gold and silver for the King and his new Queen.

Will Bryant headed up the team of nine carriages, twice as many horses, and a batch of servants, all enlisted to perform the advance preparations for our visit in town.

The Friday of Pentecost found us well ensconced in our gracious home at Charterhouse. We rose early and dressed as stylishly as we could to see the Queen. My horse was bedecked in a gold saddle, edged with white silk. I sat as erect and proud as possible. Latimer held my horse's reins and guided me through the dirty city streets.

The streets of London were thronged with people. It was years since I had visited the great city. The place seemed far more crowded than I remembered. It was a splendid May day. Everyone was overjoyed at the prospect of a royal wedding and the free wine and food that would be a part of the festivities.

Riding along the banks of the Thames was very pleasant. A few large mansions graced the water's edge. Their fine gardens led right down to the pebbly river beach. Boats with cargo would normally have plied their way up and down the river, but today every boat or tug or barge had been commandeered for the trip to Greenwich. The procession of the Lord Mayor was to be followed by at least fifty barges.

Men, women, and children, besmocked and beribboned, and dogs, cats, horses, and even the occasional goat struggled along the dirty roads. The sound of people laughing, running, playing, fighting, and singing surrounded us.

It was midafternoon before Queen Anne came out of the

palace. A gasp went up around the crowd. She looked beautiful. Her dress was of gold cloth, and the bevy of maidens attending her were all clothed in white.

The barges of her father, now the Earl of Wiltshire, of Charles Brandon, Duke of Suffolk, and of many other nobles followed Queen Anne's barge. Though we were pushed aside by this glorious throng, I made out the figures of Brandon himself, and his daughters, Frances and Eleanor, and his son, Charles. But I could not see Willy. Latimer said Willy was no doubt among them. Brandon's wife, Mary Tudor, was, sadly, too ill to attend the procession.

We followed the flotilla back downriver to the great Tower. On the shoreline, I dimly made out the grand and imperious figure of our own King Henry attended by the Lord Chamberlain and the heralds, who greeted Anne's arrival with a fanfare of trumpets.

They helped her down from the barge to a postern at the waterside and led her to the King's side. He kissed her, and a shiver went through my body at the sight of this royal passion. How wonderful the King looked! How mighty!

Anne turned to thank the Lord Mayor, before he returned to his barge. Then Queen Anne and King Henry, holding hands like any man and wife, stepped away from the river's edge and walked into the imposing gray stone Tower, the fortress of England and symbol of our security. Anne and Henry entered the Tower for a few days of royal conjugal bliss.

All thoughts of Queen Catherine had left my mind. I doubt anyone but Maria de Salinas, and maybe her daughter, Catherine Willoughby, gave much thought to Queen Catherine on this day.

Latimer and I stayed in London for a few delightful days, meeting with my sister Anne, getting to know her husband Willie, now Earl of Pembroke, and their two precious children—little Billy and his elder sister Maude. I saw my brother William, soon to be the grandiose Earl of Essex, but not his wife. Claire Bourchier, claimed our priggish brother, was out of town. My sister informed me William was a terrible womanizer and treated his wife quite hatefully.

The last day of festivities was held in honor of Queen Anne's royal progress through the city before her coronation. We were invited by Willy to view this splendid spectacle from their London mansion, Dorset House.

Latimer and I arrived around noon. Brandon was welcoming an enormous crowd to his home, feasting them with drinks and cold salmon at his own expense. We all clambered to the windows overlooking the Strand to see the girl who had won the heart of the King.

Queen Anne was a vision of silver and white. An extravagant silver mantle lined with ermine floated about her shoulders. Her long dark hair was worn loose and fell over the silver material like dark velvet. In her hair was a coif with a circlet of precious rubies. Four knights on foot walked by her sides, carrying a canopy of gold cloth to protect her head, as the procession advanced to Westminster Hall, where she was to stay with the King and ready herself for the coronation on the morrow.

Latimer wanted to hurry back to the coolness of the Yorkshire countryside, but an urgent message came from Dorset House that changed our plans.

"Brandon's wife, Mary Tudor, has passed on."

"What will happen?" I asked Latimer in a ghostly voice.

"There will be a great funeral." He sighed. "We cannot go back to Yorkshire yet." He was silent for a few minutes. "Your friend Catherine Willoughby may not find her life so pleasant now."

+

We attended the funeral, calling at Dorset House before the entourage wound its way to the burial ceremony. King Henry came to the mansion to lead the funeral procession for his sister. Queen Anne stood some yards behind him, looking bored. Obviously uncomfortable on this hot day, she was very pregnant.

Willy came forward to greet me. She shook Latimer's hand warmly. She appeared young, vulnerable and slightly nervous. There were dark circles under her pretty eyes.

As she talked I glanced over my shoulder. A pair of eyes attracted my attention. For a moment, I was unsure whom they belonged to. Then a shiver ran down my back. A mixture of excitement and irritation overtook me. The eyes staring my way were not smiling and glinting with a devil-may-care attitude today. They were brooding and mysterious—a darkly silent comment on my presence arm in arm with Latimer.

Feeling it my part to be gracious, I turned from Latimer and Willy and walked over to where the man stood alone, by a window overlooking the Strand.

"Am I right?" I proffered my hand. "Did we not meet at Sizergh Castle some years ago?"

"What an honor Lady Latimer pays me." His tone was mocking. His lips curled slightly, exposing those fresh white teeth. What was it about this man that so perplexed me? Now I was annoyed I had even come to pay my respects.

"Doesn't that seem a long time ago?" I laughed. "How have you fared?"

Bowing from his waist, one hand on his sword, the elegant, well-dressed Thomas Seymour was every inch the courteous gentleman.

"Why, Katherine." He made it obvious he was using my first name. "The courtier at the King's right hand is my own brother Edward. The young lady attending Queen Anne over there is my sister Jane. I find myself in good standing. I have become a leading member of our troops, vanquishing invaders and ne'er-do-wells. I have been honored with posts abroad on diplomatic missions for the King.

"But how, Katherine, has marriage to the devout, though surely rather old-fashioned, Latimer suited you? How is life in the dales of Yorkshire? Still racing on horseback?"

His miraculous smile was meant to unnerve.

Glancing over at his sister Jane and brother Edward, I was surprised to see how unattractive they both were compared to the beautiful Thomas. Jane Seymour lacked any of her younger brother's spirit or fire. Where her hair was pale brown, his was a vivid jet black. Her features were fine but uninspiring. Her head seemed permanently bent in either shyness or prayer. Edward was also fair, with the solid girth and straight back of a wise man of affairs. Neither had Thomas's twinkling eyes.

Smiling politely, if somewhat stiffly, I assured Seymour of my happiness as Latimer's wife.

"But surely you are married yourself, such an eligible bachelor?"

"What need have I of marriage, Katherine?" His smile was more honest than mine.

I flushed to catch his meaning. As possibly the most handsome man at Court, Thomas Seymour certainly had no need of marriage bonds to lure young women into bed.

Laughing, I smarted, "You must have many hearts in your possession."

"None that I want long enough." He sighed. We shared a fleeting moment of understanding, before I was obliged to return to Latimer. Willy wished to introduce me to the King.

"Your majesty." Willy bent her knees. "Do you know this charming lady?"

King Henry VIII, the man we all revered and held in awe, turned from his conversation with a courtier and stared down at me. He was a good figure of a man. The noble head sat atop strong wide shoulders, and he was adorned in the most sumptuous purple-and-gold clothing, albeit the occasion was a funeral.

King Henry held out his hand. I bent to kiss the back of his ringed fingers, trembling in my humility and excitement to be thus introduced.

"I don't believe I do, young Catherine."

Willy piped in, pleased with herself, "Why, this is Lady Latimer, of Snape Hall in Yorkshire, wife of John Neville. Her parents were your old friends Sir Thomas and Maude Parr. Now do you remember?"

Willy spoke with a light teasing tone, and the King appeared content with her company.

The King smiled at me, and I smiled in return. Queen Anne stared at us from behind. I felt the jealous darts from her glare. No doubt she distrusted all women at Court, particularly those not heavily pregnant. I wondered idly whether the King had a new mistress yet, now that Anne had become Queen.

To my surprise, King Henry patted me on the head, commenting on my pretty fair hair.

Willy put in, "You would admire her for her mind, if you had a chance to engage her in conversation."

"Come now, Baroness Willoughby," the King chortled. He enjoyed the sport of bantering with pretty young ladies. "I thought you were the only lady I loved for her mind!"

At which we all three tittered. Latimer came over proudly to lay his claim, bowing low to the King, forgetting for this moment his argument with his royal majesty.

Yet as Latimer walked me aside, he whispered, "Now who is the Duke of Suffolk going to make his lady wife? That's the next question. And who will King Henry *let* him marry?"

I chided my husband. "John Neville! How could you talk about his next wife when they have not yet buried the first? I thought Brandon was supposed to be in love with Mary Tudor?"

"Aye. But he loves power and prestige more."

Chapter 23

I t can't be true, Willy. You are but fifteen years of age! The position is far too grand . . . oh!"

"Brandon intends to marry me," my friend said dully in my fine chamber at Snape.

"You mean Brandon the younger, then?" I searched for an easy answer that would make *me* more comfortable.

Willy sniggered at my girlish comment.

"I wouldn't be here if I meant my own fiancé, would I? The Duke of Suffolk, my guardian, my keeper, informed me yesterday that he and I are to be married next week. I am to be the Duchess of Suffolk."

Her brave smile and jovial laugh dissolved into tears as she sobbed into a silk handkerchief.

"Oh, Willy. You can't be the Duchess of Suffolk."

"I have to. Brandon owns me, if you recall. He bought my wardship. Houses, property, cattle, and lady!" She laughed bitterly.

"What are you going to do?"

"Either marry him or run away. Which do you think I should do?"

Then she rolled over on her back, kicked her delicately shod feet so that her shoes of Spanish leather fell off, revealing beige hose of the finest silk, and stretched and yawned as though ready to fall asleep. We had only just begun our discussion when a stern-faced Latimer stormed unannounced into our chamber.

"Delia has informed me of your visit, Baroness Willoughby. I must tell you how shocked I am to see you in my home in this ungracious manner."

"Neville, please don't be hard on Willy. She had to come see me. She needed someone to speak to urgently."

"That's all very well, Katherine." He eyed me fiercely. "But as Lord Latimer, I cannot be seen accepting wild and impetuous young women who ride dangerously through the moorlands in the dead of night."

Willy stood, now obviously embarrassed. "Lord Latimer, please accept my deepest apologies for embarrassing you in this way. I never thought of what it might mean to you. I know I have brought disgrace on myself and my own family. I trust I have not so inflicted your own noble selves."

Willy stood before my husband, a woebegone figure in her simple cotton cambric dress, her hands clenched tightly together. Her long dark hair fell over her slender face, the rich ruby mouth was turned downward in a miserable gesture. Somehow, I knew Latimer would not be able to keep his bad temper in the face of such a pathetic sight.

"What does Baroness Willoughby intend to do, Katherine?"

I glanced sideways at Willy. We had reached no decision, but I knew as well as she there was only one answer.

"She will stay with us tonight, if not for a few days, as our most welcome guest. Then she will return to Grimsthorpe, in our carriage, where Catherine will gratefully accept the hand of her revered guardian, Charles Brandon, in marriage."

"Is this true, Baroness Willoughby?" he asked, his mood now changed by our humble attitude and Willy's demure and vulnerable pose.

She kept her head down as she whispered, "Yes, sire."

"Then all is well. You may stay as my guest. I will chide you no more."

"Oh, Neville," I said happily, as I ran to his side and put my arms around his waist. "Thank you. Willy has suffered enough without your taking arms too."

My husband looked down at my face. I saw water in his eyes too. "I know, dear wife. But you young women should take more care."

Willy raised her face to smile gratefully at both of us. She spoke in a rather nervous, teary voice.

"I know I shall be very happy as the Duchess of Suffolk. I look forward to welcoming you to his, I mean *our*, home."

She bowed to Latimer. He took her hand and kissed it—perhaps too long.

That night, when Latimer came to our chamber, after a splendid evening in which our dinner had been liberally laced by delicious red wines from France, I ran about the room laughing and acting wild. I was determined to stir up some feelings in him for *me*.

"So you would have Baroness Willoughby in my place tonight, would you, dear husband?" I teased, as I pulled at his cravat and watched the silk drop to the floor. Then I stripped him of his velvet doublet. I always loved him best when he wore that black velvet jacket. I began to unbutton the tiny pearl buttons that fastened the front of his shirt.

"And what makes you say that, jealous wife?"

"Just the look in your eyes. I haven't seen you look my way so intently in a long time."

"I should make you jealous more often. I appreciate the display of passion, young Katherine."

Serious for a minute, as I rubbed my hands up and down his bare back I asked, "Am I not passionate enough with you, Neville? Please tell me. You know I love you, but maybe I forget to show it."

But he shook his head sadly. "How do I know your fancy has not been attracted by a younger swain than I?"

"Never, never," I stormed, as though deeply wounded. I kissed him from his bulging Adam's apple right down to his navel, unbuckling the belt that held his breeches. I continued right down to that thick thatch of hair above his groin.

Latimer treated me well that night. Lying by his side, sleepless, thinking about Willy, I wondered if secretly she was not excited at the thought of marrying Brandon. There was something attractive in the man's sheer confidence and brash power.

Willy was married, amid much pomp and splendor, to the fiery Charles Brandon, Duke of Suffolk, on July 21 in the year 1533. Soon after, the Court was rocked by another momentous event—the birth of Princess Elizabeth. King Henry's *son* by Queen Anne turned out to be a daughter.

Willy was at Court for the birth. As the Duchess of Suffolk, she was one of the most important ladies in the land. She told me that King Henry had been stalking around the birth room for hours, while Anne was in labor. He shouted and carried on with his courtiers about the enormous welcome he was going to give his son.

> *Dearest Kate, you can imagine the confusion when the King's physician announced that the babe was a healthy and beautiful little girl! We all recoiled in horror and ran to our rooms, to avoid the King. Anne began to sob when she learned her fate and would not see the baby. King Henry refused to visit his wife, believing she had let him down on purpose. The ladies of the bedchamber were very subdued by his behavior. No one knew what to do.*
>
> *Eventually we learned that the baby was to be christened Elizabeth, after the King's much-loved mother. Once he had seen the baby, and held her in his arms, he softened. Now he seems to dote on the little princess. She's really rather a sweet little thing. She looks quite like the old devil himself, with gingery red hair crowning a sharp-featured face. She yells well, which must mean she takes after him!*
>
> *In the end Queen Anne gave up sobbing. One of her ladies says she is determined to get with child again as quickly as possible. It does seem strange that the King should only get daughters, doesn't it? But there is time! Your loving friend, Willy.*

In the spring, we received a formal invitation to visit the Brandons at Grimsthorpe. I begged Latimer to go. But he was vague, and would only talk about being too busy for social occasions. Knowing how badly I wanted to see Willy, he gave me permission to travel alone. Although I argued against leaving him, it was true I needed to get away more than he did. Delia agreed to come away this time, as well as Mary Chamberlain. Will Bryant would be our driver. I felt warm and comfortable with my friends. I kissed Latimer on the forehead as he sat poring over his books and thanked him for being so understanding.

"Get along with you, Katherine. You are young yet, and need more from society than do I. Don't ever say I held you prisoner here."

"I would never perjure myself in such a way!" I cried. "You know how happy I am here at Snape."

Once in the carriage, Delia put her arm around my shoulders. We sang most of the way like silly young girls.

⁘

Willy rushed to greet us. She was anxious, much paler and thinner than when we had last met. Trying to be gracious and charming, I greeted her as the Duchess of Suffolk. I commented on her good complexion and how married life seemed to suit her.

Willy grimaced and raised her hands in the air, as if in disbelief.

"It's fine, if you can overcome the fact my fiancé hung himself six months after I married his father, and that my stepdaughters, Frances and Eleanor, will not speak to me.

"The Duke of Suffolk," she went on rather grandiosely, "has been called back to London to speak to the King. I have no idea what is going on," she added mysteriously, "but I have my suspicions that it has to do with Queen Catherine."

Horses galloping up the long driveway to Grimsthorpe and the noise of Brandon's hasty nighttime return interrupted our visit.

"Where's my wife?" he bellowed, as he stormed through the doors. He kicked over stools and anything that lay in his path. "Where's the girl?"

Willy ran down the stairs, in obvious disarray. "I'm here, my lord. I'm here. Is anything amiss?"

"Amiss?" he yelled at the top of his lungs as if to an assembled crowd. "Amiss, the girl asks! When I've been stuck with that battleaxe of Aragon for three days!"

I froze to hear him speak so.

"God's dowry," he fumed, quieting now. "That woman is a fool. As obstinate as an ass. The King has given her an easy way out—but will she take it? No! '*I am the Queen, and will remain so*,' " he said, mimicking a woman's voice. "The woman's at death's door and here am I, sent by the King to denude her of her queenly title, pomp, retinue, and any extra she's been incurring all these years. My God, wife, how can she continue to say she's the Queen? Not only does Henry have *another* Queen, alive, well, and probably pregnant, but they even have a princess charming the pants off the whole of London! Bring me some brandy, woman, hurry up."

So saying, he slapped Willy across her behind and sent her scurrying off to find a servant—for they all had hidden themselves till the storm settled.

Delia, Mary, and I made quiet haste to depart the next morning, at crack of dawn, not wanting to be around with Brandon in such temper.

I had decided to leave without letting Willy know, and Will Bryant had already set the carriage in motion when, to my consternation, our carriage door was forced open and a cloaked figure stood in the open doorway. Fear gripped my soul.

"Let me in, Kate, let me in," whispered a gruff but distinctly feminine voice. A hand came out from under the folds of the cloak, tender, gentle, and beringed. It was obviously the hand of my friend. Without stopping to think, I grabbed her hand and, even as the carriage moved away, pulled her into our midst.

"What are you doing? He'll never accept this, Willy."

But she kept herself covered and grunted, "I know, I know, but I cannot stay."

After a short silence, she added, "Whatever will my mother say? My own husband has more or less taken the life of her friend Queen Catherine. He has forbidden her ever to see Princess Mary again! What will this do to Dame Maria?"

Willy wept silently in her corner of the carriage, while Delia wiped her brow and soothed her.

"Never mind, luv," said kind, sensible Delia. "You can come with us. Even if Latimer don't like it, we'll see he takes you in."

Beating on the front of the carriage, I indicated to Will Bryant to drive faster.

The ride continued only half an hour. We were no more than a few miles beyond Grimsthorpe's gates, Willy still hidden in wraps, when I heard horses' hooves behind us and loud shouts of "whoa" as a group of men rode up and surrounded the carriage. Bryant argued but pulled our horses to a stop.

The door on my side was rapped sharply. Will Bryant tried to stay the hand at the door, defending his ladies as best he could. But the door was pulled open and Brandon's head appeared, black with evil temper.

"Where is she?" he demanded, peering inside. He pulled her brusquely from the carriage and flung her on his saddle before him.

"That'll be all, driver. You may go on," Brandon called rudely. He threw a few coins at Will Bryant, who in turn cast them onto the dusty road behind Brandon's horse as it cantered back to Grimsthorpe.

Delia, Mary, and I stared at each other in silence. Will Bryant came to the door and popped his head around. "Did you know her, then?"

Shaking my head, I commanded, "Drive on, Will. Please let us get home fast."

"By the Lord in heaven, Lady Latimer," said Delia quietly. "I hope the young Duchess of Suffolk will be all right. I know what it's like to run afoul of a man in a temper like that."

Chapter 24

Lord Latimer called me into his library that afternoon to announce, "King Henry has passed a new Act of Supremacy, declaring Princess Elizabeth his successor, stating Princess Mary has no claim to the throne. I know I forewarned you of such events, but now the King has made things much harder for the northern gentry.

"He is demanding the peerage take an Oath of Allegiance. We must declare the King our supreme earthly authority and vow that we accept the validity of his marriage to Queen Anne, and her child as his royal successor."

Latimer coughed dryly, as if he felt unwell. Then he added, "You must know, dear wife, that I cannot take such an oath, ever. Even if it meant my life."

I cried to hear such words and dropped to my knees before him. "Latimer, please, never say such a thing. You would not treat your life so carelessly?"

"It is with deepest sadness I say I cannot take such an oath, before God, when the words would be untruths."

"But, husband, what will become of us?"

"I don't know." He sighed. "That's why I have met again

with D'Arcy. As you know, he is not a devout Catholic, yet he and many other reformists join me in their dislike of the King. We have agreed to join forces. We will take action if it proves necessary.

"Think, Kate, about your own response. If the King calls upon me to take the oath, he may expect you to do likewise, as my wife."

Was I too to be forced into a position of moral choice? Memories flashed before me—the death of Old Nell, my decision not to join Megan when she ran away from Borough. My lies to Kaitlin Neville. My secret reading of Luther's book.

✢

There was no word from Willy, though we heard that she was with child. Brandon was confidently expecting the birth of a son in September. Then, along with the rest of the nation, we had to stomach the tragic news of the execution of our beloved Sir Thomas More, who, along with the Bishop of Rochester, was led to the scaffold because he could not swear to the Oath of Allegiance for the King: not when it meant accepting King Henry as supreme head of Church and State.

Maybe it was the air of tragedy or perhaps the news of Willy's pregnancy, but the idea of her motherhood brought back distant memories for me. *How old would that baby of mine be now? Nearly five years old? How had Liza and Stephen fared? Why had I never gotten with child as Latimer's wife?*

For some time now, I had relaxed the use of my herbs. Knowing he would probably not live as long as I, I found myself dreaming of bearing Latimer's child. I began to dread the arrival of the bleed, as a mark of my failure. Latimer had seldom referred to our lack of children. But the thought of the child in Oxenholme filled me with guilt and remorse. Maybe it was my punishment not to bear any more.

Then, finally, in the new year, a long letter came from

Willy, full of news and gossip, the sort of letter to cheer me out of my winter doldrums.

Dearest Kate, You must of course have learned of the sad death of Queen Catherine in Kimbolton Castle. I wonder if you know that Dame Maria actually managed to be with her dying friend at the end. Yes, my mother, for all her age and timidity, defied the King's ruling and rode alone to the castle, on the night of New Year's Eve, demanded entry, and was able to hold poor Catherine of Aragon's hand as she passed on from this miserable life.

The King and Queen Anne acted most horrendously, however, at the news of Catherine's death. Or maybe it was just that desperate woman Anne Boleyn. She dressed herself and the toddling Princess Elizabeth in bright yellow, and danced ostentatiously the night the news was announced.

I had the honor of leading the mourners for the former Queen's funeral. We made our way from Kimbolton Castle—a terrifying place if ever you saw one—down an ancient secret route known as Bygrame's Lane, to the city of Peterborough. There, with my mother and stepsisters, we at least gave her a sincere burial. My husband was busy elsewhere.

Back in London, I was told that the King respected his former wife's funeral, but that Queen Anne—for her punishment?—was taken to her bed, where she miscarried her second pregnancy. Would you believe this, Kate, the midwives let it be known that the dead infant was a son!

You should know that the King has already made it obvious he has turned against Queen Anne. He pretends to suspect her of unfaithful behavior. But I feel that is a cover for his own sins in wooing the plain, dowdy maid of honor Jane Seymour—sister to Edward and Thomas Seymour, my dear. Why he has chosen Mistress Seymour of all the ladies at Court, who would die to be at his side, I don't know. But Anne is certainly showing her dislike of the state of affairs. She sulks before everyone, alternating those moody times with fits of hysterical gaiety. What will become of her?

With fondest memories, dear Kate. Someday soon, you must come and see my darling little boy Henry, such a little tease he is. Your loving friend, Catherine Willoughby, Duchess of Suffolk.

Queen Anne's fate was all too plain. News soon began to reach us. In May, warrants of arrest were sent out for several men with whom Queen Anne was known to be friendly. They included her brother Sir George Boleyn and our friend Sir Thomas Wyatt. Anne's brother and four other men were executed: Francis Weston, one of Henry's pages; William Brereton, a gentleman of Henry's privy chamber; Henry Norris, the King's favorite courtier and the one man he had always trusted in his own bedchamber; and Mark Smeaton, a musician and dancer. Their heads were left dangling over London Bridge.

On May 19, Queen Anne Boleyn was beheaded as a traitor. King Henry had signed her death warrant that same day, and sent Cranmer to receive her last confession. She was taken out of the Tower to Cranmer's lodgings in Lambeth, where she was asked to resign her title of Queen and give up her precious daughter Elizabeth's right of succession. Anne gave in, believing she would be offered clemency in return.

A second letter arrived from Willy giving me an eyewitness account. She had heard the details from Mary Wyatt, one of Queen Anne's serving maids who was in her attendance to the end.

> *Anne awaited her beheading calmly and heard with some measure of relief that the King had ordered a special executioner from France, who was supposed to be quick and clean, using a keen-edged sword rather than the usual blunt ax.*
>
> *No one at Court believed the King would follow through his sentence. Not only would he be putting a crowned Queen to death, but this would be the first time a woman had been beheaded. Not even our cruel ancestors have ever sunk so low as to take the blood of a woman so wantonly!*
>
> *When Anne emerged from the portals of the Tower, led by Sir William Kingston, she was dressed in a robe of black damask, with a deep white cape flowing over it. Instead of her customary pointed black velvet hood edged with pearls, the Queen wore a small hat with ornamented coifs hanging below.*

She said goodbye to Mary Wyatt and her favorite ladies, giving Mary a little book of her devotions, which the girl promised to keep in her bosom forever. These ladies then covered Anne's eyes with a bandage, and withdrew crying while the Queen knelt with her head over the scaffold. As the swordsman brought down the blade, she cried out "Oh, Lord God, have pity on my soul!"

The executioner was prepared to cart the body away, as is custom. But Mary and the other ladies, despite the fact they were faint to see the mangled heap of their mistress and so much blood shed, pushed aside the assistants and wiped the blood from Anne's face and hair.

They took the bleeding head and body and wrapped them in cloths, placing them carefully and lovingly in a chest. They walked with the men to the church where the coffin was to be interred. Queen Anne was given no ceremony for her burial, but was placed alongside her brother in the churchyard.

I hope the King will be a happier man now. The day after Queen Anne's execution, King Henry and Jane Seymour were formally betrothed at a house in Chelsea. God Save our new monarch, Queen Jane. In sorrow, your loving friend, Willy.

Chapter 25

I t was Midsummer's Eve. Latimer and I rode in our carriage from Snape Hall to Grimsthorpe for a celebration in honor of Henry VIII's triumphant marriage to his Queen Jane.

This was my twenty-third year. I felt at my most beautiful, most self-confident, and although I still had no child, at my most feminine.

I looked across at Latimer. He sat with his arms folded

across his belly, his head slumped in sleep. I loved John Neville dearly, but I wondered what more there could be to love and marriage. He had noticeably aged over this past year. Or was it I myself growing older?

Maybe it was the summer flowers or the bright green grass in the meadows, where tiny little white lambs played with their mothers in the warm June sunshine, but I wriggled with repressed excitement.

We pulled in at dusk to the manor house. Boys and girls ran around our carriage wheels, and crowds of people in their finery stood on the lawns immediately before the house. Carriages, horses, carts, and fancy litters were parked together in a meadow cordoned off for the purpose. I tapped Latimer on the elbow and told him we had arrived.

Startled, and somewhat irritated, he grunted awake, "If Brandon is too ridiculous, Kate, we are leaving."

"Just give me some time to enjoy myself," I pleaded. "It is ages since I have been to a banquet, or to a fine gathering."

The look in my husband's eye told me he felt this was one of the burdens of having a young wife. We were ushered into the house by a young steward decked out in green and white, garlands of flowers around his head. The evening smelled warm and dewy, fragrant with flower scents and mulled wine. We were led to our chambers.

Later, half-dragging Latimer behind me, I descended the stairs, feeling proud of myself in a pure white gown of finest silk, embroidered with tiny pearls. The gown was fine, so wafer-thin it floated on the warm summer breezes, flattering my slender form. I was not unaware of the spectacle I made walking at Latimer's side. His height, his stature, his commanding presence, offset by strong wide shoulders and crowned by that thatch of silvery black hair, made him the image of a nobleman, a perfect foil to my own delicately pale stature.

I emerged, as Latimer's wife, a self-confident woman, with a graceful elegance, a fine interesting face, kind eyes, and a thick mane of beautiful blond hair that poured down my back in abandon. I knew I would be noticed, that Lady Latimer would be admired.

Passing through the great hall, which was filled by dull-looking people, I stepped out onto the lawn where the groups of fiddlers, jugglers, mummers, and their happy talk lured me.

"There are D'Arcy and Megan," Latimer said in my ear. "Who's that man holding Megan's arm?"

I turned to look in his direction, and my heart missed several beats. The man holding Megan's arm was none other than her brother, my former lover, Henry Borough, Lord Strickland.

My heart fluttered up and down. It was five years since that time I had so hastily left Sizergh Castle. In the following months, I had spent some time dreaming of our "lost love," but as the years passed and I had grown used to the comfort of Latimer's mature love, I had learned to disparage Henry in my mind.

I cried out involuntarily, sweat breaking out on my forehead. But Latimer had moved forward to greet his friends. He shook hands with D'Arcy, kissed Megan warmly on the cheek, and stood back waiting to be introduced.

Megan sensed nothing of my alarm. She greeted Latimer with genuine happiness and held Henry Borough forth. "Lord Latimer, this is my brother, Henry Borough, Lord Strickland of Sizergh. You must have heard of him from Katey. We were once all together at my father's home in Gainsborough, and then Katey lived with Lord and Lady Strickland for a short while before her marriage to you, Neville."

Latimer stared at Megan. I stared at Henry. We were all unsure of what to say next.

My face flushed crimson. My white silk dress no longer felt so charming and utterly divine. I felt tawdry and commonplace. Megan was embarrassed, realizing too late what she had said.

Henry looked different. A youthful idealistic innocence had once shone through those blue eyes, making the pale strong face look like that of a classical god. His fair hair had been thick and lustrous. I had loved to brush it back with my hands. Henry Borough had been a boy-man when I had met and loved him. Now, after years of marriage to Kaitlin Neville, he looked like a man who had suffered and changed. His once classical face had filled out. The pale ivory skin had become flushed with too much wine. The good bone structure was disguised by folds of fatty flesh. Henry did not even look as tall to me as he once had. His body had bowed, no doubt under the weight of his worries and compromises. There was a slackness around his belly, which even Latimer did not have, for my husband took good care of himself.

"Lord and Lady Latimer, it is indeed a great pleasure."

Henry Borough bowed neatly, nearly spilling the wine from a pewter cup he held in one hand.

My husband bowed. I offered a hand to Henry in formal style.

"Henry, it is an enormous pleasure to see you again." I searched for words. "I have often wished to catch up on how your life has been since we last met at Sizergh. Is my cousin Kaitlin here with you?"

Henry gave me a sly smile. "Of course, Lady Latimer. My wife is over there somewhere, talking with the Duchess of Suffolk, whom I believe you know very well."

Latimer saved us both further embarrassment, obviously determined to steer me away.

"My wife has yet to greet the Duchess of Suffolk. We are newly arrived. I feel it would be impolite for us to stay talking any longer. Though of course we will both look forward to meeting Lord and Lady Strickland as the evening progresses."

So saying, Latimer put an arm around my waist and spirited me away. "Well, Katherine?" he asked, as we were out of hearing. "How does Henry Borough strike your fancy now?"

I smiled at him. "Don't worry. I am no longer in love. He does not look so good now, does he?"

"Decidedly the worse for wear, or is it for drink?"

"Both, I fear. He and Kaitlin were not exactly a love match. I wonder how he has been."

"I would rather you find that out from Megan Borough, if you know what I mean. I do not like to appear jealous, for it is not an emotion I approve of, but I will not have you publicly talking with Henry Borough."

I nodded, remembering that many people knew why Latimer had married me in such haste.

As Latimer and I walked over to a group which included Willy, we were surrounded by a gang of giggling young people who took me by surprise.

"Why, Anne, darling!" I cried, and flung my arms around my sister, whom I had not seen since Queen Anne's coronation party.

While Anne and I kissed, and held each other at arm's length for greater admiration, I said, "Don't tell me brother William is here too?"

"No, Kate. He would not come. He is so 'in' with the King, now he has been made Marquis of Northampton. He refuses to go anywhere Henry is not—a waste of his time, I dare say!"

As we talked, Latimer vanished from my side, leaving me free to mingle with the other folks. Anne pointed out many personages I might otherwise have missed. There was the young and handsome Henry Fitzroy, now elevated to William's former title, Earl of Essex, and his rather blowsy wife, Mary Howard, a relative of Anne Boleyn's. Then my sister pointed to a group of handsome, stylish young men, all dressed in the finest, most elegant fashion, laughing loudly, obviously all unattached.

Anne teased me, "Katey, they're not for you. A respectable married lady, from the North country! They are the new favorites of the King. The two tallest ones, see them leaning against the tree, are Queen Jane's brothers. The grayhaired one is Edward Seymour, whom the King seems to favor greatly; and the young dark-haired one, that's Thomas Seymour, whom *all* women adore." Anne giggled again.

As she chattered on, I was silent, preferring to watch out of the corner of my eye the antics of the King's favorites. My young soul had taken flight at the mere sight of Thomas Seymour. Maybe this was where my dreams lay? An affair with someone dashing, handsome, unattached . . . dangerous?

I stood for a long while, after Anne moved on. Men and women were huddled behind trees, in clumps of bushes, behind pagodas, and they did not seem to be in the clinches of husband and wife. If a young woman, or a couple of young women, walked past a group of courtiers, they were whistled at, talked to, sometimes even forcibly stopped. One of the men approached a beautiful dark-haired girl whose bosom was cut very low and left little to the imagination. She giggled nervously and playfully, slapping away his hand. But the man took no notice. Pretty soon he picked the girl off her feet and the last I saw of them was when they disappeared into a wood at the edge of the meadow.

The evening smells were strong as the scents of honeysuckle and meadowsweet fought with the odor of foodstuffs on the laden trestle tables, of spices from the mulled wine, of sweets and perfumes. I realized I was suffering from spring fever and it had obviously overcome my brain. I began to feel quite faint from the atmosphere.

How I wished some man would pay me ungallant court! I longed for male arms that would entwine my body with uncontrolled ardor. I was overly used to the supportive arms of my husband, who did not always need the desires of my young body.

The night shadows played tricks on my eyes and left me imagining people all around.

Then a shadowy figure emerged from the trees, disturbing my reverie. I was all set to walk quickly away, embarrassed to be so caught, but a hand shot out and grabbed my own.

"Katherine?"

"Yes?"

The fingers held mine tightly. I could not wriggle free. It was not Henry Borough. This stranger was dark, not fair.

"You never gave me another chance to race."

"Please, sir, the night is so dark. I cannot see your face."

Then he laughed, and I felt a flush rise from my toes to my head.

"Don't you still owe me a horserace?" he teased, now pulling at my hand so that I seemed to move imperceptibly closer to him.

"Thomas Seymour! Please let go of my hand. I must return to my husband and friends."

"Not before you have spoken to me, Katherine. Whatever happened to you that night at Sizergh? There was such drama going on. Henry sobbing his heart out. Kaitlin shouting. Latimer storming off into the night on horseback. Lord above! I had no idea passions were so strong in Westmoreland. I missed you later that night. And of course no one would speak a word of truth to *me*.

"The next thing I heard was you had married that old bore Latimer. . . ."

"He is not a bore. He's a very kind and loving man who

rescued me from . . . well, I cannot tell you. But he stepped in to offer me marriage, and freedom from Kaitlin's grasp." I tried to sound lighthearted, though he was still holding my hand and my heart was working extra hard.

"I've missed you, Katherine." His words scarcely registered, for they were the last sentiments I ever expected to hear from this courtly ladies' man. Surely he had no need to seduce me, to add Lady Latimer to his conquests?

"Thomas!" I was trying to free myself, though the attempt was feeble. "Don't you think we have held hands long enough for a greeting?"

He pulled me till I fell against him, smelling the musky scent of lusty manhood. My nose sank into his black velvet doublet. I was overcome by the aroma, by the power of this man. I did not want to draw my face away. I wanted to rest there, to absorb his smell and being, to become part of him. Tears filled my eyes to think what my husband would say if he could see me. I leaned back, finally righting myself.

I tried to make polite conversation, congratulating him on his sister's marriage to the King.

"Every woman's dream come true!" He winked at me.

"But her position must have secured your importance, and your brother Edward's."

"I am not complaining," he said casually, with the ease of success. "The only one who might complain would be Anne Boleyn!"

"Shh!" I cried involuntarily. "You cannot speak thus." I had noticed that at this smart gathering no one mentioned the name of Queen Anne. She had done wrong, and met her rightful punishment. Now she was forgotten. But Thomas Seymour was a man who seemed to obey no rules.

He shrugged those broad shoulders.

"I am not here to discuss my sister." Thomas was considerably taller than I. He leaned over and brushed his face in my hair, whispering, "You know I was always attracted to you."

"No, I didn't know."

Still whispering, he crooned in my hair, entwining his fingers in my locks. "So pretty, so very pretty." He sighed. "I think I was nearly struck off my horse that day in Westmoreland when I met the wild young filly astride her own horse. I carry that picture of you with me at all times—the heather, the scent of fresh grasses, the wind in your hair, your sweet unaffected face."

I gasped, incapable of taking in his meaning. Is this how a ladies' man seduces a vulnerable soul? He certainly knew how to succeed.

His strong arms were about my shoulders, caressing the silk dress and my bare flesh, as though he genuinely enjoyed the sensation.

Thomas was more mature than I had remembered him, more handsome. He was more solid, strong and determined. Even his face was fuller and better defined. The dark hair remained long and curled below his ears. He had kept the thick lustrous beard. The mysterious brooding eyes shone difficult and impenetrable. The lines around his mouth were more marked, for he was a man of humor.

Without breaking the spell, Thomas leaned farther over and brought his sensitive beautiful mouth down upon mine. Even before our lips met, I knew my own had parted to greet his. I knew deep down there was no holding myself back. Touching him about the waist, I felt we fit together. How was it possible to feel something so right when I knew it was wrong?

Thomas's mouth blended with my own. He did not force himself upon me, but drew me out. Within seconds I was kissing him back, my lips begging for more, my tongue gingerly reaching out to accept his. He plunged his tongue down into my hungry mouth. I let myself go and devoured, explored, tasted, the smoothness of his mouth. I could have expired on the spot.

"Will you walk with me over there?" He nodded his head in the direction of a thicket, a small copse of trees into which I had noticed young men leading their companions during the evening. It was obvious why a man would take a girl there, obvious I would consent. Finding words impossible, I merely nodded, dumb, overpowered by my feelings.

His strong arms held me tight about the shoulders. We stumbled, for my dress caught on brambles and twigs. I knew the grass was staining the hem at this very minute. Thomas pushed his way through the trees, smiling at the other couples making love on the dewy ground.

"Do you mind all this?" He turned to look at me. Now I was able to smile back at him. I shook my head.

"Just let me forget who I am for a short while."

He laughed genially, patting me on the behind. Then he snatched me into his arms, bruising me as he pulled me tight to his chest. My feet lifted off the ground.

"Oh, Kate, may I call you Kate? I am half mad for you, don't you realize?"

"But we have only met a few times."

"Are you sorry to be with me now?"

I shook my head, silent for a moment. A fear had flitted across my mind.

"Never ever tell a soul about this, will you? I know you have a reputation with the ladies. But I am not one of them. I have never dallied from my husband before . . . but I do feel very strongly, and . . . oh, Thomas Seymour, kiss me!"

He picked me up in his arms and walked with me deeper into the woods, until we were free of the noises and sights of other passionate couples. He placed me on the grass, then stripped off his doublet and laid it under me.

"Are you cold?"

I teased him now. "I thought it was the wild me that so attracted you. What would you do if I complained?"

"Probably very much the same as I intend to do now." He sat down beside me and placed a hand on my bare neck. His eyes were more hooded than usual, his mouth red from our kissing. The very slow and unhurried way he moved made me desire him so badly I almost took hold of his hand and pushed it down to my breast. But I dared not be so forward. Thomas was a man in control. I trusted him. And waited.

While we talked his long fingers played with the soft skin around my neck. He let them glide under my hair and around to my chin, tracing patterns on my face, brushing them over my lips. I licked his fingers, and his eyes lit up.

"Would you have more of me tonight?"

Already I was moist between my legs, and my heart was beating wildly beneath the thin silk.

"Are you offering more?"

His hand now slid down and traced the outline of the dress over my breasts.

"Thomas!" I groaned. "Please, please, don't make me wait any longer."

So saying I had unleashed the fire. He suddenly fell upon me, his mouth eating the silk that covered the flesh of my bosom until it was sodden. His hands stroked my back, my thighs, my buttocks. I was flat on the damp ground, wriggling and squirming, waiting and anxious. He pushed the dress up above my knees and to my infinite joy found his way between my thighs under the lawn garments. Sliding long thin fingers beneath the flimsy cotton, he stroked the outside of my greedy, urgent skin until my back arched. Calling his name, I begged for more. Finally with a cry I fell in a small heap at his side, sprawled across the doublet, my dress up over my shoulders, heaving a final sigh. Biting Thomas fiercely on the ear, I curled in his arms and melted into his heart.

"Dear sweet Kate," he murmured in my ear, helping me take off the dress so that it would not be further disheveled. He led my hand over to the belt and buckle of his breeches, and I needed no encouragement to discover his ardor. Thomas might have been my leader, but I wanted to make him happy too. He had freed me of many inhibitions, released a power of passion and energy, so it was my turn to rip and pull at his clothing, pushing up his shirt, tugging it over his shoulders and head. Cradling his face against the cotton of my petticoats, I knelt and stroked the thick glossy black hair, caressed the firm muscular back, carving patterns down his spine, admiring the strength of those broad shoulders.

"You're so beautiful," I whispered to him.

Though I wanted to make love to him, he stopped me. Laying me back on the doublet, he knelt by my prone body and began to kiss me from chin to the top of my thighs, and before I knew it I was lost again up the mountainside of pleasure. He buried his face under the petticoats, losing himself in the fine reddish hair that nestled between my legs. He kissed me, his tongue forcing its way deep inside me. Then, crudely, he rolled me over, pulled me so I knelt, and, finding his place with one of those long fingers, entered me from behind, rocking me back and forth on his knees. I closed my eyes, taking in the peculiar mix of evening fresh cool air, green leaves of summer, earthly smells of nature, and the perfumes of our courtly selves, all blending together to create the strongest aphrodisiac imaginable.

We slept like babes for some time. In fear, I realized I must get back to the house. Latimer would be looking for me.

Thomas lay satisfied, with a grin on his face.

"Well, Kate, shall we be lovers then?"

I wanted to hit him. *How could he say it so simply?* Already the implications of this night's actions were flooding over me.

What was I going to say to Latimer? How could I even dream of becoming mistress to another man?

"You don't really want me for a lover, Thomas Seymour," I cried. "You have made your conquest and can mark up another too-willing wife to your tally." Pulling on my dress, I tried to clean myself with bundles of grass and dried leaves. I ran from him noiselessly across the meadow back to the party.

✢

Willy let me into her chamber. She was there talking to the wet nurse about her new baby. She asked me no questions, but I told her as much as I could with the sheepish look in my eye. She patted my back.

"You're a brave girl, Kate."

"Stupid, you mean. I had to, Willy. Wait till you're my age."

I ran down the stairs and through the great hall, trying to find Latimer without looking foolish. I hoped not to meet with anyone I knew—not Henry Borough nor Megan, nor my sister Anne. But, of course, as I crossed the great hall whom should I see but Kaitlin Neville with Henry Borough, collecting their cloaks for departure.

"Kate!" called Henry. "Come and greet Kaitlin."

His wife rather noticeably turned her back. I bit my lips; I really had no patience with all this. I said, "Have you seen Latimer, Henry? I've been searching for him."

"He was looking for you some time back." My erstwhile lover gazed at me with a frown that implied: What have you been up to?

"I've been talking with Willy about her baby for quite some time. He must wonder where I am."

I knew Henry wanted to talk to me. The last thing I needed was to be trapped in a long conference with him.

As I was talking to Henry Borough, Latimer appeared at

the open doorway, looking disheveled and disgruntled. My heart skipped a beat in fear.

"Kate!" he thundered, not caring who heard what he said. He roared across to me, snatching my hand from Henry Borough's grip, and said, "I told you not to be seen speaking to this man."

"Neville!" I was shocked. "I have only just this minute met Henry and Lady Strickland." Though of course Kaitlin had disappeared, making my story appear false. "I have not been speaking with him. I merely stopped to ask if he had seen you. I have been looking everywhere for you."

"Oh, yes!" He sneered. "Then how come I have searched every nook and cranny of this house and gardens for the last hour?"

"I have been locked away with Willy, talking babies."

"I'll believe that when I see it." He was so angry, his cheeks had gone quite purple. "Come here, woman, we're going home."

With that, I was dragged from the hall. Everyone delightedly turned around to watch the scene.

Latimer pulled me behind him to the stables and ordered our carriage made ready. When I protested I had left my clothes in our chamber, Latimer would hear none of it. He even slapped my face to quiet me, something he had never done before.

Latimer was taking me home, but I did not care. I could make any man ecstatic with my body, even one so experienced as Thomas Seymour.

Once we had returned to Snape, I slipped up to our chamber, rather hoping to avoid a confrontation. I saw or heard nothing for the rest of that evening. With nightfall, I had a sense of relief that the storm had passed. Then the door was kicked open and in he marched, angry if ever I had seen a man angry. His shirt was unfastened. He held a wine goblet in his hand, a look of desperate concern on his face.

Latimer slammed the goblet down on a chest, spilling red wine over our rush matting. His face was dark with the clouds of torment.

"What has happened, Katherine?" he thundered in slow syllables.

"Nothing, I told you. I was merely talking to Willy."

"That is a lie, an outright lie. Did I not tell you I'd have none of you talking to Borough? And what do I find, after searching frantically for you, making myself a fool among Brandon's guests, but you and him talking? What am I supposed to believe but that you had disappeared for so long with *him*?"

I began to cry. "I was not with him. I do not even like him anymore. He's a drunken sop. Please, Latimer, do not hurt me . . . please believe me . . . I did nothing to shame you."

He pounced over to the bed and gripped my hand with such strength I watched the blood drain from it. Sniffling, like a dog cowering from its master, I begged, "Please, darling, get into bed. You are tired and maybe have drunk too much. I will show you how much I love you."

"I want none of your lovemaking, Katherine. Not if you have lied to me. . . . I cannot stand it. I loved you so much, to death, even, and you can be two-faced with me. I cannot take it . . . not that!"

His arm still gripped me, and I shook it, trying to release the pressure. At last, I stooped to kiss it and felt his grip relax.

"Please come to bed. I am sorry if I upset you. A wife is allowed a few mistakes, is she not? I should not have been gone so long. But Willy wanted to introduce me to some of her friends, and I didn't know how to say no."

At last he seemed to melt before me. I was feeling such shame and guilt . . . I had needed that journey into another man's heart and soul. Thomas Seymour was bold, young, driven, determined, and very skillful as a lover.

But I did love Latimer that night, and he me.

PART VI

Men
of the
North

Chapter 26

T he summer passed in a cloud of conflicting thoughts. Mostly I wanted to dream about love, to fantasize about Thomas Seymour. But politics continuously dragged me back to the reality of a country on the brink of civil war.

Megan Borough arranged clandestine meetings between me and Anne Askew, so I learned more about the feelings of the people. Anne informed me that her father, Sir William Askew, and my uncle, Sir William Parr, both of Horton in Lincolnshire, were helping the King raise money by taxing the people. One day in early October, a message was brought to me by Delia Turpin that Mistress Askew wished to speak to me in private.

I found Anne awaiting me in a private drawing room. Her face was pale and drawn.

"They've taken my father prisoner," she stated briefly. I knew she despised her father and was asking for no sympathy on his behalf. This news meant something greater.

"They've taken him before a mob of armed peasants up on Skipwith Moor, to be questioned about his work for the King."

We talked in secret. Anne returned to the D'Arcys', declaring we should join with the peasant folk on what was meant to be a march south to London. Before I could make any real plans, I was surprised by a commotion at the gates of Snape Hall.

Stable lads and servants were scurrying about, many of them leaving the gates. Suddenly my chamber door burst open and there stood a distraught Latimer, half dressed, with a kerchief around his neck and a jacket thrown over his shoulders.

"Come! You must get dressed as quickly as possible."

"Whatever is happening?"

Excitedly he explained, "Most of the populace of Yorkshire appears to be outside our gates. They demand I lead them in a march upon the King."

"Why you?" I cried, utterly cowardly, not wanting my husband to be so placed on the line.

Solemnly he pronounced, "If it is to be thus, then let it be so."

"Where are we going?" I gasped, as he took my elbow and pulled me from the room.

"To prepare ourselves. The people are going to join Robert Askew, who has led a great crowd to Skipwith Moor."

"That's where Anne Askew's father has been taken."

"I know, I know. Thousands are already converging on the moor. And we have hundreds outside our gates."

"Will you go as their leader, John Neville?" I searched his dark gray eyes with my own scared blue ones.

"Would you stop me, Kate?"

I tried to fight back tears, brushing at my eyes with the back of my hand as I spoke.

"I cannot stop you, my dear husband. But I wish we were not so placed. I am scared—very scared."

He took me in his arms and hugged me tightly. Kissing my unkempt hair, he stroked my back tenderly and whispered in my ear, "I wish I had been a better husband, Kate."

"Don't speak in the past tense. You have been and always will be the best and only husband I want."

"I wish that were true. I know you have desired more from me. But there has been so much to tend to these past few months . . ." I kissed him and tried to give him support.

"I must go now. Get yourself ready. Bring Delia or whoever will come. I shall try to persuade D'Arcy and some other true men of Yorkshire to come with us. Bring the horses and follow me to Skipwith Moor."

"Neville . . . don't go without me."

My husband marched down the elegant staircase of this home he had so lovingly built. He strode onto the front porch, then down the drive between my flower gardens to the yard, where Will Bryant waited with a saddled horse. As he mounted, the gates of Snape opened and a loud victorious roar was sent up by the mob. Within a few moments I could just barely see my husband amid a few other mounted men leading the procession of humble but determined peasants down the country lane away from this gentle Yorkshire valley.

With Latimer gone, I was thrown into a frenzy. I must contact Megan and Anne Askew.

But I had no time for words. A message came that Will Bryant was waiting at my husband's orders to be my guide to Skipwith. Lady D'Arcy and Anne Askew would meet us on the road a few furlongs hence. Lord D'Arcy had already hastened to join up with Latimer.

Our ladies' troupe, Megan, Anne, my recently returned stepdaughter Margaret Neville, Delia, and Mary Chamberlain, was several hours behind the men, but as we rode along the dry and dusty roads, we were never short of company. From every field, hut, or home streamed men and women, young and old, bearing staves or pitchforks. As we reached the lowlands before Skipwith Moor, we saw before us, like foam on the ocean, waves of men dressed in white, bearing hastily made banners portraying Jesus Christ, stained with blood symbolizing his wounds.

It was difficult to make out where the leaders were. But then an old man near our horses shouted, "There's Robert Askew!" And surely enough, astride a huge rock stood the unprepossessing figure of Askew, the self-styled Earl of Poverty. Calling the march a Pilgrimage of Grace, he exhorted the men to follow him to London and stand up for what they believed.

Askew reminded them that they were marching for the old faith, for Princess Mary, to bring back the Pope's Catholicism and to drive the heretics like Thomas Cromwell and Richard Rich from King Henry's government.

"We commoners must stick together!" he cried. "We have strength in numbers. Be not afraid. Now is the time for us to rise up or we shall be finished. Forward, oh faithful ones. Forward now or never!"

Then there was someone pushing and shoving. Askew was dragged down from the rock and in his place appeared my own husband, surrounded by the thousands of devoted and idealistic peasants. His was the voice of nobility among the poor. He was the man who was to be their leader.

"I am Lord Latimer of Snape Hall. You have asked me to be your leader in this march against the King. Lord D'Arcy and several other Yorkshire noblemen have joined me. We will light your path, but you must be prepared to fight manfully and to suffer for your deeds. Let me warn you now, the King will not take such rebellion lightly. Our mood and actions are treasonable. I cannot guarantee you a safe return to your homes, so think deeply in your hearts whether you can or will join us."

The crowd roared as Latimer jumped on his horse. Beside D'Arcy, he led the procession down the foothills of Skipwith Moor to the main road while the peasants scrambled and fell about to get closer to their leaders.

Unsure what else to do, I returned home that night. Megan and Anne Askew agreed to accompany me back to Snape Hall. We sat with Delia, and several other ladies of the area, nervously waiting for any news that might reach us of the pilgrimage.

"What do you think King Henry will do?" asked Margaret

Neville, as the great fire dwindled and shadows played around the room.

"I don't know, my dear. Maybe he'll listen to what they have to say. My dear friend Willy's husband is in London with King Henry, as is my brother William Parr. I am sure the very fact Lord Latimer and Lord D'Arcy are leading the procession will have influence on the King."

I spoke cheerfully, trying to keep everyone's spirits raised, but secretly I doubted my words.

Over the next few days, riders came to our gates with news. More and more men had joined the procession as they marched on London. King Henry ordered all the weaponry available in the Armory to be brought out for use against the rebels in an attempt to frighten the people back to orderliness. But rumors were rife that Henry did not have enough armed men to confront the rebels in war, that the Dukes of Suffolk and Norfolk were disorganized.

We cheered when we heard that the King had decided to forgive the rebel leaders, that Norfolk and Suffolk were due to meet with Latimer and D'Arcy in Doncaster a few weeks hence to see if some agreement could be reached.

With the victorious return of Latimer, riding high on the shoulders of the peasants who had encouraged him to be their leader, we were convinced we had won this battle.

But events did not progress as we had expected. Unfortunately, Latimer and D'Arcy had begun to argue. The rebels were now split over religious feelings.

Latimer insisted on a complete return to Catholicism. D'Arcy, of course, would not agree with Latimer that all "new faith" books, such as those by Luther and Melancthon, should be burned.

Both men agreed that King Henry should stop burning heretics, whether they be Papists or reformists, but the meeting would never succeed if the two rebel factions could not come together.

The sound of horses' hooves thundering in the roadway outside our gates brought us rushing to the windows in fear.

Latimer had returned from Doncaster. My heart lifted for a moment but dropped as my husband angrily stormed into our great hall. As he rid himself of boots and gloves, he shouted, "All lies, all damnable lies. I don't believe for a minute King Henry intends to stand by his word. He sent Norfolk to appease us, but nothing will be done."

Latimer went into his chamber and locked the door.

He was in a dreadful state for some time after the meeting. Then, shortly before Christmas, he called me to the library and said, "Katherine, I don't know how to say this to you, but I must go to London to plead with the King. Alone."

"What do you mean? We have never been parted. We can live together at Charterhouse. I would not be a burden to you. Please!"

"Dear wife, I dearly wish to take you. But this is dangerous work, these are dangerous times. I would hate to think of you trapped in London, possibly threatened with imprisonment or worse. I cannot, will not, put you in such peril."

I was crying heartily now, on my knees before him, hugging his waist in suppliance.

"Don't, please, Neville. If it is dangerous work, then I must be with you."

But he pulled himself free, turning to stare out the window. "I hate to do it . . . you know how much I will miss you . . ."

"Neville!" I cried from the depths of my soul.

✣

In the company of Margaret and with only occasional visits from Megan, it was a chilly, lonely winter. Like all women at such times, we closed ourselves in, devoting our time to embroidery, reading, discussion, and guesswork.

After New Year's, which passed without festivity, we received reports from Anne Askew that the peasants were once again rising, fearing that the King had bought off the rebel leaders.

Delia Turpin listened to this message as I read it aloud to Margaret Neville.

Mrs. Turpin coughed and then commented, "My lady, what Anne Askew says is right. I have not dared say anything, but maybe you should know."

"Are they planning another march?"

She coughed again, her dry throat made worse by nervousness.

"Ma'am, they are accusing Lord Latimer of selling them out. And seeing as the master has been in London so long, they now fear he has joined the King's side and might even be supplying the King with the names of the rebels."

"Delia!" I cried. "That's not true. I heard from Lord Latimer only the other day. He is eager to get back to Yorkshire but does not feel he has yet achieved anything with the King. We must trust him."

"We used to," said Delia shortly. "But since he agreed to lead the Pilgrimage of Grace, many folks now feel its failure is his fault."

I glanced at Delia's face, hearing the frostiness in her voice.

"What do you think was Latimer's position?"

"That's not for me to say, ma'am."

"All right, you may leave us." I dismissed her angrily.

We became snowbound. I spent my time with Margaret Neville, a pleasant girl, but not a woman after my own heart. She was nervous about our position, but I assured her that as the leading family in the area, nothing could happen to us.

"Besides, Latimer left Will Bryant here to protect us."

"But, ma'am," she replied in her soft voice, "I saw Will Bryant leave the castle this morning . . . and he has not returned."

Surprised and upset, I realized his leaving portended great danger.

"We must get a message to Megan," I said, trying to calm my rising panic. "Maybe we can stay with her at the D'Arcys'."

"Lord D'Arcy, as I hear it," said Margaret, "has gone back into the villages to raise the peasants. He is determined to lead a second Pilgrimage of Grace, to force King Henry to keep his word and hold a special Parliament in the North to hear the people's grievances."

"Why on earth is he doing that? He knows the King is bound to react without mercy a second time! How I wish Latimer were here. He could talk sense into these people."

"I wish Father were here, too," Margaret replied. She burst into tears and flung herself on the bed in my chamber.

"Margaret!" I snapped. "Do not be so distraught. We must be prepared to face the consequences of our position."

But my hands were sweating. I wrote a quick message to Megan, explaining why I feared for our lives.

"Ring for Mary Chamberlain and tell her to send a boy over to Megan's with this note."

As Margaret reached for the brass bell to ring for a servant, there was a tremendous thundering noise at the gatehouse.

I reached instinctively for Margaret's hands. "Keep calm, my dear. Your father would not want us to panic. We have to keep our heads and think carefully before we act. Hysterics never got a man, nor woman, anywhere."

Mary Chamberlain came to our door, and I was extremely grateful to see her.

"Ma'am, what shall we do? There's a whole crowd screaming and raging out there. They say they want to speak to Lord Latimer, and when I told them he was in London, they said they've come to take over 'is 'ouse."

"Oh, Mary," I exclaimed, emotion choking my voice. "Is

it come to this? Delia was right. They do feel we've let them down."

I knew where Latimer kept his pistols, but how could a few women defend the castle against a horde?

"Where's Will Bryant, Mary? Do you know? Margaret saw him leaving this morning."

Mary flushed crimson. For some time Will had been her beau.

"Yes, he left and indeed he's back," she replied. "But as the *leader* of this gang outside."

My face turned purple. Will Bryant had turned against me? Will Bryant! I thought he loved me. Will turned tail to join the opposite side?

"I don't understand. He's always done so much to protect us."

Mary hung her head low. "He told me last night—he believes in the rebel cause. But I don't think he's as suspicious of Lord Latimer as many of the others. Perhaps that's why he's out there in front of 'em, ma'am. To see as nothing 'appens to you."

I fought back the tears that were welling up in my eyes, and told myself not to be scared. "Lead me to the door, Mary. I will speak with these people."

With resolve, Mary, Margaret Neville, and I walked down the grand staircase to the old oak doors. The manor house that had been my home and refuge for so long had been transformed into a symbol of opulence. Although I realized the dire straits that existed for the poor people of Yorkshire, I failed to understand how they could turn against us in this way.

One of the servants pulled open the great doors, revealing a sea of faces beyond the stone steps. The peasants pushed forward in eager anticipation, as I emerged in my deep blue velvet night robe. The noise of the mob quickly subsided.

Clearing my throat, I struggled to speak as reasoningly as possible.

"Good evening. I must admit I am surprised to see you here. The last occasion such a crowd gathered outside our doors was when you were all clamoring for my husband to lead you in your march on King Henry. Now I hear you are clamoring for Lord Latimer's blood. You are convinced that my husband, the most respected man in this region, has turned coat and joined King Henry's side."

There were shouts of agreement at this. "Have you forgotten yourselves?" I cried vehemently.

"How could you imagine that John Neville, Lord Latimer, who has protected you for many years, would turn against you now? Lord Latimer has gone to London to remind and persuade the King to listen to your demands. *He has not let you down.*"

My last words rang out across the cold courtyard. But even before the final cadence fell, I could see that my words had touched barren ground.

One figure forced his way through the crowd. I recognized the brown hair and piercing blue eyes.

"Lady Latimer. We have reason to believe, despite what you say, that Lord Latimer is siding with the King. We demand access to Snape Hall and intend to go through his papers for evidence."

I was stunned by the look on Will Bryant's face. He was determined and without sympathy. I was totally outnumbered, defeated, abandoned even by those I had befriended—there was Delia, too! Resting on the arm of big Will Turpin. Instinctively, I took a few steps back, and the cry went up, "She's surrendered!"

They surged forward, forcing Margaret Neville and me back into the hall, where we cowered, taking refuge by the fireplace. They did not seem intent on harming us. The horde thronged into the hall, snatching objects as they passed, stuffing them in their pockets, raiding the kitchen and larder for food, tossing hams and loaves of bread to their friends.

Anger and hurt pride pulsed in my veins. I was about to shout out they had no business destroying my home in this manner when a hand clapped over my mouth, stifling my words. The arm dragged me backward into a small room adjoining the hall that very few people knew about. As I kicked and struggled, the door to the room closed. The hand released my mouth, and I spun around to see Will Bryant. He raised a hand and bade me be quiet.

"I'm sorry to do this to you, ma'am. But I had to come along with them to make sure nothing happened to you."

Tears of relief streamed down my cheeks, and I wept on his shoulder.

"What shall we do, Will?" I said, for I saw he had brought Margaret and Mary into the room, too.

"I'll take you all to Lady D'Arcy's."

"But I heard D'Arcy was on the march."

"Aye, so he is. But Megan has not left the house, so they are safe. Folks don't believe D'Arcy is against them."

"Do *you* think Latimer has joined the King, Will?"

He smiled. "Ma'am, I don't believe the sun shines out of Lord Latimer . . . but he is a good man and I know he's working for the people. But who can tell them that? They smell blood and are out for a fight."

"The King is bound to take revenge on them this time."

"That he will, ma'am. I've tried to talk sense into them, but they'll have none of it. They are for marching south to London, where they believe they'll defeat Henry's army. Crazy fools. But who can tell them otherwise? There ain't that much to live for up here these days."

Clutching my robe and covering my head with a blanket, we followed Will through a labyrinth of corridors until we came out by the kitchen, near the stableyard. Will had our mounts ready, two to a horse. He took me in front of him and pulled the rein tight on the girls' horse. We set off at a gallop across the fields, hoping none of the marauders at Snape had seen us. I had no time to look back, to wonder what might happen to my home. For all I knew they would burn it to the ground.

Chapter 27

arling, things are getting worse. I trust it will not personally affect your friend and mine, Megan D'Arcy. I cannot get word through to her husband now. I will send you word again when I can.

I rushed to tell Megan of Latimer's letter and found her staring out the window. Her slim form was outlined by the harsh light. Her hands tightly gripped the belt around her waist.

"Megan," I said softly, "have you had news also?"

"He is in the Tower. As is my brother."

"Megan, we must go to London!" I cried. "We cannot stay cooped up here. We must do something!"

She nodded silently. For once Megan seemed to have lost her passion and fire.

We organized our journey south, with Megan's carriage fitted out in the best upholstery. We were determined to keep up a brave face. Will Bryant had come back to our service and was to be our driver. I left Margaret Neville under Mary Chamberlain's care.

Just hours before Megan and I were to set off, a surprise letter was delivered. I thought the messenger had a strange look on his face, as though he were ill. My hand was shaking somewhat as I read the first words:

In the village of Oxenholme, this Tuesday night, writ without candlelight.

> Ma'am, I am sorry to bother you, but I write to you out of our terrible need here in Westmoreland. You will know about the Pilgrimage of Grace and the fate of the poor folk, and indeed their illustrious leaders, found to be part of that rebellious crew. I pray, your ladyship, that nothing has come of your dear Lord Latimer. We suffered much pain up here. Heaven knows, my family is not the type to take up arms against the King, as well you know. But for some reason, the soldiers of the King came marching through, murdering and hanging. Rob and two of my brothers escaped into the hills. But my Stephen was killed, gunned down. Father has died too, though not from the hands of the soldiers. He had to hide out in the barn, covered with straw and sacking. I think the mildew got to him. He lasted but three days after the soldiers left.
>
> We had terrible times here, ma'am. They left men's bodies hanging from gibbets and from church gateposts. Heads with no eyes stared down at us. Women had to creep out at night and take down their loved ones. They hid them in cellars until they could safely bury them with decency. Stephen has a fine burial place. But I sorely miss him.
>
> What I really want to say, ma'am, is we are in such straits. We lost much of our crops. Your little girl is now a fine lass nearing nine years old—Letitia, we called her. She is spirited like you, ma'am, and I think would do well in London, or in the home of some fine person in service. Could you find her a position? Mother and I have a hard time providing food for all of us. Your loving servant, Liza Harris.

Filled with remorse, I sent the messenger back with two carriageloads of food, wood for fuel, wine, and ale. I assigned several of our boys from Snape to ride back with him. I also secreted in one of the bags of flour a letter for Liza and a purse of coin. In my haste to get to London I could do nothing about Liza's personal distress or about Letitia now.

Megan was impatient to leave, and we climbed into our carriage.

As we rolled down the lane from D'Arcy's castle, I tried to warn her of what we might see.

She bit her lips firmly, scared obviously for the fate of her husband. The old determination seemed to have returned to Megan—the strength and will to survive. For that I was grateful.

The London Megan and I entered three days later was quite different from the city I had ridden through with Latimer—gone were the patriotic crowds and the atmosphere of merry-making associated with Queen Anne's coronation. Evidence of war was everywhere. Lame horses staggered through the streets. Men, women, and children begged for alms in the filthy gutters. Some of the old church and abbey buildings were now being used as warehouses, storing corn or bushels of coal for fuel. There were bodies hung from gibbets, in doorways, and across bridges. We were appalled and kept our eyes averted.

"Please," I called to Will Bryant, "please get us to Whitehall Palace as quickly as you can."

"Grim, ain't it, ma'am," Will said, turning to us with a brave smile.

Our learned and wise monarch had taken his role as supreme head of the Church seriously, weeding out all heretics or religious traitors. He constantly issued new injunctions to the clergy on what form their church services and the people's worship should take.

Excommunicated by the Pope, willingly cut off from the Roman Church, Henry had flirted once or twice with some reformist principles. But more recently, with the publication of the Ten Articles and his own book, proudly called *The King's Book*, he seemed to have returned once more to Catholic principles. He refused to banish the masses or deny that the bread and wine were the flesh and blood of Christ.

As Will Bryant once laughingly summed up the whole

mess, "He's keeping his feet in both camps, in case once he gets to heaven he finds out the other was right!"

As we approached the royal gatehouse to the Palace of Whitehall, my fingers twisted in knots wondering what I would say should the King question me on my religious beliefs.

The macabre words of Will Bryant echoed in my mind, "He hangs the Catholics who oppose him as head of the Church—and the Lutherans he burns at the stake. Choose your ending!"

❖

We settled in at Court without problem. You would never have guessed from the way people lived here that the rest of the country had seen such terrible troubles. Masques and banquets were the order of the day. Anne Herbert was cheerful and content in her position with Queen Jane. My own spirits lifted to discover that Latimer was not a prisoner but merely forced to stay within the confines of our home at Charterhouse. But I was not allowed to visit him. I was resolved to seek a personal audience with the King. My brother William, now a powerful figure in Henry's Court as Marquis of Northampton, agreed to ask the King's permission, and a meeting was set for the following week.

"He doesn't usually waste his time talking to rebel noblemen's wives," William commented.

I pointed out that Latimer had not been a rebel but rather a kind of ambassador of the people.

I kept a low profile in those first few days. I met some former acquaintances, such as Sir Anthony and Lady Denney, who had known my parents. But our positions at Court were not enviable. I was the wife of a man in public disgrace. Megan was the wife of a prisoner in the Tower. Nervously, I read all I could about King Henry's positions on faith, on reformism, on the Pope. Yet in talking with my sister Anne, I was surprised to find that she, Willie Herbert, Edward and

Thomas Seymour, and most of the other young courtiers were quite open reformists.

"Then why doesn't he have you burned at the stake?"

Anne was breezy about it all. "Oh, the King knows how most of his people feel these days. There's not much he can do about it. Only his old pals, the boring old conservatives like the Duke of Norfolk and Archbishop Gardiner, are staunch Catholics, and they are treading on thin ice. As you know, the King can't stand Papists. Just keep on good terms with Henry, treat him like a cuddly bear, and he'll be all honey. He only beheads those who stand in his way or deliberately flout his rule."

She added, "He loves wealthy, attractive women—particularly if they are married, for then they are no danger," and she burst into peals of laughter.

With great excitement the days passed. First I had the chance to be presented to Queen Jane, whose pregnancy was just beginning to show and who wore a beatific smile on her face, as though she had been sanctified by the conception. Princess Mary and Elizabeth were nowhere to be seen, for they both were now declared illegitimate and confined to their own households outside London. I should have liked to see Princess Mary again, for as girls, when I had visited Court with my mother, Mary and I had been quite good friends, though she was a few years younger than I. Mary must be nearly twenty years of age, I thought, and still unmarried. I wondered how she had fared.

When the day of my interview with the King arrived, I dressed very carefully, making sure my clothes were in the highest fashion—I borrowed a Venetian cap from Anne.

King Henry had arranged to meet me in his Presence Chamber at ten o'clock in the morning. This was his business hour.

As I approached the nest of chambers that made up the King's private world, Sir Anthony Denney greeted me and bade me sit on a windowseat while he informed the King of my presence. Eventually the door to the Presence Chamber was opened and I was ushered in.

The room was a magnificent and large columned hall; a long table with benches alongside took up the center, and the King's velvet-covered, gold-embossed throne and canopy occupied the far end. Several courtiers stood by the doorway, gold chains strung proudly around their necks. Three or four sat with the King at the far end of the raised dais that held his throne. The group of men joked. Every now and again, they would break into guffaws at the King's words. With a gasp of dismay, I recognized Thomas Seymour's shining black hair. I breathed in deeply, steeling myself for the task ahead.

The King was not as I remembered him. His fine figure had become buried under a girth so big that it now filled his throne and almost overflowed its sides. His face, which had once appeared so intelligent, so quick-witted, was now lost in the baby-fat cheeks and the rows of extra chins. His clothes were cleverly designed to cover his spreading middle and huge thighs. With the utmost of taste, he was majestically attired in a suit of crimson velvet, a stiff collar of finest white linen, and a jacket of silk encrusted with pearls and gold. A ring glistened on almost every finger. He shifted one leg constantly, and before anyone had noticed my entrance, he called sharply to an elderly man at his side, who appeared to be his physician.

"Goddammit, man, this leg aches me again. Can't you even keep a man's leg from playing up?"

The elderly physician mumbled, apologized, and bowed. He nervously scurried around trying to make up a potion to tend the King, who just as quickly forgot what he had asked the man to do.

Feeling suddenly confident, I stepped forward, dropped a curtsy, and quietly but firmly announced my presence.

"Your majesty, can I be of some assistance?"

"Does the woman pretend to be a physician?" The King roared with laughter as all heads spun around to stare at me.

Blushing to the roots, I stammered an apology. "Your majesty," I said from my knees, "I cannot claim to have the knowledge of your revered physician here. But I have had much experience with my two husbands, tending to them and caring for their sicknesses and wounds. I have some natural skill with herbs, which I only offer, in all humility, as some assistance to your painful leg."

I felt Thomas Seymour's eyes glare through the thin silk of my dress. But I would not return his gaze. However, I did recognize his voice as he was first to speak.

"Why, it is Lady Latimer of Snape Hall, with her charming Yorkshire accent!"

Again, all the men laughed.

"Lady Latimer, I am charmed. I don't believe I have had the pleasure since you were a mere babe in arms, the delightful child of Sir Thomas and Lady Parr," the King announced gallantly.

I had to remind him of our previous meeting at Mary Tudor's funeral. He looked abashed.

"Forgive me, gentle lady, the rudeness of not rising to greet you, but my leg aches me badly today. Begone, men!" he suddenly shouted. The courtiers rose to their feet and bowed out of the room.

"To what do I owe this pleasure?" He ingratiated me with a formal smile, learned from long years of public meetings.

"Your highness, I am humble at the thought of being given audience with you at such a busy time. But I come to speak on behalf of my dear husband, your devoted servant, Lord Latimer of Snape . . . and on my own behalf too, in case you should have any notion that we acted in bad faith during this recent trouble you have had with rebellious peasants."

Surprisingly, King Henry beamed at me. He offered wine,

which I dutifully took, and when he spoke, his voice was all honey.

"Lady Latimer, it has indeed been a pleasure to meet with such a humble woman, such a dutiful and loving wife. John Neville, Lord Latimer, is a lucky man to have such a splendid wife. If only I had had such success," he grumbled for a minute, then, remembering himself and his joy with Queen Jane, beamed. "Are you not going to congratulate me now that Queen Jane is carrying our son?"

Naturally I was full of praise for Queen Jane's virtue and expressed my keen hope that his son and heir would rule England with as much pride and manful virtue as his saintly father had always done. At the end of our interview, the King kissed my hand and assured me Latimer would be released any time we requested.

I glided out of the Presence Chamber feeling every inch a queen. I had achieved the impossible. I had gained my desired end and had impressed the King. He had become putty in my hands.

Scarcely noticing who stood in my way, I vaguely heard Thomas Seymour whisper behind my back, "So you've charmed the King, Kate Parr."

I wheeled around, reaching out my hand politely to shake his. "Good morning, Thomas Seymour. I must congratulate you on your sister's good fortune. I know your family must be *so* excited."

I hoped that he would not let me escape so easily. I had heard he was still unmarried, though gossip linked him with many women, particularly Mary Howard. She was Henry Fitzroy's widow, the King's bastard son who had tragically died of the sweating sickness. I was not surprised to see his eyes dilate as he looked deep into my own. Seymour obviously remembered that June day as vividly as I did.

Quietly and intimately, he pulled me aside. "I am sorry for what has happened to Lord Latimer and your friends."

There was a heavy silence between us. "Are you perhaps now going to live in London with your husband?"

I shook my head. "I doubt Latimer will want to stay here now he is free to leave. We will go back home."

Thomas touched my fingers lightly, and sparks flew between us. I shifted nervously on my feet.

"Have you nothing to say to me?" he asked.

"I have everything and nothing to say. You must know. It is not easy." Inside I was crying. "There have been times I could have written you reams of letters, whole books of poetry. But I could not let myself. I could not allow myself to indulge in the dream of love. There was my husband, there was the war, the problems of friends. What could I do?"

We were whispering urgently, and I kept darting my head to see who was looking.

"We must be so careful." I shivered.

"I know, I know," he said hoarsely. "Don't think I haven't anguished in just the same way. I dreamed of you nightly. I called your name in my sleep. I wrote you letters only to destroy them in the fire."

Now I gazed at his beautiful face, his dark eyes, his hair thick and lustrous, the body still firm.

"Don't tell me you have pined for me all these years. There have been many women, have there not?"

He nodded, and I shook my head. I wanted to get away from him. He was distressing me terribly. I had no place for him in my life or my heart—only in my dreams. He could never be a tame lover. He was too passionate, too demanding. I would never feel content, for I knew he would have too much control over me. I wished that he would go away.

"Well, Sir Thomas." I smiled brightly, seeing his brother Edward coming our way. "It has been a pleasure to talk with you again. When Lord Latimer and I are next in town you must come dine with us."

I extricated my hand and fled.

Chapter 28

The husband I discovered at Charterhouse, under arrest, was an ashen-faced shadow of the man who had left Yorkshire that winter. He was tense and deeply saddened by the deaths of friends and many of the Neville family. Henry Borough had been released from the Tower, though Robert Aske and another friend, Lord Husey, were condemned and executed. My brother had been on the jury that found them guilty. Lord D'Arcy was also found guilty, but his execution was postponed until the end of June, for no good reason other than to further torment him and Megan. I quietly placed my arms around Latimer's neck and sobbed in relief that he was alive.

"I have missed you so terribly," I whispered.

He led me to the pleasant library of our London home, overlooking the gardens where he had passed much of his time reading and writing.

We sat together on the carved settee and held hands as he described some of the terror of the past few months. We were both upset over Snape Hall, although word had come that it remained intact. Latimer felt we should retire to another of our country properties, Wyke Hall in Worcestershire, and I agreed.

That night, our first together for a long time, we lay in each other's arms and talked of the past, and the future.

Although I wept, partly in sorrow and partly in disappointment, he kissed my eyes and begged me to be patient while he strengthened and recovered. He had lost all ability or desire for lovemaking. I cradled him like the baby we never had. I wished for something else in my life—I knew not what.

✦

Lord Latimer and I rode out of London a few weeks later. From our safe retreat in Worcestershire, that summer, we heard that Lord D'Arcy had been executed at the Tower. I was nursing two wounded victims of war now—Latimer had withdrawn into himself, and Megan was pale and thin.

In October, we were among the first to learn the joyous news that Queen Jane had given birth to a son, whom King Henry named Edward. The King victoriously commanded that the whole nation celebrate and rejoice. Bonfires were lit in most villages and towns. The people danced and feasted on free wine and food, to ring in the birth of "England's treasure." Two weeks later, shortly after the magnificent christening, Queen Jane passed away, never having recovered from the difficult birth.

I spent my time furthering my studies of the new faith. With Latimer ill and often in bed, secrecy was less a problem. I had been encouraged by the reformist atmosphere at Court and corresponded with Megan, Willy, and even Anne Askew, who remained in Lincolnshire at her brother's house.

King Henry did not wear his widowhood heavily, although he adored Queen Jane's memory for giving him his much-prized son. The baby Edward survived and was kept out of the city of London, so that he would not be infected by the plague or sweating sickness. But the King, we heard, was happily flirting again, leading a merry life at Court. According to Willy, King Henry had set his eyes on a young, extremely flirtatious, wild-eyed young woman, a niece of the Duke of Norfolk and relative of Ann Boleyn. Her name was Katherine Howard. Letters from sister Anne told me the King even flirted with Willy, whenever Brandon was not around.

However, the King's Council was determined to make him a good political union and arranged a marriage for him by proxy to Anne of Cleves, a Protestant woman from the Netherlands.

Poor Anne of Cleves! Henry quite loathed her, and after spending one night in her bed he vowed he would never return. The King immediately set in motion divorce proceedings on the grounds she had been pre-betrothed without his knowing.

Anne of Cleves might not have been the beautiful simpering girl the King had dreamed of, but she had a good head on her shoulders and might have enjoyed life as his Queen. However, she accepted the terms of her divorce, her pension, and permission to live at Richmond Palace quite easily. She was no doubt content to learn she would emerge from this fiasco with her head intact.

Latimer at last decided to move back to Yorkshire, and we returned to our beloved Snape Hall, which had been cleaned in our absence and bore little evidence of the stampede of peasants through its corridors. Slowly we picked up the pieces of our former life.

The King achieved his objective and was married to the flamboyant, wild-eyed beauty Katherine Howard, who led the aging King a merry dance and was not too tactful in her tales of his inability in bed. She had bedded with many men in her uncontrolled youth, and even once lived as common-law wife with Francis Dereham, whom she now employed as her secretary.

The new Queen Katherine at least treated Princess Elizabeth more kindly than Queen Jane had, and the eight-year-old girl was brought back to Court.

By the following spring, the fifty-year-old King began to sour of his young Queen. He closed her out of his chamber and refused to hear music in Court or allow dancing to take place.

King Henry embarked on a long procession through the country to meet his subjects and talk with local nobility. He was to stay with the Brandons at Grimsthorpe as part of the tour.

For three weeks the rain fell nonstop. The roads were thick with mud, and the King and his traveling companions were wet and cold. Queen Katherine was particularly foolish and made no attempt to hide the fact she had a special relationship with a member of her retinue, Thomas Culpepper. Rumors began to circulate that whenever they stayed overnight, Katherine's ladies smuggled Culpepper into her rooms. Some surmised she was trying to get with child, hoping to keep in the King's favor. Even if their lovemaking was scant, any pregnancy might well reflect his masculinity. The Queen's position was critical.

On his return to London, the King was called to an emergency meeting of the Privy Council, where he was informed that his wife was acting like a whore, and, worse, his precious son Prince Edward was sick and likely to die.

On December 10, 1541, Thomas Culpepper was executed. Queen Katherine was taken to the Tower and kept waiting for her own trial. In early February, Katherine Howard was marched out to the same block on Tower Green where Anne Boleyn had previously lost her head.

The only feelings I suffered were for Princess Elizabeth. The child had lost her mother and favorite stepmother—both times to her father. Her plight somehow firmed in me a resolve I had been harboring in my heart.

As soon as we were settled back at Snape, I sent word to Liza in Oxenholme and bade her send me Letitia. I suggested that Liza, in her widowhood, might like to return to my household, too. Delia Turpin was no longer on my staff since her treachery, and I needed a companion. I requested Liza not tell Letitia anything about my relationship to her.

That Christmas Latimer took to his bed with a terrible attack of coughing and fever. I hoped it wasn't the sweat ing sickness. I tried all I could to curb the disease with herbal brews and bloodletting, but nothing seemed to help.

I sat with him in the bedchamber that had been the scene of so much happiness, reading to him, chatting, talking over ideas for our future.

Our friends came to help or administer comfort. I was in touch with Megan, who was now openly living with Will Bryant. I was not really alone, but still, I shivered as I looked out over the snowy lawns and imagined myself without dear John Neville.

There were tears in his eyes one snowy night when we laughed over how foolish we had once been.

"I hate to leave you, Katherine," he choked.

"Don't speak that way, darling. Of course you are not leaving me."

"It's time to stop talking that way, wife. I am going to die. You know it and so do I. We must arrange your future. Would you prefer to live here? I don't mind if you go to London. You would be better near your brother and sister. Tell me, sweetheart, have you been happy?"

Tears poured down my cheeks. I clung to John's thin chest, wrapping my arms around the emaciated frame of this once strong man.

On my soul, I swore that he had made me happier than I deserved. With those words, he drifted off.

He died that night, in his sleep. For that small mercy, I was grateful.

I arranged his funeral and his burial. Although the family cemetery was in Bedale, he wanted me to bury him at Snape Hall—the home we had shared.

On a cold chilly day, with Will Bryant as chief pallbearer, Megan Borough, Margaret Neville, young John and his wife, Anne Askew, and my thirteen-year-old lady's maid Letitia, whose hand was firmly clasped in my own, we laid John Neville to rest among the heather. His grave looked out on the dale of Wensley, his final resting place.

PART VII

Mistress
or
Bride?

Chapter
29

nne!" My voice registered a natural sense of shock at her words. "What makes you say such a thing? Surely no woman in her right mind would consider becoming Queen! The position is much too dangerous."

"Come, come, my dear sister," she remonstrated, her eyes gazing at the molded ceilings in my beautiful home at Charterhouse. "Half the women at Court would give their right arm to marry him. He may be an old devil, and a difficult grouse, but after all, to be Queen is the most important and most wonderful position for any woman. I can't imagine anyone turning the offer down, not even your old pal Willy, if Brandon were no longer around."

"Or you?" I scoffed at Anne, not particularly liking the turn the conversation was taking. "You mean you would marry him—huge waist that he has?"

We ended up laughing at the ridiculous idea of anyone's marrying the King and actually sharing his bed.

"Have you heard Anne of Cleves describe her night in bed with him?" I was laughing so hard I had to stop to wipe my eyes.

"Indeed I have," cried Anne, equally affected. "She said that he rolled over onto her and fell asleep—nearly suffocating her! Then the next morning he accused her of being frigid, and months later of being barren for not getting with child."

Anne burst into uncontrollable laughter. We were both clutching our sides when Letitia entered the room carrying a silver platter with a letter upon it. She thrust the plate toward me.

"Who's that from?" I asked carelessly.

Letita's reply was sulky. She mumbled, her head down to the floor. "Dunno, ma'am. A rider done bring it and left no word as wanting a reply."

I saw Anne's face cloud over, but I refrained from saying anything to Letitia about her manners.

Letitia's attitude filled me with remorse. To meet up with one's own child, when she was already nearly a woman, was not the simple joy-filled event in my life I had fondly imagined. I had expected to feel warmth and affection for my own offspring. I did not intend to confess to her just yet.

Letitia had been raised well by Stephen and Liza, in a loving home with Freda and her husband as grandparents, and all those brothers and sisters in the household too. But the girl was difficult, obstinate, impenetrable—there was no denying her complicated personality.

Yet her appearance attracted me. She had the same fine blond hair that I had had as a girl, silky and curly and soft to the touch. Taller than myself, and stronger in build, she already sported a well-developed bosom that would naturally bring her the attention of many young men in her not too distant future.

If only she would show some interest in the sort of life I led here in London. I sighed, not wanting my sister to perceive any of these thoughts.

"Why do you keep that girl?" Anne said sharply, once Letitia had left. "She's so rude. She's hardly going to be a gracious asset to your household."

"Maybe she'll grow out of it." I shrugged. "She's new to London and probably quite scared. Anyway, I could hardly invite Liza and not Letitia."

"You and your northern bonds," chided Anne. "I would have thought you would be glad to be rid of them."

I raised my eyes to glance at Anne, who looked somewhat matronly these days after bearing four children. A little too stout around the middle. Her face bore lines of disappointment, although to outsiders she appeared the epitome of success, with a good place at Court, a successful husband, a secure position in Henry's ranks, several children. They were not wealthy, but they scraped by. I was sure Anne was doubly delighted at my arrival in London because my own financial security after Latimer's generous bequest promised to ease their path.

I was not about to answer my sister, so I let her question drop and turned my attention to the letter.

No doubt Anne caught my blushes as I quickly pushed the note away from sight the minute I had read it. I continued the pleasantries of her visit, ordered refreshment, showed her the gardens of Charterhouse—whatever could be seen under the snow covering—and debated whether our brother William was likely to succeed in his bid for a divorce from Claire Bourchier so that he could marry Thomas Wyatt's widow, Elizabeth Brooke.

As soon as Anne left, I closed the study door and brought out the letter again. Carefully and slowly unfolding it, I was horrified to feel my heart beating like a tin drum and my palms sweating as the fingers clumsily opened the paper.

> *I cordially welcome you, Lady Latimer, to this our great city of London, though wish at the same time to pass on my commiserations for the death of your esteemed husband. Although my position here in Turkey, on the King's command, keeps me from London, I do intend shortly to return there and will immediately call to pay my belated respects.*
>
> *Your humble and devoted servant, Thomas Seymour, Lord High Admiral.*

Shaking my head in disbelief and feeling flustered, I put the note down on the small table and tried truthfully to search my heart for what I now felt.

The episode at Grimsthorpe, that hot Midsummer's Eve when I had foolishly indulged myself with Thomas, six years past. I was ashamed that the mere sight of his writing made my heart and hand tremble so.

As the evening wore on, I came to the conclusion that my nervousness was connected with the shame of having given in to Thomas Seymour. He was well known as a philanderer, with a penchant for breaking maidens' hearts and maidenheads. Irritation and annoyance began to replace instinctual yearnings, and soon I was self-righteously assuring myself I would not grant Thomas Seymour a private interview. It would not be worth disturbing my peace and harmony. For all I knew, he intended to blackmail me with his knowledge of my misdeeds!

I was in fact quite comfortable without a man in my life. In my new life at Charterhouse as a wealthy widow, I slowly developed a new social circle. I opened the doors of Charterhouse to reformist meetings, and I was excited and happy to be so openly involved in the new religion. Many evenings we held special services, using Archbishop Cranmer's prayerbook written in the English language.

I went to Court on a few occasions for some of the masques and balls, slowly building up a wardrobe of stylish clothes. I had more than enough money to live comfortably—I was able to help Anne and Willie Herbert educate their children, to lend money to some of the poorer reformists—and it gave me great pleasure to be able to do as I pleased, read whatever books I wished, and meet with friends whenever I so desired.

✣

I met Princess Mary on one of my visits to Court. The King had accepted her back in his fold since the death of Katherine Howard. She served as escort and hostess, in Henry's widowhood. Although Mary was no longer a lighthearted companion, when she invited me to visit her chambers, I accepted with excitement. To be at Court, alone, unescorted, and visit with the Princess seemed a chance I could not refuse.

But it was an embarrassing occasion, for I had chosen a fine dress of blue Spanish silk to offset my still-fair curly hair. I now wore it shorter as more befitting my age of thirty years. Poor Mary looked like a pauper in comparison, wearing a dull brown dress which matched her dull brown hair. As we were in her private drawing room, I was looking through her gowns, trying to give her some advice on how to sew this one or cut that one to make them more fashionable, when one of her serving maids came giggling along a corridor, shouting.

"My lady, your father the King is storming this way right now. He demands to speak with you."

"Now you'll see, Katherine," confided Mary. "You'll see how mean he is to me."

I blushed furiously. I had never expected to *meet* the King during this visit, but I was somehow thrilled and elated at the prospect. It would be nice to become known to him, to be at the center of his Court, counted as one of his favorites.

The door burst open like a thunderstorm, and in swaggered his majesty, wider than when I had seen him last and limping more noticeably on his swollen leg, yet still a magnificent sight worthy of our adoration.

"Mary," he shouted, "how dare you put in for more dresses when I have not given you permission?"

"But, sire, I need at least one fine gown—or how am I ever to attract a husband?"

"You'll get a husband when I arrange for you to have one," he thundered.

Mary turned to me.

"Look at the way Katherine is dressed." She flung an imperious arm toward my blue Spanish silk, which probably had cost twice as much as Henry would dream of spending on his daughter.

I dropped in a low curtsy before the King.

"Your majesty, it is an honor to meet with you, but so unexpected."

"Mary, who the devil is this? I beg your pardon, dear lady, but my eyesight fails me these days. All I can make out is a patch of bright blue—a pleasant enough sight to a man of my age, I have to admit."

"Lady Latimer, Father. Don't you recall . . ."

"Your majesty, we met maybe five years ago, when you graciously pardoned my husband, Lord Latimer of Snape Hall."

"Lord, yes, I remember. Step nearer, woman. You were devilishly pretty five years ago. How do you fare now?"

I walked toward him and dropped to my knees again, but he sharply told me to stand tall so that he could look at me. How strange to be so treated. I stared at his wrinkled, jowly face, the eyes almost sunken into the flesh, the chin disappearing in folds of flesh. Surely he must see the lines on my own face.

But the King acted pleased, like a little boy given a new toy.

"Hum, not bad, eh! So these are the sort of clothes you like, are they, Mary? All right, send to the tailor for some. Ask Lady Latimer for the pattern, and draperer. And order a new gown for Lady Latimer too!"

Then, about to swing out of the doors, he called out, "I trust we will see you again, Lady Latimer. Make your presence known at Court. I would be graced by your company one of these boring nights."

"Yes, sire," I muttered, somewhat embarrassed at his words. Surely I wasn't harboring ideas about the King, was I? I had argued so fiercely against the very thought with my sister, laughed at the notion of any woman's marrying him, and vowed to myself I would never marry again. What was wrong with me that I flew like a moth to the flame?

✤

Nevertheless I visited Princess Mary other times and noticed that the King always found some excuse to call on her. Sometimes he would join in our discussions. He enjoyed teasing Mary about her beliefs. Mary was still a Papal Catholic. He listened to my arguments on reformism and seemed in no way critical of my views. So I felt at ease discussing them.

"Come, Lady Latimer," he teased me one afternoon. "Do you believe the words of that creepy little man Martin Luther over my own?"

I was always careful to answer the King honestly, but in a way that would not offend him.

"What Luther speaks are merely words, your majesty, for every man and woman to interpret. When you speak, we are forced to accept it as right—which surely you *must* be . . . as our defender of the faith."

The King strode to the window and gazed over the frosty wastes outside the walls of Hampton Court.

"Ah, Lady Latimer, you have a good mind on those slender shoulders."

Then he seemed to drift off into his dreams. I often wondered what he thought about. Did he regret the passing of his Queens, Anne Boleyn and Kathy Howard? Did he mourn for Queen Jane? Or had no woman really filled his life?

"You see, Mary?" he went on, coming out of his reverie. "Take heed of how your friend Lady Latimer addresses me. That is how a good wife should behave. Demure, with a good mind and an ability to entertain her husband with intelligent conversation."

My back straightened of itself. This flattery was most exciting. Of course, I knew that the King was always eager to please attractive and wealthy ladies. He loved to be adored and be thought the most handsome man on earth. He loved to exert that fascinating power which still had girls and older women falling over themselves to get near to him. As for me, I was thrilled beyond measure that he seemed to have taken a liking to me, flattered that this man I once had openly hated, this man I had helped Latimer fight against, whose political and religious views I did not agree with, was paying me more than passing attention.

I was playing with fire, I knew that. Yet it was exciting, more thrilling than being the devout and sensible widow. It was also as though destiny were speaking. Those words of Old Nell's rang in my ears: "You have the sign of leadership . . . you are born for great things. I see a house, a fine house, the house of Kings. I see a crown and a large man at your side wearing a crown. . . ."

I began to have dreams about being Queen, how I could persuade the King to turn to the reformist faith, how I could endow universities and build hospitals for the poor. I could persuade him to lower the taxes and do a host of other important works.

But even as I was having these fantasies, a cold chill ran down my back. What about the rest of the prophecy? "Beware a girl child who may be your own, and who may not be." Could that be Letitia? If I were to marry the King, would he find out about my illegitimate child and make that an excuse to be rid of me, to cut off my head when he tired of me?

I returned home to Charterhouse considerably chastened. *No. Let me continue with my orderly existence.* I could not dabble with thrills and adventures in life anymore. That path had brought me nothing but trouble in the past.

The next morning the King's own messenger brought me a special note, embossed with the royal seal and borne on royal livery. King Henry had written a message of goodwill, hoping that I would be his special guest at a banquet a few days hence. I smiled to read the note, for my hysteria of last night had already faded. I was being foolish. The King was no more likely to marry me than he was any of the other women at Court.

Even so, I took great care with my dress. My gown for the banquet was of emerald-green satin, deeply embroidered with ruby beads, and a thick gold chain hung around my slender waist. The bodice was cut low, as was the fashion, but my neck was covered by a white lawn ruff, pleated hundreds of times.

But despite the splendor of my dress, as I stared at myself in the mirror that Letitia held, I had to admit that I did look my age. The King had only fallen for wild beauties such as Anne Boleyn or Kathy Howard, or for a demure, sweet little nothing like Jane Seymour. Compared to them, I was a middle-aged lady. I had no record of fertility. On the contrary, I had nursed two elderly husbands to their graves. Hardly a wild catch, I smiled to myself. Worse, I argued over religion with him.

Although my figure held firm even with age, I could not see myself as the type to attract a King. I did not have half the men at Court falling over me, like Anne Boleyn; I did not even have a string of powerful relatives the King needed to assuage. *Oh, well,* I thought, pinning a coronet of jewels into my hair, *let me at least have a pleasant evening.*

Chapter 30

As we arrived at Whitehall Palace, the King's home in London, carriages and carts converged at the grand doors. Trumpets gave us welcome, and I grabbed the arm of my brother, who had recently returned from fighting in the North and had agreed to escort me.

"Play your cards right, young woman," William said sternly.

I knew what he was implying. William wanted me to press my advantage with the King, who had already shown me some attention. I knew my sister, Anne, shared his view. They wanted me to be Queen, for it would mean advancement, wealth, and prestige for the family.

"Why, dear sister, you look beautiful tonight," he continued. "There is a radiance in that smile. I do believe you fancy your own chances!"

I blushed and said nothing, for despite myself, excitement bubbled inside me, and I had to place a hand on my stomach to quiet it.

Crowds of fine lords and ladies walked ahead of us down the halls. Everyone was dressed to perfection—the ladies in brilliant low-cut dresses, showing off their jewels and their exposed bosoms; the men with cleverly cut hose to enhance fine legs, richly embroidered jackets, and the most exquisite shirts and shoes.

I pinched William's arm, out of a childish naive excitement.

"You'll be all right," he said nervously, patting my arm as we walked.

The room was taken up by four long tables covered in the best white linen cloths that stretched their length. The hall was perhaps three times the size of the great hall at Snape, with a vaulted ceiling that rose to the heavens, and candles were ablaze on all the walls. Held in silver shields, they shone as brightly as a summer's afternoon.

Many people were already eating, as there seemed to be little control over a crowd of some hundreds. I could not imagine how the King would single me out in such bedlam and resigned myself quickly to his scarcely noticing me.

William brought me to the head table. We had marched the length of the mighty hall, weaving our way through the chattering people. From one corner of my eye, I could see the huge frame of the King, his back turned to us, indulging himself with a group of his courtiers. Charles Brandon was also there, and at his side I made out the diminutive figure of Willy, who seemed to be dancing in front of the King, attracting attention and arousing much laughter.

I froze. How could I compete with these accomplished and sophisticated courtiers? Even my extravagant dress no longer felt noteworthy among this crowd. But Willy spied me and came rushing over to take my hands. I was introduced to Brandon, who looked decidedly worse for the years, his waistline emulating the King's in excess, and his head, by all indications, had mushroomed along with the girth.

Brandon's voice boomed over the courtiers' whenever Henry was not speaking, and I felt the tension of these men fighting and jockeying for position or favor.

I grinned nervously at Willy, who tweaked me in the waist and whispered in my ear, "Relax. It'll be all right. The King probably won't even notice you. Just you watch—there are hundreds of women all fighting to catch his eye."

Sure enough, as the evening progressed and we ate our way through game, fowl, fish, and various kinds of meats, followed by cheeses and sweets, all washed down with an endless supply of wine, I witnessed a steady stream of women approach the King to pay their respects and attempt to draw him into conversation.

My, how they play for him! They are all so dazzled by the light that shines from the King. They would give up their souls to be noticed, let alone to spend some time with him.

Despite the heavy feasting, musicians began to tune up during the meal and many couples sped off into the shadows to dance. I glanced at Willy as the fifth course was brought along, yet another pewter tray, loaded with roasted venison. She put her finger to her lips and showed me how to pile my plate and then quietly empty the contents onto the stone floor, where the dogs that prowled at their masters' feet gobbled the food quite happily. Slowly tables were carried out, emptying much of the floor. I gratefully accepted offers to dance from some old and trusted friends, for, to be honest, such quantities of food did not interest me and were indeed making me feel quite sick.

The King and Charles Brandon tucked into each course and packed away plenty beneath their ever-expanding belts. *If I ever did become the King's wife, I would try to persuade him to eat less.*

After the feasting, the King ordered the masques to be brought in, and, with a squeal of delight, the lords and ladies fought over the finest masques. Masquing was one of King Henry's favorite pastimes. It meant a few minutes of delicious privacy when no one knew who you were and then the excitement of demasquing and discovering the identity of your partner.

As the music played I became quite spirited and twirled around the room with several unknown men. Then suddenly a huge figure of a man came bearing down upon me. Others quickly parted to let him through, and I knew that the King was about to ask me to dance.

"Well, pretty lady," he asked as he held my hand and walked while I pretended to dance, "how are you enjoying the festivities?"

"Oh very much, sire," I answered, trying not to give the game away.

"Are you very impressed by King Henry's Court?"

"I find it truly exquisite and his generosity without parallel."

"Do you have any idea with whom you dance?"

"Why no, sire. Though I should guess he is a handsome man by his strong figure."

"Ha, ha!" he cried as the music came to an end, and he lifted his masque and bade me lift mine. I knew all eyes at Court were upon us, and with the best acting I could I made my face express first surprise, then joy, and lastly flirtatious humility to be thus unmasqued by the King.

"Why, your majesty, what an honor!"

"Lady Latimer," he murmured, bowing over the hand held in his sweaty palm, "the honor is all mine."

Trembling and uncertain, I snatched my hand away and dropped my arms to my sides.

"Your majesty, if you will excuse me, I must return to my brother's side."

The King's fat face beamed as he yelled out loud, "But of course, Lady Latimer. The Court knows I give in to *any* request from the fair and the disarming."

I turned and fled. Searching for my brother in the sea of faces, I was overwhelmed by the crowd and became lost among some columns at the far end of the great hall. Several men and women still wore masques, which they used to tease their loved ones or those whom they pursued. I was rather annoyed, therefore, when a youngish-looking man stopped me in my flight, his face fully masked, with only a shock of dark hair protruding above.

He stood square in front of me and said in a high-pitched voice that I guessed was not his own, "Lady Latimer, I see you enjoy the attention of our beloved King."

"Sire. You have the advantage of knowing my personage while I remain ignorant of yours behind that masque. How can I speak with a stranger?"

"Oh, you have not always found that hard in the past."

Now I was afraid. Was this someone sent to torture me with my own misdoings? Was this a messenger from the King come to find me out?

"If you will not reveal your face, then I must rudely pass on," I snapped, losing patience.

"Lady Latimer, I only tease you." The voice had now dropped to its own register, and the sound rang a bell of recognition in my breast. My heart, without my knowing why, began beating very hard.

"There!" he said with a flourish, as Thomas Seymour revealed his darkly handsome face and those brooding mysterious eyes.

I scowled with anger that he could have played such a trick upon me. At the same time my heart skidded to a halt, for I had not known he was even in town. He had been in Turkey for several months, and his appearance, with such tanned healthy skin, reminded me instantly of young Thomas, the soldier, newly returned from the Scottish campaigns. His hair was down to his shoulders again, his beard neatly shaven.

"But . . ." I stammered to find words. "I believed you to be in Turkey."

"I landed at Dover before dawn, learned of the King's banquet this evening, and rode hard to London to be ready for the festivities tonight. I have been too long away and am starving for some human sport."

"Well, you have come to the right place," I said dryly.

"And how do you like the Court of King Henry, my dear Lady Latimer? I see you have quickly struck at the heart of the most notable bosom in the land."

"Oh, please," I begged him. "Do be quiet."

"Where were you running to?"

"To find my brother and see if he would escort me home. I'm tired now. With all that food . . ."

"Um! The King certainly does enjoy his food."

"Sir Thomas," I said, "why do you torment me about

speaking with strangers? I find it discourteous of you to remind me of past foolishness."

"Good lady, please forgive me. I would not wish you to believe my lips would ever mention our deeds outside these four ears."

"I hope not," I said very snappishly, for now I was convinced he saw me as an easy catch. I was a widow and wealthy. What better game was there to be had by a lusty courtier?

"I am not a . . . certain kind of woman."

"I believe you," he said too quickly.

"There are many ladies who speak highly of you," I riposted. "I hear your name mentioned quite frequently, as a wounder of hearts, and an offender of virtue."

Thomas Seymour had a playful glint in his eye. No doubt after months abroad he was eager to resume his conquest of female flesh.

"Oh yes? And who talks so about me?"

"You want me to give you all the names and make your life easier?" I laughed. Now that we had turned the conversation to his reputation it was easier to defend my own.

Although I could not fully understand why, I again felt a strong attraction to this man. I was not usually attracted to men who cared more about their appearance than their minds, nor to men who had unquestionable appeal to other women and questionable morals.

However, despite my two marriages, I had little experience with men and the ways of the world, and so when Thomas Seymour asked if he could accompany me in my search for William, I concurred.

"How have you been, Lady Latimer?"

"Quite well. My husband's death was most upsetting. I sorely miss him. My family and friends have suffered in the aftermath of the Pilgrimage of Grace, but I feel hopeful now about the future and am enjoying my new life in London."

"Your home has become quite a little hotbed of reformists, so I hear."

I was unsure whether he was serious or not. "The reformist meetings we have?"

"Aye. I would be honored, Lady Latimer, if I too might join those meetings."

"Why, Sir Thomas!" I laughed. "I did not know religion was an interest of yours."

He grimaced. "Religion—maybe not. But the politics fascinate me, and anyway, it would be a good way of seeing you."

"But you may call on me anytime," I responded, biting my lip as I remembered deciding a few days back I would not like a private interview with him.

Stopping short of the doorway to the great hall, I spoke directly. "Sir Thomas, if you intend to trifle with my affections, I must have you know that not only am I twice a widow but I have no intentions of becoming involved with a man, *any* man, ever again. I know what the morals of this Court are like, and if you wish to dally with young ladies there are plenty for your amusement."

I wheeled about and was about to storm into the hall when I felt his hand reach out to take mine.

His skin felt warm and reassuring, and his tone softened as he said in a rich, dark voice, "Kate, come back."

Not knowing why, I allowed myself to be pulled back into the darkness of the corridor and let him envelop me in his arms and, without giving me a moment of grace, plant his sensitive beautiful mouth over mine and kiss me so hard and long that my soul yearned to escape from my body.

"Sir Thomas!" I begged as he released my mouth. "Please do not do that to me."

"Why not, Kate? You like it, don't you?"

"What I like is not the question. I am more concerned with what is best for me. And kissing you is not good for me."

But I hung on to him and could not move. He was strong and firm, and the sight of his manly face delighted me.

Resting my head on his chest and gazing up at his dark handsome face, I confessed, "You are too beautiful for me."

He wrinkled his eyes as though to laugh. "*Too* beautiful?"

"I am not used to a man such as you. I come from the North, where men are down-to-earth and honest. I have been married to two older men. I don't know the rules of the games you play here at Court . . . and I cannot be involved. I have told you so."

"There are no rules in the game of love. I find you very desirable. I did twelve years ago, and six years ago, even though that was a mere moment of pleasure snatched among the bushes.

"I've had my share of lasses, Kate," he continued before I could interrupt. "I cannot deny that. But that doesn't mean I want to spend the rest of my life in their clutches. Remember, some of these young fillies chase a man till there is no turning back. You've seen what this Court is like. If a girl does not have a handsome man in her bed at night, she feels as left out as the man who strolls to his cot alone."

"Well, my cot is not for hire."

"Nor mine, Kate. I'm trying to tell you something I find hard to say. I have seldom loved. I thought women were ten-a-penny and I would take whomever I chose and then marry the one with the most wealth, or position, or whatever. But it's different with you. I have never forgotten you, and always wanted you."

I was stunned by what he was saying, and a fire seemed to be rising up inside of me. How long was it since I had felt that fire in my body? Five, six years, and these last few spent nursing my sick husband. It had all been buried along with the ashes of the dead, but now it felt as if someone had shoveled off the earth and the air was rushing to fan the flames.

"Oh, help!" I cried, and struggled to free myself of his arms. "Help, let me go! I have to go home."

Trembling, I staggered off into the banquet hall, where I found my brother dancing with Elizabeth Brooke, kissing her ear and looking not the least bit interested in taking me home. So I ran to find my lady's maid and demanded my cloak.

"But, ma'am," she chortled. "You can't go home alone. Who's to ride with you in the carriage?"

"I don't know. I just have to go. I'll ride in the carriage alone. Come along." The two of us ran down the great stairs of the palace.

But there was no escape, for as we reached the bottom of the stairs, I heard feet clattering behind me and, looking up, saw that it was Thomas, clutching his cloak and sword and leaping down the steps two or three at a time. My companion howled with laughter to see this breathless, handsome man catch me by the arm on the run.

"I can always beat you in a race, Kate!"

"How did you know I'd gone?"

"I took one glance at your brother breathing fire down the neck of his lady friend and knew you'd find no escort there. Your friend Willy told me she saw you making for your cloak."

"Friends!" I snarled. "They always let you down."

But somehow the ridiculous sight of my fighting to get my arm back made me laugh, and he swung a casual hand over my shoulder. Beneath my bravado I felt grateful that this strong and soldierly man was going to protect me on the way home.

Thomas Seymour left me at the door to Charterhouse, with a proper salute, a polite handshake, and a stolen kiss. He promised he would see me on the morrow. I retired to my room, my head giddy from the events of the night. First the King and now Thomas Seymour? *What was happening to my life?*

All night long, or what was left of it, I tossed and turned and tried to sort out the images of the evening. *What did Thomas Seymour really want with me? Was he telling the truth? Had he really desired me all this time? Did he love me? Might he even marry me—such a confirmed bachelor as he?*

Deep in my soul I longed to meet a man who would mean more to me than the strict conventions of marriage. Deep in my soul I wanted to believe that there was a bond between man and woman that nothing could untie, something akin to those first stirrings of love I had known with Henry Borough when I was but a girl. I wanted a marriage for passion, not for property.

But how could I trust him? We did not know each other, and, worse, my secret doubts came back to haunt me. He could have the pick of any woman at Court. *Why pick me?*

Then there was the King, though I did not take his antics seriously. He favored a different woman each week. It was mainly the enthusiasm of my family and close friends, who fancied the idea of my being Queen, that had spurred me on to believe the King meant anything by his play-acting. I was far too old for Henry and, by not having borne a child, showed no signs of being usefully fruitful to a man in his old age. Now my dreams were devoted to Thomas Seymour, and what sleep I fell into was colored by the look of that handsome face, by the feel and smell of his warm, sensitive body.

The next day passed in a trance, as I tried to sift dreams to reality. Thomas had promised to be in touch, and I placed all my faith in that promise. If he called, and reaffirmed what he had said, then I might be able to let myself fall in love with him. If he did not, I would quickly close myself off. I could not afford to expose feelings that would be trampled upon as a horse tramples his master when he takes a fall. I did not want to be out of control.

Chapter 31

W illy was teasing me over lunch three days after the banquet. We were preparing the house for a meeting of reformists and were both in good spirits. The events of the King's banquet had been firmly placed at the back of my mind as a self-indulgence I could do without. My energies once more were focused on the religious activities shared by myself and this group of friends.

"So, has the King popped the question?" she said.

"Don't be coarse, Willy. He merely danced one turn at the masqued ball with me. That is hardly tantamount to a proposal of marriage."

"But he did seem to pick you out as his fancy, my dear."

"He's given *you* far more attention," I chided her, for often Willy seemed to be the King's favorite.

"Ah, but I am safe, as I am a married woman. The King can enjoy my company and not imagine anything more. It's rather obvious that since you're a well-placed widow, his flirtations with you might portend a more serious matter."

"I would not accept even if he should propose," I said defiantly.

Willy cried aloud and dropped her piece of bread on the table. The sun was pouring in the casement windows and had spread its confident rays about Willy's face. She looked younger and more appealing than ever.

"Whatever are you saying, Kate Parr? You wouldn't turn down the King?"

"What if I love another?" I said mysteriously.

Willy could not help herself. She leaned toward me, breathing deeply, and eagerly inquired, "Do you really? Who?"

"Oh, Willy!" I laughed. "Now it's my turn to tease you.

There's no one. I've only been a widow a few months. How could I love another?"

"I don't know, Kate. I wouldn't put it past you. You're a strange enough woman."

Willy was lost in thought, far removed from our conversation.

"Wait a minute." She beamed. "Now I remember the night at Grimsthorpe, the flushing Kate Parr with grass stains on the back of her dress, who hid in my chamber while I suckled infant Henry and who bade me tell no one while she cleaned herself up. Who was the gentleman?" She scratched her forehead with a linen napkin, ruminating, then quickly chuckled. "But, of course, the dashing squire Thomas Seymour. And who should turn up at the King's banquet but Seymour himself? Who is still unmarried. And who was seen to disappear from the King's festivities before anyone else. Ha!"

"Stop, Willy. It's not funny. In fact, it's more than I can bear." Taking a linen napkin I dabbed at my eyes. "So I am in love with the man. But what shall I do about it? He is not sincere, I am sure of that. Yet with no more than five minutes' talk he has won my heart again! Oh, I never thought it could happen to *me* like this. I'm no blushing maiden, Willy. How could I let it happen?"

Willy became soft and quiet. "Because it does happen. Just like that, Kate. We have no control over it. Count your blessings it has come to you. Not everyone is so graced."

"But he trifles with me. He promised to see me the following day. Now three days have passed, and not a word. What am I to make of a man so free with my heart?"

"Aye, Kate. So many men have the ability to make us women weep."

"Not you, Willy. You're above all that."

"Me!" She laughed cruelly. "You must have heard about Richard." She whispered now, for she was talking of her lover back in Lincolnshire. "I have loved that man for four years, despite the face I put on here in London. I pine for him all the time that I am in town. When I am away from him I am never convinced he remains faithful to our love."

"Willy!" I breathed, deeply struck by what she had just told me. "I didn't know it meant so much to you. I thought, oh, I just thought he was somebody to have good times with in the country. What about you and Brandon?"

She shook her head defiantly. "He knows little. Oh, he heard about my love affair, of course. One of his menservants told him. He got angry with me, but he doesn't want to lose his society wife and he adores the boys. So we stick together, as most husbands and wives here do. We put up a front."

"What about you and Richard? Could anything more come of it?"

"Maybe," she said wistfully. "And don't imagine I don't spend all my time dreaming about it. Perhaps if Brandon dies, Richard would marry me. There would be all hell to pay here. The King would be furious, as would everyone else I know—Richard is not of noble birth. But after years of life at Court, I could quite happily settle in the countryside, at Grimsthorpe, puttering about, tending the gardens, and having his babies!"

What she said struck me so that I rushed to her side. We hugged each other in silence. It was not easy being a woman.

✢

Thomas Seymour was the third person who came to the door for the religious meeting that evening. He wore a splendid cloak of rich black velvet. His black hair, now cut straight over his eyebrows, was bobbed to his ears.

His eyes were dark and enigmatic. They gave little signal as to his real feelings. What was it about Thomas's eyes that so intrigued and terrified me? I never felt comfortable when he turned them on me. Yet they drew me. I danced around him fearing and loathing, seduced and loving.

Tonight he seemed to be preoccupied—deep in thoughts that I had no chance of ever sharing. His eyes seemed to shield the secrets of the centuries, at the same time promising to yield the answers to all our lives. Whenever I saw him I wanted to kiss those eyes, to make peace with them.

As he opened his mouth to speak, his eyes softened. They became smiling, happy, jovial, glinting with his accustomed humor and irreverent jokes. I knew that despite my protestations, I would quickly be in his thrall once more.

Taking my hand in greeting at the door, he squeezed it tightly and whispered in my ear, "May I meet with you alone later this evening?" Despite myself, I nodded compliantly, for my heart was in my mouth and my legs felt unsteady.

All evening, I sat in a daze watching the speakers and smiling politely at our guests. Then, as people were beginning to leave, he turned to catch my eye. I made a movement with my eyes that said, "Follow me." I led him through the dark corridors of Charterhouse until we reached my small study, which seemed as safe a place as any.

Seymour brushed nonchalantly by me into the tiny room stacked with my books. He flung down his cloak, and, before I had time to compose myself or think up a clever comment to make him appreciate my wit, he took me in his arms and smothered me with kisses.

"Kate, Kate," he breathed into my hair. "I long for you."

At first I was all aquiver to feel such ardor. But as soon as he finished kissing me, the fears and feelings of disappointment came flooding back, and I said petulantly, "But you told me you would be in touch three days ago. And I have heard nothing."

"Why, I am here, as I said I would be, sweet Kate."

"But you promised to speak with me the day after the King's banquet." Now I sounded like a child.

"Kate! Kate!" he exclaimed, wrapping me in his arms and holding me tight. "Don't hold me prisoner to exact days. I have much to do, having just returned from months away. I had appointments with the King, and my future to sort out. I came to you as fast as I could. Surely that cannot be seen as bad?"

He made me feel low, quibbling over days, but something about him still made me suspicious of his motives and to what end this secrecy would lead.

"Do you not love me, Kate?" he pleaded, one hand over his chest, his eyes turning plaintive.

I shook my head. "I cannot profess love when we have known each other for so short a time."

Picking me up in his arms, so that I felt like a straw doll in a giant's arms, he swung me around and said, "Kate, how can you talk about *time*? Love is for impetuous souls, not those heedful of time."

"But I am not impetuous by nature. And please put me down."

He swung me around one more time. Then he sat himself down on the floor, with me by his side. "There, you will do as I tell you," he pretended to scold me. "You are clay in my hands."

His commanding voice was so funny, it brought a smile to my lips. Drawing me close to him again, he buried his face in my chest, and I stroked that luxurious black shiny hair and wondered at my fate. If I let down my guard, I would fall in love with this man and he would surely hurt me. Yet why was I so scared? Could I not deal with being hurt? Many men and women had been hurt by love in the past. Would I foolishly flee the experience of love without ever having tried it, for fear of its consequences?

Soon all rational thoughts disappeared, as the soothing strok-

ing aroused passionate feelings in me, and memories of that
Midsummer's Eve in Lincolnshire, when the grass was dewy
and fresh and the air filled with the smells of flowers and
musk. Overcoming my fears, I leaned over and kissed him.
Thomas wound his arms tighter around my waist, caressing
my back. He pushed me roughly down to the floor and,
staring over me, broke our silence, bringing a smile to my
face.

"I may not be as grand as the King, but will you make do
with me?"

"Thomas Seymour!" I expostulated. "Don't tease me anymore. You know I care nothing for the King."

"And you do care for me?"

Through gritted teeth, for I could hardly control my passion much longer, I groaned, "Yes, Thomas. Yes, I do, very
much, very, very much."

But our lovemaking that night was bitter and almost angry. We tugged each other's body closer, and closer, desperately attempting to blend these two different souls and forget
our difficulties. I held on to his firm back. As he entered me,
I wanted to scream in passion and rage that I *did* love him—
but I was not sure I had enough patience and forgiveness in
my heart to allow myself to give in. And Thomas grunted
with a fury that came from deep within him. Hurriedly, he
raced toward that point of ecstasy, bringing us both, sobbing
and humbled, to the realization that we were slaves to our
own desires. We lay in a heap of entwined flesh on my study
floor, surprised at the fury we had unleashed in each other.

That night, Thomas Seymour's dark shadow was seen disappearing from behind Charterhouse, while I remained in a
state of confusion and ecstasy, wide awake till the dawn
heralded its presence with sweet birdsong.

✛

I did not hear from him again for over a week. During that
anxious time, I received a curt message from his majesty,

delivered by royal livery, requesting an audience with me at ten in the morning the following Thursday.

Almost in a panic as to what the note would portend, I waited for Thomas. And waited and waited. My spent passion transformed itself into bitter fury—to think he had made me surrender just to have one more conquest!

The day before I was to meet with the King, I sent a hurried note to Thomas Seymour's residence, begging him to meet with me, but there was no reply. When Thursday dawned and I prepared for the interview with the King, I was no longer in any mood of love. I was angry, disappointed, dejected, and bitter.

When I entered the King's Presence Chamber, announced and ushered in by his many courtiers, I was relieved not to see Thomas's handsome face jeering at me. I held my head high and my back straight, ready to meet the King as an equal, a woman he admired and respected.

Henry instantly emptied the room of all his courtiers. To my embarrassment, I was completely alone with his majesty. I was becoming used to our interviews, however, and had grown almost fond of this burly, bearlike figure whose bark, I believed, was far worse than his bite.

His size, which at first I had found offputting, was now an accepted part of him. As if to match his physical appearance, the King had perhaps the largest personality of any man I had ever met and such charisma that even his worst enemies fell at his feet. I discovered the beauty in his face that had been there when he was a young man. I remembered my mother's flattering descriptions of the youthful King, and my own childish hero worship of the majestic King Hal came to the fore.

His face might have become more fleshy, but the power was still there. It shone from those piercing brown eyes. It emanated from the very way he breathed through his nose and hissed through his teeth. It rebounded from the walls when he laughed uproariously. It sang from his lips when, in a happy mood, he turned to music and song to express feelings. Henry was a man of deep emotions, which, unlike many people, he spared no shame in exposing. I had learned to respect him as a man, as well as my King.

I was genuinely pleased that he found me more interesting to talk with than most of the men who surrounded him with flattery.

"Lady Latimer," he proclaimed as soon as the room was ours. "Do you know why I wish to speak with you alone today?"

"Why no, your majesty."

The King looked slightly uncomfortable and shifted around the room, though his great weight made walking difficult.

I stammered to find some words. "Maybe you wanted a conversation with me alone because you enjoy sparring with me on matters religious."

"Right, young lady, right," he said, and laughed, as if he were leading me through the riddle.

"And although we do not always see eye to eye, you wish to explore further some of my more controversial notions?"

I was teasing him gently, for the great bear seemed to enjoy it when I teased.

"More, more, dear Katherine," he goaded me, though I did not fail to notice he had slipped in the "Katherine" and did not address me as "Lady Latimer."

My palms began to sweat as I fished for words. I frowned. "I can guess no further, your majesty . . ."

"Henry to you, dear lady."

"But, your majesty, I could not bring myself to address you thus. I am too humble a servant . . ."

"Henry, I said it has to be."

"Yes, Henry."

"Katherine . . ." He stumbled over his sentences too. "I have brought you here today after much thought and questioning in my heart. I wanted to know if you would consider becoming my wife."

So the words were out. Despite my weeks of panic and nervousness, just to hear them voiced made me feel instantly better. Now I did not have to worry or fret or chastise myself for imagining. It was true. He did mean to marry me. What was I to do?

My mind raced like a horse freed from its stable as I chased the words around in my head. I was trying to land upon the right phrase. What did I want? What should I do? Stumbling, stuttering, I fell on my knees and, almost pleading, began to say, "Sire, I am your most humble servant, but you must know . . . you must have heard from others that . . . that I have vowed never again to marry. My two husbands have been sufficient for me. I wish to devote my life to good works. I cannot marry, sire . . . but if you wish . . . I would happily be your *mistress*. . . ."

The silence was as dense and thick as his waist. I didn't know what he would say.

The sound seemed to begin in his belly and emerged like a rumble in a thunderstorm, so in the end it resounded across the room, revolving off walls. "Katherine!"

Shivering, I remained on my knees, the supplicant to the master.

"How could you say such a thing? I am offering you the highest position in the land. I am offering you a royal wedding, a crown, and your place at my right hand as my Queen. And you want to be my scorned, reviled *mistress*? You know how I have been betrayed over the years by these wenches, who come to me promising their innocence and then trick me with their inconstancy. I cannot stand the abomination of infidelity. I can take no more of the cuckolding bitches! I could never marry a young woman again, Kate. I need to be wed to a widow, so you do not have to lie to me about your innocence. I know you to be a good woman, Kate. Above the rest. With a soul that is pure, and a mind that was created in the heavens. We shall be happy together. I may not be as young as I was, but I shall be devoted to you. I need a friend in a woman now, not a coquette. Won't you have me, dear Kate?" And he fell onto his throne, looking so troubled and petulant that he could have been a little boy.

His words made me tremble with fear. He knew nothing of my past. What if he found out? Would I go the same way as Anne Boleyn and Katherine Howard? Should I hide my past or confess all? It might be better to go to the block tomorrow rather than to wait and worry when the day would come.

What was I to do about Thomas? How would I tell him I had agreed to marry the King? Sweating and feeling faint, I asked the King for at least some time to think his proposal over.

"I am but recently widowed, your majesty, as you know. And I have deep respect for Lord Latimer. I could not marry you straightaway. It would not be proper. Pray let me return with my answer after some thought and prayer, and then I shall respond in some way that will please you."

The King grudgingly agreed, but he insisted I come back on the morrow, to give him my word. It was rather obvious he would not take no for an answer. Had anyone ever turned down King Henry? What would the great King say if I should refuse his proposal?

✜

Thomas was waiting at Charterhouse when I returned home. He had received my note only an hour before, as he had been out of town on important business. He knew I was angry but, again, had little to say by way of apology. I looked at him with deep sorrow and resignation. I knew what I had to tell him, but obviously it was for the best. Further involvement with Thomas would only lead to tears on my part and anguish for both of us. I could not be happy loving Thomas; that I now knew for sure.

He was sitting by the fire in my library, where Liza had seated him. He watched as I threw my cloak, mittens, and hood on a chair, slipped my overshoes from my feet, and moved toward the fire to warm myself.

"I came as quickly as I could, Kate. Are you cross with me again?" he pleaded. All men played on you in the same way, I reflected.

I was tired and scarcely up for any games with him.

"Thomas, I have something terrible to confess, something to tell you that you may not believe."

"You're not ill, are you?"

A vague smile passed my lips. How neat that would be. Why could I not invent a mysterious illness and be too sick to marry the King?

"Not yet!" I tried to make a joke of it. "I have just come from the King, and . . ."

"He's proposed?"

"Yes."

Silence, while Thomas tried several facial expressions to find the one that best suited his feelings. He was unable to speak and choked somewhat, as words tried to come out.

"You've . . . you've accepted?"

"I asked for time to think it over. He said I must return tomorrow."

Silence again. Maybe Thomas would want me to be *his* mistress, if I married the King? But no, that would be impossible. The King would never allow that.

"Then I must leave town."

Shocked to hear his words, for I never really imagined losing him, I said angrily, "Is that all you can say? That you will go away from me, deserting me to my destiny?"

Thomas's eyes glinted with hurt male pride. "Who has deserted whom, Kate? I came today to propose marriage myself. For the first time in my life I have found a mate I wish to make my wife, and you accept the King. What am I supposed to do? Duel with the King over you? There is no place for me and you in London, if you marry the King. You know that. He will suspect me if I so much as glance your way. If he sees us whispering together, he will lock me, or you, away. He's an old man, Kate, and certainly more vain than ever. He tries to compete with the young courtiers. No, it would be far too dangerous."

I knelt down, tears flooding my eyes, as my future revealed itself in all its grimness. "You mean you will leave me to my lonely fate, married to him?"

"I cannot stay around to hold your hand. You brought this on yourself. Don't tell me you weren't tempted by the gaudy bauble that will be your crown. Don't tell me you weren't seduced by the idea of being Queen, even though it still only means greater servitude than ever you suffered before. You might fancy the freedom of wealth and power. But he'll keep you on a tighter rein than any man ever has. He has the ultimate power. And you will be his slave. Mark my words."

"Thomas, please leave this house," I cried in anger, calling for Liza so vehemently that she came running, imagining I was being attacked.

Thomas backed away from me with a sardonic smile on his lips and quickly took his leave. I sat down on a bench in my library, stunned by the turn of events in my life. I had recently felt so happy, so content. Liza tiptoed in quietly. She stood in the cozy room, waiting, questions begging from her silent lips.

I looked up at the kind, patient, lined, and weathered face of my longtime friend who had endured so much with me and yet who suffered far greater tragedy than I had ever known. Shaking my head in disbelief, I said, "The King has proposed marriage to me. I just told Thomas, who informed me he had meant to ask me to marry him. There is nothing I can do. Thomas has stormed out of my life forever."

"My lady." She dropped to her knees before me. "The King has actually proposed? You will be Queen? Oh . . ."

Taking her friendly face between my hands, I smiled.

"I shall be Queen. What do you think of that, Liza?"

"Why, it's wonderful, ma'am. Aren't you thrilled, and honored, and excited beyond belief? You'll get over Sir Thomas. I never thought he was right for you. Reminds me of that time you were so much in love with Henry Borough. All heat and fire, but no substance. Whereas, the King . . . oh, ma'am." And I could see tears streaming down her face.

By next morning, I was composed again. I had cast Thomas from my mind, as an obvious mistake, a selfish man who could never have made me happy, a sensual bondage of the flesh that was exciting to have known, but without which I would be much freer. He called marriage to the King servitude. But I knew that the feelings I had for him were so intense, so blinding, so overwhelming, that I would easily have been much *more* bound as a slave to that kind of love. No, this way I would marry, and have liberty at the same time. Maybe not liberty of flesh, but certainly of mind.

In many ways, the King reminded me of Latimer, who had always been so good and kind to me. I knew I would feel safer married to an older man again.

Marriage to the King was infinitely preferable. I admired his mind, sympathized with his health problems, and even *liked* the man. He made me laugh! If I had to marry again, then all I asked for was safety and security—the easy communication of like minds.

I delivered my acceptance to the King in person, and was kissed hotly on the lips. I begged time before the wedding. I must first pay due respects to my dead husband. I knew full well the King would admire that.

Henry agreed. He held my hand all morning and insisted

that we spend as much time as possible together in the coming months, for he was only happy when I was with him.

My own King, I laughed to myself. The King Hal I dreamed about as a girl and chatted to Liza about in the woods in Lincolnshire, saying, how I would love nothing better than being his Queen. The King I had admired and been in awe of all my life. Of course Old Nell had been right—I was born to wear a crown and have authority.

I felt supremely happy as the days passed in festivities, and congratulations poured in from all sides when our engagement was formally announced.

Thomas Seymour left London within ten days, having been appointed special ambassador to the Queen Regent in Brussels. I did not see him before he left but noted his departure with relief. I did hear from him some days later; a note was delivered to me, sweetly requesting a picture from a collection of miniature portraits of myself. I duly sent it on to Brussels, feeling that in no way did it perjure my position with the King.

PART VIII

His
Royal
Pleasure

Chapter
32

The morning of Thursday, July 12, 1543, was blessed with summer sunshine. Any doubts I had harbored over becoming Henry's Queen had vanished as he made it more and more evident how much he favored me and how happy he was with our union.

I was brought to Hampton Court a week before the celebration and was installed in my own apartments, known as the Queen's Rooms. As yet I had been given no allowance to redecorate the apartment to my own taste, and I had the disquieting feeling that Katherine Howard had last lived here, though in reality Anne of Cleves was my predecessor.

The marriage took place in my own rooms very early in the morning. I invited Willy, of course, and Anne and Margaret Neville. We were also graced with Willie Herbert, Edward Seymour and his wife Anne Stanhope, Sir Anthony and Joan Denney, and Margaret Douglas, as well as my new stepdaughters, Princesses Mary and Elizabeth. Prince Edward remained at Ashridge. The King would not have him near the city for fear of his health.

Liza and Letitia were already dressing me for this, my third marriage, when Willy came to the chamber door. Liza was brushing my hair and we were gently gossiping, sharing a laugh over the circumstances of my two former marriages.

"Remember, ma'am, the day Lord Borough wed you?"

"How could I forget?"

Our laughter was too loud, for Willy begged us to hush. "What if the King should hear you, Kate? His chambers are adjoining."

"He might think we were laughing at him. Oh, Lord, Willy. Can I really go through with this?"

"You haven't much choice, dear friend." She kissed me warmly on the cheek. "You'll be all right. We'll look after you."

Keeping a tight hold on Willy's hand, I glanced down at my fine dress of purest white silk, covered with a swirled pattern of pearls and golden embroidery. I had never seen anything so expensive.

"Where are you and the King honeymooning, my dear?" she asked cheekily.

"He has mentioned taking a progress through the country-side, beginning in Surrey and working our way up to Hertfordshire. I should enjoy some time in the country air, I must say. But, Willy, what am I to do on our wedding night? I can hardly pretend to be madly in love!"

"You'll find a way, Kate. We've all done it before!" Again we laughed, that mysterious laughter of women that should never find an audience outside such walls.

Anthony Denney came to announce that the King was ready. A silence fell over our party. Willy grabbed my hand once more, Liza leaned forward to kiss me, her eyes glistening with tears, and Letitia meekly accepted my kiss.

As we emerged from my chamber into the anteroom that was to serve as the chapel, I saw Archbishop Cranmer clutching a small Bible in his hand, and I smiled at him. Cranmer and I had managed to persuade Henry that the service should be in English and not Latin. I glanced over at my husband-to-be, so stout, so sick, yet still so charismatic a figure. A glow of pride washed over me that he should have chosen *me* among all others to care for him at the end of his life.

Walking quietly to Henry's side, I smiled up at him, wondering if he would have been more delighted had I been a younger woman. Henry took my right hand in his and spoke for the first time the new marriage lines written by Cranmer.

Then he released my hand, and I clasped his, as I said nervously, "I, Katherine, take thee, Henry, to be my wedded husband, to have and to hold from this day forward, for better for worse, for richer, for poorer, in sickness and in health, to be bonair and buxom in bed and at board, till death us do part, and thereto I plight my troth."

Henry placed an enormous gold ring on my finger. We kissed, then I turned, beaming with pride, to kiss my step-daughters, Mary and Elizabeth.

Musicians piped as Henry, walking fitfully on his sore leg, led me out of the room, through his own chambers, to the great hall, where the palace staff and the invited guests were gathered for the wedding breakfast.

✣

So it was done. The knot was tied. I was Henry's wife, his sixth. Queen of England.

Willy came up to me immediately. "How does it feel to be Queen?"

"Be gone with you, foolish woman! How can I possibly know one minute after the event?"

Despite my worldliness and comparative sophistication, I was as nervous as a child bride. I was determined to continue my life as happily as I could, love my stepdaughters, look after my own friends and family, and try to love the King and make him happy in his old age.

Mary came to offer congratulations.

"Well, Katherine, now you are our stepmother, I may find it hard to address you thus."

"Princess Mary. Think of me as no more than your old friend, Kate. Life will continue as normal. Maybe your father will be a little sweeter if I can keep him happy."

Then it was Princess Elizabeth's turn to approach and pay her respects. Elizabeth was ten years old and quite sweet-looking, but she had unfortunately inherited the looks of her father, not of her exotic mother. Elizabeth's face was very pale, but neatly shaped in a pure oval. Her hair was rather wild, carroty, a strawlike mess. She had a haughty distant look in her eyes, a look that said, "Don't cross my path!" We had met a few times in recent weeks, and though she had always been charming with me, I distrusted her.

Now Elizabeth walked over, after chatting to many of the nobles present. She took my proffered hand, kissed it, then dropped in a low curtsy.

"Come, Princess Elizabeth," I chided. "I'm your stepmother, not someone to be curtsied to."

"You are Father's wife and my Queen," she said as if she really meant, "How do I know how long you'll be around?"

"I would like to be your mother, Elizabeth. I think we can have some fine times together with our studies. I know you have a far brighter mind than I do. Maybe we can learn from each other."

To my complete surprise, Elizabeth suddenly flung her arms around my neck. I grabbed her around the waist and held her tight. Of course the girl wanted someone to love! How foolish of me not to think of that. She had lost every mother she had ever been offered, and now she must be scared of giving any more love. But I would work on her. I meant to try.

"Oh, Elizabeth," I sighed into her neck, as we held each other close. "I would be happy if you would love me, if we could be like mother and daughter. I lost my father when I was a baby, and I have never had a child. Will you be my daughter?"

I guessed she was speaking from her heart when she whispered, "Yes, Queen Katherine."

"Then I will save a special place in my heart for you. We've all had a difficult life. Let's hope it will begin to get easier now. You are back at Court and I am going to arrange things so that we all spend time together, as every family should do."

Our little tête-à-tête was interrupted by other well-wishers. My sister beamed, and my brother, having chatted with the

King for a long time, wandered over to my side and said, "Well done, Kate. I knew you could do it." I had to take it as a compliment, although I knew his own future was secured with his sister as Queen.

I noticed Edward Seymour give me a strange look as he came to kiss my hand. I imagined Thomas's and the late Queen Jane's brother thinking, "Let her have her moment of glory, and let her brother bask in that majestic sunshine for now. It won't last long."

I held my head high and enjoyed nothing more than seeing Anne Stanhope, Seymour's wife, curtsy, in deference to my position as Queen. An arrogant woman, she seemed to set herself up as my enemy, but I wished secretly I could bring her to my side, as her husband was powerful and rising daily in the King's esteem.

The King presented me to his chief courtiers, and to his councilors. Although not yet ready to face my full burden as Queen, I gathered from the look in the eyes of the staunch conservatives, such as the Duke of Norfolk, Archbishop Stephen Gardiner, and Chancellor Wriothesley that my new position of power in this land was a questionable pleasure in their minds.

My brother had warned me to tread carefully where Gardiner and Wriothesley were concerned. More than ever, such men of the Papist old guard would fear my reformist influence over the King, and most certainly over Prince Edward—heir apparent to our nation's future and their own.

Then Henry was impatiently at my side, like a young bridegroom lusting after his bride. The Court laughed politely when he tugged at my arm and said, "Come, Queen Katherine, let me show you the King's private chambers."

Blushing, I squeezed his hand and smiled with joy for the assembled company, then followed his lead from the great hall, through the waiting room, the Presence Chamber, and the Privy Chamber, until finally we came to his private quarters, made up of a bedchamber, closet, and drawing room.

Generally speaking, Henry was never alone. Courtiers or servants attended him all the time, so I was concerned to see him banish everyone from his bedchamber.

The King was dressed in white for our wedding, with gold, silver, and pearls adorning every inch of his body, like a galleon in full sail. His bed, I could not help but notice with a smile, was in the correct proportions for one so large, being, some said, eleven feet square, under a canopy of silver and gold.

"Tonight, Kate, you will sleep with me in my bed."

The words of Anne of Cleves flashed through my mind: "I pity the poor lady saddled with such a burden! Can you imagine tiny Katherine Parr and great Henry in bed together?"

"Of course, dear husband," I replied with a smile. "Nothing would give me greater pleasure."

He pulled me to his side on the bed and bade me place my hand under his breeches. I sighed to myself, knowing that this, of course, would be my position as his wife. I had learned over the years with Latimer how to keep an older man happy, especially a man like Henry who had lost the ability to rise for a woman.

"That's good, Kate. You have cool soft hands. That's what I like."

Indeed he was happy, for he kept me at my labors for nearly a full hour, and when I had worked him sufficiently so that his member was somewhat soldierlike, he pushed my head down and bade me bring him to ecstasy. So my life as his Queen began, head down between his legs.

But I did make the King happy on our wedding day, even if the same could *not* be said for myself.

Afterward King Henry fell into a deep sleep which lasted most of the day. And I slumbered at his side. He would have had my head for treason within a minute if he could have read my thoughts, for all I could dream about was Thomas, and how my body ached for his caresses and lovemaking.

I was woken abruptly, some hours later, by one of the King's gentlemen of the bedchamber, who had come to dress Henry and offer us supper in the adjoining closet. When Henry slowly awakened, his breeches down around his ankles, a broad smile of pride covered his face, for he was thrilled that one of his gentlemen had caught us together in bed—knowing that word would now fly around the palace about our sex life. I had done him proud and he was pleased to be with me. I had not mentioned a word of my own desires, or begged him to make love to me, or even hinted at any displeasure. He could never have married a young wife; only someone with my own experience would take on this aging bear, I reassured myself. I woke feeling quite content. *My life may not be full of sensual pleasure, but there will be other rewards.*

❖

Two days later, the King and I made a trip to Oatlands in Surrey. We stayed in the country mansion and partook of the outdoor life that Henry had so loved as a young athletic man. We went riding together most days, though Henry had to be hoisted onto his horse, out of the view of most people. We hunted venison and enjoyed eating our kill that same day. I was quite happy and wrote letters to my sister and brother, telling them I was content to be Queen, knowing full well that the import of those letters would quickly work its way back to the King and could do me no harm.

Henry was genuinely elated, and many of his courtiers and ambassadors congratulated me on reviving the spirit that had disappeared since the fiasco with Katherine Howard. I smiled enigmatically and kept my inner life a secret. There were some things to be said for being thirty-one. I might have lost my youthful enthusiasm and enchantment, but at least my maturity brought wisdom and tolerance in its path.

It came, therefore, as a great shock to see the tearful face of Liza as she came running into my chamber at Oatlands. She was bearing huge bunches of freshly cut flowers from the gardens of the manor but looked quite distraught.

"Whatever is the matter?"

"Ma'am, I find it hard to break the news, but one of the menservants has galloped over to Windsor. Archbishop Winchester, Mr. Gardiner, has taken prisoner some of your reformist friends from Windsor, and they are under arrest with the promise of being burned very soon."

"Whatever for?" I said angrily, thinking how, after our recent talks, the King had agreed to let up on enforcing the Six Articles and would not commit reformists to the fire anymore.

"Ma'am, they searched all the houses at Windsor for books in the new learning. They found some notes on the Bible and a Latin concordance in the house of John Marbeck, a chorister, and in the homes of three others. Didn't they come to Charterhouse a month or so back?"

I sighed with resignation. I could see that we were going to have trouble. Although Henry enjoyed talking to me about my ideas, others in his staff feared my influence over him. Men like Gardiner and Norfolk were still trying to sway the King back to Catholicism. Anger seethed through my body, though I knew it had to be controlled if I was to fight their reformist hatred and political maneuverings.

I cornered Henry when he returned from hunting. "Henry, dear husband," I called as he walked through the great hall, kicking mud from his boots and leaning on the arm of one of his servants. "Could I speak with you?"

Henry beamed, still very jovial. "Of course, my own sweet. What ails thee?"

I had to be careful how I presented my fears. "Henry, I

am troubled because I hear news from Windsor that some God-fearing churchmen have been arrested for having books of the new learning in their houses. Isn't that just what we spoke about the other evening? That we were no longer going to commit heretics to public burnings?"

"Come, Kate," he said brusquely. "Don't bother me with these trifles. Who is it you are concerned about? Do you know these Windsor men?"

Blushing, I said, "John Marbeck, the chorister, has many times visited my house and sung most beautifully, my own darling. I would hate to think of him and his family suffering."

"Then I'll reprieve him, dear wife," said Henry coldly. "I have to make a spectacle of these people. Otherwise the whole country could go against me."

"But, Henry, it is not the reformists who rise up against you. They believe you to be on their side. They no more adhere to the Pope than you do. Remember, when the peasants were up in arms in the North, during that Pilgrimage of Grace, they were the Roman Catholics, not the reformists."

My voice did not falter, nor did it ever lose its soft cajoling tone. To provoke Henry was to engage him in battle. To engage him in battle was to lose the war. One had to be subtle with the King.

"Confound it, Kate. You may be right. But I don't trust any of 'em. Let me continue to take action against them, if I want."

"But why should Gardiner act against reformists, Henry, when it is the Papists you hate most? I do not understand, dear husband. Isn't he taking too much power into his own hands?"

"You're right, Kate." Henry frowned, scowling as he continued on his way.

I returned to Liza, worried but slightly relieved. Recently, Liza too had joined the reformist ranks. The movement for the new church had swept the nation. Most people under fifty were now committed to the teachings of Luther, to the idea of saying our prayers in English, to the abolishment of those Catholic rituals such as kneeling to the cross, or the transubstantiation of the bread and wine. But Henry remained doggedly in the middle, his faith his own Henrican code.

"He says he'll reprieve Marbeck. But the others may die. Do you think Gardiner is doing it deliberately to scare me?"

"Lord, ma'am, I don't know," she said nervously. "There are times I wish we was back in Westmoreland."

Fear had come to my soul, and instinct told me to respect that fear.

Three men from Windsor were burned two days later, after a quick trial. Out there, at Oatlands, just ten miles away, we could smell the roasting flesh on the summer breezes. Marbeck was forgiven and sent me a secret note of thanks.

If Gardiner was to act against me in this way, I now knew it was even more imperative to keep the King on my side.

❖

By August, we had visited the countryside around London and were in Hertfordshire, on our way to visit Ashridge, the home of my stepson, Prince Edward.

As Henry and I traveled through the green and pleasant counties surrounding London, the people crowded the road-sides to greet the King, whom they still adored, and to glance at the new Queen. We gave gifts of food and money to the villages we passed, where our visit was the main event of the year.

I was excited at the idea of meeting Prince Edward, know-ing that my enigmatic and difficult husband had given his precious son's education into the hands of two learned re-formists, Richard Cox and John Cheke. Edward had been brought up in a monastic way, studying hard and playing little, so at the age of six years, he could read and write in Latin, but knew little of the life of the heart.

When our coach pulled into the impressive drive of Ashridge

and servants came out to greet us, I noticed the fair-haired boy staring at us from an upstairs window, his nose pressed against the glass. Poor Edward, trapped in his kingly fetters.

Without waiting for the King's word, I tripped out of the coach and ran into the palace. I raced up the stairs and, seeing worried faces standing in the corridors, decided that that was where Edward was to be found.

"I wish to see Prince Edward. Tell him his stepmother, Katherine, is here."

Several pairs of feet scuttled within the chamber. Then servants emerged, pulling the boy behind them. I kneeled on the floor, my arms out to him.

"Edward, I have been dying to meet you. Elizabeth told me all about you."

"Is Elizabeth already your friend?" he asked curiously.

"Why, of course. And I want to be your friend too."

Edward had never known a mother. Jane had died in childbirth, Kathy Howard had had little time for the infant, and Anne of Cleves had remained like an aunt to him.

"Come here. Kiss me on the cheek, Edward," I encouraged him, as one would a wounded bird.

Slowly, the sweet-faced little boy stepped forward and gingerly placed his lips on my cheek.

"Now I will kiss yours," and I held his arms as I kissed his soft, downy cheek.

"There, doesn't that feel nice?"

He looked at me with huge, doelike eyes and said words that struck my heart. "May I kiss you again, Queen Katherine?"

"Of course, of course," I said, laughing. Then I took hold of his little body and hugged him. He buried his head in my neck, and when he brought his face out, he raised his lips to mine, and we kissed like young lovers.

"Oh, Prince Edward," I exclaimed, sensing the child's

stiffness, "we are all going to live together from now on, one big family."

His face lit up. "With Elizabeth, too?"

"And Mary," I chimed in, knowing that Elizabeth was his favorite.

"Oh, good." He sighed, as if he had been offered a sweetmeat. "Oh, goody!"

Triumphantly I came down the stairs, hand in hand with Edward, both of us grinning. The King looked up and said peremptorily, "I see you two have struck it off well. How are you, son? How are the studies?"

"Very well, Father."

"We are not going to talk of studies today, Henry," I ordered. "Edward is to enjoy the company of his mother and father. We are going to spoil him and play with him, and then, tomorrow, Elizabeth and Mary will come join us. We shall have a real family party. Won't we, Henry?"

The King looked quite pleased. "Why yes, sweetheart, of course. Instruct the staff on what to cook, will you? I don't know much about these things."

All through the autumn and into the winter, I kept the family intact and was delighted to see how Elizabeth and Edward were such friends. We shared our study times, and those bright children taught me much I had let lapse.

That Christmas and New Year's we indulged in festivities the like of which the Court had not seen in years. All family members were invited, and our gifts to each other were thoughtfully made. Elizabeth gave me a beautifully wrought translation from the Italian, and Edward addressed a special piece of his own handwriting to his loving stepmother.

Anne Herbert had her dream come true when she was granted position as lady-in-waiting to her sister the Queen. Willy declined an offer of a position at Court, but she was around so much it really did not matter. I brought Megan D'Arcy from her isolation in Yorkshire to work for me, though

I was surprised she agreed to come, for Megan had borne two children to Will Bryant and was quite happy in the North. I felt somehow safer with all my old friends around me. Margaret Neville also came to live with me as a maid of honor, and so my family was complete, with the young faces of Jane Grey, Frances Brandon Grey's daughter, Margaret Douglas, and Princess Elizabeth occupying the palace schoolroom.

Henry granted the Parr family many honors. Brother William was finally made Earl of Essex; Anne and Willie Herbert were given large grants of land, plus a gift of the dissolved Wilton Abbey outright. Henry made over to me a life interest in much of the land inherited from Anne Boleyn and Katherine Howard, plus gifts of so many manors, castles, and boroughs that I felt quite dizzy. As Willy wryly noted, his gifts made me the richest woman in the country.

Most important, Henry gave the succession to any *son* of mine, while Queen, second only to Prince Edward. To my greater pleasure, he granted first Mary and then Elizabeth their rights of succession, again after a *son* of mine. Never mind that there was no law allowing women to rule the kingdom, at least Mary and Elizabeth were of Henry's blood; if Edward, who was never a strong boy, should die, and if I had no issue, then the country would be thrown into civil war if the King did not name a further heir.

Chapter
33

I felt as if my life had reached a new high, and nothing could go wrong; our life together had settled down. While the King was frequently moody, I felt more and more confident of my ability to please him. Now Henry was girding himself, and his nation, for war with France. I pleaded with him against the idea of going himself, for he was far too old and infirm for such a journey. But by the early summer of that year, he had made his decision. He was going to war with the other men.

Then Thomas Seymour returned from Brussels, and immediately made an impression at Court. He still had his youthful good looks, vigor, and enthusiasm and could entertain with funny stories from his fiery imagination. Henry was instinctively jealous. I wondered if that was why he was so determined to go to war and fight like the younger men.

"Katherine, come here, sweetheart. We have need of you."

The King's voice called to me from the chamber of the Privy Council. I was shocked, for I never entered that realm of government with him or his courtiers. But Denney held the oak door open, and in I slid, walking past the assembled men, aware that all enemies such as Gardiner and Norfolk were eyeing me, as well as friends, crouched in positions of deference before their King on low stools. I joined my husband by his throne.

Henry took my hand lovingly in his, rubbing it warmly.

"Gentlemen, you know I intend to leave the country to join my men in France for the fighting. I feel my soldiers need my strong spirit behind them. I have called the Queen in to announce that in my absence she is to be Regent of our nation. She will meet with such councillors as are here each day, pass judgment, and make decisions for the good of our nation. Katherine is a serious and honest woman, whose opinions I abide by."

Maybe he felt the sweat in the palm of my hand, for he dropped it by my side.

"Why, Henry!" I turned to him with surprise.

The Privy Councillors also expressed their reservations.

"Your majesty, the Queen, with all due respect, has no training in government, no status worthy of such a position. She has been Queen but a few months."

"Aye, my lords, but I have made her Regent in my absence. And that should put an end to any wrangling and conniving among you. You will show her respect and courtesy, and obey her word. Understood?"

"Yes, sire," they murmured, and I feared their treacherous looks that spoke volumes of contempt.

"But, sire." I felt the need to speak up myself. "With your noble personage away at war, I hate to say this, but if something should befall you, some dread accident, then Prince Edward will be in power, as a minor. Am I to remain as Regent until he comes of age?"

"Yes, sweetheart. Whom else could I trust so implicitly."

How my heart thudded. This was a dream come true. To be Queen in my own right, acting Regent for King Henry! This was a far greater honor than merely being his wife. This indeed put me in a position of power and advantage.

✢

The only communication Thomas and I exchanged during this time was a meaningful look, thrown my way one evening after dinner, when Henry was sitting in his usual position. His diseased leg was upon my lap. I petted it lovingly for all the world to see, chatting and laughing with his courtiers.

Thomas's look read, "Is this what your life is come to? Is this why you turned me down, for the diseased leg of a fat old man?" But I refused to be led into any conversation with Thomas. Nor did I believe he wanted to risk his neck or position by dallying with me. Ever the handsome courtier, he flirted ostentatiously with all the women.

Once Henry had left the country in July, my life took on new meaning. For the first time ever, I had duties beyond that of wife or stepmother. There was no time to be sitting sewing, or chatting with my ladies, for I had matters of government to attend to.

Each morning, as was Henry's custom, I met with the Privy Council to discuss the day's dispatches. I had pressing issues to deal with, for we were at war with Scotland and it was my decision when to direct the troops to attack and when to let them rest. I also had to intercede on matters of law, on judgments for local people, on gifts or taxes. I met the foreign ambassadors, and we talked of policy and friendship. Each day, I met with Archbishop Cranmer, for I was helping him translate and rewrite our prayerbook.

I had been at work on my own small book, secretly scribbling in the quiet morning hours. I called it *Lamentations of a Sinner*, and though I was proud of my work, I was also concerned it might too obviously be seen as the work of a reformist, if ever it came to public attention.

Once, when Willy and Megan were with me in the privacy of my chambers, I shyly let them read from my writing.

Willy sucked in her breath and called Megan over, then giggled as she read aloud. " 'Send forth the hot flow of my love to burn and consume the cloudy fantasies of my mind. . . . Gather, O Lord, my wits and the powers of my soul together in thee and make me to despise all worldly things, and by thy grace strongly to resist and overcome all motions and occasions of sin.' "

Willy paused, scratched her head, then surprised me by saying, "You *are* missing something, Kate, being married to the King."

"Whatever do you mean?" I was embarrassed that they had read aloud something so intimate, felt naked that they had seen my innermost feelings.

"Listen to this stuff, Kate. It reeks of a woman whose body yearns for happiness. Maybe you *should* have run away with Thomas after all."

"Oh, do stop," I chided. "You know I am perfectly happy with the King."

"Happy being Queen, you mean," put in Megan rather critically.

"Why do you say that?" I snapped, having long ago stopped feeling sorry for her over D'Arcy's death.

Megan shook her lovely red head. "You should never have married him. I was surprised at you. He is a murderer."

Her words left us in stunned silence.

"You must be careful how you speak, Megan," cautioned Willy. "All walls have ears in a palace."

"But he burns those who follow our belief," she cried.

"What would you have done?" I replied heatedly, angry to be so attacked in my own home. "If the King had proposed, what would you have done?"

"Refused . . . politely."

"I did try. I offered to be his mistress rather than his wife."

Willy burst into laughter, clutching my hands in her glee.

"You did what?" she cried. "Offered to put your head on the block?"

"Well, it was all I could think of to say at the time. I didn't want to marry him. I wanted to marry Thomas. I thought maybe he'd let me be his mistress. I'm sure Thomas wouldn't have minded that."

Megan hugged me. "I'm sorry. I didn't know about you and Thomas. I'm very sorry."

"You and Willy have found your happiness, even if out of bounds of convention. I'm in a much greater trap. And now

Thomas is back, yet I cannot be seen even to smile at him, for someone will surely tell the King."

We three women ended amicably enough, but Willy's words had unsettled me. She believed I wrote with such passion because my body was denied the gratification it desired. Perhaps she was right. I had forgotten about sensuality since becoming Queen. Instead I'd immersed myself in my work, my duty, and my stepchildren.

But I was angry with myself and with her. What was the point of thinking about such things? To remember the times I had spent with Thomas was foolish and dangerous. Soon Thomas would be married to someone else and I would be too old to care or to attract attention. Now I must accept my fate. Being Queen had many mercies that these two women could not enjoy.

✣

In October, Henry returned from France, and we met him at Greenwich. The war had been a failure, but he was sufficiently excited by all the fighting to be in a good mood. He had appreciated my letters while he was away and had managed to write pleasing notes to me.

I had no reason to fear he was tiring of me, though, on his return, he commissioned the Dutch painter Hans Holbein to paint a new portrait of himself and his family, and, mysteriously, Holbein omitted to put *me* in the painting. Instead there was the ghostly presence of Jane Seymour's face in the background.

A nagging thought began to dog me. Was Henry disappointed I had not gotten with child? He knew we had never made love as must man and woman to create a child, so how could he expect otherwise?

We were dancing at a private banquet given by Henry to cheer Willy, in her widowhood. After the trials of war in France, Charles Brandon had returned home and suddenly died from illness within barely three days. I was feeling

omewhat uneasy, for my husband had not paid me any
ttention all evening, but rather had escorted Willy around
he dance floor, and was even holding her firmly to his bosom.

I despised these jealous thoughts but could not help wondering what was going on between my husband and my
closest friend.

Then Megan was at my elbow, whispering in my ear, so
when I stopped to listen I realized the fear that was spread-
ng throughout my body was not without reason.

"They've taken Anne Askew."

"Who has?" I whispered over one shoulder, keeping the
smile firm on my face.

"Gardiner's men," whispered Megan. "They've arrested
her under the Six Articles, for things she once said in
Lincolnshire."

My face fell. Gardiner had arrested Anne Askew, knowing
he was my friend and a guest at Court!

Megan went on, "I'm going down there, right now. To the
Sadler's Hall, where they are questioning her. I cannot leave
Anne to face this alone. I'll take Letitia, if that is all right.
She will report back to you."

Of course I had to let Megan go. I could not run from
Court myself. But I was determined to act for Anne's immediate release.

The evening dragged on. The King kept Willy close to his
side, and I knew she was embarrassed, because she kept
trying to catch my eye to beg forgiveness. But I was angry
with her now. Why should I forgive? She was endangering
my life and position. Her husband was no sooner dead than
he was playing with mine!

My mind raced over events of the day. Anne Askew had
been arrested for breaking the Six Articles, for not paying
obeisance to the King, for her devout belief in reformism.

I suspected strongly now that Gardiner was after *me*, that
he was looking for a scapegoat to bring me down. I was

sweating, extremely uncomfortable, and desirous to retire to the oblivion of my chambers.

When I caught Liza's eye, I signaled that I wished to leave the banquet. She came across to help, pretending I was suffering a stomach upset. Neither Willy nor my husband made a move. For all I knew they could have become lovers from that moment on.

A little after midnight, there was a scuffle by my door. I stirred in my bed, having had a terrible nightmare of people burning at the stake. Letitia crept in like a mouse.

"Ma'am?" She came straight to my bedside. "Megan asks for money. We need some coin to bribe them to let her go."

"Take any amount you need, Letitia. Liza, help her find money and stuff the bag down her bosom, or anywhere to hide it. Letitia, can you venture out again alone?"

"That's all right, ma'am. Lady D'Arcy has a man who is safe to walk with me."

"Trust Megan to know such men!" I said peevishly. "What are they doing to Anne?"

Letitia yawned, sleepily. "They's just questioning her, ma'am. Lady D'Arcy has got herself into the room, to watch after her. I'm sitting outside."

"You poor girl," I said apologetically. "Liza, get her something to eat. Then be gone with you. I'll see what influence I can have in the morning."

I called in Sir William Laxton, the Mayor of London, and demanded to know on what evidence they had arrested Mistress Askew. Laxton shook his head, somewhat nervously but confessed that he had been involved in the questioning and was helpless.

Megan returned toward noon, looking frustrated.

"It's all nonsense," she exclaimed. "Anne has made mince meat of these men, yet they have imprisoned her for ten days and she may speak with no one. They are taking it very seriously."

"What did they ask?"

Megan sat on the edge of my bed and looked disdainful.
It was pitiful. They kept asking her if she refuted that a
priest could make the body and blood of Christ from bread
and wine, of the holy sacrament, and Anne replied, 'I have
read that God made man, but never that man can make
God!' They did not catch her humor, of course, and became
more and more irritated at being unable to defeat her. They
kept calling her 'a foolish woman,' which she patently was
not. They asked again, 'After the words of the consecration
is it not the Lord's body?' And Anne replied again, 'No. It is
but consecrated bread, or sacramental bread.' She is so straight-
forward, she leaves them dumbfounded. And," said Megan
proudly, "she shows no sign of being afraid."

We lost contact with Anne for those few days, but I was in
touch with the Bishop of London to make sure she was being
treated fairly.

All of us—my sister Anne, Megan, Joan Denney, even
Willy, who had come back into the fold without mentioning
the night of play with my husband—were up in arms about
the affair, determined to do anything we could to rescue
Anne, and to save our religious beliefs at the same time.
Equally frightening to us all was who or what was behind
this persecution and what it boded for the future. The King
as always seemed unconcerned about my religious leanings.
Yet he refused to discuss the situation of Anne Askew.

Then, as suddenly as the case had arisen, it dissolved.
Anne was released on bail in March. We had two days of
celebrations, and many a wild party in my chambers, so
much so that word came from the King for us to be quiet, for
he could not sleep.

I turned to Megan, during one of the parties, and remonstrated with her. "I do feel we should lie low about our
beliefs for a while. I will keep Anne living here with us at

Court, so that they cannot touch her again. But let's not be too outspoken."

Megan looked at me as if I had been touched by the devil "What you do in your own conscience is up to you, Kate. could not lie low or lie at all about my faith."

I sighed. Megan had always been more radical than I. Wa I afraid for my own life in this mess, or for their lives?

Willy came up to me and put an arm around my shoulder "Never mind, Kate. It will be all right."

"How do you know?" I snapped, for I was still angry wit her.

"Because you are the Queen, and they cannot touch you, she said, surprised.

"Queen for how long?" I shot back bitterly, giving he such a stare that she blushed.

"Kate, let's not argue. I'm sorry about the other night. did not want to attract his attention in that way. I did m best to discourage it, but there was little I could do to refus his offers to dance."

Pulling my arm away, angry, I said, "Dance? He wa flirting quite openly with you, and you did nothing to pre vent it."

"I hoped he was just trying to cheer me up, because Bran don had died."

"He has always been attracted to you, and you know it. My voice was rising. "And now you're widowed, young beautiful, and obviously fertile. He is wondering what o earth he is doing encumbered with me. He is no doubt plo ting to marry you next!"

"Kate!" she exclaimed, shocked at my statements. "Ho could you? You know I'd never step between you and you husband. How dare you imply I would endanger your life? have loved you like a sister for years!"

She was genuinely hurt, and I softened my stance, bu

remained tearful. She went on, talking fast, no doubt to soothe my fears.

"Let's be frank about this. He was *trying* to come between you and me, because he knows we are such good friends. We're a threat to him with our secrets and our loyalty to each other. Maybe he does have a notion to divorce you and marry me. But he won't have his way." She stamped her foot and took me by the arms firmly, and planted a kiss on both cheeks. "We're friends above all else, Kate."

I fell into her arms. The fears of the last days broke out of me, and a torrent of tears flowed forth. We hugged each other, vowing eternal devotion.

Chapter 34

L ife quieted down for the summer. I left London, taking Elizabeth and Edward to Ampthill to be clear of the plague. Henry left again for war in France, and I escorted him to Greenwich. We were still a loving husband and wife. He returned for Christmas and New Year's, and, although he still flirted with Willy quite openly, I now knew *she* would do nothing to hurt me.

In the spring, the King and I enjoyed a few weeks of victorious celebrations when the French ambassador came over for the signing of the peace treaty. Henry ordered festivities, the likes of which had not been seen since his early days. He gave Prince Edward, now just turned nine, the lead in the show. My stepson was magnificent astride an enormous charger, leading all the other riders. Henry adorned me with new jewels, for my own keeping, and granted me money to refurbish my apartment.

But my mood was to slip quickly off its pedestal. One evening, as Henry and I were chatting, his diseased leg resting in my lap, Stephen Gardiner, who I had long guessed was my chief enemy, joined us. Liza had brought in new jugs of wine and ale for our entertainment, when the King began to be annoyed with something I said. He was often irascible if his leg hurt, and I shivered when I overstepped my mark.

The King snapped at me, "This is a fine state of affairs, when my wife turns teacher on me."

"Why, Henry, your majesty, I had no intention. I was just teasing, my darling."

Gardiner coughed unctuously and made as if to leave the room, but first he stopped, bent over in a deep bow, and let slip the sly words, "Of course, your majesty is right. No one knows better than the King, our superior in all ways."

I glared at Gardiner for flattering Henry in this way. It always made my husband more difficult to manage if someone told him how *right* he was. There was a fire in Gardiner's eyes, however, that further scared me.

"I see you two men do not really require female company tonight. I shall retire to my bed, sweet husband. Look after that leg now."

So saying, I curtsied and made for my own apartments.

Liza scurried around clearing dishes away, and she did not emerge for some ten more minutes, by which time I was in my chamber.

"What did they say after I left?"

Liza looked pale with concern. "My dear lady. It was not good. Gardiner dared to imply that you had overreached yourself, that you are influencing Prince Edward in the ways of the reformist faith. He mentioned Anne Askew, who is your known friend, and implied they believe Megan D'Arcy to be a heretic."

"The cheek of the man!" I exclaimed. "What else?"

But Liza had fallen into a chair and I had to lift her head to hear her next words.

"He . . . he asked the King if it would be all right to investigate you, my lady. He is going to draw up a list of points that will necessitate your interrogation. Oh, ma'am, we should never have left the North . . . we should never have got into this. I'm so scared."

For a moment my own fear was drowned by my need to care for Liza. But then it dawned on me. Everything I had feared since Henry first proposed marriage was now falling into place—the flirtation with Willy, his recent irritation with me, his distrust of my religion. Now I was to be disposed of, just like Anne Boleyn and Kathy Howard. My religious interests were to be the excuse.

The next morning, there were many long faces in my apartment. Most of my women friends were there, not to protect me, but to complain about warrants they had each received from Gardiner and Chancellor Wriothesley. My sister Anne, Megan, and even Willy had been summoned on accusations of heresy and were to be investigated.

There was no doubt in my mind that they were out to get me. They were sure they could force one of my ladies to confess about my part in the "heretic" religion.

Matters worsened. Anne Askew was once again whisked away from the center of our world for her trial. Richard Riche, assistant to Chancellor Wriothesley, came to take her to the Tower.

Again we sent Megan and Letitia to smuggle money and food to her, for the only way to survive in the Tower was to buy food and fuel and perhaps bribe one of the guards to be lenient. Anne was determined and clever, and I knew they would find it hard to convict her.

That night, Megan came rushing back to the palace, her hair unkempt and her face wan from fright. She had left Letitia there, for the girl seemed to have befriended the wife of the warden of the Tower, so she could continue to advise us.

Megan's news fell from her lips. "They're torturing her to confess that you are a heretic. They want *you*, Kate."

"What do you mean, torture?" I snapped, frantic with fear.

"They've put her on the rack!"

"Who has?" yelled Willy, as though she were a vengeful warrior who would rescue Anne.

Suddenly our center of power had disappeared. Our strength as a group of women cast no sway. Wriothesley and Riche had put Anne on the rack, to torture her until she would give them names of others involved and say who was sending her money.

But Anne Askew said nothing to her torturers. Riche even pushed aside the man whose job it was to turn the screws and, so Letitia reported, ripped off his own coat, pushed up his sleeves, and turned the screws tighter until the young woman was nearly dead.

Anne fainted, but they poured water on her face and revived her. For two hours she sat on the dirty floor. Even covered with the vomit and blood of other torture victims, she had the strength to lecture Wriothesley. According to Letitia, they tried to bribe and flatter Anne to change heart. Then they threatened that they would take her to Newgate to be burned as a heretic.

"I would rather die than break my faith," was Anne Askew's brave response.

We were stunned into a deathly silence in my apartment. None of my ladies would retire to her room that night. We sat up whispering and talking, fatigued with fear and exhaustion.

+

The King had taken a turn for the worse, with his painful leg. I had not seen him for several days. It was Megan who came racing into my bedchamber, where I lay dozing that afternoon, clutching a piece of paper which she almost victoriously thrust under my nose.

"Look at this, Kate, and tell me the King is not evil! You must escape, my dear friend! I will help you run to Yorkshire now! I have sent for Will to bring horses and men. I will not let them get away with this!"

Tired, I grabbed the paper. When my eyes read the words, it was as though someone had taken a knife to cut out my heart. Was this really happening to me?

The paper listed all the grievances and sins committed by Queen Katherine against the Six Articles, and recommended her arrest and immediate transportation to the Tower for imprisonment awaiting the King's pleasure. *Pleasure*, I murmured to myself. I remembered the hours of hard work I had undertaken to bring him some "pleasure." I remembered the self-sacrifice I had made to marry him. What could I have lost, by marrying Thomas Seymour?

And then, to compound the injury, I noticed the handwriting of my own dear husband in signature at the foot of the incriminations. He had signed my death warrant.

"How did you get this?" I asked Megan dully.

"Outside your apartment, on the floor. I was passing and naturally picked up the piece of paper. Someone must have dropped it." Then, panting, she gained her breath. "Don't just sit there, woman," she shouted at me, frantic with fear, trying to gather clothes and money together.

Liza came running in, having been alerted to the escape, but I could take no more. I wished for death, for a release from this deception and double destiny.

A man told you he loved you, and when he grew tired of you, he cut off your head.

A man begged you to be his, and when you gave in and became his, he wanted to be rid of you for some other delight.

Feeling so tired, I sank under the bedcovers and gave in to tears. I began to cry and cry and cry. I wept for Anne Askew, and for Anne Boleyn, and for Kathy Howard. I wept for us all. I screamed for mercy. I wracked the walls with my pain and anguish. I could think no more. Act no more. Do no more. *Let me out. Let me out.* I screamed and raged.

Liza came and went, wiping my brow and bringing me a hot herbal tea. Megan stood glaring angrily at me, that I should go so passively, give in to my fate in this way. Willy came and tried to talk to me.

But I'd have none of it. *Go away. Go away, world.* How many hours I was in this condition, I do not know. But darkness was falling outside and I was still in bed, weak, drained from crying, mindless as a young lamb with no mother, when my husband's doctor, a learned elderly man called Dr. Wendye, knocked at my chamber door and begged for entrance.

Megan raced around trying to build some defense, like a lioness protecting her cubs, but one by one the women fell back, and Dr. Wendye came straight to my bedside.

"My lady, our most revered Queen," he started.

"Speak up, man," said Megan crossly, in the emergency throwing caution out the window.

He looked archly at her and returned to my side.

"The King wants to know what ails you, dear Queen. He cannot believe you are crying, so rent with misery."

Willy laughed contemptuously, for we were all broken up by fear.

Dr. Wendye leaned his venerable head farther over my bed. "Dear Queen, be advised that I am aware of the contents of that note and told the King as much. Whereupon the

King groaned, for he is sorely sick today, and in need of your good favors, and said he would like to see you this evening!"

My eyes were like hot balls of lead in my brain. The last thing I wanted to do was see my perfidious husband. "I cannot go to him right now, Dr. Wendye, but do give him my kind regards."

"Your highness, dear Katherine," he said. "I have it on good faith from the King that he did not mean so to scare you with that paper. In fact, I believe it was left lying on the ground specifically for you to find. He does not mean to further your arrest. He plans a plot to trap Gardiner."

"Oh, come now," exploded Willy. "That's preposterous. He would use his own wife's life to bait his archbishop and adviser?"

Dr. Wendye continued quietly, "Do come and see him, Katherine. It will help enormously."

As soon as Dr. Wendye left, the chamber was a gabble of voices, most in disagreement. Megan did not see the point of humbling oneself to the King, but Willy favored the visit. After all, she argued from her years of experience with Brandon, these old men were like bulls when they were feeling unloved.

"You can usually get around them, if you sweet-talk them," she said.

"Why should she sweet-talk that ogre?" snapped Megan.

"To save her neck," put in Willy crossly.

"I'll go," I said to calm the fray. "Help me get ready, clean me up."

Liza, Megan, Willy, and my sister Anne strove for an hour or so to repaint my face, adorn my hair, dress me in suitably plain but neat clothing. Then the women tossed dice as to who should accompany me. I went down the corridor to my husband's apartment with my sister Anne, and Lady Jane Grey, the King's niece, carrying the candles.

My lines had been rehearsed among the company of women;

Megan played the ogre-King. As Willy pointed out, Anne Boleyn and Kathy Howard got nowhere, once his heart had turned against them, by begging and acting hysterical. As far as we knew he had no sexual fears on my behalf, no plans to marry elsewhere, so the only thing against me was his adviser Gardiner's evil word.

I should sweet-talk him, as Willy put it—gently reason my way into his good wishes. I had been in this position before with my previous husbands. I prayed now, if ever I had prayed, that my common sense would prevail.

Jane Grey set down one of the lighted candles outside the King's door. The courtiers stood back on seeing our procession. They disappeared into the tapestries, letting us through the Presence Chamber and Privy Chamber, until we were by the door to the bedchamber itself.

I heard the voice of Anthony Denney telling the King that I was without. Then I heard Dr. Wendye's soothing words. Henry called out to me to enter and not keep the door open, letting in the drafts.

Tiptoeing nervously, leaving my supporters, I walked through those doors I had so seldom entered during our three-year marriage and went immediately to his bedside.

Henry bade me kiss him on the forehead, which I dutifully did.

"Why have you come to visit me tonight, wife?"

"Because I heard that your leg was making you suffer, and I came to be of some help."

He looked proud and distant, as if he were talking to an enemy, not a friend.

"And are you sure you have not come to lecture and teach me again?"

"My dear husband." I spoke nervously. "I never intended to teach or preach to you. If I have engaged you in religious debate it is only because I know you to be so much more clever than I, and such debate will help broaden my own outlook. Moreover, I thought the debates were lively enough to distract your attention from personal discomfort. I never, ever intended, my lord, to make you uncomfortable in my presence. Why, my darling, you are my anchor, my supreme head and governor. I always defer to your majesty's wisdom. How could you believe otherwise of me?"

"But Kate," he sulked, "you have not been to see me for a long time."

"Sweetheart," I cried, grasping his head to my bosom. "I have not come to visit because I thought you were displeased with me. Oh, we have been so foolish with each other! You know I believe that God has endowed man with special gifts of perfection, so that he, *man*, may contemplate heavenly matters. It is not for women to meddle in such affairs. I am just a silly, poor little woman. . . ."

Henry's face visibly changed as I coaxed him with these words. Henry took one of my hands and stared at the rings on my fingers, then his voice changed tone and brightened considerably.

"Sweetheart, is it so? Then let us be friends again. I have missed you so terribly!"

Kneeling at his side and covering his face with kisses, I wept as I said, "And I you, my darling King."

Henry reached his arms around me and promised, "Never again will I mistake your intentions, sweetheart. Stay and be friends. Bring some wine, Denney."

The next morning, Henry invited me to sit with him in the gardens at Hampton Court, for the day was pleasant and sunny. We were sitting in chairs, side by side, holding hands, with Willy and sister Anne proudly in attendance. To our surprise, we heard the sound of horses' feet clip-clopping toward us.

Worriedly, I looked around and hung on to Henry's hand. There before the palace gates rode Stephen Gardiner and what looked like some forty mounted guards.

The King shouted, "What brings you here?"

Gardiner replied, "I am come for her majesty, the Queen, your majesty."

"Be gone, arrant knave! Fool!" shouted the King, and a shamefaced Gardiner turned tail and retreated.

Henry and I never once mentioned the note, the list of accusations, or the fact I had narrowly escaped being taken to the Tower.

"Why did you send Gardiner away, dear?" I asked sweetly.

"Oh, Kate." He sighed pompously. "You don't know how evil that man is and what he has tried to say against you."

I smiled, and my ladies smiled—with enormous relief.

Megan, however, was not in our midst, for she had raced back to the Tower gates upon hearing word that Anne Askew's end was near. There was nothing I could do, in the light of recent events, to free her, though I cried for her soul.

When an ashen-faced Megan returned, she reported that Anne had been unable to stand at the end and was carried to Smithfield bound to a chair, which was then tied to the stake. She was placed between two other prisoners.

Megan watched Anne's final hour in stark disbelief.

The torturers cruelly offered her King Henry's pardon if she would recant, but she refused. The Mayor of London then gave the order for the fire to be lit.

Anne Askew prayed and smiled while the flames leaped around her, refusing either to cry or to scream. The crowd was shocked to see how brave she was.

When Letitia came back to the palace later that evening, for she had been with Megan to see Anne's end, I wiped her tear-stained face clean and held her thin sobbing body to my own chest. We stood silently for some time. If I could not help Anne Askew, maybe I could give some warmth and comfort to this my own child . . . whom I now loved dearly and to whom, one day, I would tell the story of her beginnings in an attempt to make amends.

PART IX

Beware
a Girl
Child

Chapter 35

T he air at Chelsea was so clear that I would spend hours gazing out the windows at the crystal waters of the Thames flowing by my home.

It was midwinter and frosty cold, but I felt peaceful and rested. Six months had passed since the death of Anne Askew, and many wounds had healed.

Early in the new year of 1547, my husband passed away. The King had lain ill through Christmas, and I stayed at his bedside through his final pain and misery.

Henry would not mention the word *death*. The King of England was immortal, and Henry refused to believe otherwise. As his last act, Henry had organized a Privy Council to run the country while his son was a minor. Edward Seymour was to become the boy King's Protector, thereby placing him above me in station. I was not to be Regent until Edward came of age.

As sleep slowly fell away from eyes and mind, I woke to the dull fog of a new reality. Disappointment skewered my soul.

I was Katherine Parr again. Not Lady Borough, nor Lady Latimer, nor Henry's Queen. But gradually I became cheered. I was a widow, with enormous wealth, which gave me means to be independent for the rest of my life.

"You loved him, didn't you, Anthony?" I asked Denney.

He bowed his head sorrowfully. "We all did, ma'am."

"Yes, we all loved him. Great Henry is gone. England will not be such a wonderful place again . . . at least not till Edward grows up. There will be trouble, won't there?"

Denney did not reply.

The next few days passed in a flurry of arrangements.

Henry was embalmed and readied for the funeral. I did not see his body. I had no wish to. The man I had married rested in my soul as basically a good man, driven to excesses by his own emotions. He had been kind to me as a husband, and except for this last year, I had not been unhappy.

I was allowed to take Princess Elizabeth and Lady Jane Grey with me, to remain under my care, when I moved from the royal palace at Hampton Court to Chelsea House. I wished to keep the girls, for we were happy together. I had set up a flourishing school where they could continue their education.

Our quiet life began to take a certain shape, as it had nearly four years ago. Again I concentrated on the reformist movement, and lent my house to its meetings, lectures, and preachings. Emotionally exhausted by the events of the months before the King's death, I was determined to live my life in peace and harmony. I was thirty-five years old, and ready to retire from active service.

✣

Elizabeth was changing every day. The ten-year-old I had grown to know and love when I first married her father was now a highly precocious thirteen-year-old woman. Aware that she no doubt would be betrothed quite shortly, I was contemplating a suitable marriage for her. The King had decreed that neither Mary, Elizabeth, nor I should marry without Edward's, and implicitly the Protector's, permission. Our inheritances and, in their cases, the right of succession were at stake.

Elizabeth was a formidable young girl, with a magnetic personality which more than compensated for her lack of beauty. She flirted with the courtiers and enjoyed leading them on.

Letitia, too, was growing haughtier every day. Her northern accent had long since been forgotten, replaced by the more cultured London tones.

"Letitia, come here," I called to her one morning. She was

huddling with Elizabeth in one of our drawing rooms. The two girls looked up, instantly abashed, and tried to conceal a piece of paper under the embroidered cushion of a chair.

"I thought you were at your studies this morning?"

"Queen Katherine, we are doing nothing wrong. I was just showing Letty a poem I had written. I felt it would be beneficial to her education. You know how her command of the written word is improving."

"May I see the poem too?" I asked, holding out my hand. But the paper was not forthcoming. I knew the power of that inner world shared by young women.

"If you will not show me, then tell me, Letitia, why you are wearing that splendid new ring on your little finger?"

My eyes were pinned to a glittering ruby-and-gold ring the young girl certainly had not received from me.

Letitia blushed, making her look very much like me, with her large dark eyes and pert mouth. She put her hands behind her back.

"Come, tell me." *Men are far easier to deal with than these young women.*

Elizabeth piped up, "I gave it to her. As a mark of our friendship."

Though I knew Elizabeth was lying for Letitia, there was nothing I could say.

Later that day I found Liza tidying up my bedchamber.

"Do you know where Letitia got that new ring, Liza?" I asked as I brushed my hair before dinner.

Liza mumbled, "No," but her obvious unease made me concerned.

"Liza, what is going on here? First Letitia sports an expensive ring, and then Elizabeth hides a letter, or so it looks, under a cushion, and tells me it is a poem. Do you know something I don't?"

"I know nothing about the letter, ma'am, or poem or whatever of Elizabeth's. Her little highness never imparts any secrets to me. But, ma'am, I was wondering whether I should tell you about the ring. Don't you know about Letty and him?"

"Him?" I frowned. Surely Letitia had not found a beau so early in life? I had not even thought about arranging a marriage for her. I intended to leave her much of my wealth when the time came.

Liza fidgeted nervously in the room. My old and trusted friend, her hair now shot with streaks of gray, her face lined from the cares she had seen in her life, would have to tell me the truth.

"A man has been visiting Letty, ma'am," she stuttered, obviously wishing she did not have to tell.

"Without my knowing? How has that come to pass?"

"You have been in London these past few days, taking care of business. And when the man came, I could not refuse him entrance."

"Why could you not, Liza? You don't act in authority here."

"No, ma'am, but I knew him well . . . and it was such a shock to see him standing there, at the porch, that I nearly dropped dead on my feet."

Now my heart and mind were stirring.

"Tell me, Liza, before I take a broom and beat you!"

"It was Henry Borough, Lord Strickland, ma'am."

I very nearly fell off my stool to hear his name. I had not seen him since that night at Grimsthorpe so many years ago.

"What on earth was Henry Borough doing here? What right has he to come calling at Chelsea House?"

Liza looked uncomfortable again. "He came to visit Letty, ma'am. I had to let him see her, for he believes she is his daughter, and I did not know what to say. He came in here and took her into the library, ma'am, and I heard much talking, and then weeping, and laughing, and they came out arm in arm like young lovers. She was wearing this ring and acting proud as a peacock. What was I supposed to do, ma'am? I couldn't say she wasn't, for that would have meant saying whose she was . . . if you see what I mean."

Why would Henry Borough come and claim Letitia for his own? I tried to interrogate Liza more, but though she confessed that he had once visited them in Oxenholme, I came away with little other than the impression he had *never* believed my tale of the stableboy and had, over the years, convinced himself that Letitia was his daughter.

"What about Kaitlin Neville? Is he not still living at Sizergh?"

Liza laughed. "Lord no, ma'am. They separated years ago. After the Pilgrimage of Grace, I think. He set up home with a lady friend here in London. I'm surprised you haven't come across him."

"He wasn't in Court circles, was he? How strange it all is. What about Kaitlin? What has happened to her?"

"She's been trying to get a divorce from him for years, ma'am, an annulment or something. She wants to marry again."

"Did they have any children?"

"None. I imagine they hardly gave it a chance. . . ." Her voice trailed off as though she feared she was overstepping her place.

"No, I could never imagine them as lovers!" I giggled, remembering that night I had nursed Henry Borough from his terrible drunkenness and had crawled into the bed with him, so very much in love. But my fond memories were not working in his favor now. I was irritated at this intrusion into my life, at his taking over Letitia. I would have to break the real truth to her.

"I don't want to meet with him myself, Liza. Do you

understand? And please try to curb these meetings of his with Letitia. Tell him I have forbidden him entry to the house."

"I'll try, ma'am." She sighed, not relishing a fight with Letitia herself.

"Are you getting yourself ready for this evening, ma'am?" Liza changed the subject to something she knew was more to my taste.

As the brush ran through my hair, I realized I had been staring at myself in the mirror, counting the lines on my neck and under my eyes, with growing despair.

Thomas Seymour was coming to dine tonight, and Liza knew I was in a confused state of expectation. He had dropped me a courteous note just the other day, and with mounting anticipation I had agreed to entertain him this evening. What he wanted I wasn't sure. Maybe I was ready for the affair I had been planning some four years ago when the King had so rudely interrupted my dreams.

Thomas had been out of London for the past eighteen months, as warden of the Cinque Ports in his rank of Lord Admiral of the Fleet. His position was elevated now; his nephew Edward was the King, and his brother Edward, the Protector, had been made Duke of Somerset.

Searching through my array of fine clothes for the perfect dress for the evening, I fingered the Venetian silks, Spanish brocades, special little caps from France, and shoes from Italy, wondering at the blessings my life had brought me. When I left Westmoreland with Liza for my first marriage, I had been dressed mostly in fustian, cotton cambric, and solid wool weaves. Now I had at my fingertips the most beautiful clothes, richest jewels, and a choice of fine homes to live in. What more could a woman want?

But there was a small nagging somewhere in the recesses of my soul that told me I craved something more. I wanted a grand passion with a man that would mean more to me than my life. I wanted the thrill of bearing a child to that man, a child born of love, and a child whom I could love from the beginning.

Chapter 36

The servant came to announce Thomas Seymour's arrival, and pairs of feet scurried in all directions. This was an all-female household, and the entrance of a man as dashing and handsome as Seymour was enough to reduce us to fluttery moths. As I made my entrance into the great hall, attired in a dress of purest ivory velvet, a heavy gold chain at my waist and neck and a fine white cap on my head, I was startled by the sight of Elizabeth and Letitia running hand in hand to take their places of welcome by the doorway.

The great oak doors swung open, and the magnificent figure of Thomas Seymour strode in. Elizabeth giggled, while Letitia hid her face in shyness. Both girls dropped their knees slightly to curtsy to him. Seymour burst out laughing at their antics. He took Elizabeth's hand and kissed it fervently, bowed very low over that hand, and begged her humble forgiveness, for he should be the one to curtsy.

"But, Lord Admiral," she chirped, very aware of her own youthful appeal, "how could you curtsy, when you are a man?"

He dropped his legs in the required bend, saying, "There is no law requires skirts to curtsy, Princess."

"I could never imagine to see a man so handsome as you, Thomas Seymour, in a skirt." And this set the two girls off into giggles again.

Deciding to put an end to this nonsense, though pleased to see my troublemakers so cheerful, I stepped forward, my own hand outstretched, my perfect, charming-hostess smile practiced on my lips, and was stunned when Seymour proceeded to drop a curtsy to me.

"You may rise, Lord Sudeley," I teased him, using his new title in the peerage, as though I were a Queen. "You have entered a house full of would-be Queens here!"

At that we all laughed. Elizabeth had confessed to me how she dreamed of being Queen some day, and we discussed then how difficult it was for a woman to wield power effectively. I was determined to teach Elizabeth some of the lessons of my own life.

The girls, and Lady Jane Grey, joined Seymour and me at dinner. Indeed, we appeared a splendid family group, though every now and again I had odd flashes of being the outsider in my own home.

Somehow, it was as though I were losing Thomas to my stepdaughter. Elizabeth was hanging on his every word. She laughed very loudly at all his jokes.

Secretly I disapproved. If he had come to pay me court, he was not making a very good job of it. Some of my former misgivings and suspicions about Thomas Seymour flooded back. I had once decided he would be too dangerous a man to love. Before our dinner was complete, I had made up my mind I would entertain a casual love affair with him, but most certainly I would *not* fall in love.

Thomas rose from the table overlooking the beautiful garden at Chelsea House and asked the younger ladies to return to their own chambers.

"I came this evening to spend time with the former Queen. Katherine and I now wish to be alone. Much as we adore your company . . ." He teased them and kissed each tender cheek as they eagerly proffered them.

I found my palms sweating rather too much at the idea of being alone with him. I tried to summon words that would show my disapproval and indicate that our evening was now coming to an end. But as soon as the girls had departed, he walked over to my side, took hold of my hand, and pressed it to his lips.

"Do you remember me in your heart, Katherine?"

I was completely and quickly thrown. It had not entered my head that Thomas Seymour might still be in love with *me*, only that I had suffered a dangerous passion for him. The very thought was instantly overwhelming and quite disturbing. All those years of repressed passion, of bottled-up feelings, seethed within my veins, and my body felt hot and uncomfortable.

I wanted nothing more at that moment than to be lifted in his arms and transported to some other heavenly sphere. I wanted to float in his love, forget my own identity and become merged into his. As I said nothing, but stared doe-eyed at him, he pulled my face toward his and kissed me softly, and so caringly I wanted to break down like a little girl and cry on his shoulder.

"Will you take me to your chamber, Kate?"

Looking him straight in the eye, knowing I had no more strength to fight this passion, I yielded utterly to him.

He moved to pick me up in his arms, and I lay between his firm strong hands like a young deer he had found in the woods. He spirited me up the stairs, while I directed his movements toward my chamber.

He kicked open the door with one foot. Liza had already absented herself. Perhaps she, too, was giving in to this fate. My bed had been prepared for the night, with clean white linen sheets and a thick white damask counterpane. There were winter roses in the room that lent my chamber a fresh springlike atmosphere, and a bright warm fire to light our way.

I felt completely secure as Thomas laid me on the bed, threw off his clothes, and agilely, for he was so athletic, took his place at my side. Very gently, he caressed my body through the ivory gown, taking away my jewelry, my ruff, the signs of my social status, never once stopping his hands from exploring my every curve, my every mountain and valley of feelings, till I had begun to moan and cry with pain and happiness, till I had begun to exclaim that I could take no more. Yet still Thomas continued and begged me to wait for him, for he wanted to make real love to me and not rush our time together.

I began to feel myself blend with him. My flesh was no longer merely my own. It had reached out to meld with his. My body was united with its partner. Somehow, together, we made a union. I felt most exquisite and ethereal and holy, in a state of bliss. I cried out to my God, to His Holiness, and to Thomas, for making me so happy, so elated, so ecstatic. The sensations were all sufficient to justify my existence.

"Thomas, I love you," I whispered in his ear, as he lay at my side, spent.

"I love you too, Kate. That's why I waited and came back."

"I cannot believe you really waited for me. That's too, too good. I do not deserve such bliss."

"My dear Queen Katherine, you deserve anything for your endurance test!" he teased me. "You fell for the bauble of a crown and suffered three years, six months, and fourteen days of bondage, my sweetheart. But now I want you for my own. I want us to be married, Kate."

There it was again, like a death knell. Each time I found some personal happiness, each time I felt at liberty, capable of conducting my own life, someone tried to snatch away that liberty.

Yet I had dreamed of marrying him and yearned deeply for a love like ours to take seed, flourish, and grow. So it took me barely a few minutes to work through my confused state and accept his proposal.

"But not for a couple of years, Thomas. We could not marry immediately, not so soon after King Henry's death. It would look terrible."

"I don't want to wait and lose you again."

"Lose me to whom?" I scoffed, as I caressed him from the tip of his neck to the bone between his buttocks. What a fine sturdy back.

"Thomas, we have to bide our time. If we are seen rushing into marriage, your brother will be suspicious, and by Henry's will, King Edward has to agree to my remarriage. Oh, my darling!" I gasped with horror as a new thought entered my mind. "What if I have become pregnant this night? It could as easily have been the King's child, and then there would be all hell to pay—for my child would take right of succession after Edward."

Thomas leaned back on the pillows, so I could stroke his chest, weaving my fingers through the dark hair that covered his chest like a thick rush mat.

"I'll sort Edward out. You know he loves me. I'm his favorite uncle, even if Somerset is the Protector. The King knows I am much more generous than the Protector, and I make him laugh. The boy appreciates my company."

"As do many others," I commented peevishly.

"Come, Kate, don't be cross with me. I have to be charming to everyone. There are so many spies and double-crossers around. I prefer to walk an unknown middle course, keeping friends with everyone I can. Don't breathe a word of this, Kate, but I have plans to marry our little Lady Jane Grey to young Edward. She is King Henry's niece and has the closest claim on the throne after Mary and Elizabeth. It would be a perfect marriage. Jane adores you and is a devout reformist, as is Edward. They are devoted to each other. We would have the throne in our power, rather than the Protector's, darling."

But I did not take in the import of his words at the time.

"Everything will be all right soon. I just want us to love each other and be happy. We should ask *our* stepson Edward what he thinks of our marrying, himself," he reassured me.

"Thomas." I pressed my fingers to his lips. "I beg of you, be quiet about our love for now. Let's do nothing till the situation settles for the new King. We can meet in secrecy, can we not?"

Taking hold of my breasts and licking my nipples with his tongue, Thomas roused my furious passions once more. My heart felt it would overflow. My voice lost all desire to speak. He laid his strong body over mine, convincing my pulsating thighs to open once again.

"I *have* to have you, Kate. I have to . . . I may be a madman, but I want you, for mine, and I want to keep you. I want your child to be mine. And if you get with child after this night, I will marry you whether the King agrees or not, and you *will* be happy and grateful to have found me, forgetting all others. . . ."

I gave in to everything, losing caution and regard for propriety. He roused my passions three or four times that blissful night. We were wide awake and smiling at each other as the first birds began to sing in the early dawn.

"You must go, Thomas. We cannot have people seeing you here. But come back, soon. I shall be waiting for you. If you come by the fields, and get a message to me, through Liza, I shall either wait for you myself or send Liza with a torch, by the porter's lodge at the field entrance. No one will know if you leave by dawn."

"Lord above, Kate," he exclaimed, with that humor I so admired in him. "Those fields are treacherous. There's any amount of robbers and murderers lurking in the dark between the city and Chelsea!"

"You're a brave man, Thomas," I said, tugging at the gold chain he wore round his neck. "You said you would do *anything* to have me!"

Jumping from the bed, he pulled on his clothes and turned to bid me farewell, forcing his mouth down over my exhausted lips once more. "I'll be here one dark night, never fear."

"And I'll be waiting," I murmured in ecstasy, yearning only for sleep now, and to dream about my newfound pleasures.

All morning I tossed and turned, trying to understand that this dream of all dreams had finally come true. Was this my reward for former sufferings? I writhed in a state halfway between agony and ecstasy, imagining all sorts of further delights. I arose from my bed around noontide, having snatched just a few hours' sleep.

Willy came to visit, and before I knew what was happening, Liza had let my friend into the bedchamber.

"How come you are still in bed, Kate? You're getting lazy in your old age." She moved over to sit on the edge of the bed. Breathlessly, she took my hand into her own. "I have come with wonderful news! Richard and I are to be married."

Rising from dreams, like a newcomer to this world, I struggled for energy to express my delight in her rash move.

"But, darling Willy, how and where?"

"I shall move back to Grimsthorpe," she said with a defiant toss of her head, her black hair glinting and blue eyes shining. "It is sufficiently distant from Brandon's death now. My widowhood has been served. I want to be Richard's wife and have his children."

I should have been jumping up and down with glee at this great move in her life. But something puzzled me. "What will the King do about your title, Willy? Will you be Duchess of Suffolk? Richard is untitled."

Willy laughed, got up from the bed, and paced around like a caged lion. "Don't ever let such things come between you and a man you love, Kate. I was married once for social reasons, and I'd never do it again. What's more, I'm bringing up my sons to believe they may find a partner they love, not one who fits the social register. I believe I *may* keep my title. Our oldest son will inherit it. Richard will always be Mr. Bertie." She pealed with laughter. "Mr. Bertie and the Duchess of Suffolk! Can you imagine us being introduced at Court! Oh hell, Kate. I've had enough of this city life. I'm retiring from it all. I'll still visit you, and you will come see me. . . ."

But before she went any further, I had to tell her my news about Thomas. In her turn, she blanched rather noticeably and those blue eyes pierced my bosom.

"And you dare to criticize me, Kate? What on earth will the King say about your dallying with his uncle before his own father is scarcely cold in his grave?"

She knelt by my side. "You must be *very* careful. You're not going to marry Thomas, are you?"

Now it was my turn to blush. "Yes—at least, I think so. He wants to be married as quickly as possible."

"But you are the Dowager Queen, and he is far below you in rank. What will people say?"

"No more than they'll say about you," I retorted.

"But with Brandon dead, I'm a nobody. They don't really care where I go or what I do. They care about their Dowager Queen. The people still love you as their Queen. They adored King Henry. They'd be so disappointed. And what will Elizabeth and Edward say?"

Willy's stern words annoyed me, for her warnings did not fit my ecstatic mood.

"You cannot tell a woman in love such things."

Willy looked sorrowful, for she knew it to be true. Quietly

she added, "I hope that Thomas Seymour is not merely after your status and wealth, Kate . . . I really hope so."

Haughtily, I glared at her. "Why? Is Richard Bertie after your status and wealth? Did he crave Grimsthorpe Manor and seduce you to get his hands on your property?"

Willy sighed. "No, Kate. But Thomas is a different fellow. He's a political schemer. He's not a safe sort of man."

Mournfully, I agreed. "None of my men have been the safe sort. . . ." And at that we hugged each other in sympathy.

"Good luck, Kate." She kissed me on the brow.

"Good luck to you, Willy."

❖

Three days later, all misgivings fled as a note was passed to me by a worried Liza. I was instructed to be at the porter's lodge at midnight. Thomas would brave the journey across the fields to Chelsea House. I sent him a note by return messenger, confessing most honestly my love for him. My heart had now gone over to him in total surrender. There was no holding back.

Although it was cold on this March night, I stood at the porter's lodge, my long thick robe enveloping my body, a candle flickering in my shaky hand, praying he would hurry, for my passions were harder to ignore than the cold. There was a rustle in the grass, then a shivering, angry-looking figure stole through the gate and wrapped his arms around me, breathing in the warmth of my own body.

The night was clear, and I stared at his beautiful personage in the moonlight. Holding hands, and still in secrecy, we made our way up the paved path to a side entrance of Chelsea House and tiptoed up a dark back staircase, my heart beating wildly all the time. When we entered my bedchamber, the fire was roaring. I had instructed Liza to leave us food to eat and wine to drink. I had laid out clean clothes for him, and I slipped off my thick robe to reveal a thin muslin nightgown beneath.

Thomas grinned at me mercilessly. "So you were ready for me."

"I've been waiting for what seems an eternity."

"But we agreed on meeting at most once a week, sweetheart."

"I could not wait so long. The days are long out here at Chelsea. I have nothing to do other than think of you, which I have done every waking and sleeping minute. My body feels full of you, and my heart sort of contented."

Pulling me onto his lap, he sat me down, his arms around me, and we both stared into the roaring flames.

"That's how it should be. I want you to be part of my soul. I want you to be in the very core of my body, and I shall be in yours. I want us to be more than just each other, we must be a new whole person, a pure person, a Thomas/Katherine. Can you do that for me, my Queen?"

"Thomas, I am not your Queen. I am your Katherine."

"Oh, you are my Queen, my sweet, and my slave. . . ."

"Thomas," I groaned, turning to nibble his ear, while his hands strayed over the thin nightgown. My legs felt like putty, and between my thighs was moist and welcoming. "Do not tease me now."

"What should I do, my darling?"

I untied the scarf around his neck, unbuttoned the shirt that covered his dark chest, buried my head in the mounds of dark hair, biting at his breast, tasting the sweat from his skin, reveling in the smell and aura of him, as he caressed my breasts, stroked my hair, and pulled up my nightgown, till I wanted to shriek with pleasure.

He took me there on the chair by the fireside, his breeches still half on. He brought fire from my loins to such a pitch I nearly fell from his tight grasp. But afterward I wound my arms around his neck, so contented, so happy, so much in love.

He picked me up then, laid me in the bed, and after he

had undressed himself, returned to me. Opening my eyes, I saw he was very much alive and ready again, and I smiled with pride at this strong lusty man.

"You have no shame, Thomas."

"Oh, I have had shame in the past, Katherine. But this is far from shame, this is bliss. It's not just me that makes it happen, you know. It's you, you beautiful lady."

Then he buried his head between my thighs, and any words of warning from Willy, or Liza, or the King himself would never have been heeded, for this was my fate, my destiny.

Thomas slipped out of the house before dawn had really broken the next morning, leaving me tired and somewhat dissatisfied. Now we were so close to each other, I craved marriage. What if I became pregnant? I would be so happy to have a child with him. I encouraged him to meet with King Edward, who, I knew, adored both Thomas and me. Thomas was less confident about the Protector's approval, but assured me he would make approaches to Edward and see what the eleven-year-old boy felt.

Chapter 37

I t was that very same morning when Henry Borough arrived at Chelsea House, begging to be allowed to see Letitia. I was in no mood to meet him. I was angry that he should disobey my word and presume to call on her. Nevertheless I made my way down to the great hall to speak to him. Complicated images flashed through my mind as I glanced at the man waiting by my fireside.

It could have been his father, the mean Edward Borough, whom twelve-year-old Kate was being sent downstairs to marry. Only the male figure was the one in penitence and I was the one with the power. How the scales swing. How the balance changes.

The Henry Borough who stood there so nervous and jittery was not the beautiful young man I had known and worshiped in Gainsborough. He was fatter, red in the face, with the appearance of a dissolute. No doubt he spent his time wastefully. I wondered what had happened to the poet and man of ideals I had known as a girl.

"Queen Katherine." He dropped to his knees as I approached.

"Henry, Lord Strickland." I held out my gracious hand. "Please do not fall to your knees like that. I am hardly Queen anymore, and were I Queen I would not call for such obeisance from you, an old and trusted friend."

"Oh, Katherine!" He stumbled for words, his red eyes looking sick and old. "It is such an honor to meet you again, in this beautiful house."

"Come, sit down by the fire." I moved us slowly from our stiff standing positions. "How have you been, Henry, over all these years? I am sorry we lost touch, and, somehow, I never heard news of you from our mutual friends. Megan from time to time alerted me of your condition. How is Megan doing?"

Henry scowled, so his fat cheeks looked even more ugly. How could I have passionately loved him? Compared to Thomas, he was nothing. Compared to dear John Neville, he was a nobody.

"Megan," he said contemptuously, "has shamed the family. First she has those two brats by this Bryant fellow and now she has gone and married him."

"I hope she is happy," I said mildly. "Megan has had such a difficult time."

"It was a tragedy D'Arcy went. He was the best thing that ever happened to that headstrong, insensitive woman."

"But what about you and Kaitlin, Henry?"

He laughed and threw back his head, so his teeth showed in an expression that jarred memories out of deep recesses.

"Our marriage was a sham. You must have known that all along, Kate. Oh, Kate . . ." he said, with a sob in his throat, so I recoiled in horror. "Oh, Kate, I have only ever loved *you*, don't you know that? I loved you as a girl and followed your life all these years. You made my life a tragedy, sweet Kate. It is because of you I am the wretch I have become."

"Lord Strickland!" I was alarmed and now stood up on my feet. "Please stop this talk. I will not hear it in my house. The King is not long dead, and I cannot accept this kind of conversation."

Henry faced me squarely.

"Don't speak to me in that haughty, queenly way. Speak to me as a woman. Do you not have any love for me in that hard heart?"

I grimaced. I did not need this harangue right now and wished there were a way to be rid of him, without a disgrace.

Sitting again, I softened and whispered, "Henry, do not carry on so. I have always harbored fond memories of you, and of our love for each other. But I was a girl then, and you were only a young man. That love was pure and wonderful, and I treasure the memory. But it cannot survive the years. Our lives have taken such different paths. I have been married twice since then and . . ." I wanted to say that I was about to be married again. "And I have loved those men in my way too. I cannot claim to still love you, Henry. I . . . I do not know you now."

He would not let the matter drop and took the opportunity of my sitting by him to grab my hand and hold it warmly in his rather clammy grasp.

"Kate, that is why I came to find my daughter. I knew all along she was mine. I went and found her with Liza at Oxenholme. I have sent her gifts and money over the years from an unknown admirer. She is a wonderful girl, and someday soon, when . . . when my finances are sorted out, I intend to bring her to my home and give her a start in society. But Kate," he begged, "just think, if you would marry me now, we could make it known that Letitia was our child, born of innocent love, born out of wedlock but with passion those years ago. We could bring her out as our loved daughter and find her a good marriage. . . ."

Recoiling in horror, I opened my mouth to reply, but no words would come. Abruptly I found my mood shifting. Why insist on the truth? Why not let Henry continue to believe Letitia was his? Maybe it would be better all around this way, for everyone's sake. No one remembered the details of that pregnancy. Wouldn't Letty be happier? Wouldn't it save this man's soul? I decided to play along with his fantasy.

"Does she know yet she is your child?" he asked me patiently.

"No, and you must not tell her. I intend to break it myself when the time is right. If it comes from your mouth, I shall see you are publicly disgraced."

I rose to my feet and walked away, trying to dismiss the conversation and him.

"Shall you leave her some of your inheritance, then, Kate?" He finally was brave enough to ask.

Then the picture became clear. Henry Borough was broke, in debt, probably two feet short of debtors' jail. He needed Letitia for a hold on some of my wealth.

Sighing, for I knew no other way out, I said, "Most likely,

most likely, when I have found the time and place to tell her. Henry?" I coughed, because the question was indiscreet. "Do you need some money?"

His head bent down toward his feet, and I had never seen a man so broken and dejected. "I cannot say no, Kate. My life has not been a good one. Kaitlin kept most of our jewelry, plate, and houses. I came to live in London and have kept up a life that is expensive. I am . . . in quite severe debt."

Now I had truly softened toward him. "But, Henry, you should have come to me directly and asked for money. Come by the house tomorrow and I shall have arranged for a loan to help you out. I would not see you starve, not for old times' sake."

His eyes were moist as he approached me to shake my hand and press it to his lips. I felt from the way he held his body that he intended to make a move to put his arms around me. I stiffened and edged back. No doubt he would continue his shenanigans with Letitia, but I was tired and did not know what to say. I bid him good day and retired to my room.

✣

Thomas quickly worked miracles. He approached King Edward at first teasingly, asking the boy whom he would like his Uncle Thomas to marry, and King Edward replied, innocently, Anne of Cleves, his other former stepmother. Thomas then pressed the point further, asking how Edward would feel about a marriage between his Uncle Thomas and his own dearest stepmother, Queen Katherine. He softened the questions, no doubt, with gifts of money, for the Protector was notoriously tightfisted with the King, leaving him nothing to spare for small treats or gifts to his family. Thomas received word from Edward that the boy would be *delighted* with such a marriage, and he came swiftly over to Chelsea House, bringing me gifts of jewels, and a fine gown, to break the news that we were to be married *within the week*.

Needless to say, my head reeled at the information. I was not yet out of widow's weeds for the revered King Henry.

"But, Thomas," I stuttered, nonplussed, as we sat that evening sipping wine, scantily dressed, on a fur rug I had in my chamber, lying back in each other's arms, blissful as we usually were in the radiant glow from the fire. "We cannot have a public wedding. It would be a scandal for King Henry's widow to marry so soon after his death."

"My darling." He sat up, taking my face between his hands, staring deep into my eyes. "There is no need for a public wedding. I am not such a showman just because I am wedding the Dowager Queen! No, let's have a simple secret celebration, confirming our feelings for each other, here at Chelsea House. Surely, your own chaplain, Miles Coverdale, will perform the covenant . . . and, my sweet, you can write the words to your very own marriage ceremony."

Peevishly, I retorted, "I already did that. I helped Cranmer write the new English marriage service."

Thomas raised his eyebrows. "And is it just as you would wish . . . as a woman?"

I furrowed my brow, for there were some ideas I would have changed, given a chance. "Maybe . . ." I said. "Maybe I could change something. Hmm! Now you have planted thoughts in my head."

He squeezed my hands. "Don't be frightened, sweetheart. Everything will be fine. When we are married, I shall spend much more time here . . . and if you should get with child, then we will have nothing to fear."

"Oh, Thomas," I groaned, for now he was stroking my belly, as though there were already a child within. "You know I have never been with child from my other husbands. . . ."

"Why, never from the King?"

"Oh, do not say that. You know it was impossible."

"I had guessed, or hoped, as much," he whispered. "Tell me the King never possessed you, Kate."

"Never." I shook my head. "Never."

"Then I shall have you all for mine," he said so proudly.

"Do you very much desire a child?"

"Of course I do," he said lightly. "What man would not want a son?"

So the joy went out of our conversation, for me. How could I promise him a son? How could I even promise him a child, after so many years of not conceiving? Letitia had been such an accident, almost as though she were not mine. I doubted very much I could get with child again at thirty-five years of age. Surely a woman goes stale and dried-up after so many years?

Tears began to spill from my eyes, and I rolled my body away from him in distress. Thomas was oblivious to what was happening, and rose to dress himself. He was excited now that he had won over King Edward and me. Everything was going his way.

Shivering in the firelight, I refilled my glass of wine. Maybe the nourishing red liquid would warm my soul, which felt cold. Everything would be all right, as Thomas kept reassuring me. We were in love, weren't we?

✜

Early in the morning, on a beautiful sunlit May day, when the blossoms were sufficient to catch the nose and portend of a sweet life, Thomas Seymour became my husband, and I became Katherine Parr, Lady Sudeley, my fourth and, I hoped, final change of name.

If my marriage to King Henry had been complete with pomp and royal circumstance, this wedding was its exact opposite. My sister Anne and her husband Willie were present to witness the ceremony. I was attended by Lady Jane Grey and Princess Elizabeth. The service was read by my friend Miles Coverdale. No other friends were invited, for our marriage was a secret, until Thomas had worked the permission of the Privy Council.

Although I was dressed in one of my finest robes and wore a crown of woven flowers made for me by Letitia and Liza, it was not a ceremony of great import. Yet I felt proud of the fact that our marriage vows were changed by my addition of the words "to love, honor and obey," which I felt were lacking in the prayer as written by Cranmer. Thomas believed in the totality of our love, and so did I. He enjoyed the notion that we were a unity, obeying the laws of love and of each other.

I clutched his hand nervously after we exchanged rings and kisses, like a child bride. Gazing up into the eyes of my new husband, I thought I saw a halo around his head, as though he were a saint sent to save me.

Chapter 38

Married life with Thomas did not change our routine very much. He was still absent for long days at a time in London. I kept our family life going in Chelsea. He visited the house secretly, and my sister, being my most frequent visitor, transported love letters between us. It was, perhaps, the finest time of our love and marriage. The long absences kept our passion alive, and neither of us so far had disappointed the other.

Shortly after the marriage, however, Liza upset me by saying she wished to leave my service and return to Westmoreland.

"But why?" I cried, having become so accustomed to having her with me again.

"I'm getting old, ma'am. You are married and a happy woman. Soon you will have a child with him. I'm not needed now. Besides, I want to go back and settle in the North. I'm tired of all the politics here in London."

"Liza, don't go." She had been such a bulwark of strength. "The only time you left me was when I married Latimer. And he has been the only husband who really looked after me. Even Thomas is not so supporting."

"No, ma'am," she said curtly, "he's not."

Looking at her askance, I said, "Come now, Liza, what are you hiding from me? Why do you really want to leave?"

Liza was as obdurate as ever, with that northern silence that passes for wisdom. She looked the other way when she finally spoke to me.

"I can't say as I'm any too fond of your new husband, ma'am. He and me don't get on. I'm not really happy with him around."

Shocked at her disloyalty, I said, "But, Liza, you haven't given him a chance. You just see that flamboyant careless side on the surface. The charmer, the court flirt. But he is good and kind and loving to me. You know that."

"Aye, ma'am. But there's so many rumors from Court about his flirting. It upsets me."

Now I felt so worldly, compared to this poor innocent from the North! After all, in her only marriage, she had been wed to a churchman. What did she know?

"Oh, my dear friend," I said, holding her hands, as if she were in need of sympathy, "I know there are rumors. I get to hear them too. But they mean nothing. Thomas has often told me how women chase him. You know how handsome he is. For fear of hurting their feelings, he has to play them along. Remember, too, we have not announced our marriage yet, so, to keep up the pretense, he has been flirting more ostentatiously than ever. Besides," I added confidently, "I don't care. I know he loves me, more than he ever could those other women. Let him flirt if it keeps him happy. You don't marry a man in his middle age and expect him to settle down overnight."

I laughed happily, knowing about the tales of trysts between Thomas and Mary, Duchess of Richmond, and knowing, in my heart, how much he despised the foolish woman but had to pay her some attention for fear of reprisals from her powerful family.

"We'll announce the marriage just as soon as we get the Protector's consent. Then things will change, you'll see."

"And you really think the Protector is going to let his younger brother get away with marrying the Queen?" Liza snorted miserably.

"Why ever not?"

"The Protector knows as well as you how much King Edward adores you. He much prefers his Uncle Thomas to the Protector. So with you as Thomas Seymour's wife, you could easily sway King Edward to your side, make him desert the Protector."

Now I looked furiously at Liza for daring to meddle in my affairs so deeply.

"Really, Liza, you talk like one of these foolish women at Court. Everything is not political, even here. Men and women can still marry for love, you know."

Liza just grunted and continued about her business. I noticed she did not bring up the idea of leaving my employ again, so I assumed I had won her over.

It was in June of that year that I received a letter from King Edward telling me not only how much he loved me, but how he thought it was a splendid idea for me to marry his Uncle Thomas. I was excited when I received the letter and sent urgently for Thomas to visit, so I could show him our victory.

Thomas did not share my excitement. "I know Edward wrote that. I encouraged him to do it, one afternoon when we were alone. It's the Protector I'm still concerned about. He doesn't trust me any more than I trust him. And his dreadful wife has been so awful to you. I could smack her across the face myself."

Soothing his fevered brow, for he had raced here on horse-back, believing something was badly wrong, I said calmly, "I gave up worrying about your brother's wife a long time ago. Anne Stanhope never liked me even when I was Queen. Now she has robbed me of jewels and money left to me, by King Henry's will. She claims, as the Protector's wife, she has a right to them. Anne Stanhope thinks she's so almighty grand as the Duchess of Somerset. But there is really nothing she can do to harm me. I am the Dowager Queen, and shall remain so until King Edward marries and gives the country another Queen."

Thomas grabbed at my arm thoughtfully, while I massaged his sore shoulders. "But what is my lady Duchess of Somerset going to say to her archenemy the Dowager Queen when it is learned that the Dowager Queen is now her sister-in-law, Lady Sudeley?"

I bit my lip, for obviously the status problems involved were quite complex. "I shall walk ahead of her with dignity and calm, upon *your* arm as *your* wife."

Thomas grimaced. "*My* wife. But who is the most powerful? The new King's Protector and his wife, Lady Somerset? Or the ex-King's widow and her husband, the Protector's brother?"

"Why, we are, my darling!" I said, astonished. "I am still King Henry's widow."

And so we hugged and he bade me goodnight, for he had urgent things to attend to back in London. I hated to see him go but could do nothing to persuade him. More and more, people were getting to know about our secret marriage. He had to find a way of letting the Privy Council know.

❖

Later that summer, our marriage became public. I received masses of letters, either from well-wishers or from shocked and angry people. I was mortified at the amount of hostility I had invoked by remarrying so shortly after the beloved King Henry's death. Princess Mary, Elizabeth's sister, sent me a very curt note avowing to our former friendship but expressing her deep concern over the impropriety of the act.

That same morning, Elizabeth came to see me in my study. She walked in very gently and calmly, clutching a letter to her bosom. This small girl, my stepdaughter whom I loved so much, was about to turn fourteen years. She was lovelier than I had ever known her, now that the carrot-colored hair had come under some control and had been trained to emphasize her neat, small features.

Elizabeth's body was thin and delicate. Her small breasts budded for all to see. Her skin was white and firm. I felt proud to have helped mold her.

"Ma'am." She nodded to me, as she entered the sunlit room. She came to stand beside my desk, where I was busy writing. "I have received a letter from sister Mary."

"So have I. How is she from your letter?"

Elizabeth frowned. "Not too good, again. She requests I leave this household and live with her at Hunsdon."

I sat upright, and a moment of fear gripped my heart. "Oh, Elizabeth, I am disappointed. Do you wish to leave?"

Elizabeth sat on a stool at my side, taking my hand in her own and kissing it. "No, dear stepmother. I do not want to leave you. Mary suggests that your marriage to Thomas Seymour was improper, an insult to Father's name, and therefore I should remove myself from this 'house of iniquity,' as she puts it. But Mary is such a miserable person, and . . . oh, Katherine, I am happy here, happier than I have ever been. I do not think your marriage to Uncle Thomas was improper. I know how content you are with him. It is only natural. And anyway," she added peevishly, "it's a lot more fun here than it would be with Mary!"

Laughing, and taking her face in my hands to kiss her, I said, "Then, Elizabeth, you shall stay here as long as you wish. Write politely to Mary telling her just that. She will understand. Maybe Mary will find herself a husband soon, and that will make her a lot happier. And you, too, Elizabeth. It is time the Protector or I was working on a marriage for you."

Elizabeth jumped away from my hands like a faun caught in a trap. "Oh no, Katherine. Please don't arrange any marriage. I am *never* going to marry."

I smiled at the vehemence in this young woman, remembering how I had not wished to marry at her age either.

"I will not force you," I said gently. "Things have changed from when I was a girl. You will fall in love one day, and then marry."

Elizabeth smiled firmly. "I expect to fall in love, indeed I want to fall in love. But I will *not* marry."

"There'll come a time when you will have to, my dear. What about children?"

Elizabeth pouted. "I do not want children and I shall not marry. I do not intend to let any man master my life, Katherine. To marry is to sell yourself to a man. I will rule my own life, thank you."

I laughed and sent her away, thinking of the foolish arrogance we have when we are young, before we are aware of the passions that come along to set the steady boat off its well-planned course. I thought of the number of times I had determined the future course of my life, only to have the wind change overnight and the boat sent in a totally different direction. How can women be masters of their own lives?

I moved the household away from Chelsea to escape some

of the bad feelings. I had another dowager house left to me by King Henry at Hanforth in Middlesex, where the air was even fresher than in Chelsea village, and where I felt we could all breathe more easily.

On occasion, I returned to London for some special reason at Court. King Edward granted me my former Queen's Chambers at Whitehall Palace, and, of course, my husband Thomas would stay there with me.

❖

It was in the autumn, when the mists were returning to London and the atmosphere was tinged with the acrid smoke of wood fires burning in household grates, the air chill with an early wintery grip, that Thomas and I prepared ourselves for a banquet at Whitehall Palace, given by my eleven-year-old stepson, now also nephew by marriage, and presided over, of course, by brother-in-law Edward Seymour, the Protector.

Thomas and I had been feeling very happy that day. He was more secure about his future now that our marriage was public. He had been chiding me for not getting with child. I stopped brushing my hair and ran to him as though to attack with the hard ivory handle of the hairbrush. My fair hair had grown long again, at his wish, and although I pinned it under a cap in public, when we were alone together it hung straight and loose down my back, for Thomas loved to feel and stroke its silky strands.

I doubted at that moment that a woman could feel more happy. I was halfway dressed in a camisole of finest lawn over my undergarments, ready to put my head through the neck of a splendid new gown of deepest midnight-blue satin, embroidered with gold and encrusted with pearls and rubies. Thomas snatched the brush from my brandishing hand, grabbed me by the waist, and threw me onto our bed. Giggling furiously, I tried to stop him, for we were already late for the banquet.

"Thomas! Thomas!" I gasped for air. "We have no time for such play."

"If there is no time for play, there is no time for life, my sweet."

"Oh, come, husband dear. The only person you play with is Elizabeth! I should never have arranged it so beautifully, that by marrying me you gained a nubile stepdaughter as pretty and flirtatious as Elizabeth."

I was teasing him, but there was some truth in my words, for Thomas had been paying almost excessive attention to Elizabeth since our marriage, and since the move to Hanforth. Part of my cheerful mood that day was because Elizabeth and Jane Grey had not accompanied us to the city for this banquet. I had Thomas to myself for once.

He cooled visibly as I spoke. "Katherine, don't tell me what I may or may not do in my own house. I have married you. We are happy together. I find Elizabeth a perfect playmate, and an adorable young woman. There is nothing wrong with what I do. If I were her natural father, you would not criticize me. What's wrong with my actions? Is it because she is a Princess you find my attentions improper? If it were Letitia I teased so much, you would find nothing wrong."

Now I was mournful and angry with myself for having changed our loving mood. Yet I could not stop.

"But Elizabeth is going to be a very powerful young woman quite soon. Once Edward comes of age and is King in his own right, Elizabeth will be as important as King Henry's sisters used to be. And besides, you should not play with a young woman's emotions like that. She is at that age when her heart can be tricked and deceived."

Thomas pounced on me again, beating all the breath out of me. "Wife, you are sometimes too serious to be true! Forget Elizabeth! I was about to make love to you, and you bring up such dreary subjects. The young Princess is my stepdaughter. I can act with her as I please. If you open your mouth again, I shall be off this bed in a trice."

I smiled. "Then how can I kiss you if I may not open my mouth?"

"Kiss me with your mouth closed, woman," he said, forcing his mouth down upon mine, so very soon I could do no other than open my lips and welcome his beautiful mouth on mine.

Thomas ripped off my camisole and made passionate love to me there on the bed at Whitehall, while we were supposed to be attending the banquet. But my mind banished all such social niceties as I lost myself in the sheer joy of our lovemaking.

Thomas had taught me so much about ecstasy that I was continually humble before him, like a pupil before a teacher. I wanted him to lead me, guide me forever into eternity. I remembered the words he had used to me not so long ago, that I was his Queen and his slave. . . . He was right. If ever I had been a slave to a man, it was to Thomas. For my passions knew no holding back. My sense of caution and reason were blown to the winds, and I was his obedient handmaiden, prepared to do anything he wanted.

I lay on the bed, our passions spent, remembering the exquisite moments of our lovemaking. Then I recalled our social commitment.

"Hurry, my darling. We must dress and go down to the great hall. They will be waiting for us. Can't you just see Anne Stanhope's face now we have kept them waiting? She will be convinced we did it on purpose to show her who is in the more powerful position!"

Some half hour later, dressed and at peace with each other, Thomas and I descended the fine staircase to the great hall, where the many guests had gathered to be led into the state dining hall.

The Protector and his wife stood fuming at the open doorway. As Thomas and I walked through the crowds, greeting our friends, shaking hands, expecting to take up the lead, to my horror I saw Anne Stanhope push herself forward, grab the Protector's hand, and move ahead of us.

I pulled Thomas and tried to squeeze past to our correct position, but the upstart Anne Stanhope pushed me back, quite forcibly, and was heard to mutter under her breath—so all around could hear, of course—"She married that disgusting old and lewd King Henry, when no woman of virtue would have considered letting him come near. Now she marries a younger brother. And she expects me to give way to *her*! Come, husband, we will go first."

Sensing Thomas's temper rising, I strained to hold him back. I knew he was willing to defend my honor by fighting his brother right now, in the palace, before all the nobility, which would only have led to one of their deaths.

"Don't," I hissed desperately. "Leave it for now. You know she is crazy. She has not long ago borne a child, and I fear her mind has become deranged."

Pulling Thomas back into the shadows, I wrapped my arms around his neck, so all could see our show of love and affection. I whispered in his ear, "Kiss me now, and let them see we don't care."

Thomas looked around, no doubt angry with me for controlling his true feelings in that way. "I wish you'd let me go for him," he snarled. "My brother fancies himself King, and she, that whore, has decided she is definitely Queen. Look, she is wearing some of your jewels in public."

"I know, Thomas," I said soothingly. "But I love you too much to let you fight. I don't want to lose you."

"Nor I you, sweetheart," he said, so kindly and genuinely I felt my heart jump and something inside open and give in to him that night. Maybe my pregnancy began right there and then. It certainly happened around that time.

Chapter 39

ying in my bed at Hanforth one dark December morning, feeling quite ill, I wondered why Thomas had risen so early again and wished that he were at my side so that we could talk before the day began. Suddenly I was disturbed by a knock on the door. Liza entered to tell me Kat Ashley, Elizabeth's young governess, wished to speak with me.

"Oh, Liza, I feel terrible. Does she have to come now?"

Liza busied herself in the room, tidying up, and said, "I think she *has* to come and see you now."

"Liza, you haven't said anything to me about my sickness. What do you think is happening?"

Why was she being so uncaring?

"Ma'am, I was waiting for you to tell me the good news. Has it happened?"

"I think so. Oh, Liza! I'm excited but scared. I'm so old now. This is like a first pregnancy, and I'm thirty-five! Is it safe, do you think?"

Liza had come over to me now, and she put her arms around me, in support and tenderness. "Oh, ma'am, I'm so happy for you. Maybe a child will make everything right with you and Lord Sudeley."

"Yes, Liza," I said dreamily, not realizing her meaning. "Maybe it will."

Then she left my bedside and returned to the door. "What about Kat Ashley?"

"Let her in, let her in. She'll have to accept me still in bed. I'm not rushing for anyone. Don't breathe a word of my news, till I have told Thomas."

Kat Ashley was quite a pleasant young woman, though not the type I would have personally chosen to care for Elizabeth's personal life. She did not seem solid enough. But she loved Elizabeth, I could see that. They had been together since Elizabeth was a baby.

But now Kat was here by my bedside, humbly prostrating herself. I beckoned her to sit in a chair by the window. She crossed her hands, and hesitated before speaking.

"Mistress Sudeley." Kat coughed nervously. "I have begged this audience, though I really do not know how to express my intent. . . ."

"Hurry, please, Mrs. Ashley. I have yet to dress and face the day's business. Lord Sudeley and I have much to do today."

She coughed again. "It's about Lord Sudeley I came to speak, ma'am."

"Oh yes?" I said, quickly and crossly. "What about him?"

There was a long pause, and I was about to ask her to leave when she braced herself to say, "Ma'am, I am unhappy about his sporting with Princess Elizabeth. It does not seem somehow right and proper."

Angrily, I snapped, "He is her stepfather. If he wishes to tease and play around with her and Letitia, he is perfectly within his rights."

"But, ma'am, he came into Elizabeth's bedchamber this morning, before my mistress had risen. He opened the curtains . . ."

"So what, in heaven's name, is improper about that?"

" . . . then he pulled back the curtains to her bed and began to tickle her under the sheets."

"Really, Mrs. Ashley." My temper was up, that she could speak to me in this way. "Be careful what you say, or I might suggest to Elizabeth that you be dismissed. If my husband tickles his stepdaughter, it is only because he cares for her deeply. He is her uncle, after all, and has known her since she was a babe in arms. What can you see that is improper in his actions?"

Kat Ashley shifted nervously in her chair. "Well, the young lady was not up, nor dressed. She was in her nightgown. And the other servants and I stood and listened to this noise of squealing and tickling, and, ma'am, it sounded quite awful to us. We all love Elizabeth and would do her no harm, but some of the other servants, the local ones from the village, have been gossiping and implying that your husband is really carrying on with the Princess, and that the Princess even, Lord be, is with child! You know what these local people are like. And how their tongues love to wag."

"Yes, and I would love to cut out those tongues that wag," I said, angry at being so humiliated in my home.

I sighed resignedly, for I too had felt Thomas was overdoing his playing with Elizabeth. But how could I speak to him so he would listen? Maybe now I was with child, he would reform. Everybody saw Thomas in the wrong light. He was merely flirtatious, charming, and very handsome. These dull country people were just not used to someone as attractive as he.

"I'll speak to him, Mrs. Ashley. You may leave my room."

As soon as Kat had departed, I turned to the pillows and beat them with my fist. Here was I, about to feel so joyous, for I was almost certainly with child after all these years, and by a man I loved deeply. Here I was about to announce the news, at the height of my new happiness in life, and the truth was my husband had been flirting too ostentatiously with my stepdaughter and I really did not know what to do about it.

Elizabeth was as bad as Thomas, that I could see. All that giggling between her and Letitia had not stopped. In fact, it had grown worse. Letitia was obviously party to Elizabeth's acts. They found it exciting, and I knew deep in my heart that Elizabeth was as guilty of leading Thomas along as he was of trying to string up her heart. It was a game they both enjoyed playing. In that sense they deserved the trouble they were going to bring each other. Yet how could either of them deceive me and cause me such pain, so willingly, so knowingly?

The next morning, I caught Thomas by his arm as he was about to jump agilely out of bed.

"Kat Ashley came to speak to me yesterday."

"What about?" he said impatiently, already throwing on some clothes. "Don't start one of your tedious conversations now, Katherine. I have much business to attend to. Speak to me in the evening."

"But you are never here in the evenings, Thomas, and . . ." Tears began to trickle down my face. "I have been waiting for days to tell you my news, yet there never seems to be a time you want to speak to me."

"What news, Katherine? Whatever are you talking about?" he said snappishly.

Still weeping, I said miserably to myself, but so he could hear, "I never thought it would come to this. That the happiest day of my life, when I can bring you such pleasure, should turn into an argument between us."

Then, drawing in my breath, for suddenly it seemed like a chore, rather than a gift, to be giving him the news, I said, "I am with child, Thomas."

At least my words stopped him in his tracks. He dropped the breeches he was pulling up his body.

"You are what?"

"I am with your child. I believe it will be born sometime in the summer of next year."

He dropped to his knees, as if in prayer. "I cannot believe. I had given up all hope. Oh, Kate." He sounded near tears himself. "You are to have my son . . . ?"

Now I smiled, for he was so sweetly childish about wanting a son. "Why do you hanker for a son? You are the second son yourself, so cannot pass on a title. Would you not love a daughter as much?"

Thomas had come to the bedside, where he sat stroking

my belly. "This is such wonderful news, Kate. I wish I could have the church bells rung and announce it to the world. My first baby . . ."

"Oh come. There must have been others . . . ?"

He shrugged. "Maybe. I don't know. But this is *my* son, *my* child."

"I am very happy to be pregnant, darling. Even though it scares me, at my age . . . labor cannot be easy."

"You'll sail through it, sweetheart. With all your knowledge about medicine and all, you'll be fine. Oh, this is just wonderful!"

Snatching his hand, I pressed my advantage. "Thomas, don't go in to Elizabeth again, not this morning, please?"

"What?" He sounded so irritated.

"Kat Ashley came to tell me yesterday that all the servants are gossiping. I know there is nothing wrong with your actions, you have told me before. But it's these local girls from the village we hired, they're all saying you and Elizabeth are having an affair, and even that Elizabeth is with child."

"Oh, good Lord!" he shouted. "Why should we take heed of what they say?"

"Because word might get back to your brother and to the King. And you would not want the Protector thinking you were seducing Elizabeth, would you?" I said sternly, to make sure he got my message. Then soothingly, I added, "Anyway, darling, I'm beginning to feel unsettled by it, and now I'm with child, I would prefer it if you refrained from the horseplay. It would look better."

"Katherine," he exploded. "That's all you care about—what things *look* like. You were the same when I wanted to marry you. We had to consider what people would say—it's always the same with you. Where's your spontaneity? That's why I like Elizabeth. She's such fun. She goes along with me, and we have wild times together."

"But Thomas!" I cried. "She is but fourteen years old,

unmarried, and the game you play is dangerous. What if she begs you to make love to her? What would you do?"

I was shouting at him now, not caring if the whole house heard. I felt my marriage and love disintegrating before my own eyes.

Maybe because of the state I was in, Thomas returned to my side and stroked my hair as he used to do. "Don't get so upset, Kate, sweetheart. I just don't like being criticized by these ignorant country bumpkins. I don't want you to endanger that sweet baby of ours. Look, why don't you come with me to visit Elizabeth this morning, so they'll stop talking? That way they'll see it's just normal, human behavior, nothing bizarre, just a mother and father who love their step-daughter and who greet her in the morning. I promised to walk with her in the garden, anyway, and I don't see why I should have to break my promises to her just because of evil gossip."

So I rose from my bed and, at Thomas's insistence, did not change from my night robes, so all could see how happy Thomas and I were, and how his morning antics with Elizabeth were quite innocent.

I felt all their eyes upon us as we walked past the assembled servants in Elizabeth's outer chambers and entered her little bedchamber. Because it was winter, the heavy bed curtains were not yet pulled apart, but I could hear her light breathing from within. I shivered with fear to think of that vulnerable child, playing with such dangerous fire, and what might yet be in store for her, if she did not learn to control that impulsive, spontaneous will Thomas so bragged about. Spontaneity was not likely to advance her in this world, any farther than to prison or to the block.

Thomas yanked back the bed curtains, and a startled Elizabeth woke from her slumbers. I was pleased to see that even before she knew I was also in the room, she scurried down the bed, hiding under the blankets, so he could not reach her.

"Good morning, my pet," he said lightly. "What, not awake yet? Naughty Elizabeth. It's time you were up and about. Did I not promise to walk with you in the garden, this cold day?"

"Good morning, stepfather." Her voice came muffled from under the covers. "Please, you wake me too early. You must wait outside till my servants have dressed me."

"Elizabeth!" he cried. "Look, Katherine is here with me this morning. She wanted to join in our playful antics. Isn't that fun!"

Elizabeth sat up and smiled feebly at me, with a hint of red blushes about her face. I bent over and kissed her good morning.

"Well, Elizabeth," he went on. "We have some news for you. We are to have a baby!"

"Oh, ma'am," Elizabeth stuttered. "Why did you not let me know sooner? I am so happy for you both." She grinned with genuine delight.

"I had not told Thomas till this morning. There never seemed to be the right opportunity."

Then Thomas jumped on her bed and grabbed hold of the girl's thin little arms and began tickling her chest, his hands brushing over her small breasts. I said to myself, *I'm not surprised the servants prattle!*

"Come, Katherine, Beth loves to be tickled," and he pulled my arm, so I too had to join in the game until Elizabeth was sprawled on top of the covers, writhing in ecstasy and agony from tickling, her nightgown ridden up over her knees. I glimpsed her small private parts and wondered whether Thomas had caught the same intimate view.

Gloomy about his antics, but quietly relieved we had quashed rumors by coming to her room together, I vowed to accompany him more often.

✛

The winter passed, and Thomas, as an expectant father, became a more attentive husband and a proud parent-at-large. He bragged about his child, his wife's health and fecundity. He faced the world as though he had finally been proved a real man.

My pregnancy made me more contented too, and life seemed to sail by happily that spring.

The weather had become much warmer, so warm in fact for the time of year that everyone was lazing in our garden at Hanforth.

Thomas was talking with Elizabeth under a bower, and I was sewing quietly in my own favorite garden, thinking of my growing baby, who kicked and moved around with quite some fury. Already I felt that she, for I knew this child was a girl, and I were good friends.

Letitia sat at my side, scowling, for whenever Thomas was with Elizabeth she was left out, as the no-longer-needed friend. Elizabeth was dressed this morning in a very somber black dress.

Suddenly, Letitia and I were forced to look up, by the squeals and shrieks of laughter coming from their bower. Thomas was tugging at her dress, and Elizabeth was laughing as though she would burst, trying unsuccessfully to push off his hands.

"Stop, Uncle Thomas, please, stop!"

"No, young lady. I told you I cannot abide this dull black dress. You must take it off, or I will rip it off you!"

"Thomas!" I yelled out, alarmed at what he would do.

"Come here, Katherine!" he called to me. "Bring me the scissors from your sewing box. We must get this dress off Elizabeth, for I keep telling her she must learn to embellish her looks, not play them down."

He ran over and snatched the scissors from my hand. I

leaped to my feet, though I felt the baby move within, as if she were saying, "Don't get up, sit down, I need the rest."

Letitia grabbed my hand, and we ran together to where Thomas had already begun snipping at Elizabeth's dress. I tried to stop his hands from cutting, but he pulled hunks of dress from her body, first the skirt and then the bodice, until she stood with tattered clothes, her camisole and underslip exposed to all who were watching. Without a doubt, there were many pairs of eyes now glued to windows.

"I shall cut this dress from her back," he chortled.

"Stop, Thomas, stop," I shouted angrily, staying his arm. "You don't know what you are doing. Everyone is watching."

"Goddammit, Kate, I don't care if they *all* watch. Bring 'em in. Charge 'em a groat. If a man cannot play in his own gardens, then where can he play?"

Turning to me, he snarled angrily, "Would you rather I went into the city and played behind your back, with girls of the night?"

"Oh!" I stepped back as though I would faint, clutching my belly, for the baby now seemed most disturbed, and was writhing around. *Oh, no, don't let me lose this baby, not now. She's all I have.*

Elizabeth managed to collect herself and, looking most embarrassed, wrapped her arms around herself, a pathetic sight in the white cotton camisole.

"Elizabeth, you must not let him act like this with you!" I now screamed at her, turning the full vent of my fury on the young woman, who I knew was goading him on. "It's not right or proper. Already they are gossiping too much about you. If this gets back to your brother the King, and to the Protector, there will be all sorts of questions to be answered and trouble ahead. Be sensible, young lady."

I turned my back on both of them. Leaning on Letitia's shoulder, I held my belly and headed for the house and my bed, knowing I must rest and not get too excited or I might lose the baby.

"Oh, Letty, my love, help me," I whispered, as we tiptoed into the house. "Help me lie down. I don't want to lose the baby."

"Ma'am, don't say that. Liza will help. She knows all about these things."

"I know, Letty . . . I know," I muttered as they helped me lie on my cool bed and brought me wine to sip, to stop the movements of my belly, which was tightening too hard for my peace of mind. "I know, Letty, I had a baby once before . . . this is not my first."

"What's that, ma'am?" the girl said, leaning over and trying to make out my words. "What's that you said?"

"Move along, Letty," Liza commanded, pushing Letitia out of the way so that she could wipe me down with cool water. "Leave the mistress alone. She's had enough to contend with today—she doesn't need your questions."

"But she was just telling me something peculiar, about having had a baby before." Letty was nonplussed.

"I said get out of the way, girl. You'll find out soon enough, no doubt," grunted Liza, obviously angry at what had taken place.

⁂

Thomas was kneeling at my bedside that evening when I woke to feel refreshed and no longer in pain. The baby had settled; my belly had stopped moving about in that alarming fashion.

"I am so sorry, sweetheart," he mumbled at my side, kissing my hand, though I snatched it back. "I did not mean to upset you. I do not want to harm our baby, sweetheart. Please forgive me." He stroked my belly and caressed me, so I began to feel better and trust him again.

We had had no lovemaking since I announced the pregnancy, for fear of disturbing the baby. I sensed he was suffering from the desires of his body . . . and heart. Maybe that was what led to the excesses of play with Elizabeth.

So, that evening, to show that I loved him and forgave him, I bent down over his strong, muscular, hairy body, took his sex in my mouth, and tried my best to please him, so hard in fact that I ended up exhausted and spent. But he was delighted and called me all sorts of endearments, vowing to be a good husband.

"I think we should leave Hanforth soon," I whispered, as he lay prone at my side. "Could we retire to the country for my confinement, darling?"

"Why yes, sweetheart. Anything that would make you feel better. We shall go to our country home in Gloucestershire. Sudeley Castle is supposed to be very beautiful."

"I would love that." I sighed. "I'll take Jane Grey with me, Liza, and Letitia. But Elizabeth will have to move elsewhere."

"I understand," he crooned in my ear.

I fell into a sleep wracked by tortured dreams of this baby.

Old Nell's fortune: "Beware a girl child who may not be your own, or may be." Who did she mean? Letitia or Elizabeth? They were both partly mine, and partly someone else's. What was going to happen?

Chapter 40

ane Grey scampered over the lush green lawns to the nearby castle entrance. I squinted my eyes against the noonday sun, wondering why the girl had decided to run inside. Jane was such an endearing person. A head on her shoulders like a woman my age, an intellect brimming with information and wisdom. I shook my head to think of what would become of these young women. Elizabeth seemed hell-bent on a dangerous racing current, riding whim and spontaneity. Jane was on a boat being dragged through lockgates against her will.

Jane was happy with me; happier, she kept confessing, than she had ever been at home. Poor child, despite the fact she was King Henry's grandniece, her mother and father treated her abominably, beating, pinching, and scolding their own flesh and blood until Jane had readily accepted Thomas Seymour's request to buy her wardship for £2,000 (£500 on deposit). Indeed, Jane revered her Uncle Thomas in a manner these young things all seemed to share. He now had King Edward, Princess Elizabeth, and Lady Jane Grey quite under his spell.

Jane reappeared from the castle doorway, running in her delicate way, skipping over the nettles in the grass until, breathless, she reached my side.

"Letters have arrived, Queen Katherine, from your husband and from Princess Elizabeth!"

Thomas had not spent much of the summer by my side at Sudeley. But at least he was now behaving more like a husband with his almost daily letters and concern for my health. I patted my stomach again, and a smile flitted across my face to remember the last letter I had written Thomas. "The little Babe became quite active when I told it about you." The letter must have touched a nerve in Thomas's soul, for now he was writing in total adoration and as though already a devoted father.

Separating Thomas and Elizabeth had been the wisest move. Time and distance had made me see Elizabeth in a warm mood again. *I hope she finds a good man, someone strong enough to curb her spirits, yet able to give her freedom to move. She needs a man like Latimer. Thomas is far too headstrong for her. They are like fire with fire. Give them a few months together and they would explode.*

I looked up to find Jane waiting with bated breath to hear news from these two members of her family. "We'll invite Elizabeth to visit once the baby is born. She will enjoy that, don't you think?"

"Oh, ma'am," sighed Jane, relief in her voice, for she had shared the concern at Elizabeth's disgrace. "Elizabeth would be thrilled, I am sure. She loves you so . . . you must know that." Then Jane paused.

"And how is your good lord?"

"He fares well in London. He had audience with dear King Edward yesterday and has once more lent him money. The Protector is incredibly mean with his charge, considering he is *King*!"

We laughed, relaxed, contented, as if there had never been any trouble on our horizon.

"I feel somewhat faint. I will retire to my bed for the afternoon. You may continue with your studies if you wish."

Jane jumped from her perch on a garden bench and ran to help me indoors. Everyone was so concerned for my health that it made me nervous. *I wish they would just assume I was going to be fine. Then I could sail on quite happily too. I wish I did not feel so terribly tired, and so sick all the time. I hate to think I am not really quite well . . . to scare myself this way.*

Aided by Jane, I entered the castle through the kitchen entrance. We passed Liza and Letitia, who were eating a late meal on the old wooden table. The sun shone into the enormous kitchens, and I stumbled for a minute, for the baking ovens were roaring away, suddenly making the atmosphere overpowering.

Liza jumped up, aghast. "Ma'am, are you all right?" she said, rushing over to me. She held my arm, pushing young Jane out of the way as though the girl were a mere nuisance.

"It's just so hot and stuffy in here," I mumbled, mystified

by my feelings. "I'm on my way to lie down. I must have overdone the walking this morning."

"I told you not to spend so much time in the outdoors, ma'am. Lord knows what my mother would say about you," Liza grumbled and led me to bed.

Later that evening, Letty came and sat on the edge of my bed. Suddenly she began to talk as though nothing would stop her.

"Why did you never tell me? I can't believe it! I am horrified, appalled. . . ."

"Whatever is wrong?" I stirred myself.

"Liza has just told me the *truth*. That I am not Lord Strickland's child at all . . . that . . . that you are my mother and I was fathered by a stableboy at Sizergh. Only you were too ashamed to be seen! They hid you and me away at Oxenholme. All these years! All these years, I grew up loving Liza as my mother, Stephen as my father, and Freda as my grandma. I can't believe it. I don't want to believe it. I don't want you to be my mother," she snapped with all the vengeance her wounded pride could muster.

I groaned. So it had come out and in the worst possible way. Of course, I should have told the girl years ago. It was my responsibility.

"Letitia, please. Don't. You must understand." I spoke with difficulty, for my breath would not come easily; I only managed short phrases, and even then had to pause between.

"I was trying to do the best for you. I wanted you to be happy. To have a good start in life. I did not want you to hate me. . . ." My voice died away, as Letty jumped from the edge of the bed and strode to the window, staring out at the beautiful gardens of roses and honeysuckle, the perfectly laid-out lawns, the fine yew hedges.

"All this," she muttered evilly. "All this you have, and I . . . I have nothing."

Trying to lighten the conversation, I said, "We may not

have this for long. You know Thomas was only given Sudeley as a gift from King Edward when he came to power. The way Thomas is going about things, I imagine the Protector could quickly snatch it away again."

" 'The way Thomas is going about things,' " Letitia said in a mocking tone. Then she turned to me with a new sense of power, throwing back her head and laughing. "You should know some of the ways your husband 'goes about things.' "

"Whatever do you mean, dear girl?" My stomach was moving in an uncontrollable fashion, and I really had not the strength to deal with this emotional scene.

"If we are telling truths, then maybe you should know what your husband was up to just before he proposed marriage to you, ma'am," Letty snapped.

Now I willed sleep so as to avoid this scene, but Letty went on remorselessly. "He proposed to Princess Elizabeth, that's what he did."

I put my hand on my stomach and closed my eyes.

"You remember that day you caught me and Elizabeth with a letter we were giggling over? And you asked me where I got the new ring? Well, Lord Strickland gave me the ring, and Thomas Seymour gave *her* the letter. Before he ever came to see *you*. You should have read it! He told her he'd adore her till death, that he was pining for her, couldn't get her out of his mind . . . that her beauty bewitched him and if she would just write two simple lines of acceptance, he'd be the happiest man in the world!

"Elizabeth didn't accept him, of course. She knew their marriage would never be acceptable to the King and the Protector. But she was in love with him, too. Passionately." Letty emphasized the word with great relish.

"She turned him down. Told him she had to learn to enjoy the state of maidenhood first. Didn't intend to marry for some years, at least until she'd finished mourning her father. Then . . ." Letty paused for effect. "A few days later, who should turn up at the house again but Thomas Seymour, and lo and behold, we hear that *you* are going to marry him."

It was as though someone were stabbing me, as though my blood were draining out, but I had not strength to move, only to watch as a bystander to my own destruction and death. I had no emotion left to respond to this news. I did not want to feel anguish, or misery, or sadness again. I wanted to blot out the words, pretend I had never heard them.

❖

I stifled my fear, kept quiet about things I yearned to discuss, preferring to keep up a pretense of harmony. How simple it would be if I could sit down next to him and say, "Is it true that you proposed to Elizabeth before me?" How simple it would be if I could say, "Then, Thomas, I will let you go. Go to her. I will be quite happy on my own."

But we were married. We were lovers. I was bearing his child, and I had to live with the torment. The confused emotions. Could I ever love him again knowing this? That one question wracked my mind and heart, night and day.

❖

Just before August sank into September, under an amber moon that was huge and round, the peasants in the fields were enjoying haymaking and celebrating harvest home, and I knew my time was come. I had been feeling sick all day, and my back hurt so much that I could scarcely walk. My hands were sweating.

Liza sent word for the midwives to come from the nearby village of Winchcombe. Messages were sent to Thomas in London, to my sister Anne, and to Willy in Grimsthorpe.

Liza leaned over my face, wiping my brow with cool water.

"Will it take long?" I begged.

"Why, it's hardly begun yet!" Liza was resolutely cheerful and optimistic. "You're feeling nothing right now. You're young and healthy. You'll get through it in no time."

"I am neither young nor healthy, Liza, and you know it. Don't lie to me.

"Why did you tell Letty?" I gripped her hand with the pains.

"I'm sorry, ma'am. It slipped out that day."

"I shall tell her you were mistaken, that she is the daughter of Lord Strickland. I shall treat them both handsomely in my will—and you, dearest Liza."

I felt Liza bend over and kiss me on the brow.

It was a long, hard, and unpleasant labor.

On the second day, Letty was alone with me in the afternoon.

"Ma'am," she whispered, "I've come to make peace with you. I have to apologize for what I said about you and Sir Thomas. I didn't mean to cause you pain. I was just upset. I want you to know I'm very happy you're my mother."

"And I want you to know, Letitia, now and forever, that you are Lord Strickland's child . . . the seed of a love we shared many years ago . . . a love that was forbidden and one that we had to hide. Hence the story of the stableboy. I was never sure how to tell you, whether to tell you. I was so ashamed of myself. Liza spared me my reputation, enabled me to marry Lord Latimer. But I have always loved you in my heart."

Letty's face changed as she sat there. A smile widened, and she leaned over to kiss me. "Thank you, ma'am. You have made me very happy. Lord Strickland is a fine man."

"And I shall see you both looked after in my will. As soon as I have recovered from this birth, I'll set you up with a dowry. You may leave my service if you so desire. . . . Oh, this is too painful. It was easier by far with you, my child. You just slipped out." Letty held my hand with a renewed determination.

Thomas arrived with a Dr. Huick he had brought from

London, and the pains became so intense I could not think or hear what they were saying.

I could hear shouts from Dr. Huick and Thomas, and surprised gasps. My head was floating, and I almost believed myself dead. Was the baby here? Had I died and the baby lived? Then I heard a small cry, as though from a baby lamb in the farmyard at Snape Hall, and Dr. Huick spoke into my ear.

"You have a fine daughter, Lady Sudeley. What shall we call her?"

Liza came to my bedside to wipe my brow once more with cool water. "You did wonderfully, ma'am, I'm proud of you. The baby is so sweet! She has your fair appearance. Your husband is quite doting. He has already held her in his arms. Shall I bring the baby for you to hold? Seymour says you will call her Mary, after Princess Mary. I think that's a good idea. She's in the nursery you prepared for her, with the little red counterpane and the white crib. She has so many gifts of silver and gold, you'd be proud to see her there. Maybe in a few days you'll be well enough to come to the nursery. The wet nurse says she's a good sucker and will be hale and hearty."

Now we can invite Elizabeth. Soon it will be her fifteenth birthday. She may come visit us, to see Mary Seymour—the fruit of my loins, of Thomas's and my love. I do love him, oh I do.

And then Thomas was there at my side. He kicked off his boots and climbed onto the bed, lying beside me holding my head in his arms. Knowing about him and Elizabeth had changed nothing. My love went out toward him in a tremendous surge of warmth. Ours was no romantic foolish dream, but a real marriage, of two imperfect, slightly marred human beings, who tried their hardest to be good and faithful to each other. I reached out to stroke his chest, tired, spent, drained, but in love again.

My handsome, braggart husband, soldier on horseback,

racing wildly across the moors to Sizergh Castle, skillful courtier so funny and entertaining; ardent lover and my own dear
friend. I stroked the thick black hair on his head that now lay
limp and damp on my chest. I cradled him in my arms.

"You'll never be perfect, will you, Thomas? You'll always
cause me some pain. But you are mine and I am yours. And
I love you. Are you happy with your baby Mary?"

"She's the most wonderful little girl I've ever seen. So
beautiful, just like her mother. Do you want to sleep, sweetheart, or can I stay here with you? I'm the luckiest man alive
tonight."

"So am I, dearest. We will be happy, won't we, Thomas?"

"Why, of course, Kate. Weren't we ever so?"

And Thomas Seymour fell asleep, his head on my chest,
while I closed my eyes and drifted off happily to catch up
with his dreams.

Epilogue

Seven days after the birth of Mary Seymour, to
everyone's surprise, Katherine Parr died of puer-
peral fever. It was two days before Elizabeth's
fifteenth birthday. Thomas Seymour fell to pieces at the loss
of this source of strength and stability in his life.

Edward Seymour learned of his brother Thomas's antics
with Princess Elizabeth, and he managed to poison King
Edward's mind against his favorite uncle. A Bill of Attainder
accusing Thomas Seymour of treason for attempting to seduce Elizabeth was signed in Parliament on March 5, 1549,

by his nephew. He outlived his wife by just six months, being executed on March 20. When Elizabeth heard of his death, she said, "There dies a man of much wit, but very little judgment," and she vowed never again to let love or passion make her lose control over her life.

The orphaned baby Mary Seymour was taken by Willy, Duchess of Suffolk, to live at Grimsthorpe Manor in Lincolnshire. The baby was treated as a royal Princess, though Thomas Seymour had been stripped of all his and Katherine Parr's property and wealth, which had gone to the Crown, by the Act of Attainder. When Mary Seymour arrived at Grimsthorpe with full retinue of a Princess, she had no money or possessions—just a large and costly staff, which fell on Willy and her husband Richard Bertie's shoulders to provide for. Historical records run out on the fate of this child. Willy fought with the Protector for money, jewels, and nursery equipment.

Edward Seymour, the Protector, was himself executed just three years after his brother's death, in the scramble for power during the years King Edward was still a minor.

The last mention of Mary Seymour is that, at age thirteen, she was wedded to a local nobleman, Sir Edward Bushel.

Some say Mary Seymour died in childbirth, others that she died without issue. But one Suffolk family claims its descent from the daughter of Mary Seymour and Edward Bushel. And I know my own family claims distant descent from Katherine Parr.

I believe her spirit, so common in many women, does indeed live on. She would hope her descendants in the twentieth century find life easier than hers was in the sixteenth.

2°